More From ~~Barnacle~~

Chains of Nobility: Brotherhood of the Mamluks (Book 1)
by Brad Graft

A Lion's Share: Brotherhood of the Mamluks (Book 2)
by Brad Graft

The Swamp: Deceit and Corruption in the CIA
(An Elizabeth Petrov Thriller)
by Jeff Grant

Meeting Mozart: A Novel Drawn From the Secret Diaries of Lorenzo Da Ponte
by Howard Jay Smith

Labyrinth of the Wind: A Novel of Love and Nuclear Secrets in Tehran
by Madhav Misra

The Living and the Dead
by Brian Mockenhaupt

Three Days in Gettysburg
by Brian Mockenhaupt

Senlac: A Novel of the Norman Conquest of England (Books 1 & 2)
by Julian de la Motte

Vetville: True Stories of the U.S. Marines
by Mike Sager

The Devil and John Holmes, and Other True Stories of Drugs, Porn and Murder
by Mike Sager

#MeAsWell, A Novel
by Peter Mehlman

HOLES in the SOLES of his Gucci Loafers

A BEN JENNINGS LEGAL THRILLER

BY BILL WALK

Cover and Interior design by Siori Kitajima,
SF AppWorks LLC.

Cataloging-in-Publication data for this book
is available from the Library of Congress.
ISBN-13:
Paperback
ISBN: 978-1-950154-47-0

eBook
ISBN: 978-1-950154-48-7

Published by The Sager Group LLC
TheSagerGroup.net

HOLES *in the* SOLES *of his* Gucci Loafers

A BEN JENNINGS LEGAL THRILLER

BY BILL WALK

THE SAGER GROUP

Artifex Te Adiuva

To MY MAN KEVIN,

DUDE, YOU ARE A FORCE OF NATURE. YOU LIVE TO DOMINATE! THANKS FOR BEING A FRIEND AND ALLOWING ME TO HANG WITH YOU GUYS. I TRULY APPRECIATE YOU TREATING ME AS ONE OF YOUR OWN!

To my wife, Maggie
And to my children,
Madison, Thomas, Will & Henry

BILLY

Contents

PROLOGUE

"There is a reason they don't show this part on *Law and Order*," Ben Jennings mumbled under his breath.

He was sitting through yet another monotonous seven-hour deposition of his client with the defense lawyer asking what kind of grades she made in fourth grade math, what breed of dog she has, and where her cousin's ex-husband lives. Ben spent most of his waking hours in these unadorned, soulless conference rooms of glass and marble listening to lawyers ask endless, inane questions they hoped might someday support a withering cross-examination of his clients. Defense attorneys look for the nugget, vulnerability, contradiction, exaggeration, or outright lie that they can use to destroy the credibility of Ben's case. Also, they are required to bill a minimum number of hours to support their status and value within their firm so they can retain their small office with a window, mortgage on the house in the suburbs, tee times at the country club, private schools for their two beautiful and well-adjusted children—and bankroll spring break skiing in Colorado, summer vacation in Europe, and fall break at Rosemary Beach in Florida. On the other hand, Ben holds his breath and crosses his fingers, hoping his star witness does not lie, exaggerate, or say something incredibly stupid that will crater the case and prevent him from maintaining his South Main modern, exposed wooden beam office, outrageous mortgage on an old, classic house in the funky part of town, tee times at the country club, private schools for his two beautiful and semi-well-adjusted children—and then, alimony, child support, spring break skiing in Colorado, summer vacation in Europe, and fall break at Rosemary Beach in Florida.

Ben is a trial lawyer in Memphis, Tennessee, and his job requires him to wear nice suits, Hermès ties, and chestnut Alden's to present fascinating cases to juries whom Ben hopes might actually listen to the words he spent so many hours crafting. Ben tells stories for a living, hoping to convince a jury to buy what he is selling.

When he started, Ben believed in the goodness of people and their desire to do what is right and carry out their civic duty, much as did the jurors in the classic film *Twelve Angry Men*. After twenty years of countless jury trials, Ben's romantic ideals about the practice of law evolved into the Brooks Brothers-clad sausage factory that it really is. Those years fed his previously dormant cynical urges. Trial after trial in those twenty years taught him that jurors come to court with their own personal and political agendas that are unlikely to be moved by a carefully argued closing statement. Those jurors arrive with hardened beliefs that only get harder when a fellow juror of a different race, religion, sex, or ethnicity challenges their validity. In Tennessee, all verdicts must be a unanimous decision of twelve jurors. In this political climate, it is difficult to get twelve jurors to agree on lunch, much less a major tort case with millions at stake. Conversely, Ben's opponents on the defense side need only one juror to side with them. Anything other than a unanimous verdict ends in a mistrial, which means the lawyers, clients, witnesses, and experts must come back in a year and retry the case. For a defense attorney, the older the case gets and more the plaintiff's lawyers spend, the better.

Being a trial lawyer is one of the few occupations outside of professional sports that is a zero-sum game. For one to win, someone must lose. Trying high-stakes lawsuits is like hitting big league pitching. When big money is on the line, scrubs need not apply. The insurance companies have bottomless budgets and pay great lawyers princely sums to the bring the heat so that a jury will not award Ben's client the entire kingdom. Ben knows all too well because he spent eight years of his career as legal mercenary and verbal pugilist, throwing haymakers meant to smash plaintiffs' dreams of lottery-sized jury awards. Prior to representing people injured by hospitals and doctors, Ben defended the very groups he now sues. Ten years ago, he surprised the legal community by leaving the highly respected Thornton Firm, a boutique group of lawyers who represent doctors and hospitals. He went out on his own, determined to listen to his calling to represent little David against Goliath.

This is not a game for the faint of heart. Heart attacks, suicide, and divorce rates are much higher among trial lawyers than any other profession. As the old saying goes, if you can't run with the big dogs, stay on the porch. When you do battle in big tort cases, lawyers better leave their feelings back at the office and lace up their wingtips for a roller coaster ride. At least in professional sports, the players get long-term contracts that guarantee them those big bucks whether they win or lose. If an NBA player misses a three-pointer that costs his team a championship, he is still getting paid his millions. If the defense lawyer loses, he is still paid his high hourly rate by the insurance company. When a lawyer for the plaintiff in a personal injury case loses, the lawyer earns a goose egg. No, wait, not only does he not get paid, but he is also in the hole tens of thousands of dollars for the expenses fronted during the three years of sweat and toil put into the case. Big verdicts inspire headlines and glamour, but a losing lawyer is an orphan. Ben Jennings gambles for a living. He puts more money on the line a year than the most degenerate gambler during an NFL season.

Early in his career, Ben spent hours researching poignant quotes and parsing over word choices, trying to bring home the brilliance he had long admired in fictional television and film trial lawyers. Paul Newman's brilliant three-minute summation in *The Verdict* and Matthew McConaughey's riveting closing in *A Time to Kill* set the standard in Ben's mind. It took twenty years of practice before Ben learned that few if any jurors paid attention to his verbal flourishes, instead focusing on the clothes his client wore and if she laughed in a hallway during a break. He held on to the illusion that he was a teller of truth and champion of underdogs and that juries would right wrongs and compensate his clients generously for their pain.

At some point along the past two decades, Ben realized that instead of that fantasy, he was working in on an assembly line where people loved the final product but did not want to see how it was made. For every hour in the courtroom, Ben spent weeks and months in depositions and legal motions all over the country trying to build a case that a jury would love or an insurance company fear. Many times, a client's brother-in-law would read on the internet that her case was worth $50 million when, in fact, it was only worth $50. Ben deals in the seedy underbelly of plaintiff's practice where clients shop their cases to various lawyers as though they were a five-star recruit choosing between Duke and Kentucky. When a catastrophic injury happens in Memphis, some lawyers of little integrity actively recruit clients with promises of millions of dollars without knowing the facts to convince them to sign the employment contract. Consequently, wily family members of the injured will attempt to act as agents, shopping the cases around looking for upfront payments or backend kickbacks. For every case he takes, he rejects nineteen.

There is little drama in an eight-hour mediation set in a conference room that has the ambiance of a car dealership. If a trial lawyer is in court, he is losing money. All the good cases settle. If the case goes to trial, it has very large weaknesses, or the defendant is a sadist who loves punishment.

In the waters of medical malpractice, cases that go before a jury in the ultra-conservative state of Tennessee are decided in favor of the doctor or hospital 80 percent of the time. The paradox is that by trying those cases, others get settled. If the insurance companies know that a lawyer will not push to trial and "put twelve in the box," referring to jurors, there is little impetus to offer a deal. Insurance companies do not pay money if they do not first dread what the lawyer can do to them.

Ben can talk a dog off a meat wagon and will shamelessly attempt anything in a courtroom to help his case. Lawyers are distinct animals with their own culture, smells, sounds, and rules, both spoken and not, that they had better learn early or be thrown to the wolves. Despite his inner apprehension, Ben outwardly projected fearlessness and earned a reputation among the Memphis Bar as a worthy adversary. Many come to court thinking what lawyers do is easy. It is not. The complexity of mental and social talent necessary to successfully litigate a jury trial is monumental. There are very few lawyers left who consistently try jury cases. Those lawyers are dinosaurs. Today, most cases end in mediation, arbitration, or some form of dispositive motion. Many lawyers outwardly front as though they try cases when, in actuality, they do not ever pull the trigger.

Ben Jennings has been in the fire and lived to tell about it.

CHAPTER 1

Chaos descended on forty-five-year-old Memphis trial lawyer Ben Jennings like a summer thunderstorm rocketing through the Mid-South on one of those steamy August afternoons when it feels like you are breathing dry ice through a wet sheet. Not the everyday-witness-lies, cannot-pay-the-rent, expert-witnesses-quit chaos, but real disaster. Two hours earlier, Ben found out that his business and law partner for the past two years, Marco Alexopoulos, stole millions from clients while running a shadow law firm from within their own firm. Marco's house of cards collapsed after the criminal court judge shipped him off to rehab for the fourth time after two DUIs in consecutive weeks exposed the juggling act that likely caused the relapse. In two weeks, Ben will start a huge medical malpractice trial against Marston Owens III, the toughest defense lawyer Memphis has to offer. That means Ben preps extra hours every night, focused on this case with no time to pick up Marco's slack. All day, his phone rang off the hook with calls from Marco's anxious clients screaming and crying about the state of their cases, alarmed at citywide rumors of Marco's nefarious activities. Peggy did everything in her power to manage the crisis, but she was ill-equipped to handle the deluge of panicked and angry people flooding the office and phone. Ben needed to get to the office, set aside everything else he was doing, stop his trial prep, and just try to dig to the bottom of what it is Marco did and how bad the damages were.

As the thunderstorm abated, steam rose from the ground. As the sunlight returned, the early evening transformed into full sauna mode. Ben's ex-wife, Lisa, whom he divorced eight years ago, called to tell him that their sixteen-year-old daughter, Annie, was off her meds and having another anxiety attack. Their daughter's illness had stressed Ben and Lisa's marriage to the breaking point, and there had been cracks developing before. The two now worked hard to manage the daily situation that was Annie Jennings.

Ben navigated his black Range Rover for the ten-minute trip from his downtown office on South Main Street to Central Gardens located in tree-lined Midtown. His mind raced through a decision tree of what to do next. Jason Isbell's "Goddamn Lonely Love" pulsed through the stereo. As an answer man, Ben chose his own path, rarely deferring to others for solutions. His deceased old-school father did not suffer fools gladly; he rose from the depths of poverty during the Great Depression and allowed no sympathy for whiners or indecision. Ben adopted his father's edict of self-reliance and dig-it-out-of-the-dirt frontier mindset, determined to prevail no matter the personal cost.

Sweat seeped through his Zegna suit, and his Hermès tie hung halfway down his Egyptian cotton dress shirt. Ben's typically perfectly coiffed sandy-blond hair, now showing twinges of grey at the temples, was wet with droplets streaming down his face. His tall frame, previously lean and muscular body had aged in the past twenty years but not so much that a good tailor could not conceal. Ben arrived at his ex's house, the one they had lived in on Peabody Avenue, one of the most beautiful streets in toney Central Gardens. The Samuel Rucks house, built in 1910, was the first homes in the neighborhood, originally owned by a wagonmaker. The "four square"-style grey limestone and stucco house stood prominently on small hill. He rolled up the narrow driveway to find Annie curled up in a ball on the walkway connecting the sidewalk to the front steps, rocking back and forth and chanting indecipherable noises. Annie's long blonde hair was now kinked from a week of not bathing, a sign of a bad patch of anxiety. She constantly twisted a strand around her fingers and swayed back and forth. A day of tears crusted on her face and framed her large, round, red eyes. She had draped her athletic figure in torn, faded blue jeans and a ripped shirt. Despite the circumstance, her natural beauty still shone through. When she was like this, she wouldn't listen to Lisa. Ben was the only one who could break through the trance.

He sat next to her and tenderly rubbed her shoulders, patiently waiting for her to respond. After ten minutes, she stopped rocking and looked at Ben with a pain that destroyed him every time.

"Hey, sweetie, what's going on?" Ben said in a quiet, gentle tone that was almost a whisper.

"Oh, hey, Dad, all good, just hanging out. I feel great." Annie answered innocently, as she always did, as if the previous minutes of tears and agony had not occurred. Annie's self-denial of her reality made dealing with her condition more difficult. Whenever Ben had tried to talk with her about her rocking and chanting, Annie refused to acknowledge it existed. Lacking any medical insight or psychological experience in handling his once-perfect daughter's struggles, through trial and error, Ben had learned that a calm, patient approach worked best.

"Well, baby, you don't seem to be great. How about going to get some ice cream?"

Annie looked at him with her kind and haunting eyes, searching for answers in the face of the man she relied upon most. She took a deep breath. "No, thanks, Daddy, I think I'll just stay here for a while."

"Is it okay if I just sit here with you?" Ben responded optimistically.

"Sure, Pops," Annie said, as if indulging a kind but annoying stranger.

During these times, it took everything Ben had not to break down himself. A parent is only as happy as their saddest child, and his daughter suffered. Ben's two children, Annie and Max, meant the world to him. The change in Annie arrived suddenly two years ago. As a star athlete and honor student, Annie had been everyone's friend. She had the soul of a poet, feeling the world more than others, looking for kindness and meaning in every human transaction. She found goodness in small things, and her empathy for others created a gravitational force around her, attracting and charming people she met. Annie spent her life bringing people together with kindness, humor, and grace. She had the heart of a lion about school and athletics. She had a dogged determination to compete and succeed. Three years before she became ill, Annie, Ben, and Max capsized their canoe along a rough stretch of rapids on the White River in Hardy, Arkansas. Fearless Annie stood in frigid water helping to flip the canoe back to its proper position all while comforting her frightened little brother. With cuts, bruises, and a sprained ankle, Annie, without complaint or objection, helped Ben pilot the canoe down another six miles of rapids to safety.

When she was younger, Ben used to coach her basketball and softball teams, developing an unspoken language only known by the two of them. Annie dominated in athletics, excelled in academics, and truly loved people. Back in 2008, when Ben's beloved Memphis Tigers blew an eight-point lead in the final minutes of the NCAA National Championship game against Kansas, it was the eleven-year-old child, Annie, who comforted her inconsolable father, their bond earned from years of mutual support and understanding. Ben, Annie, and now thirteen-year-old Max had been closely knit and went to every Tigers' game. The three of them spent weekends in the gym playing endless games of HORSE and Around the World. Max, an eighth-grade basketball prodigy, gave Ben a respite in his tumultuous life as a trial lawyer with their time in the gym.

Ben's marriage had ended eight years prior, when the demands and mercurial life of a trial lawyer became too much for him and Lisa to handle. Trial lawyers experience an unusually high level of divorce and make for difficult spouses. As trained verbal pugilists, trial lawyers find it difficult to put down their gloves in personal relationships and are reluctant to cede ground on even the smallest points of domestic life. A spouse grows weary of listening to lengthy and exquisitely worded arguments about the correct manner in which to load the dishwasher. Good trial lawyers win every argument, even when they are wrong, but compassionate relationships are based on mutual respect not domination. Left alone to manage households and children while cases were prepared, settled, and argued, wives of trial attorneys grow accustomed to handling life solo; it can be challenging to shift into Husband Knows Best when he finally comes home.

Ben met Lisa in law school; she was a smart cookie with great legs and a terrific sense of humor, and she helped make the stress and workload bearable. They married out of law school and were deliriously happy for eighteen months. Then something. And he worked more and more, saw her less and less, and she handled the kids solo and grew resentful. She asked him to change, he knew she was right, but he didn't want to—he wanted the work and that world. So they stopped loving and appreciating each other, and he started sleeping with colleagues and secretaries.

He was outgoing and social, while she was quiet and preferred solitude. The two never fought but seemed to lack the chemistry as a married couple that they had had single. Ben felt the long hours and pressure of being a lawyer and needed time to decompress and blow off steam. The two devolved into roommates, and neither felt the spark for the other.

The stress and long hours of handling big high-risk cases drive trial lawyers to blow off steam through drinking and boys-only activities that don't require much self-reflection. Golf. Hanging out with the guys. Hitting the bars. Ben thought he was protecting Lisa and the kids from the tension of his work while providing for their every need. They thought he was hiding from them. A trial lawyer's life pits him or her against the world, a lone hero versus everything else. Ben knew that had prevented him from being emotionally available to Lisa. On the other hand, Ben was frustrated by the pretentious façade Lisa put on: Her family and marriage had to look perfect for her family, her friends, the neighbors, the school. Behind doors, Lisa brooded for days on end, refusing to discuss the origin of her melancholy either because she was stubborn or did not know. The two grew distant over the years, surrendering to their own corners of the house, avoiding any real conversation only to reconvene and present the perfect family postcard when they left the beautiful home with their gorgeous children in tow. Ben responded to his ever-decreasing connection with Lisa by thrusting himself into the lives of the kids, coaching their teams, playing endless games, and creating their own world of three, in which Lisa appeared uninterested. Ben took the kids to Grizzly and Tiger games, even traveling for the NCAA Tournaments. On Annie's seventh birthday, Ben, dressed in full tuxedo and hired a horse and carriage to transport her and her friends, dressed in princess costumes, around the neighborhood. Ben's relationship with his children was easier for him. With them, he relaxed; he felt like himself; and he laughed. Among the three of them, there was not the upspoken disappointment, discontent, and layers of scar tissue formed over the course of a marriage that demanded hard work and painful self-examination. Lisa had them go to counseling, but after a year and many visits, it did not help. They finally decided to end it.

The decision to divorce had been a tough and painful one. Ben worried about Max and Annie; the statistics regarding children of divorced parents concerned him. Divorce made him feel as though he failed, which he had. He rationalized that if he were single and happy, he would be a much better father. And the truth was that Ben was happier and spent much more quality time with the kids.

After the divorce, Lisa kept the house to provide some continuity for the kids, and Ben rented an apartment on Mud Island for two years. He and Lisa shared week-on, week-off custody. He loved the weeks he had with Annie and Max and relished playing football and baseball on the green separating his apartment from the Mississippi River. The car rides to school were epic, playing loud music and grabbing donuts. He and the kids talked easily and openly about everything and laughter abounded. The children appeared to adjust well and loved the new adventures that awaited on Mud Island. After a few years in the apartment, Ben bought a house in Hein Park, and things with the kids seemed to be going fine. He and Lisa got along better divorced than they had married. He had given her the house and generous child support.

Ben dated a string of interchangeable women, stemming from his disappointment from failing at marriage and a desire to avoid repeating the same mistake. He kept his women and children separate. He could not conceive of a woman that he would ever want to bring home to Max and Annie. One day, Ben got a call from school and was told that Annie had curled up in the fetal position in her counselor's office and would not move or speak. Ben raced to the school and managed to get Annie up and out but could not get an explanation from her as to what had happened. Overnight, Annie transformed from the model child into a lost and troubled soul. For the next three months of school, she became increasingly worse, unable to complete assignments and having inappropriate outbursts in class and at home. Annie could no longer write simple words on a page, and at night, Ben heard her weeping in her bed. Her friends abandoned her as if she had contracted a contagious disease, thrusting a troubled adolescent teenager into complete isolation. The shunning she experienced forced her deeper inside, spinning into a cycle with no bottom. The school had been understanding. Annie managed to complete the semester with Ben and Lisa handling most of her homework and generous teachers ignoring academic standards. Annie still had not returned to a conventional school environment. Ben's sister, Kimberly, homeschooled her with a combination of books and online learning.

The next two years were spent in visits and sessions at Lakeside Mental Health, sometimes for thirty days at a time, the psychiatric department at Vanderbilt Hospital, and a variety of other facilities attempting to answer what caused this sudden, dramatic change. After two weeks of tests and evaluations at Vanderbilt, there were no answers. Every conceivable examination had been run, and there were no objective findings of organic injury to Annie. She did not have a tumor, cancer, or anything else that showed up on scans or radiographic tests. Annie denied to doctors, counselors, and her parents that she had been physically or sexually assaulted. Looking for a root cause, Ben questioned this assertion and had her seen by several psychiatrists and counselors, none of which found any evidence of assault or physical abuse. For her part, Annie never acknowledged a problem and claimed that everything was perfectly fine. Still, she clutched things likes keys or crackers and carried them around for weeks at a time, refusing to let them go. Taking a shower made for a stressful day. She could no longer dress herself, catch the school bus, or manage her homework. Annie refused to bathe herself, brush her hair, or engage in basic hygiene.

The working diagnosis was acute anxiety manifested in extreme OCD. In the modern world, everyone assumes that all conditions are knowable and treatable. However, when it comes to mental health, there are no real answers. Doctors cannot tell which drugs will work, which ones will not. It is all trial and error with no one having consistent, reliable answers. In the cloistered Southern world of upper-class parents, the number one concern is always keeping up appearances and acting as though there is nothing worrying or troubling as they watch their children melt around them. The need for appearance and perfection is so great that children do not imagine that they can be anything less. When that fiction is punctured, the results can be catastrophic.

Paradoxically, the prescription of the medication that treats the illness also confirms to the patients that they are crazy. They resist treatment and get worse. When Annie avoided taking medication, her condition deteriorated, and she had more anxiety and increased symptoms. Now, it was time for Annie's recurrent OCD to kick in. The two of them could be here on the front stoop for the rest of the night while Annie worked to get order in her head. Ben had learned the hard way that he could not hurry the process. Her problem could not be fixed through the force of his or her will and personality. The answer man did not, in fact, have all the answers. How many dinners were delayed for hours while he and Max sat in the driveway waiting for Annie to get herself into the car? During those times, Annie sat at the door fighting her mind, hoping to trick it into submission, allowing her the simple act of walking to the car. They would sit at a table in a restaurant while Annie quietly moaned, cried, and did not allow Ben or Max to move until the feeling in her head was just right. Intellectually, she knew her compulsions were illogical, but still, she was emotionally unable to overcome them.

During those times, Annie sat perfectly still, the gears in her mind turning viciously until finally they aligned to allow her movement. Ben hated himself for the many mistakes he had made attempting to force her out of her trance and screaming at her about indulging herself in White girl diseases and first-world problems. Ben grew up in the lower-middle class and had been bussed to schools in the all-Black neighborhood of Orange Mound. The physical and mental abuse he suffered there forged a toughness in him that he feared was lacking in his children. Ben could not bear subjecting his children to the hostility and danger in the Memphis City Schools, so placed his kids in private school. This decision had both positive and negative effects.

As Ben sat on the front porch steps with his arm around Annie's shoulder, gently rubbing her back, the events of the day squeezed his head like it was in a vice. The cascade of angry clients, his poor choice of partners, and stress from a trial he feared he could not win felt like the Sword of Damocles. Ben's confidence disguised inner insecurities which invited bouts of self-flagellation from poor choices and past defeats. Since his youth, he had been thrust into sink-or-swim situations where the outcome had been solely dependent on his wits and quick action. After being shoved into inner-city schools, Ben had been the victim of violence and intimidation. Through that experience, he honed his wits and used the beatings as fuel to get tougher and stronger. He learned psychological tells and used humor to defuse otherwise violent confrontations. He still refused to sit with his back to the door.

After sitting on the front steps quietly together for forty-five minutes, as quickly as Annie's episode came, it left. The once-curious neighbors had grown accustomed to Annie, and in a show of benevolence, they now embraced her in any way they could, even at times protecting her from outsiders who stopped to witness the seemingly aberrant behavior. There was never a tangible trigger to break her out of the trance. The more Ben hurried her, the longer it took. Annie had somehow untangled what was eating her up from the inside long enough to get herself together and go back inside her mother's house. Lisa came to the door twice to check, and she and Ben exchanged a knowing look of experience. Annie vexed Ben in that there was no rhyme or reason, cause, or effect to solving her issues. Annie turned to her father and embraced him, pulling him tight for a minute. Her eyes watered, reflecting pain and thoughtfulness.

"Dad, I am so sorry I put you through this. I am really trying to get better. I know it doesn't make any sense to you, but I just get stuck in my head and have to go over it until it feels right."

"What do you mean, you get stuck?" Ben asked softly, his watering eyes mirroring those of his child.

"I don't know how else to describe it, Dad. Before all of this happened, my brain just worked normally. Now, it's as if there is nothing in my head, and I have to work to put all my thoughts back in. I keep trying to get to where I think like I used to, and I can't make that happen. I know it sounds strange."

Ben reached back and hugged her again, whispering in her ear, "Baby, it is going to be alright, I promise. It's not your fault, sweetie. I love you more than anything in the world and will always be by your side. We are going to get through this together, no matter what. You are noble and brave, and we will figure it out."

Annie smiled sadly as if indulging an uncomprehending child. "Thanks, Pops. I love you too. I'm okay," she said, trying to convince herself more than her father. "I am so sorry; I didn't even ask you about your day. How was it?"

In the deepest recess of her pain, Annie's still showed her innate thoughtfulness to worry more about her father than herself.

Ben's heart melted, "It was just fine, sweetie. Kind of you to ask."

"If it's okay, I am going to go back inside. I love you."

"I love you, too, Annie."

She turned and went into the house. This hurt Ben because he knew she could not control what was happening to her. Annie's kind heart and genuine warmth made her condition more painful because there was nobody to direct his anger toward.

As Annie opened the door to the house, Lisa stepped outside. Annie's condition had resulted in more collaboration than had existed during the marriage. Their divorce and spending time together in mental health facilities with their daughter removed all pretense and artifice of their once seemingly perfect family. They had been laid bare for all to see. The two reached a mutual respect and knowledge that no one else in the world but the other knew exactly what they were going through.

"How has the day been?" Ben asked quietly.

"Not good," Lisa responded. "She keeps getting stuck, as she calls it, and the periods last longer and longer."

"What about her meds?" Ben asked.

"It's a fight to get her to take them."

"We have to figure something out. But for the life of me, I don't know what that is."

"I agree. Looks like you have put that suit through the ringer."

"It has been one of those days."

"It's gotten to where there are more of those days than the other." She smiled plaintively.

"We will get through it. Call me if you need me tonight. Please tell Max I said hello."

Ben turned to walk down the steps, climbed into the Range Rover, and drove off. Since his youth, Ben had found solace and peace on a golf course. A natural player, he honed his game as a child by mimicking the swings he saw on television. The Jennings were not a country club family, so he grew up on the hard scrabble Memphis municipal courses, such as Fox Meadows, affectionately known as "The Rock" for its hardpan surfaces and lack of grass. On summer nights, Ben and his childhood friends, Joe Carrol and Freddie Franks, would sneak onto The Rock from the adjoining apartment complex to get in eight holes on the back nine. If the notoriously cranky starter, Rallo, had gone home by the time they reached his shack, they would play the remaining eleven holes, usually in the dark. They invented ridiculous short game and putting contests by placing the balls in impossible positions, betting Cokes on who could execute the shot. The games produced short-game magic. Ben and Joe competed and won local tournaments, Ben securing a scholarship to play golf at the University of Memphis and Joe going on to play basketball at Purdue University where he would make all Big 10 his senior year. Despite incredible talent, Freddie refused formal tournaments for a "piece of metal" but instead concentrated on money games with the muni-course regulars.

Ben had to get some relief from Annie's illness, Marco, the impending case, and stress of financing his law practice. Incessantly, he ran his fingers through his hair as he drove more aggressively than safety allowed through congested Midtown traffic. His phone chirped from the console. Ben's friend Matthew Graves, a genuinely devout Christian who was kind to a fault, dealt personally with Ben's crisis of faith that had developed during the past several years, genuinely attempting to help Ben back to what he considered the right path. Matthew, a fellow lawyer and member of the Lunch Crew, frequently offered a kind voice and empathetic heart to Ben's sometimes chaotic life.

"Hey Matthew," Ben said in the calmest voice he could manage.

"Hey, Ben, I was just thinking about you and wanted to reach out and see how you were doing?"

"Matthew, you are too kind, my friend. Honestly, it is not going too well. I don't have the time to go through it, but it's a real shitstorm at the office, and Annie has not been taking her meds."

"Dear Lord, Ben. I am so sorry. Is there anything I can do?"

"I wish there were. Matthew, I have been thinking a lot about what you have been saying. I must tell you that I now believe that God exists and is real."

Matthew's voice was joyous. "Ben, that is marvelous! I am so happy! This is terrific news."

"And do you know how I know he is real?" Ben continued.

"No, but please tell me. I am so excited to hear."

"Because he hates me. God fucking hates my guts. That is how I know he is real!"

"Oh, Ben." Matthew was ever calm. "Come on, my friend. This is not healthy."

"Nothing in my life is healthy. I am going to die and go to hell. I am a sinner and a loser. Life sucks, and then I will die. I am sorry."

"Ben, we can get through this," Matthew urged. "Where are you? I can come meet you."

Ben quickly calmed down. "Man, I am really sorry. You didn't deserve that, and I am an ass. I apologize. Thanks for the offer, but I can't right now."

"No sweat, brother. I am a big boy and your friend. What can I do to help?"

"Matthew Graves, you are a good egg, and I love you for it. But right now, the only one who can get me through this is me. I do appreciate you."

The two hung up the phone. What a jerk he had just been. Ben immediately hated himself for his misdirected explosion. The stress of the day had reached peak, and poor Matthew was the undeserving recipient. He knew he had to be better.

Dusk set in and a brilliant sunset of reds and oranges, like cotton candy, streamed in the western sky over the ancient oaks when Ben pulled up to the back of Galloway Golf Course, a pretty but short little muni course in the heart of Memphis surrounded by stately homes on estate lots covered in beautiful hardwoods. He popped the back, pulled out the three Titleist Pro V1s and his Scotty Cameron Newport 2 putter and headed to the putting green. The cart guys grinned and yelled his name as he walked by. Ben offered a high-five and then a wave at the lady who ran the snack bar walking to her car after a long day. Here, watching perfectly rolled putts dive effortlessly into the cup, Ben felt most at peace and able to unpack the catastrophic events of the day.

There in the darkness, putting by the light of the clubhouse, he heard a familiar voice: "Heard you got your ass kicked today."

Ben shook his head, smiling. Without looking up, he said, "Partner, you have no idea."

It was The Sage.

CHAPTER 2

Alicia Landers was a beautiful woman with skin of mocha and a smile both alluring and intelligent. She came from poverty in North Memphis but set her sights higher than her immediate surroundings. When her classmates skipped school to smoke weed and party to the latest beats from the popular rappers of the day, Alicia studied and read. Her mother was sixteen when she had her, and Alicia was not going to make that mistake.

Alicia's English teacher took her under her wing and encouraged Alicia to plan the steps necessary to achieve her goal: to be part of the bigger world and leave her to leave cyclical poverty behind. Alicia became determined to graduate college, become a lawyer, and return to her community to help others see the value in hard work, discipline, and accountability.

Alicia earned a scholarship to the historically black college, Mississippi Valley State University, located just west of Greenwood in tiny Itta Bena, the birthplace of blues legend B.B. King. She majored in English, determined to improve her communication skills. Alicia abhorred her friends teasing for her proper diction and academic effort, knowing those skills were imperative to a better life. At Mississippi Valley, she met Marcus Jones, a biology major from Jackson, Mississippi. Marcus was the son of a schoolteacher and foreman at the local casket company and second in his family to attend college. He hoped to go to pharmacy school after graduating.

The two became inseparable and quickly fell in love. As seniors, they made plans to marry and start a life together. During their senior year at Valley, Alicia got pregnant.

Despite pressure from her family, she refused to terminate the child. Alicia saw the child as a gift and believed her pregnancy to be all part of God's plan. Marcus hung in there all the way and was excited to start a family, even though the conditions were not ideal.

In July, Alicia went into labor eight weeks early and gave birth to Sydney at Lutheran Hospital in Memphis. A beautiful child, Sydney suffered many of the complications associated with premature babies. The most serious was necrotizing enterocolitis, a dangerous condition wherein a baby's digestive track is not fully functional, and the intestines have difficulty moving food through the digestive track. The danger is that the food that does not move through can cause a hole in the intestines, allowing bacteria to enter the bloodstream and cause a potentially deadly infection known as sepsis. Sydney had been in the neonatal department of Lutheran Hospital for almost thirty days when she began experiencing fever and agitation. The next morning, before she could be taken to surgery, she suffered respiratory arrest. The doctors managed to revive her, but over the next weeks and months, it was clear that Sydney had suffered brain damage during the anoxic event. A nurse whispered to Alicia that it should not have happened.

The strain of the situation affected her relationship with Marcus, and his trips to Memphis became less frequent. Alicia faced huge medical bills and a future of supporting a child who would require a lifetime of special care. Then, one day at church, Alicia met Stephanie Mann, a sixty-two-year-old lawyer who came to the law after serving in the Navy. Stephanie had graduated nursing school and practiced as an ER nurse for ten years. She began law school at night when she became disenchanted with the unanswered mistakes she witnessed daily in the emergency room. As a malpractice attorney, Stephanie possessed a tremendous grasp of medicine. As a trial lawyer, she struggled to effectively communicate her medical knowledge to a jury.

Stephanie knew her strengths and limitations, so she teamed up on a case-by-case basis with veteran trial lawyers to assist her. Ben worked with Stephanie many times, and they quickly developed a chemistry. Ben hated grinding for weeks over thousands of pages of medical records looking for the needle in the haystack, while Stephanie relished the forensic drilling down deep into the details. As "first chair," Ben directed the strategy and formulated the approach to handle depositions and the presentation at trial, akin to the British system where a solicitor prepares the case in the early stages, leaving it to a barrister to conduct the trial. If only a case, from start to finish, lasted one hour in real life like it did on television. Instead, most medical negligence cases take three to five years to get to trial. The entire process is designed to deter and discourage unhappy patients from bringing cases. Memphis had more than one million residents and no more than six lawyers who handled medical negligence cases on a regular basis because of the technical and financial requirements necessary to bring a case.

The Health Care Liability Act was a draconian labyrinth of onerous and technical requirements; the failure to adhere to any single one would lead to complete dismissal of the case. Many legal malpractice cases stemmed from rank-and-file lawyers attempting to take on the Healthcare Liability Act, following the allure of a big payday, and big defense firms licking their lips in anticipation of a lawyer who doesn't know their way around medical malpractice attempting to sue one of their doctor clients. Defense lawyers could easily exploit a novice's lack of understanding of the arcane requirements of the Health Care Liability Act, drafted by the medical lobby and rammed into law by the most conservative legislature in the United States. Interestingly, when those same legislators' families suffered medical negligence, the legislators pursued cases against hospitals and physicians with the zealousness of the converted, seeking to put a pox on the house of any offending medical professional.

In Memphis, those six hearty souls were pitted against the hospitals, doctors, and resource-rich insurance companies, who aimed to rid the state of the trial lawyer pestilence much like what had been successfully accomplished in Texas years before. Prior to the medical lobby becoming involved, citizens of the state of Texas enjoyed protections from negligent acts of doctors and hospitals, allowing Texas jurors to determine a fair amount to award without interference from the legislature. However, the strong medical lobby had persuaded the Texas legislature to place artificial "caps" on damages that could be awarded, thus making it financially unfeasible for private attorneys to accept those lawsuits on a contingency fee basis. A contingency fee is one where the lawyer does not receive an hourly rate but instead waits until the end of the case and receives a percentage of the proceeds of either a settlement or jury award. If lawyers do not get a settlement and lose at trial, they are not compensated for their time or expenses in advancing the case, thus risking thousands of dollars of their own money and hundreds of hours of time they can never recover.

The insurance companies of doctors and hospitals spend untold sums of money on every aspect of a case affecting their clients and leave nothing to chance. For starters, the insurance companies pay health care lobbyists to pour millions of dollars into the elections of state legislators and judges to garner support for tort reform and favorable laws to protect doctors and hospitals. Next, they create faux grassroots organizations dedicated to convincing uniformed citizens to support laws that are actually against their own interests. Then, the medical insurance companies heavily fund local chambers of commerce in their states to work in concert with these

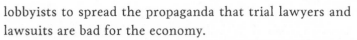

lobbyists to spread the propaganda that trial lawyers and lawsuits are bad for the economy.

Once the special laws protecting doctors and hospitals were in place in Tennessee, medical insurance companies dedicated millions of dollars to hiring white-shoe law firms to stamp out every conceivable case brought by a plaintiff's attorney. The doctors in Tennessee and many other states created their own insurance company wherein each physician is a shareholder and benefits financially by keeping all cases to a minimum. For this reason, it was next to impossible for a patient bringing a case to get a Tennessee physician to testify as a medical expert against a fellow doctor because of their shared financial interest was at stake. To testify would damage the company in which they were both part owners. Every doctor in Tennessee who was being sued by an unhappy patient could count on a retinue of local and state doctors lining up in support, closing their eyes to errors and flaws, and saying what needed to be said to protect the home team. Tennessee hospitals have a system in place, employing fellow physicians to investigate bad outcomes and determine the fault, if any, of the health care providers. However, Tennessee has a specific law that prevents this very relevant information from ever being released. One must be a masochist to represent a Tennessee plaintiff against a doctor or hospital. There is a reason that, in Tennessee, more than 80 percent of all jury verdicts involving doctors and hospitals result in their favor.

Stephanie spent the first year after taking Alicia's case scouring over thousands of pages of medical records and piecing the case together like a jigsaw puzzle. A jackass can kick a barn down, but it takes a carpenter to build one. Stephanie meticulously reconstructed what had happened to Sydney from scores of nurses' notes, physicians' orders, x-rays, and laboratory reports. In this area of the law, it was the plaintiff's lawyer's task to boil a maze of scientific information down to a basic concept that uneducated juries could understand. It was the job of the lawyers protecting hospitals and doctors to muddy the waters and complicate every aspect of every medical procedure, convincing jurors that magic, not science, was being performed, and they best not even attempt to understand what these medical miracle workers were doing.

Ben Jennings had a well-earned reputation for connecting with juries. He grew up with the very working-class people who typically served on juries. He understood their backgrounds and feelings because he shared them. Ben's standard for taking a case was simple: If he could not tell a non-lawyer's spouse at a cocktail party the story in one minute and have her shudder and gasp, the case was not worth taking. Stephanie knew she had some convincing to do anytime she wanted Ben to join up.

Ben met Stephanie for lunch at the Choctaw Country Club. The Chock was second in line to the Memphis Country Club, a club that refused membership to those who could not trace their Memphis lineage four generations back. Ben's foray into the upper-middle class and exceptional golf game produced enough sponsors to gain admission. Every time he stepped foot on the grounds, he smiled at the irony of his membership and thought of the famous Groucho Marx quote: "I would never join a club that would have me as a member." Ben was troubled by the club's historical racism but loved the golf course and easy access to a quick round and place to hit range balls. Such dilemmas occur most weeks in the South. For all its history of reprehensible behavior, Memphis had made great strides in righting past wrongs. While vestiges remained, private clubs now had open membership policies. Memphis had more Black judges than White on the bench. Its city council sat a majority of Black members and the director of police, city attorney, and superintendent of schools were all Black. Access to economic levers had been slower, but most contracts with Memphis City government required a substantial minority participation. Blacks integrated private schools throughout the city, and the athletics in those leagues was more diverse than the public schools.

As a member, Ben delighted in bringing Black guests to play the course and eat in the dining room. Southern society had progressed enough to not make verbal statements when Black guests arrived, but their appearance still annoyed the blue-haired ladies of society. Ben strolled into the main dining room, oozing his most syrupy Southern charm, greeting each bridge club member by name and walking that line between grace and condescension.

Stephanie entered the dining room; she wore a tailored blue suit, white silk blouse, Hèrmes scarf, and high-heeled black Christian Louboutins with the signature red sole. Her hair and makeup were without flaw. Ben could not guess her age but knew she had two grown kids and three grandchildren. While petite in stature, Stephanie walked confidently through any room as though she owned it. The elder ladies stole glances but were too proper to stare. Stephanie, all too familiar with Southern customs, paid them nary a notice, walking directly to her old friend and colleague. Ben stood up, arms open, grinning from ear to ear, and wrapped her up in a bear hug. Not ever the touchy type, Stephanie indulged Ben like a little brother.

"Stephanie! How are you doing, darling?"

"You know, I could always be better, but the Lord has blessed me." Stephanie always played down her success, not wanting to jinx it. She worked hard and was successful but tried to cry poor. Except for the Hèrmes and the Louboutins. They sat down and chatted about their families and courthouse gossip. Stephanie adhered to the Southern custom of small talk but could never get down to business fast enough.

"Ben, this is the one," she said. "It's a terrible case, and I think we can really do well."

"Stephanie, you have never met a case you didn't like." She aggressively took on way more cases than Ben felt comfortable handling. Stephanie ignored Ben's flippant remarks. The two had been to trial five other times together and settled another twenty. They were comfortable with each other, neither feeling the need to sugarcoat the truth. They had danced this dance many times, and Stephanie blew right through his teasing, getting down to the sale.

"No, no, this is different," she said. "This one is special."

"You always tell me that. Although, to your credit, most times you are right."

"Not kidding, I promise. This one has everything."

"Stephanie, of course, if it is good, I want it, but I am just so stacked up right now. I am just not sure I can give it the time and attention it needs."

The waitress approached the table to take their order. Ben gave Stephanie some recommendations and then said, "I don't know why I went through that because I know you're going to end up with a salad."

She smiled. "True to that." And turned to the waitress and ordered the house salad. Ben went with crab cakes and a bowl of gumbo. As soon as the waitress left, Stephanie dove right into her pitch.

"Beautiful young woman whose newborn was deprived oxygen because the doctor messed up. Alicia Landers was twenty-two and had a premature baby. The child was premature but doing pretty good. Then, little Sydney stopped pooping for several days. When that happens, the biggest concern is NEC. When a baby gets NEC, the doctor's standard of care requires them to perform several x-rays per day to make sure she doesn't get a hole in her bowel, which can cause sepsis and death."

"So did they not run the x-rays?" Ben interrupted.

"That's the thing. The x-rays were run, but the doctor read them and not the radiologist."

"So what? Can't a doctor read an x-ray?"

"Not if he gets it wrong. Lutheran Hospital has an entire squadron of radiologists on call, ready to read these very x-rays. The doctor did not call them and instead read the x-ray himself."

"And?" Ben asked.

"And he read the damn x-ray wrong. Sydney got septic and went into cardiopulmonary arrest."

Stephanie started with Ben's hot buttons, knowing he was a sucker for children and beautiful women. If she could only add a dog in there somewhere, he would surely be hooked. Ben viewed a lawsuit and trial as almost a dramatic production of pitting good versus evil and beautiful versus ugly. Ben needed a narrative and a hook to take a case. He had lost enough of them to not jump as quickly as he once had. His lack of discretion taking cases with no chance of success had cost him thousands of dollars.

"What the hell is NEC?"

"Necrotizing enterocolitis. It's a condition in preemies. The food doesn't move properly through the intestines and sits too long, causing it to rot part of the intestine and cause a perforation, which then leads to bacteria in the blood."

"How is the little girl now?"

"Not sure completely, but very developmentally delayed. It seems likely that she will have permanent brain damage. Her pediatrician diagnosed her with cerebral palsy secondary to her lack of oxygen to the brain."

"What about the husband?"

"Unfortunately, she is a single mom. The father has kind of disappeared because the pressure was just too much. He still comes and goes. If he is like a lot of other guys, when he finds out there may be money involved, his interest in little Sydney may go up quickly."

"Have you filed the lawsuit yet?"

"Statute runs next Tuesday. That is why I need you on board now."

"Dang, Stephanie, you always do this to me."

"Come on, Ben, everyone knows you are the patron saint of lost causes."

"That is pretty tight window to get a medical malpractice case together."

"Ben, you know me. The complaint is drafted and medicals summarized and organized."

"Who are we suing?"

"Dr. Robert Kirkwood."

"I don't know him."

"I didn't either before this. I checked him out, and he has a pretty good reputation."

Ben paused, steepled his fingers under his chin, and looked up to nothing in particular. "Stephanie, that sounds pretty good, but I want to think about it. Do you have an expert?"

"Oh, yeah! I forgot to tell you. He is the best part of the case. Dr. Bell is one of the foremost experts on the topic. The criterial for measuring degrees of NEC is called the Bell Criteria."

"Wow! You have certainly piqued my curiosity."

"I tell you what. Alicia is coming to my office tomorrow. How about I bring her by your office, and you can at least meet her before you make a decision?"

Ben sighed. "Fine, I will be there."

The food came out.

"You have got to try some of these crab cakes. They are terrific."

Stephanie picked at her salad. "Does it feel like all of these White folks are staring at us?"

Ben grinned. "Absolutely. Isn't it scandalous? Come close and give me some sugar. That will really rile them up."

"Boy, you better stop that. They will have me hanging from a rope on the eighteenth hole over there. You are one crazy-ass White boy."

"You know what Jimmy Buffet says: 'If I weren't so crazy, I would go insane.' By the way, get an extra order crab cakes to take some home to John. I know you aren't cooking."

Stephanie lifted an eyebrow.

Since his divorce five years ago, Ben Jennings' love life had been quite the hot topic of discussion, debate, and wager among lawyers, colleagues, club members, and wives looking to pair him up with single friends. He was often seen at restaurants, charity events, and dinner parties with a statuesque model or one of those Ole Miss types who are stunningly beautiful yet eerily indistinguishable from one other, with long legs, a year-round tan, hourglass figure, perfect teeth, and perky bums. At dinner and cocktail parties, his buddies' wives were gracious when meeting these women but gave each other a knowing look, making private wagers on when the next one would appear. It is a solemn duty among married southern women to aid and assist in getting every available bachelor married as soon as possible. While ostensibly done to help a single friend, it is really self-preservation to keep their own husbands from thinking the single life is better.

Ben maintained cordial relationships but never let a woman get too close. The rumor among the boys was that when Ben broke up, the lady received a generous parting gift. The information always came from the women, as Ben stridently adhered to the long Southern tradition of gentlemen never discussing such matters.

Like most of his friends, Stephanie could not resist landing a not-so-subtle jab.

"By the way, with all of those girls chasing you around, when are you going to get married?" Stephanie waggled her fork at him.

Ben set down his napkin and looked her in the eye pensively, leaning into her, almost invading her personal space. Ben spoke in a low earnest voice, "Stephanie, in my experience, a man does not realize what true happiness is until he is married."

"Ben, that is so sweet." Stephanie glowed at the unexpected insight. After just a second, Ben had leaned back in his chair with a gleam in his eye.

"And then . . . it's too late."

"Boy, you are out of your mind." Stephanie shook her head in disbelief.

CHAPTER 3

emphis's revitalized South Main district is a stone's throw from the Mississippi River, lined with rows of three-story buildings constructed in the early 1900s that are now occupied by restaurants, boutiques, and small professional offices. Ben's office occupied the third floor of an old dry goods store overlooking the National Civil Rights Museum and the balcony of the Lorraine Motel where Dr. Martin Luther King Jr. was assassinated from a next-door boarding house in April 1968. As Ben hung up the phone, he looked out his window and noticed an older Black couple approaching the commemorative plaque marking the sacred spot. Ben could see the man bow his head, pull out a handkerchief, and dab his eyes as his wife put a comforting arm around his shoulder. Ben felt a lump in his own throat and welcomed the reminder of the historical significance of the ground he occupied.

His third-story office had fourteen-foot ceilings constructed of exposed heart pine timbers from a virgin forest in Louisiana. The floors were a patchwork of hardwood that could be dated like a geologist could estimate the age of layers of rock formations. Ben loved the exposed aluminum ducts and the irregular brick patterns running the length of the north wall. Natural light flooded in through the length of the southern wall, allowing a view down South Main to the Arcade Restaurant and Central Station. The Arcade is a classic art deco American diner with neon lights and a colorful interior famous for the back booth that was always reserved for Elvis, who frequented the place before his death. Tourists pass available tables to wait for a seat where the King used to have meals. Across the street, the famous juke joint, Ernestine and Hazels, is known for soul burgers, a great juke box, and a former brothel upstairs that is known to have a resident ghost.

Ben and his law partner, Marco Alexopoulos, each had a corner office on the front eastern-facing wall. Their offices were separated by a large conference room with a sixteen-foot heart-pine table Ben designed and had constructed by local craftsmen. From his window on the northeastern corner, Ben could see the street North toward the famous Beale Street and the FedEx Forum. He often walked in that direction to grab lunch at the Green Beetle, the oldest tavern in Memphis and the place Machine Gun Kelly holed up in, avoiding the long arm of the law. Years ago, Ben had insisted that the renovated office have clean lines and be devoid of superfluous ornamentation. Instead of conventional doors, Ben designed a series of huge eight-by-six sliding wooden "barn" doors below glass transoms throughout the office, allowing the spaces to adapt and morph into the specific need of the occasion.

South Main was Memphis's art district, and Ben adorned the common areas with modern, colorful geometric abstract paintings, sourced from local artists, placed on white walls, lit by modern LED tracks lights contrasted with well-placed vintage fixtures. Guests entering the large space were welcomed with a life-sized cutout of Elvis in one corner and an antique coffin-style Coca-Cola cooler stocked with Cokes and Ghost River and Wise Acre Beer produced a couple of blocks away. Guests sat on a large distressed leather sofa or one of two facing tobacco-colored Barcelona chairs and ottomans, first made famous in architect Phillip Johnson's Glass House. Strategically placed throughout the office were several bourbon barrels surrounded by stools and a dart board in a small nook, working in unison to create a modern but welcoming environment.

In his personal spacious office, Ben displayed prints of architect Frank Lloyd Wright's masterpieces, Falling Water, and the Imperial Hotel of Tokyo, beside E. Fay Jones' autographed sketch of his AIA gold medal-winning Ozark Mountain chapel, Thorncrown. In front of Ben's simple cherry desk and table sat a long mustard-colored leather sofa. Beside it, Fredrick Remington's bronze sculpture "The Mountain Main" stood on a pedestal, facing a vintage leather club chair. On the west wall was a low blonde-wood book-case holding sports memorabilia and photographs of his children from some of their memorable journeys.

There were crystal glasses and decanters filled with bourbon and scotch. While there were many Southern traditions Ben found arcane and silly, he loved the South's strict adherence to manners and hospitality. It was an unpardonable sin to not rise when a lady entered the room, not open a door for her, or not send a timely handwritten note in response to a kindness, gift, or death. Northerners are quick to deride the Southern ways but, once here, always go away having been charmed by its simple graces. At his core, Ben was a son of the South and, for better or worse, loved this place and its people.

Precisely on time for their meeting, Stephanie strode into Ben's reception area. Stephanie was dressed to the nines but was quickly eclipsed by the stunning woman of regal bearing who accompanied her. At five-nine, the now-twenty-three-year-old Alicia Landers looked like bronze sculpted by Rodin. She had mesmerizing, sparkling round brown eyes, shoulder-length, straight dark brown hair, and a dazzling smile she demurely revealed upon first eye contact with Ben. She wore fitted tan riding pants, black boots, and a crisp white button-down shirt. The usually ebullient Ben was at a loss for words. Stephanie broke the silence by greeting Ben and quickly introducing him to Alicia.

"Alicia, I want to introduce the man who is going to save you." Stephanie took one look at Ben and knew his signing onto the case was a fait accompli. Ben met Alicia's eyes and saw her blush under his gaze.

"Hello, Ms. Landers," he said, taking the hand she offered. "It's a pleasure to meet you." She smiled, and Ben gestured toward his office. "I am so sorry it is under these circumstances."

"Mr. Jennings, the pleasure is all mine. I understand you are a miracle worker, and it's a miracle worker I need. And please, call me Alicia."

Ben put his hands in his pockets and ducked his head ever so slightly, "Alicia it is then. And of course, please call me Ben."

She smiled, seemingly embarrassed, and said, "Ok, Ben."

The three walked to his office. Ben served fresh pimento cheese and egg salad with crackers, green olives, and Coca-Cola over cracked ice. Another steadfast Southern edict is that prior to discussions of a business nature, one must get to know the other on a personal level. Anywhere else, folks ask each other where they went to college. In Memphis, it is always where they attended high school. Ben loved the shocked reaction when he told people had had attended Sherwood Junior and Wooddale high schools, which are both mostly Black, rough-and-tumble public schools. Very few Memphis lawyers started in the public school system, and even fewer White ones did. Ben's insecurity about his background in the lower-middle class caused him to scrupulously remove the obvious tells of clothes, shoes, and diction, but age and perspective offered him a certain pride in having overcome those obstacles. The ladies sat on the sofa facing a coffee table with the refreshments on antique china, and Ben sat down in the leather club chair facing them, his Coca-Cola already resting on a coaster on the bookcase beside him.

"So Alicia, where did you go to high school?"

Actually

"Actually," she said, looking straight ahead, "I went Trezvant." It was a notorious, tough school located in the center of gang-infested North Memphis.

"Oh, yeah, up in Frayser. I played basketball there."

Alicia raised her eyebrows and tilted her head, "How in the world did a guy like you play basketball against Trezvant?"

Ben smiled warmly. "Because I played ball at Wooddale."

Alicia shifted in her seat and pointed her finger at Ben. "You went to Wooddale?"

"And before that, Sherwood Junior High," he bragged.

"Wait, what? You went to Orange Mound to school and then to Wooddale?"

"Yes, ma'am, I did."

"Get out of here. How did that happen?" she asked incredulously.

"It's a long story, but I come from a background similar to yours."

Stephanie, who was well-aware of Ben's background, could not resist poking at him. "You have to watch out for Ben. He went to those tough public schools with all of those Black folks and sometimes thinks he is a real brother."

They laughed at Stephanie, not usually known for her humor.

Ben raised both of his hands in mock surrender. "Guilty."

The other safe topic for polite Southern discussion is college football. It is said that in the South there are two seasons: football and spring football. "Stephanie told me you went to college at Mississippi Valley."

"I most certainly did."

"How about those Delta Devils? Did they have a good season?" He referred to the nickname of her school.

"Yes, we have some really good players this year and we're going to be good. You know, by the way, that Hall of Famer Jerry Rice played there in the 80s," Stephanie said.

"Oh, yes," Ben moaned. "That is the first thing anyone who went to Valley tells me."

Alicia's shoulders noticeably relaxed, and she unclenched her hands and leaned in for the first time to grab a cracker and spread pimento cheese. Ben bent forward at the same time to join her, the two sharing a smile before leaning back. They needed to talk about the case.

"Alicia, Stephanie has told me about your situation and the case, and I am just so sorry. I have two kids of my own, and I cannot imagine what you must have gone through."

Alicia tilted her head down and frowned for the first time.

Ben continued, "How is Sydney now?"

Alicia gathered herself and looked him in the eyes. "Ben, she is almost one and the sweetest thing you have ever seen but struggles mightily."

"Please tell me about it, if you would."

"She has missed every milestone. She cannot crawl, is not close to speaking, and cannot swallow food, so she will be on a feeding tube her entire life. She smiles beautifully but does not seem to understand any word or gesture. Her pediatrician told me that she would likely never walk or talk. Just think, she will have to wear diapers the rest of her life."

"Goodness, gracious, Alicia. I am so sorry."

"The doctors tell me she has cerebral palsy and will always require special care. I am at my end and don't know what I will do. There is no way I can work and provide her care. My mother has been great helping, but how much can I ask of her? The doctors tell me that when Sydney gets older, there are therapies that can really help her quality of life. But how can I ever afford those? If I work, I can't take care of her. If I don't work, how can we pay our bills? Ben, I have a stack of medical bills nine inches tall on my kitchen table. Without your help, we will never get out of this hole."

Ben sighed and leaned back in toward them. "Alicia, there is no guarantee in a case like this. These things are hard. Stephanie is as good as gold, but man, this is a really tough case. The entire thing rests on whether a jury will rule against a doctor because at 6:00 a.m., he missed a little spec of free air that would have saved Sydney. He is going to look the jury in the eye and tell them he did the best he could. He is going to tell them that even today, that x-ray does not show free air. The doctor's lawyers will traipse a parade of fancy experts through the courtroom who will tell the jury how good a physician Dr. Kirkwood is and how many lives he has saved."

"But we have Dr. Bell. Stephanie told me he is the leading expert in the world."

Ben nodded his head. "That is a fair point."

It was Alicia's turn to lean in. She placed her palms together in front of her as if praying. "Please, I will be eternally grateful if you will take this case. Because at least if we have this case, I can have hope. And that is more than I have right now."

Ben leaned back and ran his hand through his hair. He felt her words in his gut. Annie had serious mental health issues, and he could afford to get her all the treatment she needed. This just was not fair.

After a few seconds, Alicia continued. "Ben, you are all I have. If we do not get help, I do not know how I will raise her. I always planned on law school, but now I have to figure out how to get a job and still take care of her. I have no one to help me, and you just have to do this."

Ben audibly let out a deep breath. "Alicia, I'm your guy. I am going to do everything I can for you and Sydney. And if we go down, the three of us will go together. But I am not in the business of going down. We are going to get Sydney justice. You both deserve it."

Tears ran down Alicia's eyes, and Stephanie handed her a tissue. Stephanie, who was also wiping her eyes, looked at Ben and silently gave him a nod of appreciation.

"Ben, I can never thank you enough," Alicia. said "Everyone should have hope. You have just given it to me. I know you can do this. I feel the connection. I cannot wait for you to meet Sydney."

Ben reached out for Alicia's hand and clutched it tight when she put hers in his. "You are welcome. Go take care of that little girl of yours, and Stephanie and I will get the ball rolling. These cases can take years, but I will do my best to get it on the court's trial calendar as soon as we can." Ben turned. "Stephanie, what do we need to do to get the complaint ready to file?"

"I will email you my draft tonight along with the medical records and a medical summary."

"God, I hate medical records." Reviewing medical records was Ben's least favorite part of being a lawyer. Cases like this would have thousands of pages. His dyslexia made regular reading challenging, but deciphering the scribbles of doctors and reading the various lab studies and progress reports would prove truly daunting.

"Ben, I have you covered," Stephanie said. "I have a ten-page summary that gets you everything you need to know now. Then, you can gradually dig in more as we go. You have me by phone and email. I have already prepared a rough draft of the lawsuit, so that won't take long to finalize."

They stood up, and as they walked toward the door, Alicia took Ben's right hand in hers and placed her left hand on his elbow. "Thanks, Ben. You don't know what a relief this is."

"You are welcome, Alicia. Here is my card and cell number if you need me for any reason. Don't hesitate to call me."

***

Ben spent the weekend reading Stephanie's summary and matching it with the records. The records consisted of over five thousand pages contained in three banker's boxes. It was a forced discipline that Ben resisted, but he knew that to handle the case properly, he had to do it. Whichever lawyers defended this case would know every record backward and forward and to cede superior knowledge to them would be suicide.

Ben's mild dyslexia was a closely guarded secret. When he was a child, he believed he just was not smart until a helpful fourth-grade teacher diagnosed his problem and did her best to help him cope with his processing issues. People with dyslexia have difficulty reading due to problems identifying speech sounds and learning how they relate to letters and words, commonly known as decoding. Reading dyslexia is similar in that it affects areas of the brain that process language. If Ben did not hyper-focus, he would read a paragraph and skip entire lines and many words. Sometimes, he would read the words backward or not be able to decipher what the letters added up to spell. However, there are strategies of accepting the brain's natural tendency and decoding the written work into understandable language. There were many people with worse cases than Ben, but not being able to read easily like others caused him great inner turmoil.

Part of the reason Ben wanted to play pro golf was that the only reading required was that of the greens. He wanted to face his challenge head-on yet tried to take the easy way out by playing golf. When his professional golf dream ended, Ben had no choice but to tackle his problem. The virtue in his dyslexia was that it had forced him to develop an almost photographic memory. He became an uncanny listener, focusing intently on the spoken word to compensate for his reading challenges. He laughed at his own hubris for choosing a profession that relied on reading more than anything else.

Monday morning, he felt sufficiently versed in the case to work on the draft lawsuit Stephanie had started. The lawsuit—or complaint, as it is known in legal parlance—is the document that begins a case. The document is designed to put the person being sued, known as the defendant, on notice as to the legal claims being made against them. Also, the document contains technical assertions that the lawsuit is filed in the correct court, county, and state, otherwise known as venue and jurisdiction. The document must next lay out sufficient factual allegations to properly put the defendant on notice as to the specific claims of negligence being made against them. The complaint must assert a factual basis for the causal connection between the negligence and damages claimed to have been suffered, which must also be specified. Finally, the complaint must ask for relief in terms of the money the plaintiff seeks to compensate them for the damage suffered.

The following Tuesday, Stephanie filed the complaint electronically along with a summons, which a sheriff's deputy physically served as a document to the defendant. The computer randomly selected Judge Jerome Jones to preside over the case. This was great news. Judge Jones, a tall, serious Black man, previously handled medical negligence cases on behalf of plaintiffs before he ascended the bench. He was not known for doing plaintiffs favors, but he had impeccable integrity and a razor-sharp mind and was both knowledgeable and capable of handling a complex medical negligence case without hedging to either side. At least we have that going for us, Ben thought as he tried to rally some positivity going into the game.

Within one week of filing the complaint, the sheriff returned notice that Dr. Robert Kirkwood had been physically served. He would have thirty days to file a responsive document known as an "answer" to respond to the specific allegations contained in the complaint. They would soon know their opponent, and the battle would be joined.

CHAPTER 4

One Commerce Square lords over the center of downtown Memphis. The square tower of concrete and glass was constructed in the 1970s, providing one of the centerpiece structures to the Memphis skyline and now the home of iBank, whose sign is proudly displayed at the top. Located on the twenty-ninth-floor penthouse are the ornate offices of the Thornton Firm. Strangely, it was named for Archibald Thornton, a successful and famed Memphis lawyer, who never practiced in his namesake firm. Thornton was the mentor of senior and founding partner Marston Owens III, who named his firm in Archibald's honor. Marston's father died when he was a teenager, and it was Thornton, a fellow church member, who took Marston under his wing, shepherding the wayward but precocious young man, mentoring him toward a career in law. Marston would spend the rest of his life honoring the man responsible for his success.

When clients entered the building from Monroe Street, they walked into a space that quickly blossomed into an open four-story lobby supported and surrounded by large, fluted marble columns. Years ago, the once heavily trafficked bank had moved out of this grand space and into online banking and small satellite locations at suburban strip malls. Its lobby had been converted to an event space for weddings and big parties.

After taking the elevators to the penthouse office of the Thornton Firm, which occupied the entire floor, guests were greeted in a grand office that had all the trimmings expected in a brass-plate silk-stocking law firm that exclusively represented doctors and hospitals. Dark oak paneling with wainscoting, oak floors as palettes for elegant oriental rugs, tufted leather sofas, Queen Anne chairs around antique cherry side tables set with colorful Tiffany lamps. On the walls of the spacious reception area hung large paintings of scenes of the Mississippi River, the Memphis skyline, and of the firm's namesake, Archibald Thornton who, with his grey hair and steely eyes, resembled an oil baron from a hundred years past. Bordering the ornate reception area, a floor-to-ceiling glass wall allowed visitors to see the expansive conference room which had a glorious view of the Mississippi River and seemingly all of eastern Arkansas. In the conference room, sat a thirty-foot oval table of highly polished cherry accompanied by eighteen modern, expensive black leather high-backed chairs on rollers, spaced apart in precise distances, all slightly tilted toward the even larger chair at the end of the table reserved for Marston. A large video monitor covered one wall and an original Carroll Cloar painting the other.

Floor-to-ceiling glass opened the expanse in three directions to the most exceptional prospect in all the Mid-South. From here, an expansive view of the Mississippi River and eastern Arkansas gave witness to the most beautiful sunsets one could imagine, changing color and angle with the evolving seasons along the Big Muddy. Guests could watch long barges meander lazily under the old and new bridges, as they were known to locals. Four main bridges span the Mississippi River at Memphis: the Frisco Bridge, the Harahan, the Memphis and Arkansas, and the Hernando DeSoto. When it opened in 1892, the Frisco was the third longest bridge in the world and first to span the Mississippi south of St. Louis. The Harahan Bridge opened in 1916 for railroad traffic. In 1949, the Memphis and Arkansas bridge, now known as the "old bridge," was constructed, linking Tennessee and Arkansas via Interstate 55. The Hernando DeSoto, or "new bridge," constructed in 1972, is a modern structure with the metal supports above the road forming an elongated "M." At night, the bridges put on a light show with a rotation of multiple colors and themes, depending on the occasion. The view also allowed guests to see the buildings making up much of downtown, from the Pyramid to the South Main District. When on the outdoor patio, one could hear the trolley cars passing below, blowing their familiar whistles. On nice days, lawyers of the Thornton Firm enjoyed lunch on the terrace with the tantalizing aromas of the Rendezvous Restaurant's BBQ pit wafting to their perch.

From the reception area, wide hallways pointed north and south and eventually in a square around to the eastern "city" side where the support staff occupied the lower-status wing of the office. In the Thornton Firm, a person's status could be deduced by the size of their office, view of the river, and proximity to Marston's office. From reception, ninety feet north down the hallway, the suite of offices dedicated to Marston Owens III, occupied the corner. Prior to entry, one had to pass Marston's secretary and, to either side, paralegals manning a mini-reception area to the senior partner's office.

Once inside Marston's office, a visitor encountered an almost surreal twenty-by-forty space that, for all its size, was minimally appointed with a modest and simple three-by-six desk devoid of any paper, file, or object. It was uncomfortably cold, always at a chilly 66 degrees. The desk had been Mr. Thornton's and was treated by Marston as a priceless masterpiece. Two simple antique wooden armchairs with brown leather cushions faced the desk at precise 45-degree angles, symmetrically placed to the inch. Behind the desk was Marston's two-by-six credenza that matched the desk and was identically lacking in having anything on its surface, save the black modern office telephone. The corner windows offered glorious north and west views of downtown and the Mississippi River, similar to those in the conference room. To Marston's left, a wall was covered with a curtain of cabinets and bookshelves filled with ancient books with leather-tooled spines, etched in gold and frayed at the edges, including first editions of *Don Quixote*, *The Sun Also Rises*, and *The Great Gatsby*, supplemented with shelves of Russian novels bound in yellowed and distressed leather, including Dostoevsky's *The Brothers Karamazov* and *Crime and Punishment*. Between the books were collections of antique fountain pens in ornate brass stands and a substantial collection of Russian nesting dolls. Perfectly placed, small, elegant objects from a lifetime of world travel acted as bookends. If one looked closely between those books and artifacts, they could see two five-by-seven black-and-white photographs framed in brocaded, antique gold frames. One, an image of an eight-year-old boy with who appeared to be his father standing on a boat dock, the boy holding a fish and the father staring down proudly at the child. In the other, the same boy at about thirteen standing next to Archibald Thornton in front of a church altar.

On the far end lay an antique conference table and six straight-backed chairs below a massive oil painting of a riverboat. Like the reception area, this room had polished oak floors with an oriental rug, but in a Chinese style not matching the Persians in the lobby. Despite the natural light afforded by the windows, the office was surprisingly dark, cold, and Dickensian. Marston Owens III occupied this space.

Marston and Ben both loved architecture. When Ben worked for Marston, they discussed, debated, and argued the merits of every building, structure, boathouse, and park they walked or drove past. Marston favored the Walter Gropius–Bauhaus movement with cubist, box-like structures and military precision and symmetry. Gropius took the great Louis Sullivan's edict of "form follows function" to grotesque ends. Marston pointed to Sir Christopher Wren's St. Paul's Cathedral as the perfect religious space and Ben countered with Frank Lloyd Wright's Unity Temple in Oak Park,

Illinois. It did not take Freud to connect the two lawyer's architectural tastes to their personalities. Marston once repeated the common complaint that all Frank Lloyd Wright buildings leak. Ben countered with, "That's what happens when you put a piece of art out in the rain."

Marston was the senior partner of the twelve-person law firm, but he was the only partner who made decisions, set policy, and dictated how the firm was run. The other three partners were partners in name only, because no one had the courage or leverage to cross Marston on any issue large or small. The firm had a high level of turnover among associates because while the pay was excessive, the pressure was even greater, and few lawyers had the intestinal fortitude to produce the level of perfection demanded by Marston on a full-time basis. To lose a case, make a mistake, or fail to achieve a successful result unacceptably besmirched the firm's holy escutcheon. There was no room to be a human being.

Marston was perhaps the city's most enigmatic lawyer. He personal story was known to few and mysterious to the rest. His success was not given but forged by years of work, toil, and pain. As the brilliant and precocious eldest child of a mechanical engineer, Marston worked hard to live up to his father's high expectations. Marston's family came from the middle class, and it burned a hole in his gut not to be a member of the higher classes he felt he deserved. His childhood intensity made social interactions awkward, and after school and work, Marston retreated to his books of war and adventure. He fantasized about the heroic characters in those books, determined to one day be seen and admired in that same light. Because of his lack of interpersonal skills, Marston asserted his power through intimidation with word and deed. His classmates learned to befriend him less they become the victim of razor-sharp putdowns or physical insult from the largest kid in the class.

When Marston was twelve, his father died suddenly and tragically in an industrial accident. Marston had a grieving mother and little sister to attend to. A fellow church member, then forty-five-year-old Archibald Thornton, took on the challenge of mentoring young Marston. Thornton had long respected and admired Marston's father, whom he believed to be a serious man of inscrutable integrity. All was not easy as the hard-headed and passionate Marston went heavily into drinking and drugs at the age of fourteen, attempting to self-medicate the pain he had long felt, first from a child different from the others and then at twelve, losing his father, further isolating him from a perceived normal life.

Even before the death of his father, he felt different from his peers, and during his teenage years, the differences became more pronounced. Archibald did not give up on this gawky kid, who had risen to a height of six-four with a booming baritone voice. Marston soon realized that control over others offered a poultice to his extreme anxiety and drive for success. His OCD quietly informed his ritualistic life as he secretly counted steps and overtly obsessed over order and cleanliness. His house was like a museum; his closet, a showroom. From his secret obsession, Marston knew the number of steps in every walk he took; thirty-one from the reception to his office, fifty-eight from his car to the parking garage elevator, forty-two from his front door to his mailbox.

***

When Marston graduated law school in 1974, he prepared for the bar like no one else, even though he was smarter than any of his colleagues and likely to pass without such efforts. Marston's photographic memory of the dictionary facilitated his use of obscure words and gave him the slightest edge, forcing fellow students to anxiously look up the meaning.

He learned to dominate and control people in every forum. However, when the bar exam came, he succumbed to anxiety and inner insecurity, freezing to the point of not completing the written portion of the exam. He had studied so hard and felt so much pressure he simply could not put pen to paper, overwhelmed by the thought that his answers might not be perfect. Marston could not perform. He studied even harder for the next time, and in February, when he retook the exam, it happened again. One of the smartest people in the state of Tennessee could not pass the bar exam. After the second failure, Marston crossed the river Styx. He had read about drugs that could help mute his anxiety and was willing to try anything. On his third bar attempt, he attained the highest score ever recorded. Thus began a lifetime of self-medication to numb his feelings of anxiety and insecurity. However, the drugs masked any empathy he previously possessed and turned him into a brilliant, determined lawyer but untethered to conscience or feeling.

This singular experience informed his entire career. Never would he not be the most prepared lawyer in any room. There would be no stone unturned. Every conceivable scenario charted and dissected. Marston kept four associates going at any given time along with a secretary, paralegal, and two nurse paralegals. The associates worked eighty to ninety hours per week and always kept their cell phones turned on, frequently receiving middle-of-the-night calls, emails, and texts requiring immediate response and attention. His maniacal chase of perfection in his own preparation extended to that of his colleagues and limited the typical shelf life of his associates to two years despite the generous salary. Twenty-four months was all most young lawyers could take of the around-the-clock emails, calls, and demands for perfection. No document escaped his red pen, and even the most innocuous email could be subject to ridicule for improper punctuation or grammar. Marston liked to say he looked for strong backs and weak minds, but the truth was just the opposite. To remain with Marston, a lawyer better have a strong sense of themselves and the stamina of a Kenyan marathoner. Past associates formed a survivors' club who met regularly to process the PTSD from their experiences at Fort Marston.

Marston started at the lowest rungs of the legal food chain, representing insurance companies in car accident cases. He tried hundreds of cases and honed a powerful and aggressive attack persona, bringing fear to his adversaries across the aisle. He burned like the sun and took no prisoners. His reputation and firm grew, and soon, companies that wanted a killer knew the place to go. But Marston did not just want to be good; he wanted to be respected. And the only place he saw to obtain that respect would come from that highest of callings, defending doctors and hospitals. Despite now having an abundance of money, he cared little for what it afforded him and only saw it to satisfy the ever-widening hole in his soul. If Marston were poor, he would be called crazy. But because of his wealth and power, he was considered eccentric. He rarely ate meals with others, used a drawer of colored markers to code every calendar event and written word. Social situations were awkward, but Marston managed to memorize a few soundbites of normal human interaction when forced to attend a cocktail party with doctors or lawyers.

He had never lost a jury trial, and the thought of it possibly happening kept him up most nights with a whiskey in his hand. When he was younger, his firm went undefeated in basketball and won the law league championship. He refused to ever play again for fear of ruining his perfect record. His entire identity was tied up in winning.

The current senior associate was Kip Lane, who had lasted a nearly unprecedented four years and was on his way to a record. Along with the newest plebe, Steve Francis, Kip had been summoned to the quarry, as Marston's office was known among his minions.

They were granted access by Marston's secretary, Nancy, and entered with as much self-confidence they could muster. Marston never engaged in small talk of any form unless politically necessary to achieve a goal. In his office, lawyers and staff knew better than to even try. The two young men entered quietly, raising their heads high enough to belie confidence, but not enough to make eye contact with Marston, and took a seat in the two side chairs facing Marston's desk. While Marston's office was a fascinating space, the two feared looking around too much in anxiety of drawing his ire. They learned early with Marston that it was best to stay quiet with eyes straight ahead until spoken to. And then, the answers should be thoughtful, concise, and accurate. Offenders to this edict suffered a range of reactions, from the Marston tapping his fingers on his desk in repetitive form while nodding in impatience to outright cruel condescension.

As soon as they were seated, Marston looked up and began. There was no introduction or small talk. Marston looked at a manilla folder with a single sheet of paper and got right to the point.

"I need you to drop everything you are doing and jump on this project." Marston spoke in his baritone. "It's of tremendous importance. Dr. Bob Kirkwood has been sued, and I want the full treatment performed. There will be no stone unturned, no scenario unevaluated. Nancy will Dropbox you all of the medical records, the complaint, and information you need."

"What are the allegations?" Steve asked. Kip winced, furrowed his brow, and looked down at his shoes.

Marston tilted his head and squinted as if attempting to solve an indecipherable riddle. That look quickly converted to that of a steely killer. "Goddamn it! Is English your mother tongue? What did I just tell you?"

Kip looked up, and Steve, shocked by the aggression, attempted to recover. "I'm sorry. I was just asking."

"You are not being paid to ask; you are being paid to answer. I just told you that Nancy would provide you the file. Before you ask me a question, first read the file. If you are still unsure, ask Kip, who has learned to not ask stupid questions. So get the hell out of here until you have answers." Marston, clearly still agitated, did a double take toward Steve. "And what the hell kind of shoes are you wearing?"

"Sir?" the clearly shaken Steve stammered.

Marston stood up, the height difference pronounced against the five-seven Steve. "Brown shoes with a blue suit. What are you, some kind of dandy?"

"S-s-sir?" Steve now could barely get a word out.

"We are lawyers, real lawyers. This isn't some television show. We wear black lace-ups with our suits and white shirts with rep ties. This is not a fashion show. We do serious work here. We dress accordingly. Understand?"

"Yes, sir," Steve managed to squeak out.

"Get the hell out of my office, pretty boy."

As they left the Marston's suite, Kip looked down at the floor, shaking his head at Steve's perceived impertinence, and managed a gallows laugh. "Welcome to the show, rook!"

Steve, crestfallen, his mouth and throat too dry to speak, just kept walking and shaking his head.

Back in Kip's office, Kip powered up his large computer monitor to pull up the new assignment. They handled dozens of cases per year, and Kip had never seen Marston with such an initial reaction to a case. Marston was always short and to the point, sometimes annoyed, but usually saved the harsher words for trials and depositions. Kip went through the complaint and saw nothing noteworthy until he got to the signature line.

"Oh, now I get it," Kip said.

"What?" Steve asked, while nervously scrolling through his phone.

"The lawyer representing the plaintiff is Ben Jennings."

"Who is he?"

"Oh, you will figure that out very soon. Ben Jennings, or he-whose-name-must-not-be-spoken, is Marston's kryptonite. Ben was Marston's associate until eight years ago and, according to legend, his favorite. Marston considered him a son. He trained him, mentored him, and even had meals with him. Ben practiced here eight years and became Marston's right hand. Ben is the only lawyer that Marston ever respected. Word is that Marston was almost human back then. After that, never again has anyone seen that side of Marston. When Ben left, I hear tell it turned this place upside down."

Steve looked quizzically. "Why? What was the big deal? Shit, the way I hear it, Marston goes through associates like most people do socks."

Kip turned his head from the computer now looking Steve in the eye. "Dude, I wasn't here, but Ben was somehow special to Marston. From what the older guys tell me, Marston was obsessed with Ben. He actually spent time with him outside of work. They used to go to lunch, have drinks, and eat dinner. They say Marston was almost human around him. Ben is a hell of a lawyer, and Marston let him take lead in depositions, handle jury selection in trial, and in some cases, trusted him to be first chair. No one before or after has ever gotten that kind of respect from Marston."

"Why did Ben leave?"

Kip raised his palms face up. "Nobody knows."

"So what happened?"

Kip waived Steve to sit down in his side chair. "Not only did Ben announce his departure, but when he told Marston he planned to switch sides and now sue doctors, Marston went over the edge. This place almost imploded. Marston screamed and yelled at everyone. The partners locked themselves in their offices. Marston fired Ben's secretary, believing she had somehow been disloyal and complicit. Marston changed the locks and had security prevent Ben's entry to the premises. Then Marston disappeared for two weeks but kept sending drunken emails to Ben at all times of day and night, copying the partners and associates, saying the most insulting things. Marston forbade the mention of Ben's name, and anyone who was ever seen or heard speaking to or about him would be fired. In the eight years since this happened, this will be the first case in which they are opponents."

"Oh, shit," Steve moaned.

"Oh, shit is the least of it. Our lives are about to be a living hell."

"Do you know Ben Jennings?" Steve asked.

"Everyone knows Ben Jennings. He is the all-American guy. Great-looking with an easy smile and great golf game. He's never met a stranger and is loved by lawyers and judges alike with all the traits Marston wanted but never had. Ben Jennings is the guy the girls want sleep with and the guys want to drink with."

"Why did he leave Marston?"

"That, my friend, is a question that has never been answered. A funny thing for those of us who have served at the Thornton Firm is that since leaving, Ben has never been seen in another white shirt. Blue shirt, pink shirt, striped shirt, but never a white one. And if he is not wearing brown shoes, he is wearing those Gucci loafers that Marston hates so fiercely."

"Sounds like my kind of guy," Steve said wistfully.

"Ben is everyone's kind of guy," Kip responded. "It's why Marston hates him."

CHAPTER 5

M edical malpractice cases initially proceed at a snail's pace. It is like two big armies gathering weapons and supplies, preparing for the great collision. Each side poses written questions to each other, which take months to answer. Then every medical record, school record, criminal record, social media post, and any other conceivable document or photograph taken throughout a plaintiff's life is produced by the parties and examined by lawyers, paralegals, and experts. This process takes months. After that, the real work begins. Depositions are recorded, and testimony is taken outside of court in a conference room with the lawyers, a court reporter, and a videographer present. While depositions are not generally exciting, they are exceedingly important. A case cannot be won in depositions, but it can certainly be lost. A lawyer can effectively cross-examine a witness only once, and he or she doesn't want to waste the pyrotechnics when the jury is not watching. Young lawyers often make the mistake of shooting all their arrows in a deposition, only to find at trial that the witness has suddenly developed better explanations for the glaring conflicts that were previously exposed. Experienced lawyers wait until cross-examination happens—in the court room with twelve jurors in the box—before pinning down a witness.

Lawyers spend countless hours preparing clients for handling questions during depositions from the opposing attorneys. Lawyers playing the role of opposition counsel prepare their clients with video-recorded mock examinations which are done over and over until the answers take on just the right tenor and tone.

Alicia came to Ben's office on the Friday afternoon before her Tuesday deposition. Alicia wore tan chinos and a periwinkle cotton sweater with sensible navy-blue flats. With no court appearances or other appointments, Ben dressed down in blue slacks, a pink dress shirt, his Rolex Submariner, and black Gucci loafers without socks. Stephanie was stuck in a weeklong deposition on another case and could not be there.

Alicia surprised Ben when she arrived pushing a stroller. Inside, Sydney Landers sat peacefully, having fallen asleep during the car ride down. Ben's face lit up.

"Well, hello, who have we got here?"

"This is my little bundle of joy. She is asleep, but I'm pretty sure it won't be long before she joins us."

Ben knelt to a foot of Sydney's face and smiled at the sight of the innocent child.

"Alicia, she is beautiful. My goodness, she takes after her mother."

Alicia smiled warmly. "You are sweet, Ben. She is everything to me."

They went to Ben's office and sat down-Alicia on the sofa and Ben in his leather club chair.

"Alright, Alicia, next week is your deposition. Do you know anything about them?"

"Not a thing, Ben. I am very nervous. What is a deposition?"

"A deposition accomplishes three things for the opponent: First, they want to evaluate you as a witness and decide how a jury may perceive you so that they can know whether they can attack you or not. Second, the opponent wants to determine every bit of information you possess so that nothing you say at trial can surprise them. The biggest fear of defense lawyers is for a witness to say something they have not heard. And third, they want to put you in a box, so to speak, which means they want to completely lock you down to what you are going to say under oath so that if you deviate in any way, they can use the deposition to try and make you out to be a liar."

"Wow," she said, "But what actually happens in the deposition?"

"Alicia, you are going to be in this conference room right here," Ben said, pointing to the big room next to him with the large, long rectangular table and accompanying eight black high-backed leather rolling chairs. "Marston Owens will be there as will, most likely, two of his associate attorneys. A lady will sit next to you with a stenographic machine taking down every word you say, which will later be in written form just like this." Ben showed her a transcript of another deposition which laid out in question-and-answer form every word spoken, including "ahh"s and "um"s. "Every word you say will be reduced to print, so remember to say 'yes' or 'no' as opposed to nodding your head or saying 'uh-huh,' which people do in regular conversations. Before answering any question, make sure you understand the question. If you do not know the definition of a word used, do not be embarrassed. Simply ask Mr. Owens to repeat the question or explain what the word or question means. There is no shame in not understanding a word or question. There is great shame in answering one that you do not understand, so never do it. It's most important that you tell the truth, because even if they catch you in a small discrepancy, they will twist it around and make the jury feel that they cannot believe a word you say."

"This sounds scary," Alicia said.

"Don't be scared. Be you. You are smart, thoughtful, and kind, and the truth is on our side. There is nothing to fear. Just make sure you tell the truth no matter how embarrassing you believe it is, because chances are, as long as you are truthful about it, the judge will likely not ever let the jury hear it. But if you lie about anything, Marston will be allowed to hit you over the head with it. The most difficult witness in the world to cross-examine is one who is honest and does not exaggerate because there is no ammunition to contradict your testimony, embarrass you, or make you look bad. Even the slightest contradictory statement can be used by the opposition to suggest, 'If you will lie about that, what else are you lying about?' For a plaintiff's lawyer, the best depositions are the boring ones. So, if you don't hear another word I say today, make sure you tell the truth no matter what. They have already had a team of private investigators comb every inch of your life, so don't think for a minute they don't know everything about you and your family."

Alicia squirmed in her seat. "Ben, you know my life hasn't been perfect. My mother has had a lot of issues with drugs and drinking. We have moved around a bit, and she has done things to feed us that she is probably not proud of."

"That is just fine. We will likely use your sister and not your mother, so they will not be able to use that information unless you lie about it. Also, there will be folks on the jury with similar experiences to yours, so the defense knows they risk alienating part of the jury if they come down on your humble beginnings."

"Okay, got it." She took a sip of her water. "What else do I need to know?"

"There will also be a person videotaping your testimony, so be conscious of your facial expressions and reactions. No matter what, do not let Marston get a rise out of you or make you angry. I will defend you, but at some point he will test you to see if you will take the bait so that at trial he will know what buttons to push to try and get you say something you will regret. He will have the tape of your deposition ready to play in the event your testimony changes or you act less than ladylike."

"How long will this whole thing take?"

Ben smiled. "Funny you ask. Marston will be taking the deposition himself, so it will likely take two to three hours. If it were one of his young associates, it would take all day."

"Why?" Alicia furrowed her brow. "I would think the more experienced lawyers would take longer depositions."

Ben chuckled to himself. "You would think, but it's just the opposite. Young lawyers take eight-hour depositions with two goals: rack up billable hours and miss no detail that an insurance company could later question. There is a direct correlation between the length of the deposition and the trial experience of the lawyer. The more trials a lawyer has handled, the shorter the depositions last because experienced lawyers know that in trial, it will not matter what the plaintiff made in fourth-grade math or what breed of dog she has. Inexperienced lawyers go down rabbit holes asking about your babysitter when you were five or the names of every neighbor on your block. It can be maddening listing to the drivel when you know none of it is relevant to the case nor will ever be heard by a jury."

"I'm just so worried. I don't want to mess up my case."

"You are going to be fine, Alicia. Remember, take deep breaths, listen to the questions, answer the specific question, answer the questions truthfully, and look him dead in the eye. Don't show any weakness or hesitation. Hell, you have faced worse interrogations at Trezvant High School. This will be a walk in the park. Marston won't be pulling a knife on you."

She smiled for the first time. "Ain't that the truth."

Alicia and Ben spent another two hours going over every conceivable fact of the case and question that might be answered, practicing making sure the words and tone were just right. Ben pretended to be Marston and asked several hard questions in a harsh tone to give her a feel for what she could expect. At the end of their meeting, Ben left her with a last thought: "Look him in the eye and tell the truth. You are ready for this. I know you can do it."

***

Alicia's deposition was significant in several ways: First, she was the most important witness in a very big case. If the jury did not like Alicia, the rest of the case would not matter. Ben had seen many witnesses perform well in office preparation only to fold up like a cheap suit when the hot lights of the real deposition were on them. Also, this would be Marston and Ben's first case against each other since he left the Thornton Law Firm ten years earlier. Every time they had run into each other at the courthouse, they intentionally avoided each other, one of the two changing direction or pulling out his phone to feign a conversation. When they found themselves stuck in the same courtroom, they scrupulously avoiding even the chance of a forced interaction, sitting on opposite sides, separated as far as possible.

Very few senior partners take the depositions of plaintiffs, feeling it is a task beneath them. Senior associates who learn from the rigorous process of having prepped partners' question lists, begin taking depositions of smaller witnesses and then progressively move up. The big firms have boilerplate deposition outlines that establish every line of questioning that must be completed. Marston operates differently. If he is going to cook the dinner, he wants to buy the groceries. He will not allow anyone else to question the plaintiff. Marston uses his six-four height, deep voice, and intensity to intimidate and scare plaintiffs. He does not consider a deposition successful until he makes the witness cry.

Marston, Steve, and Kip arrived at Ben's South Main office at the appointed time. It is a time-honored tradition among defense lawyers to bring two associates—not for assistance but to triple the hourly rate and intimidate the other side. Also, lawyers of Marston's stature do not look for documents. They hold their hand out and an associate who damn well better be reading his mind places the document in his hand like a caddy would a 9-iron for his golfer. Ben usually wore a suit, shirt, tie, and lace-ups for depositions, but today, he changed the tone. To poke the bear, he wore slacks, a striped shirt, no tie, a blue blazer, and black Gucci loafers with no socks. Marston strode into every room as though he owned it. Ben was only six-one, but he was still built like an athlete, with lean muscles and upright posture, while Marston's six-four frame was lean and gaunt from years of torturing his body with long-distance running. William Faulkner once famously said, "The past is never dead. It's not even past." The old tension between the two was just under the surface.

"Hello, Marston, so good to see you." Ben delivered a hearty greeting, but his handshake was noticeably withheld.

"Hello, Ben, the pleasure is most assuredly mine. It sure is a nice office you have here. I see you indulged your taste for the modern," he said with a hint of sarcasm used effortlessly among the higher classes to strain the line between sincerity and derision. Ben was not having any of it.

"Well, it seems like all the wood and marble have been done, and I wanted to change it up a little bit. And besides, the art galleries were all out of boat and skyline pictures."

Marston pressed and raised the ante. "The only taste you ever had was in your mouth. By the way, I love those shoes. What pimp did you have to kill to get them?"

"We can't all have your exquisite taste in clothes. I don't know how I would ever decide which white shirt to wear each day with which blue suit." The two traded barbs like schoolyard kids, both unable to exercise the discipline they had always prided themselves on as higher-level attorneys.

Lawyers of this level of practice hardly ever exchange petty taunts.

"I guess you spent so much money on the office and shoes, you couldn't afford to buy socks."

"I find not wearing socks keeps me a little less uptight, unlike the boys with the knee stockings and garters."

"I see there are no books on any shelves. I guess it is all the better since they would just collect dust," Marston retorted.

"Well, clearly you have done a great job of hiring erudite staff, so I know you have improved the collective IQ of the firm vastly since I left," Ben said sarcastically and then added, "If they would only stay more than a couple of years, you would really have something going."

And then Ben crossed the line. "Hey Marston, is it too early for a Bourbon or, better yet, maybe too late?" referring to Marston's penchant to get into the cups at all times of day and night.

Marston's glare could have melted diamonds, and it appeared he was deciding whether throwing hands would be the next move. Neither man seemed aware of the three other lawyers, court reporter, videographer, and Alicia Landers in the room, all standing mouths agape at the acrimonious tone. Stephanie, having known both men for over twenty years, quickly moved between them, offering a warm greeting to Marston to break the standoff.

"Marston," she touched his arm. "Are you not going to speak to me? It has been too long! How is your lovely wife?" Manners around ladies are the one constant in the South that cannot be broken among gentlemen. Marston reluctantly drew his attention from Ben and redirected his countenance and gaze.

"Stephanie, it is such a pleasure to see you." Marston's shoulders relaxed, and a smile came to his face. "Rachel is doing very well. Thank you so much, and I will tell her you asked about her. How is John?" Marston hated these social niceties, and Ben knew it. While Marston was capable of enormous grace and charm, he loathed small talk and what he perceived as the antiquated pretense of such exchanges.

"He is just fine, thanks. Why don't we move into the conference room? Gentlemen, can we get you something to drink?"

Ben, recognizing his lack of courtesy to the other lawyers, quickly jumped in. "Gentlemen, I apologize. I am Ben Jennings, and it so nice to meet you. Kip, I have heard a lot of good things about you but have never had the pleasure." The two men shook hands, and then Steve Francis offered his hand and introduced himself."

"Mr. Francis, so nice to meet you as well. I do not recognize the name. Have you been with Marston long?"

"No, sir," replied Steve deferentially.

"Brother Francis, my father was a sir, I am just plain ole Ben. Please call me that, and if it's okay, I will just call you Steve,"

"Um, uh, yes, sir. I mean, sure, Ben."

Ben then offered up the guest of honor. "Gentlemen, may I introduce you to Alicia Landers." Her stunning beauty and self-confident posture gave Marston and his associates momentary pause before catching themselves and offering appropriate greetings. Marston was a slave to habit, and Ben knew every move in his book. Marston's game was all power and no finesse. He made no bones about it and would come at lawyers with both guns all the time, offering nor requesting quarter from any opponent. Ben wanted to throw him off his tone and lighten the mood, making it slightly more difficult for Marston to frame the day as gladiatorial. As three defense lawyers assembled in line around the oak conference table, he asked, "So, I know who spit-um is. Which one of you is tote-um, and which one of you is sit-um?" These were old pejorative thrusts at defense lawyers traveling in packs.

"Boys, your affective rate must be $1,200 per hour. You are at the foot of the master of billing. Marston is just like the army; he bills more before 9:00 a.m. than most people do all day." This was a direct attack on Marston's notorious and questionable billing practices among his clients. Marston, brushed off the remarks, never raising his head from his notes.

This tone and behavior fell right in Marston's wheelhouse but was anathema to Ben's character and personality. Ben was the likeable guy who got along with every lawyer and judge. It was not an act. Ben genuinely liked people and always believed that good relationships with adversaries were prudent and beneficial both professionally and psychologically. In reviewing the day's events later in his mind, he would be angry with himself for taking the bait and showing that side of himself. Marston brought out the very worst in him. Ben was not wired that way; showing off demonstrated weakness not strength. He had allowed his competitive instincts and inner demons to get the best of him, and he knew he would have to do better over the course of this case. Conversely, Marston's wiring suited him precisely for this type of warfare. He knew Ben as well as he knew himself. He smiled to himself, aware he had rattled his protégé.

Alicia Landers was a born performer and witness. While she had never faced someone with the language skills of Marston, she had grown up tough, and he was not the first bully to attempt to intimidate her. The only difference between this world and her former life in the hood was that in the streets, the insults are clear and not clothed in false civility. Lawyers smile and project manners, all the while belittling the other while trying to win the case.

Marston went back and forth, showing Alicia various documents, including Alicia's sworn interrogatory responses and Sydney's medical records, attempting to confuse and incite contradiction, but Alicia was too smart to take the bait. Alicia disarmed Marston with her poise, candor, and sincerity. The more agitated he became, the calmer and more serene she acted. A lawyer wants his witnesses so prepared that, during the exam, he can feign indifference and appear as though none of the questions or answers offers the slightest reason to worry. A lawyer is never truly indifferent, but litigation is a combination of war and college theatre. Never let the other guy see you sweat no matter how much the question or answer hurts.

Toward the end of the deposition, Marston, having already obtained all the information he needed, wanted to see if he could rattle either Ben or Alicia.

"So Ms. Landers, back to Sydney's father, Mr. Marcus Jones. You two were never married, is that correct?"

Alicia never lost eye contact. "No, we weren't."

"And you contend he is, in fact, Sydney's father?"

"Marcus Jones *is* Sydney's father!"

Marston nodded his head. "I see. But was there ever a DNA test to determine if he indeed is the father?"

"No," she said curtly. "There was no need for one."

"No need for you or for him?"

"Neither."

"I see. So where is Mr. Jones now? Does he financially support Sydney or even bother to show up and see his child?"

Alicia retained her dignity. "Marcus comes to see us when he is able. He is in school attempting to become a pharmacist, so he is very busy."

"Too busy to come see his only child? Sydney is his only child, isn't she? Or not?"

"Sydney is his only child." Alicia stared Marston in the eye, ready to take whatever he could dish out.

"Does he support Sydney financially?"

"When he is able, yes."

"Oh, I see, when he is able. What does that mean?"

"It means just what I said. When he is able." Alicia stared at Marston as if to gain sharper focus.

"Are the two of you still intimate?" Marston pressed.

"What do you mean, intimate?" Alicia asked.

"I mean, do the two of you still have sexual intercourse?"

Alicia cocked her head sideways and pursed her lips. "Mr. Owens, I am not answering that question."

"Ms. Landers, I am entitled to an answer, and I will get one."

"Not from me, you won't. You are just being disrespectful."

Marston raised his voice. "Oh, you will know when I am being disrespectful, and there will be no ambiguity."

Ben interrupted. "Marston, come on. This is ridiculous. Either move on or end the deposition. You know that question is irrelevant and unnecessary."

"I am entitled to an answer, and I will get one," Marston barked.

"Not without Judge Jones ordering her to do so. I tell you what, let's get Judge Jones on the phone and tell him the question you are hung up on getting an answer to."

Marston, aware he miscalculated, stood up and in an angry voice said, "If Ms. Landers is not going to cooperate, the deposition is over."

Ben, no rookie to such theatrics, did not move a muscle and said with the utmost calm, "Marston, you are free to end the deposition whenever you choose. However, this will be the only day that we submit voluntarily to such an interview. If you are finished, fine. If not, I suggest you cease peddling your empty threats."

Lawyers are given one shot at deposing any given witness. There are no do-overs. However, if the judge finds the witness did not appropriately cooperate, he or she can order the witness to reappear and face attorney's fees and court costs for causing the court to intervene.

Marston responded. "We will see about this. Judge Jones will hear about this, and I will ask for costs and expenses to reconvene."

Ben knew he had Marston committed to a losing position and added a little syrup to his already Southern accent. "Marston, as my daddy used to say, you do whatever you are big and bad enough to do. But we both know Judge Jones is not going to take your side on this, so I suggest you finish your deposition and take those young men of yours over to McEwen's for a proper lunch."

Ben knew it was not worth the time and energy for Marston to go to court over a temper tantrum involving a question that had no relevance to the case. The testimony was all on video, and Judge Jones would side with Alicia. Marston took a ten-minute break with his associates and came back composed-looking to preserve dignity from outkicking his coverage.

"Ms. Landers, we will reserve our issues with the court on the previous question and move on to other matters." Marston invented ten more minutes' worth of questions to deflect his defeat. After three-and-a-half hours, the deposition of Alicia Landers was over. Marston knew that not only was his legal opponent up to the challenge, but the jury would also love Alicia Landers.

CHAPTER 6

The order of discovery requires all written questions to be completed prior to depositions. Next, the depositions of the parties to the lawsuit are taken, followed by those of non-party witnesses, and lastly, the depositions of the experts. It is customary for the plaintiff to be deposed first, since she has the burden of proof in the case. Also, local custom allows the plaintiff and defendant to be deposed at the office of their respective lawyers. The day after Alicia's deposition, Ben was scheduled to take Dr. Kirkwood's deposition at the Thornton Firm. Ben had not stepped foot across that threshold in ten long years. So much had changed since that day, and so much water had passed under the bridge. He was a different man now, having matured into a successful attorney in his own right. He had tried thirty jury trials on behalf of plaintiffs since his departure. Significant successes mixed with some tough losses.

Today, Ben dressed in a formal blue suit, blue shirt, and a green Hèrmes tie with brown Alden lace-ups. As Ben entered the reception area of what some referred to as the "big law firm in the sky," a couple of long-time staff members moved to greet him, only to stop themselves and nod a restrained formal hello. Only his former paralegal, Kelly, greeted him with a heartfelt hug and warm smile.

"Hey, Benji! Long time no see. How are you?"

Ben smiled broadly. "Kelly, you are a sight for sore eyes. I am doing better than I deserve. How is Cody?"

"Ben, he is as tall as you and a freshman at the University of Alabama."

"I can't believe it. Show me a picture."

Kelly obliged. "Heard you and Marston had quite the warm reunion yesterday."

Ben laughed. "Right. Not the sort of behavior the American Bar Association recommends in their lawyer civility classes. Truth is, I lost my cool and shouldn't have."

Kelly patted him on the shoulder. "Don't sweat it. That guy can bring it out of you. By the way, how are your little ones?"

"Not so little anymore. Max is great, and Annie is doing her best."

Now that Kelly had broken the ice, a couple of other staff came to speak. It felt so strange for Ben to be back in the setting of the formative years of his career. He noticed a pit in his stomach and had to confess to himself the nerves he felt walking into this space. Whether he would admit it or not, his time with Marston kept a hold on him that he could not release. Ben still needed Marston's approval.

Many at the firm had heard through Kip and Steve about the fireworks on South Main and were both fearful and excited about the prospect of a rematch today. They would be disappointed. After the loud roars on their first meeting, the two lions appeared to have decided to settle in for the long haul, knowing a medical negligence case is a marathon and not a sprint.

Kip soon arrived at the reception area and greeted Ben. The two exchanged handshakes. "Ben, welcome back. Has the place changed much in the past ten years?"

Pondering the question, Ben looked all around. "Nope. Not a bit. Same old bad feeling. I don't envy you guys."

"We are just fine. Don't worry about us," Kip said, pointing to the conference room. "I think you have been in there a time or two. I will let Marston know you are here."

"Thanks, Kip."

Kip took his place at the giant table and began arranging his notebook and documents to be exhibited during the deposition. Five minutes later, Marston entered the room followed by Dr. Kirkwood.

"Ben, this is Dr. Robert Kirkwood."

Ben walked across the room and formally shook Dr. Kirkwood's hand.

"Nice to meet you, Dr. Kirkwood. I am sorry it's under these circumstances."

Dr. Kirkwood raised his eyebrows. "Nice to meet you, Mr. Jennings."

The men took their places around the table with Dr. Kirkwood at the head, where witnesses traditionally sat, with a court reporter to his right and video camera at the far end.

One strategy when preparing a physician for a lawsuit and trial is to counsel him or her to deny independent memory of the events in question and rely strictly on the medical records. Doctors see hundreds of patients and might not even be aware that one suffered through a bad outcome. When they get sued, they claim a lack of memory and hide behind medical records that many times do not record the negligent acts committed. This forces the plaintiff to construct a case from multiple nurses, technicians, and other physicians, making the presentation extremely complex and layered, often confusing a lay jury. Further, the doctor relies on a band of experts who confidently take the stand, extolling the virtue of the defendant doctor's care and professionalism.

The other strategy requires the doctor to be an active participant in the defense of the case. He or she acts as his own best expert with knowledge of the facts, the patient's care, medical history, and science on the specific topic. This can be a powerful defense, but if the facts are against the doctor, it leaves him vulnerable to a skilled cross-examination. Experts will still be crucial but are more limited by the testimony of the defendant doctor (so as not to contradict him).

Dr. Kirkwood and Marston chose the first strategy of feigning memory loss about any specific facts of the case. Dr. Kirkwood testified in his deposition that he lacked any memory of the specific facts of Sydney's care on the morning in question other than the information contained on his singular note drafted the morning that she suffered the cardiopulmonary event. This defense strategy limited the scope of the deposition because Ben's job would be to lock him in to his testimony and prevent any movement from the stated position. With no memory to any fact outside of his singular note, there would not be a lot to question Dr. Kirkwood about. In this case, out of five thousand medical records related to Sydney's treatment, thirty documents were actually important to the case, ten were vital, and one was crucial.

Part of Ben's strategy when deposing Dr. Kirkwood was to employ sleight of hand in disguising which of the case documents he truly valued. During discovery, Marston had dumped five thousand records on Ben's doorstep, none of them in any discernable order. Ben knew Marston would take advantage of Ben's reading challenges by attempting to hide the needle in the haystack. If the defense was not careful, there might be records inadvertently omitted from the document dump.

Stephanie was crucial during this deposition because her expertise was medical records, and there she shined. Stephanie had reviewed the records for three months before contacting Ben. She continued reviewing for the several months between the filing of the lawsuit and Dr. Kirkwood's deposition, scouring them for the nugget supporting the case. Ben knew much of the glory he received for his courtroom prowess on cases he had co-tried with Stephanie was predicated on the thousands of hours of hard work she put in behind the scenes. On the cases he tried without her, Ben hired nurses and doctors to review and organize the medical records, looking for those same obscure but crucial documents. In this case, Stephanie had found the essential hospital protocol for treatment of NEC. A protocol helps to establish the standard of care for the people who work in a hospital. It is a set of rules set forth in manuals so accreditation agencies can ensure continuity and consistency of care throughout the country. Hospitals play coy to accreditation agencies and plaintiff lawyers with these protocols because they are required to have them and the associated accreditation necessary to receive Medicare and Medicaid reimbursement from the federal government. In another case, Ben had discovered the hospital had kept one set of protocols for the accreditation agency and another different one that the doctors and employees were expected to follow. In Alicia's case, Stephanie had managed to unearth one of the obscure hospital protocols that required radiologists to review all x-rays in patients diagnosed with NEC. This was gold. Ben and Stephanie could use Dr. Kirkwood's failure to follow that protocol as evidence that he was negligent in his care of Sydney and caused her brain injury because of a lack of oxygen during her cardiopulmonary arrest.

Ben spent an hour asking Dr. Kirkwood questions about his background, training, education, and job history before moving on to asking him about medical records.

"Dr. Kirkwood, we have been provided with over five thousand medical records related to the care and treatment of Sydney Landers. Of those, how many did you author yourself?"

"One."

"You mean with all these records, you only drafted one?" Ben sounded incredulous.

"Yes, it was on the morning of her arrest. Exhibit 4 that you marked a minute ago is the only one."

Ben continued. "I see there is some computer printing and a handwritten note at the bottom. Is that your handwriting on the bottom of that page?"

"Yes."

"And just to make sure, is it your testimony today under oath that other than that single document we have marked at Exhibit 4, you have no independent memory of any other treatment you provided Sydney Landers?"

"Yes, that is correct."

"And just so we are clear, you are not going to come to court having suddenly remembered additional facts that you are not telling me here today."

"Correct."

Dr. Kirkwood committed to his position and could not easily change it at trial. Ben locked in an airtight commitment from Dr. Kirkwood that he had no independent memory of Sydney Landers, and his treatment on the morning in question was contained in the medical record he had personally authored. This small victory would hopefully lead to a major win at trial.

**

The case would come down to the testimony of Dr. Kirkwood, Alicia, and the opposing medical experts on each side. After the depositions of Alicia, Dr. Kirkwood, and the nurses, there is break in the action so that transcripts can be provided to the experts, and the lawyers could draft lengthy Rule 26 disclosures.

Ben and Stephanie identified Dr. Martin Bell, for whom the criteria of measuring the degrees of NEC is named, as their expert world-renowned pediatrician—a strong cross-examination weapon. Marston took Dr. Bell's deposition in St. Louis three months after Ben took Dr. Kirkwood's. Marston's client paid for Dr. Bell's time in submitting to the examination. Dr. Bell testified that Dr. Kirkwood deviated from the acceptable standard of care, the precise phrase used to describe medical negligence, by failing to follow the protocol requiring hospital radiologists to review all x-rays in babies diagnosed with NEC. Dr. Bell also testified that Dr.

Kirkwood's negligence led directly to Sydney's cardiopulmonary arrest, brain injury, and lifetime of damages. Dr. Bell was a consummate professional. Marston explored his background, opinions, and the factual basis for each, ensuring there would be no surprises from Dr. Bell at trial. Marston saved his cross-examination for trial.

***

Thirty days after he deposed Dr. Bell, Marston identified eleven expert witnesses of his own who would testify on behalf of Dr. Kirkwood. They were drawn from Vanderbilt, Duke, Emery, the University of Kentucky, and Memphis-area hospitals and medical groups. Marston would never actually call that many experts to testify at trial, but his strategy for naming nearly a dozen of them was two-fold: identify so many experts that he would exhaust Alicia's money and Ben's time attempting to depose them, and along the way, Marston could judge their performance and choose the best for trial. Ben could not afford the cost of deposing so many experts, so he developed his own strategy for handling defense experts. He did not take a single deposition but instead relied on the defendant's obligation under Rule 26 to give precise substantive grounds and factual basis for every piece of testimony offered at trial. Rule 26 disclosures is a document whereby each lawyer must spell out with specificity the names and qualifications of their experts, followed by a detailed synopsis of their opinions with a detailed summary of the factual basis for said opinions.

This posed a huge risk for the plaintiff because Ben had no idea how any of these experts of Marston's might present as witnesses. But it also provided multiple benefits unforeseen by the defense. First, the expert would not have a deposition transcript to use to prepare for his cross-examination. Second, the expert will not have met Ben and have no idea what Ben's plans of attack were. And third, defense experts usually appear in the second week of the trial when fatigue and stress take their toll on the lawyers, who have already spent the day in the meat grinder of trial.

But perhaps most importantly to Ben's case, Marston would not be able to evaluate which of his many experts handled Ben's cross-examination with the most equanimity. Marston could not assess which of his experts would be best before the jury. Marston would not have the benefit of the audition of depositions to evaluate their performance. He would be putting them on the witness stand cold for the first time at trial, not knowing how they would handle questioning from Ben. Judge Jones would likely only allow Marston to have three to four experts, so it would be a big decision on Marston's part as to whom to call.

The obvious counterpoint to Ben's strategy was that Ben, not knowing what Marston's experts might say, would also be flying blind. Ben would have to bring his best game to court if he were to score any points against the leading doctors in the field of their subject of expertise.

Ben took no defense expert depositions but instead sent a formal letter to Marston stating specifically that he would be relying on the four corners of the Rule 26 disclosure and any testimony offered outside that document would be subject to objection. The case was ready to be set.

***

Ben filed a motion for trial setting. In what amounted to miraculous luck, the day Marston and Ben appeared for the motion, another medical negligence case had just announced settlement and would no longer need its trial date of September 14. Most medical malpractice cases took three years to bring to trial. Alicia's would go to trial in just over a year from when it was filed. Trial would begin in just four months.

CHAPTER 7

Marco Alexopoulos was born into second generation wealth. His Greek immigrant father clawed his way through law school and established a practice representing the lower socioeconomic classes. After getting a license to practice law, Alexi Alexopoulos overcame not being a native Memphian or blue blood by outworking and outhustling the competition. Alexi was a large, brawling man known among friends and colleagues for his passion for alcohol and prostitutes. When he began his practice, his clientele was the invisible class—Blacks, immigrants, and the poor—who were by and large ignored by the doctors, lawyers, and political power structure of the city, taking what scraps they could get from the table of the marginalized. The Civil Rights Act of 1964 was a mere suggestion in the South, so Black people still did not have a real voice if they had been victimized. The tongue-in-cheek saying that being a lawyer was a license to steal was a permission Alexi took literally. If he settled an immigrant's case for $10,000, he would tell his client it had been only $3,000, hand them $2,000, and demand that they be thankful for his efforts. Many of these clients could not read or write and were forced to accept what he gave them even though they suspected a wolf in the henhouse.

Alexi acquired wealth but never acceptance in the Memphis community. He polished his rough edges via his children by sending them to the prestigious Presbyterian Day School in Memphis, dressing them impeccably, and providing nice cars. The boys took music lessons and were encouraged to develop friendships among children of the wealthiest men. Alexi was lewd and lascivious. He had long, slicked-back, greasy hair and reeked of cheap cologne. He often made crude remarks to ladies about their attire and commented on his perceptions of their sexual desires. Many women described the horror of finding themselves alone on an elevator with Alexi as he looked them up and down, licking his lips. His aggressive and ungentlemanly nature made women worry about calling him out for fear of what he might do. One Saturday morning in November, on the corner of Madison and Cleveland Street, Alexi jumped out of his car to punch the lights out of a driver who had the temerity to honk at Alexi's horrible driving of his full-sized Lincoln Continental.

The Memphis police were regular visitors to Alexi's house to handle scuffles between him and his long-suffering wife, Sophia. She always refused to press charges, probably because doing so would have enraged her already irrational husband more.

Marco and his older brother, Nicholas, used the advantage of private school and coupled it with the one Southern commodity that transcends class: football prowess. The brothers, four years apart, shared their father's tenacity. At an early age, they distinguished themselves on the gridiron with a barbarism that gained them attention and popularity as they helped their schools win championships. Alexi injected a profane, boorish aggression around the polite crowd, making the high-brow folks uneasy. At the PDS football games, Alexi cursed loudly at opposing players and referees and outwardly relished an injury on the other team. His vulgarity shocked the genteel crowd, but his sons were so damn good, and those same folks valued football wins over manners.

They were both blessed with classic Greek good looks: jet-black hair, chiseled jaw lines, and broad shoulders. Both were killers at heart, but Nicholas masked his tendencies with a rakish charm and endeared himself to boys and girls alike. Marco had no such charm. People who exchanged a few minutes of casual conversation with him at cocktail parties or business meetings could not quite put their finger on what was off about him but would later say he made the hair on the backs of their necks stand up.

After graduating sixth grade from PDS, Marco and Nicholas spent the next six years at Memphis's most prestigious all-boys academy, Memphis University School. There, they dominated on the football field and held their own academically at the highly competitive school. Nicholas went on to play football at the University of Tennessee and later attended the University of Memphis Law School. He turned into a replica of his father. Nicholas's charm got him passes for most of his transgressions until he was finally disbarred for stealing clients' money, much in the fashion of his father. The US attorney's office indicted Nicholas: After a trial, he was sentenced to twenty-four months in federal prison.

Marco's good looks and alpha personality made him popular with the girls as well as the boys at MUS's sister high school next door, the all-girls Hutchison. Alexi gave Marco a new Corvette for his sixteenth birthday. Marco's future looked bright. He often brawled with groups of kids from the rival all-boys Catholic school, inflicting carnage and refusing to quit. This singular trait defined him: No matter the circumstance or setback, he plowed ahead and never quit. An admirable trait contained in an evil vessel. Marco went to school at Ole Miss and came back home to law school at the University of Memphis where he clerked for his father. In his life, he had never worked for anyone outside the family and had the outward confidence of the privileged born.

But no matter how hard he tried, he was never fully allowed into Memphis society because of his father's rough and questionable ethics and his older brother's increasingly bad reputation. Marco's good looks, football prowess, and status as an attorney required recognition but acceptance was another thing entirely. The Alexopoulos firm represented poor people who had suffered or claimed to have suffered personal injuries. The Alexopouloses' methods and practices with clients and cases were not always those used by white-shoe lawyers, but it was hard to put a finger on what exactly the Alexopouloses were doing. Other lawyers whispered rumors of unethical conduct. The Alexopoulos firm perpetually delayed paying bills from experts and court reporters. Alexi and his sons used charm and intimidation in equal measures to calm the rough waters when an aggrieved client or lawyer made claims against them.

The family lived an ostentatious lifestyle reeking of success. Alexi taught Marco and Nicholas that clients would not respect you if your car were inferior to theirs. Alexi wore expensive, oftentimes garish clothes sprinkled with gold rings and bracelets. They lived in the exclusive part of East Memphis and drove expensive cars. Alexi made an overt effort of showing success and wealth in every purchase.

When Marco was in law school, Sophia died of complications from years of alcohol and drug abuse. Two years later, shortly after Marco began practice, Alexi died of a heart attack while in the middle of an alcohol and drug-fueled night with several prostitutes. The boys were orphaned and left to their own devices.

In the aftermath of Alexi's death, Marco screwed Nicholas out of his part of their inheritance by claiming Alexi's investments were part of Marco's law firm. While they shared a suite of offices, Marco and Alexi's firm was separate from Nicholas's, who practiced alone. This caused a split between the brothers. They each began practicing law on his own with no guardrails. Nicholas and Marco were the only ones who truly knew the family history of lying and deception. Instead of being angry at his brother, Nicholas almost admired Marco's cunning machinations to claim both their inheritances. Nicholas set about stealing it back. To both of them, it was just business. Neither of the Alexopouloses had to deal with burdensome ideals like conscience and morals. They were predators and respected only power. To the people they manipulated and stole from, the boys rationalized that the suckers had it coming. Much like their father, Nicholas and Marco used clients' money as if it were their own. When a case settled for $300,000, instead of paying the client their two-thirds share, Marco and Nicholas would dole it out in $2,000 increments, creating their own lawyer Ponzi scheme.

***

The first Christmas after Ben left Marston, Ben ran into Marco at a party thrown by mutual friends. Marco sought Ben out from across the room.

"Ben Jennings! Merry Christmas!" Marco offered Ben a big smile and handshake. "How is it going?"

"Hey, Marco, same to you." Ben smiled politely. "Everything is going great."

"I heard you left Marston a while ago?"

"I did. I just needed to go a different direction."

"I also hear that you are in the plaintiff's racket now. Any truth to that rumor?"

"As a matter of fact, there is." Ben took sip of his cocktail and looked around the room. "I am doing a little bit of everything, but with my background in medical malpractice, I would like to break into the plaintiff's side of things."

"Funny you say that. I have been meaning to call you. I have never handled those cases but happen to have a couple of great ones I am trying to get off the ground. Are you interested in discussing joining a couple of them?"

"Yeah, sure, sounds great," Ben replied eagerly.

They met the following week at the Alexopoulos Law Firm in the Raymond James Building located on North Front

Street. It was a modern-looking building from the early 80s with an irregular shape and spectacular views of the river. Ben strode through the marble and glass lobby and took the elevator to the ninth floor. It was a richly appointed office with modern furnishings made to look expensive but lacking the taste seen at most defense firms, which had the money to buy originals. Defense lawyers love to make fun of plaintiffs' lawyers' flashy cars, tacky clothes, gawdy offices, and stereotypical brash manners. Marco perpetuated these stereotypes in dress, jewelry, and cars. His reputation was that of an intelligent and talented lawyer but rumors about his family lingered, and Nicholas had been disbarred. Marco marched out to greet Ben. Marco's million-dollar smile was almost too white, aided by expensive veneers. He was handsome, mannerly, and gracious.

"Ben Jennings! I am so glad you came." Marco grabbed Ben's hand like it was a life preserver. "Everyone knows what a badass you are. I am just so glad that you have switched to the side of angels."

"Well, thanks," Ben managed. "I am not so sure about all of that."

"Stop being so modest. If you are going to be a plaintiff's lawyer, you must sell yourself, or nobody else will. We are about to make some real money." Marco put his arm around Ben and led him back to his office.

Marco hit all the right buttons with Ben, whose divorce was fresh and bank account was stretched. Ben had much to consider: alimony, child support, and private school tuition obligations along with the cost of running his own firm. He had cashed out much of his savings and always seemed to be behind. A couple of big paydays was just what the doctor ordered.

Marco gestured to a leather chair and sat opposite him. "Ben, these two cases are giant! We are going to make some cash money together."

Ben shifted his weight in the chair uneasily, not sure what to make of Marco's over-the-top delivery similar to that of a car salesman. "Marco, I appreciate what you are saying, and I am glad to take a look at your cases."

Marco hit his intercom button. "Kim, come in here and make copies of the Williams and Johnson files for Ben. He is going to help us out." Marco's secretary quickly entered, grabbed two large accordion files, and smiled broadly at Ben as she walked out.

"Ben, do you mind if I smoke?" Without waiting for a reply, Marco lit up a fat cigar. "Do you want one?"

Ben waved his hand. "No, thanks. I'm good."

The two spent several hours going over two cases: one, an accident where a truck had rear-ended a man, causing brain damage; and the other, a malpractice case where the client's vocal cords had been damaged during a surgery. Ben expertly pointed out strengths and weaknesses of each case, suggesting how they might divide work and responsibilities. So they struck a deal, and a working partnership was formed.

Marco enjoyed poring over huge document dumps; Ben strategized and planned tactics. They took several depositions and pressed aggressively on the two cases. The two worked well together. Within six months, both cases had settled for substantial amounts. For the next eight years, they repeated this formula, working together on a case-by-case basis, usually handling no more than two at a time. They never socialized but had a good working relationship. Ben never saw Marco consume a drop of alcohol or behave badly.

Just two years ago, and eight years after Ben left Marston, Marco proposed that he and Ben form a formal partnership and split all cases, expenses, and profits equally. Ben had trepidation about another partnership, so he sought out an old friend, one of the most successful attorneys in town, a senior partner at one of the largest law firms in Memphis who specialized in medical malpractice defense. The Sage had acted as a mentor to Ben ever since they met at Henry "Fats" Feldstein's office when Ben was a first-year lawyer. The two developed a close but private friendship. Ben relied on his counsel and judgment.

The Sage believed Marco to be a top-notch lawyer but had past negative encounters with Alexi. The Sage did not come out directly against Marco but damned him with faint praise.

Ben pressed. "Come on. Tell me what your problem is with Marco."

"I'm not condemning the son for the sins of his father, but I am just not sure about him. He is clearly smart and successful. But some in our firm have questioned his tactics a time or two. Nothing they could prove, but they suspected Marco didn't always play by the rules."

Ben sighed. "But can you give me anything concrete? This guy gets great cases and will give me a bigger platform to grow my practice."

"Ben, you are a big boy. Make your own decisions. I have no evidence that I could ever put on against Marco Alexopoulos. I just have a bad feeling. Take that for whatever it is worth."

Even Ben had to admit there was something different about this guy that he just could not quite articulate. The Sage warned against Marco. One of Ben's weaknesses and strengths was the good he saw in people. Sometimes, people had taken advantage of Ben's good nature and tendency to overlook flaws in others. In his Marston days, Ben had blindly focused on the good in his partner, defending him to outsiders who questioned Ben's sanity for practicing law with a psychopath. Now on his own, Ben let hope prevail over experience and chose Marco as his new partner.

Ben and Marco settled into the South Main office. Marco didn't care for aesthetics and allowed Ben to create his dream workspace. Ben indulged his love of architecture and immersed himself in design, light, and structure. It seemed that every lawyer in Memphis had some derivation of the traditional clubby-looking office, which seemed to be what clients expected. Ben reasoned that a different look might set his firm apart. He created a modern office with glass and light and made spaces allowing for easy movement and collaboration. Clients and lawyers alike were amazed at the place and found themselves smiling at the open spaces, natural wood, and sunshine pouring in.

While the office felt perfect, the partnership gave Ben a strange feeling from the beginning. Marco kept bizarre hours, coming in late or in the middle of the night. The first month together, he disappeared for a week without telling Ben and refused to answer his phone. Soon thereafter, Marco announced that he and his wife were divorcing. Between Marco's mortgage, child support, alimony, and private school tuition for his children, his first $30,000 every month was already spent. Marco lived like a rock star.

Marco's behavior became increasingly unusual. He fell asleep at his desk and missed deadlines. Ben noticed Marco did not seem right in his speech and demeanor when in the office. Scruffily dressed, unusually smelling people who were not clients regularly came to the office and left threatening messages with Peggy demanding to speak to Marco. On more than one occasion, Marco met with men in his office who yelled and screamed at him. Marco reacted calmly and quietly like it was a normal event in a routine day. When Ben and Peggy asked Marco who the threateners were and what the yelling was about, Marco said they were old clients of his father asking for money.

Then, one Friday afternoon, Marco's brother, Nicholas, called Ben with news that he had sprung Marco from jail after being charged with a DUI. Nicholas said Marco had been dealing with a persistent drug and alcohol problem since college and now needed long-term care in rehabilitation. Ben offered to help, making calls to the Tennessee Lawyers Addiction Network to find a suitable rehabilitation placement. Ben called several clients and told them he would be taking over as lead counsel for the case.

The next day, before arrangements could be made for rehab and while Ben was focused on the detailed preparations for the Alicia Landers pre-trial motions scheduled to begin in twenty-four hours, Ben received a second call from Nicholas, who reported that Marco, out on bail, had just been arrested for another DUI. He had spiraled out of control and needed help badly. Nicholas drove him to a Texas rehab facility and checked him in. Then, people started calling the firm and leaving messages for Ben with Peggy. People who said they were Marco's clients, though Ben had never heard of them.

That alone shocked Ben because he believed he and Marco shared every client and were both aware of what was going on with every case at the firm. Now, Ben learned that Marco made promises to off-the-books clients with whom only he interacted and that Marco had not answered his phone or called them back in a month. Ben asked Peggy to gather together all the names she could find of Marco's irate callers and visitors. He looked up their names on the court's website and found that they were plaintiffs in lawsuits and represented by Marco. From the same website, Ben retrieved the various defense counsels' names.

The first defense lawyer he came to was a friend, Craig Evans. Ben picked up his cellphone and immediately called Craig.

"Craig, what is going on with the McMullen case?" asked Ben.

"Ben!" Craig sounded frustrated. "What are you talking about? That case settled six months ago. I sent Marco $250,000."

"What?" Ben screamed into the phone. "Can you send me the releases and orders of dismissal?"

"Sure, bud." Now, Craig sounded worried. "What's happening over there?"

Ben sighed into the phone and ran a hand through his hair. "I'm not sure, man, but I think the world is about to cave in around me."

Ben quickly called Charles McMullen.

"Mr. McMullen, my name is Ben Jennings. I work with Marco Alexopoulos."

"I am glad someone finally called me," McMullen said angrily. "That son of a bitch Alexopoulos will not return my calls. I have been trying to track him down for three months."

"This may sound silly, Mr. McMullen, but have you received any money on your case?"

"Hell, naw! That is what I am trying to find out. He told me five months ago it was about to be settled. And now, he will not talk to me. I need some goddamned answers, and I need them now!"

"Mr. McMullen, have you signed any settlement documents on your case?"

"No! Are you telling me that bastard settled my case and didn't pay me?"

Ben drew a deep breath, his heart now racing. "Mr. McMullen. I am not sure what has happened, but I am trying to get to the bottom of it."

"And who in the hell are you again?"

"Ben Jennings. I work with Marco."

"That's funny. I have never heard of you. But someone better have some answers fast."

"Partner, I am doing everything possible to get you those answers."

Ben hung up the phone and reviewed the documents Craig had just emailed him while he was on the phone with Mr. McMullen. They were purportedly signed by McMullen. The documents had been forged.

Ben looked up the next case on the list from Peggy, Earnest Saulsberry, another closed case listed on the Shelby County Circuit website. That meant it had been settled or dismissed. He called lawyer Charlie Hill, who was listed as defense lawyer on the case.

"Charlie, this is Ben Jennings."

"What's up, Ben?"

"I am sorry to bother you, but did you defend a case with the plaintiff by the name of Earnest Saulsberry?

"Of course. You should know, your partner represented him."

"Well, Charlie, humor me. What is the status of the case?"

"Ben, I paid Marco $150,000 on that three months ago. You need a copy of the settlement agreement?"

"Yes, please," Ben replied and hung up.

Shit! Ben had felt this weak in the knees before but never without first having consumed copious amounts of bourbon. He uncharacteristically yelled at the office manager, "Peggy, get in here now!"

"What the hell?" Peggy ran to the door, pen in one hand, file in the other. She was shocked by the stricken look on Ben's face.

"The dam has broken, and we have a huge problem. We have to go through Marco's office and figure this out. I think he has been running a shadow law firm and stealing money from clients."

Peggy's mouth was agape. "Are you serious?"

"As a heart attack. Call the tech guys and have all of Marco's emails forwarded to me. Also, have them lock him out from the server remotely. Then, we have to go through his Marco's office and computer and attempt to figure out the damage."

On a good day, Marco's office looked like an episode of *Hoarders*. It had always been a mess too chaotic for neat-freak Ben to enter. Peggy bravely waded in and spent the next hour combing through the piles of paper, stacks of mail, and notes scribbled on legal pads. While Peggy organized and searched, the tech guys quickly flipped the switch on Marco's email, allowing Ben began the long task of reading through Marco's emails looking for more evidence. Checking the email of clients that did not add up would take days, if not weeks, to complete.

Then, Peggy yelled from Marco's office, "Ben, come in here! I think you will want to see this." Ben arrived to find Peggy shaking her head, one hand on her hip and the other on her brow. A file cabinet behind Marco's desk held thirty perfectly arranged red files bearing clients' names Ben did not recognize. In those files were releases, dismissal orders, and even sheets of paper on which Marco had practiced forging his clients' signatures. Before Ben could look closely at the first one, his cell phone rang, and Ben recognized the number of his ex-wife, Lisa. Ben showed the phone with Annie's contact photo on the screen to Peggy and looked plaintively at her.

"Oh, sweet baby. That poor little darling." Peggy gave him a concerned look.

"This is never good news."

"Hello." Ben tried to muster a positive tone.

"Ben. Annie is curled up in a ball on the front walkway. She had a terrible day. I am not sure if you are free, but I would sure appreciate it if you can come by and see what you can do."

"I am on my way." Ben hung up the phone and looked at Peggy as if she had an answer to all of life's mysteries. "It's

Annie. I've got to go. I am so sorry to leave you with this mess . . ."

"Stop it." Peggy looked at him intently. "That's your baby girl. You go do what you need to do, and I will handle things here. I will call you if anything else develops."

"Peggy, you are the very best."

"Yes, I am," Peggy said with her warm smile and a wink.

CHAPTER 8

The Memphis legal community is a microcosm of the city's society. Both are based on a heretical culture of money, arrogance, and entitlement from years of profiting on the backs of the less advantaged middle and lower classes. The Sage, a senior partner in one of the state's most respected insurance defense firms, now in his late seventies, long ago learned how to succeed in law without being the progeny of old Memphis. The Sage achieved access to the children of wealth and power as the son of a well-respected Presbyterian minister at an affluent Memphis church. While accepted, he was subtly reminded by the wealthy of his lack of breeding and legitimate standing. He was an honorary member allowed in because of their good Christian charity. Memphis Country Club or just "the Club" was the central connector among wealthy Memphians. The Sage's father had been given an honorary membership as a perk for his ministry, but when they amended the tradition of free admission to certain clergy and required him to pay a paltry seventy-five a month, he would have none of it and dropped out. To be part of the blue blood of Memphis, one had to be a member of the Club and participate in the annual Cotton Carnival where debutantes were introduced.

The Sage attended Ole Miss in the early 60s during the turbulent time of James Meredith and glory of the 1962 undefeated football season. The Sage took the unpopular position of supporting Meredith's admission and spoke passionately to students and faculty as president of his fraternity. What followed Meredith's admission was one of the ugliest and bloody riots ever seen in a state which already had its share of historic conflict. The Sage often found himself caught between his ambition and his suspicion of money and power. Upon graduation from Ole Miss, he served in Vietnam as an officer in the Marine Corps and carried that tradition and ethos throughout his life. The Sage came home and excelled at Vanderbilt Law School. Because of his undeniable talent and intelligence, one of the large Memphis law firms scooped him up, knowing with all the average lawyers hired by virtue of nepotism, someone had to do the hard work. Within five years, he made partner, and after ten, he commanded a seat in the main power structure.

As a senior partner in one of Memphis' biggest law firms, every November 10, he orchestrated the traditional celebration of the Corps' birth in 1775. The celebration was entered into the Marine Corps Drill Manual in 1956 and outlined the ritual slicing of a cake, of which the first piece is given to the oldest Marine present who, in turn, hands it off the youngest Marine present, symbolizing the old and experienced Marines passing their knowledge to the new generation of Marines. The celebration includes a reading of Marine Corps Order 47, issued on November 1, 1921, summarizing the history, mission, and tradition of the Corps; it is read to every command on each subsequent November 10 in honor of the birthday of the Marine Corps.

Ben first met The Sage while Ben worked as a first-year lawyer under Henry "Fats" Feldstein, a shyster street lawyer who hustled his way to a lucrative cash business before the IRS began requiring cash transactions over $10,000 to be reported. Fats was a character out of a crime novel: five feet, nine inches, 325 pounds, thick, brown hair, and a walrus mustache. He wore glittering custom three-piece pin-striped suits, a diamond-studded Rolex Presidential, plank gold bracelets, diamond rings, and gold rope necklaces. He represented Memphis's drug kingpins and wealthy divorce clients who wanted a bulldog on their side. One of his more notorious clients had presented him with a large gold nugget ring with a seemingly real green human eye center stone. Fats used a gold lighter to fire up the menthol cigarettes that he chain-smoked, making a distinctive popping noise with his lips with each drag.

A brilliant man, Fats grew up tough and fought for everything he got, if he had not already stolen it. You knew he was lying when his lips moved. He yelled, screamed, lied, cheated, and stole, yet possessed an unmistakable charm that was sometimes hard to resist. Fats mastered the wry smile with a sparkle in his eye, letting willing co-conspirators in on whatever absurdity he advanced.

The meeting with Fats was conducted on the thirty-fourth floor of the 100 North Main Building. An old 60s-style building, its only positive distinction was that it was the tallest in the city. The building had never been updated and captured the era's style with a lobby of terrazzo floors and black granite-framed bronze elevators. Collections and criminal defense lawyers occupied the building, attractive for its close access to the courthouses and low rents for lawyers with clients unconcerned with the thirty-year-old thick mustard-brown carpets with bathrooms requiring a key for entry, plain fixtures and appointments, and industrial tile suitable for a 50s East German bureaucrat's building.

However, Fats' office seemed to have no connection to the outward edifice and all the other offices with their grass-cloth wallpaper with cheap, old, mismatched furniture. Occupying the premium floor in the building, Fats' office covered the entire floor and welcomed visitors to an oasis. Its grand entry had a floor-to-ceiling glass wall and accompanying glass doors. Patterned white-and-green Italian Verdi marble led to a semi-circular, custom-built oak reception desk occupied by a young receptionist who appeared to have a nighttime gig at a local strip club. Instead of paintings of boats, the office walls were adorned with high quality, limited numbered Dali and Picasso prints separated between plaques ascribing to the greatness that was Henry Feldman.

Fats' personal office was something to behold. In keeping with his pattern of doing everything in flamboyant over-the-top style, his twenty-by-forty office, the largest in Memphis, represented decadent, if not gauche, excess. Entering through twin oak doors, the sheer space alone took a visitor's breath away. The decor offered one potential insight as to why King Louis had inhabited Versailles. Six large windows with remote-controlled blinds surrounded the mini village of marble and wood that was Fats' office. The desk was large enough to land airplanes on, the credenza, the size of a twin bed. Fats sat behind the huge structure on an oversized decorative chair better described as a throne. Two oversized wooden armchairs with imported fabric straight from a Byzantine ruler's closet faced the aircraft carrier-sized desk. In the middle of the room lay a ten-by-four polished cherry conference table with ornate carved legs topped with a luxurious leather inlay surrounded by gold leaf brocading. Around the table sat ten wooden chairs matching the table with thick leather cushions. At the far end of the office were two eight-foot-long leather sofas and two leather club chairs placed around a large square carved coffee table holding an antique Chinese vase overflowing with a stunning bouquet of fresh flowers, changed weekly. All of this faced a large fireplace framed by a massive white marble mantel. To one side of the fireplace were glass shelves filled with crystal decanters of the finest scotch and bourbon along with a bar that'd make the Peabody Hotel envious. On the other side of the fireplace, shelves held crystal glasses and another vase of birds of paradise. Above the mantel, an oil painting of ole Henry Feldman himself, albeit forty pounds lighter, looked down on the viewer. Opposite the windows, the walls held two large, colorful original abstract oil paintings between a tapestry sourced from a former king's palace in Bombay.

Ben and Fats were in a heated and contested case the day Ben met The Sage. Ben was twenty-four and just out of law school, working his first job as a lawyer for Fats Feldman. At the time, The Sage was approaching sixty but maintained the straight military bearing signaling his Marine Corps roots. The man stood at a lean six-three with a close-cropped haircut, but his perfect posture and a resonate feel of authority made him appear three inches taller. With efficient and crisp speech, The Sage possessed perfect manners, but they seemed a forced construct rather than genuine nature. He did not mince words nor abide nonsense, and his rapier wit readied to any ill-considered sentence of an opponent. Fats asked The Sage to meet him, ostensibly to negotiate a solution to their impasse, but in reality, it was to give Fats an opportunity to simply to force his will upon him. Fats always insisted meetings occur on his home turf to gain whatever psychological advantage it may garner.

The case involved a dispute between the contractor and owner of a large commercial project. Over the months, like every case involving Fats, the case became contentious because of Fats' unreasonable demands and lack of connection to the truth. The man who would become known as The Sage and Fats agreed to a face-to-face meeting to iron out the dispute. Fats asked Ben to join the conference because he had performed most of the work on the case and knew every detail.

Before the meeting began, Fats energetically spun tales of his exploits to The Sage, while walking around his office, describing the origin and value of each piece and the price of the office and its contents. The lawyer and Ben took seats in the large chairs facing Fats' desk. Once settled, Fats quickly ramped up the civil tone by screaming and yelling- with what Ben knew to be a completely false narrative. The Sage was unflinching, like a Marine. Ben never spoke in these meetings; he just took notes and acted as accoutrement and back-up to Fats. However, on that day, things took a decided turn. After Fats' lengthy bluster that had no relationship to facts or truth, he suddenly turned to Ben and demanded, "Isn't that right Ben?"

Ben, completely stunned by the request to offer verbal affirmation of outright lies, was forced onto the horns of a dilemma. To disagree with Fats would result in Ben losing his first job as a lawyer and having no way to pay his bills. To agree with Fats' perjurious contentions would be to compromise any ounce of integrity Ben possessed and place him on the path to becoming a legal hack, whom no one would trust or have any voluntary dealings.

Ben considered his options, looked Fats right in the eye, and said, "No, Henry, that is not how I remember it."

Sitting beside Ben, the former Marine and now prestigious lawyer, whom Ben had met for the first time five minutes prior, swiveled his head, and looked at Ben with equal parts shock and awe, personally witnessing a young man commit career suicide right in his very presence.

Fats' eyes nearly popped out of his head. He exploded. "What!!!! You sorry, no-good piece of shit. You don't know what you are talking about. Pack your stuff and get the hell out my office! I want you gone in ten minutes!"

Ben stood up and dutifully walked out of the office without another word.

Ben threw his coffee mug and his law school diploma into his briefcase, went down to his car and tossed his stuff in, and walked the streets in despair. When he returned to his apartment that evening, he found the man he had just met, the former Marine, still wearing his elegant suit and spotless, shined shoes, sitting on his doorstep reading the newspaper, drinking a six-pack of Bud Light, and smoking a fat cigar. Ben was shocked to see the lawyer who had witnessed his humiliation in Fats' office and did not think he could abide another scolding.

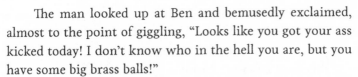

The man looked up at Ben and bemusedly exclaimed, almost to the point of giggling, "Looks like you got your ass kicked today! I don't know who in the hell you are, but you have some big brass balls!"

After having pouted for the past three hours, Ben could not contain his own laughter, even at his own expense. The two men sat on the doorstep and drank the remaining beer along with two more six-packs retrieved from inside and a couple of cigars. Ben told him the short version of his story, and the two talked and laughed well into the night. The man whom Ben would come to consider "The Sage" told Ben about his background and the challenges of growing up an honorary but subtly scorned part of upper-class Memphis society.

After a period of silence while the two enjoyed their cigars and cold beer, the man spoke in a serious tone. "Ben, what you did today surprised me, and I am not often surprised. It took a lot of courage to stand up to Fats knowing you were about to lose your job. I don't know another person in this town who would have done that. You are either crazy or brave, but either way, I love it. This business is hard as hell, and you can easily lose your soul if you allow it. And let me tell you this: Those wealthy blue-blood lawyers are no better than you. They have a huge head start on you because of generations of money, access, education, and experience. But you also have an advantage. From what I heard tonight, you come from relatively humble beginnings and went to the tough schools. I figure you got your ass kicked more than a few times. Lawyers born to privilege have literally never been hit in the face, and I would not give a quarter for someone who hasn't. Your self-esteem comes from having actually earned something. Theirs is false, and they know it. They fear losing their money and their prestige because they do not have confidence they could make it on their own if their money disappeared. Use that against them. Exploit the fact that you have the ability to talk to real people about real things, and the only Black people they have ever interacted with either cleaned their house or served them a mint julep."

Ben was almost speechless. When the day began, he had been a first-year lawyer working for the hated and disrespected street lawyer, Fats Feldstein. Now, freshly unemployed, he had just spent the last several hours with one of the most respected lawyers in the city who received a PhD in the actual practice of law.

"I don't know how to thank you. I appreciate your words. Would it be okay if we talked again sometime?" Ben asked.

The Sage responded as only he could. "Ben, don't be a bitch. You are grown man and a licensed lawyer. We are colleagues. We have the same license. Of course, I make a hell of lot more money than you do, and I have a great job, but you get my point. You are going to be fine. You have all the stuff that's hard to earn. The rest of it is easy. You need to believe in yourself. If you ever want to talk to me, pick up the damn phone and call me like a grown-ass man."

Ben could only laugh. "You are one interesting guy. I have never met anyone like you."

As The Sage stood up to leave, he said, "Ben, my boy, I tell you what—my firm is not going to allow me to hire a poor-ass public school kid with no experience. But you have something. I am going to call my friend Marston Owens and see what he can do. He is a son of bitch in a different way than Fats, but a son of a bitch, nevertheless. If you can do what you did today, you can handle Marston."

***

And so began a beautiful friendship. No other attorney knew the depth and importance of the relationship between The Sage and Ben nor would they understand. The Sage, a fiercely private man, did not believe in revealing or commercializing his personal relationships. Ben felt so lucky to have this wise man as a close confidant and feared disclosure could risk The Sage's friendship. The Sage swam in the waters of the privileged where class, status, decorum, and seriousness were the order of the day.

His friendship with Ben allowed The Sage to indulge his real self, the tough son of a preacher, who had a wicked sense of humor and looked down on the kids born on third base thinking they had hit a triple. They wrote each other profane and insulting letters and played elaborate practical jokes, raising the stakes each time. After Ben bought his Range Rover, he bragged to The Sage about the outstanding gas mileage. For the next month, The Sage surreptitiously filled Ben's tank every day he could, causing Ben to marvel at the magic of this wonderful vehicle. After a month of that, The Sage siphoned the gas every day, turning Ben's joy into vexed mania. Once exposed to the prank, The Sage laughed until he cried at Ben's exasperated response to The Sage's little caper.

The outwardly conservative and sober Sage, a bleeding-heart liberal at his core, could only act on those impulses privately or rarely lest he risk losing his club status. The Sage and his wife adopted two refugee children from Vietnam and secretly paid tuition for several underprivileged children to attend private school. As with Ben, because of The Sage's age, haircut, dress, and military bearing, people were often unaware of his gritty upbringing. During a deposition of a young Black man, who was speaking in a diction and language The Sage did not understand, he became frustrated with the answers and uncharacteristically asked, "So homey don't really know?" to a shocked court reporter and plaintiff's counsel._

Once Ben heard the story, he could not resist and sometimes referred derisively to The Sage as "homey." Ben called The Sage's firm and demanded to be buzzed through to homey, mortifying the restrained receptionist with such a reference to the stoic, conservative senior partner. When she asked who was calling, Ben gave her the name of a famous old baseball player, forcing her to buzz the corner office and say, "Sir, I am sorry, but Honus Wagner called and demanded to speak to you." Sometimes, Ben called and told her he was "Lou Gehrig calling for the homeslice." Soon, the receptionist was in on the joke, and she would giggle at each call. When she put Ben through, The Sage picked up the phone and, without any greeting, immediately launched into to a comedy routine, telling Ben some outrageous story. Every so often, Ben appeared unannounced at The Sage's office, an unheard-of practice in the prim and proper old-world law firms. Associates and junior partners could not believe this nobody showed up out of nowhere and was immediately directed to the corner office where he was warmly welcomed. Many of them had worked years at the firm and never seen the inside of The Sage's office.

The two also had serious discussions. The Sage became a father figure to Ben and offered much-needed advice served with sarcasm and wit. The relationship was complicated by Ben's employment with Marston, who was possessive of his own connection with The Sage and would have likely been hurt by the close and comedic relationship of which he was incapable. It was the Sage who had first introduced Marston to the elite level of Memphis lawyers by sending Marston his first medical negligence case from one of The Sage's conflicts. The Sage knew Marston well and, at times, acted as a ballast to curb some of his more outrageous urges of cutting ethical corners and scorched-earth tactics that burned bridges with lawyers and judges. Ben and The Sage had long discussions about navigating the murky waters of Marston's psyche, his heavy drinking, and his prescription drug abuse.

The Sage offered this explanation: "Ben, Marston's a tortured soul, and the problem is not an addiction to alcohol or drugs; it's his addiction to the practice of law. His identity is tied up in being a successful lawyer, and he is frightened to death he will be exposed one day as not being good enough. He is petrified of losing a case because he thinks that means he will lose his reputation. That fear keeps him up at night and fuels him and sometimes his lower instincts."

"Well, why doesn't he quit the practice?" Ben asked. "He is a smart guy. There are dozens of things he could be."

"Because then he would not be a lawyer. He can't live with being one and can't live with being anything else. Marston is chasing a ghost. His father died when he was twelve, and that frightened Marston to death. The loss of a parent to any child informs much of who they will become. Then, you add Mr. Thornton. Believe me when I tell you that Mr. Thornton was no saint. But he was a hell of nice guy, and he rescued Marston from a sure path of destruction. Marston idolized him and wants to prove Thornton's faith in him deserved. Even though Thornton died twenty years ago, Marston will always chase the approval and the myth of Mr. Thornton. It is a standard that no human can attain. His rose-colored view of his mentor saw him in much greater stature than had been earned. Marston has a biological need to win and succeed, and his conduct is rooted by that singular force. He has nothing else to be. He never had kids for fear of the father he would be. He is not a bad guy. He does bad things and treats people terribly, but it all stems from his overwhelming insecurity that he is just not good enough, despite overwhelming evidence that he is a tremendous lawyer. It is not an excuse but an explanation. I have tried to my best to ease him off the gas, but I fear it is a lost cause."

When Ben made the decision to leave Marston, The Sage gave his blessing and approval. Ben, the Sage, and Marston were the only three people who knew why Ben left. Marston remained bitterly jealous of the relationship that Ben and the Sage had. Second to Thornton, it was The Sage's approval that Marston sought most.

The Sage thought it hilarious that Ben now represented plaintiffs in medical negligence cases—The Sage and his firm even defended a few of them. When they both had to depose experts on a case, they scheduled their out-of-town trips around major league baseball games. They ate great dinners, shared rental cars, and stayed at the same hotels. The Sage and Ben shared the same moral code regarding the ethics and duty to their clients. Their friendship outside the courtroom did not affect their fierce representation of their opposing clients in the courtroom. They had too much respect for their profession and each other to compromise. However viciously lawyers fight for their clients during the case and in the courtroom, when they step outside, they are often collegial and even friendly.

The Sage was a brilliant lawyer. In follow-up questioning of the opposition, Sage could eviscerate an expert in fifteen minutes. The Sage had an economy of language and action and an abhorrence of the superfluous. He mocked lawyers on either side whose elevated sense of self exceeded their ability. Fortunately, the two never had a case that went all the way to a jury trial, but it likely would not have mattered.

CHAPTER 9

There, in the darkness, he heard a familiar voice.

"Heard you got your ass kicked today."

Ben smiled. "Partner, you have no idea."

As darkness fell over Galloway Golf Course, Ben recited the day's events to The Sage. While Ben offered excruciating detail of what he had uncovered of Marco's crimes, he continued putting while The Sage stood near the hole tossing the balls back to Ben as they had done dozens of times before.

"That son of a bitch should be shot." Sage nodded and just let Ben vent. "That coward was given everything, yet he still felt the need—no, he felt entitled—to take people's money that he had no right to. I have watched this guy smile and hug and charm people while he stole their entire settlements. I saw an email from one of them who can't get back to North Carolina to take care of her terminally ill child, because Marco stole her money. It is heartbreaking. What the hell do I do? I have pre-trial motions tomorrow, trial in two weeks, and I have just discovered that my partner stole God-knows-how-much money from God knows who. He's stripped our operating account dry, and I have to come up with twenty grand to get our experts in town and on the stand."

Ben stopped putting, and the two walked quietly to the short stone wall bordering the green and sat down. Ben propped his chin on the butt end of the putter like a child.

After a few moments quietly pondering the significance of what Ben had just told him, The Sage finally spoke. "Ben, this is serious stuff. I think we need to employ the elephant rule here." Southerners have a saying for every situation and often don't even state the complete saying. In this case, The Sage meant: How do you eat an elephant? One bite at a time. "First things first. In the morning, you must call Sally Edwards at the district attorney's office and the Tennessee Board of Professional Responsibility. You have an ethical duty to report him to both places. Then, you and Peggy work out a system to inform the firm's affected clients of what you have discovered. Then . . ."

Ben interrupted. "Pards, maybe you forgot. I have pre-trial motions beginning at 9:00 a.m. with your boy, Marston."

"Then save those calls until the afternoon. First, handle those motions. Anything crazy about them?"

Ben sighed. "It is Marston freaking Owens. Everything about them is crazy. He has thrown everything but the kitchen sink at Stephanie and me with his ten-person trial team and will be looking for the early kill."

"How do you feel about your case?"

"It is a really tough one. My client is as good as gold, and her little girl is this precious little thing who has permanent brain damage. If I hit, I hit big, but the odds are against us. My best proof is the hospital protocol that Dr. Kirkwood clearly violated. In a rational world, it would be game, set, and match. But today, right before I left to pull Annie out of the street, I received a hand-delivered amended motion moving to exclude that protocol document."

"On what possible grounds could Marston get that protocol excluded?"

Ben snorted. "Here is the kicker, typical Marston. He's claiming an administrative error and that the protocol we used was not in legal effect at the time of the negligence."

The Sage shook his head. "That is such horseshit."

"You're damn right it is, but would you expect anything less from Marston? He claims he has a witness ready to testify that the administration possessed that document as a proposed protocol, but in fact, the actual effective protocol surprisingly excludes all of the language that puts Kirkwood on the hook. Judge Jones will have no option but to exclude the protocol that helps us and allow them to use the protocol that hurts us."_

"Jesus, Mary, and Joseph." The Sage raised his eyebrows, the lines on his forehead pronounced. "That boy will absolutely do anything. It is the biggest mistake I ever made, getting him into the med-mal game. Marston thinks whatever the means necessary justifies the end. He is so obsessed with beating you that he has lost all perspective. When I heard the insurance company was about to assign the case to Marston, I tried to get them not to do so. They said Dr. Kirkwood insisted on Marston. Then I called Marston, and I tried to get him to let someone else handle the case, but he would not hear of it. He cursed me out. Me!! Do you think you can get the trial continued?"

Ben shook his head. "I cannot afford to continue the case. I have so much money invested that I cannot wait another year. Not only do I have to try this case in two weeks, but I also have to win this case in two weeks, or my whole existence craters under the pressure. I was already at the saturation point with Annie, work, trial prep, and now the Alexopoulos stuff. If I do not make something happen, I will just have to fold the tents up and close the circus."

The Sage set a hand on Ben's shoulder. "Ben, you are going to make it through this. I know it sounds corny, but one step at a time, one day at a time. This is survival mode. Focus on the task in front of you that day and then wake up and start again. First thing to do is handle those motions and do not let Judge Jones hit you too hard. Then, as soon as you get out of court, make those calls to the DA and the board. Do not miss sleep. You have to be rested to handle this stress. Be careful with the brown water. Times like this can make it a problem. And by the way, how is my girl Annie?"

"Pards, she is the most noble soul I have ever known, but she is exhausting. Guys like us are used to controlling things with the force of our wills, and she is one thing that cannot be moved. I found her curled up on the sidewalk in front of the house. I talked her down a bit but not all the way. Finally got her in the house, and Lisa was there to help.

"Man, I am really sorry. That really sucks." The two stood up, and The Sage handed him his three golf balls. The Sage looked for a positive note to end on. "How is Max?"

"Max is the greatest kid that has ever lived. This Annie thing has been hell on him, and at thirteen, he already has enough going on in his head. He never whines and never complains, which is a little scary. His team is going to be great this year."

The Sage lived a good pitching wedge away in a stately home located on the tenth hole. "Ben, want to come over for some dinner? I know Jane would love to see you."

"Thanks, but I better go. Please give her my love. I will see you guys soon." Ben took his Scottie Cameron putter and balls and put them in the back of the Range Rover. People who frequently rode with Ben had to get used to the sound of three golf balls rolling back and forth in the back of the car. For Ben, instead of an annoyance, they acted as a metronome, and the balls' rhythmic sounds soothed him.

"Hey, Ben." Ben turned around.

"Don't forget to hydrate!" The Sage yelled.

Ben shook his head, laughed, and gave him the thumbs up. The Sage always made things better.

Ben climbed into the Range Rover and began the ten-minute drive home to Hein Park, comprised of the original Jewish neighborhood in Memphis with beautiful estate lots and uniquely crafted homes. The neighborhood abutted the lovely Rhodes College on the west and the old woods of Overton Park on the south.

Ben did not get three blocks from Galloway when the Rover started steaming, made the most horrific sound—the sound of money leaving, Ben thought to himself —and then rolled to a stop. "You have got to be kidding!" Ben screamed to no one. Then, he called Triple A to tow him.

There truly was not a better-looking SUV in the world. Ben loved the Range Rover but described it like being married to a stripper. You had a smoking hot chick with amazing sex, but you were always going to have some drama and crazy issues that got expensive quickly. It had been his dream car when he was in college. Four years prior, when he got a nice check, Ben went straight for the Range Rover. As good a lawyer as he was, his money skills were horrendous. He had no business spending so much money on a car with such a dubious record. Growing up with little caused him to pounce on shiny things when prudence suggested otherwise. Annie named it the Royal Motor Coach after seeing some of the British royal family riding in them. It had been a source of great joy and great angst. With every repair came huge bills and a shrug from the service manager, "Hey, it's a Range Rover." The joke was that there were a lot of people who owned one Range Rover but far fewer who owned two.

While waiting on the tow truck, Ben reflected on the Rover and all the fun he and the kids had enjoyed over so many long rides. When Annie was going through the worst of times, they crawled in the Rover and blasted Taylor Swift through the speakers. Swift was the only one who brought Annie any measure of peace. Ben learned the lyrics to all her songs and sung them along with Annie with the windows down and wind blowing. Once, while waiting in line at Target, Ben sang the song "We Are Never Getting Back Together" to himself—and in front of a young girl at the register and a young mother. The two stopped what they were doing to watch this middle-aged White guy pound out Taylor Swift lyrics using a basket of cleaning supplies as a rhythm section. When Ben noticed shocked looks, he shrugged his shoulders. "Don't be hatin' on Tay Tay!" That got him a hearty laugh. Ben's musical taste ran the gambit from his favorite, Jason Isbell, to classic Johnny Cash, Waylon Jennings, and Willie Nelson. He loved 60s classics and 70s rock anthems and jammed to the Almond Brothers and Lynard Skynard. James Taylor and Billy Joel calmed him down, Lyle Lovett made him laugh, and Bob Dylan made him think. When he and the kids listened to music together, Ben made the kids identify the artists. They were the first in their classes to know Bob Seger and Neil Young.

When it was Max's turn to choose the music, he went straight to rap with J. Cole, Yo Gotti, Young Dolph, and of course, Drake. Ben tried but could never quite get on board with that sound except for his three guilty pleasures: Ludacris's "Area Codes," the Ghetto Boys' "Damn It Feels Good to Be a Gangsta," and Kanye West's "Gold Digger." Annie loved Taylor's upbeat, catchy pop tunes, but Ben was surprisingly moved by her ballads. He secretly listened to "New Year's Day" and "Lover" on his morning walks through Overton Park. The song "Fifteen" brought tears to his eyes, noting the struggles his own fifteen-year-old confronted.

Forty-five minutes later, the tow truck came, the driver an old country guy with a big gut and trucker's hat. There is a difference between a Southern and country dialect. Based mostly on education, it has nothing to do with intelligence. Many a Southern gentleman and Northern asshole have made fatal mistakes underestimating the Southern country man. Ben grew up around country folks and never made that mistake, especially when dealing with someone about to help him.

"Wow, that's a hell of a nice truck. What happened?" the driver asked in a country twang.

"It freakin' blew up!" Ben was still salty about his day.

"What do you mean?" The driver wanted to tweak this fancy-pants yuppie.

"What do I mean? The damn piece of shit blew up! No lights, no warning, no shut off, just blew the freak up!" Ben screamed, knowing the guy was condescending to the perceived rich guy, but still unable to control his temper.

"Well, you know what they say about those Range Rovers." The man continued the needle.

"Yes, yes, I do. I know everything they say about them. I have said everything about them. There is nothing you can say about them that I have not said about them."

"It's my second one this week," the driver offered, still deadpan but loving his power.

"You don't say."

"Yup, those sure are some pretty cars but don't seem to last worth a shit."

"You don't say. Can you just tow the car?"

"How much did you pay for it, if you don't mind me asking?"

"A fortune."

"How many miles?" the driver was having too much fun to stop.

"104,000." Ben knew he was stuck and had to play along.

"Jeez, I cannot imagine paying that much money for car and only getting 104,000 miles on it. My Ford truck has got over 200,000, and all I have had to do is change the oil."

Ben finally surrendered. "Partner, you got me. I am a dumbass lawyer with more money than sense, and I bought a piece-of-shit expensive car because it looks cool. Can you please tow us both?"

The driver grinned from ear to ear. "Oh, sir," he feigned innocence. "I didn't mean anything by it. I just seem to tow a lot of these cars, and it never made sense to me why people bought them."

Ben's sweat now soaked through his suit. It was evening, but the oppressive August humidity stubbornly refused to abate in the slightest. It had been the day of days, and the pain was just starting. The next two weeks would be more than he could stand. The tow truck left the Rover and Ben at the locked gate of the closed East Memphis dealership. The dealership was no stranger to such orphan vehicles. Ben walked up to the key box and dropped his fob; the service department would attend to it when they arrived the next morning.

He took an Uber home, stripped off the wet suit, and put on a pair of shorts and tee shirt. He poured himself three fingers of Woodford Reserve over a huge ice cube from his whiskey ice tray and sat on his porch trying to make sense of it all. Tomorrow was going to be a tough day.

CHAPTER 10

The next morning, Peggy picked up Ben from his house at 7:00 a.m. and drove him to the office. They both were still rattled by and struggling with the idea that they had been working alongside a criminal sociopath. Peggy, who was in her late forties, wore a red floral sundress. She had short hair and a radiant smile that had served her well through her life. She was genuinely charming; Ben had never heard a bad word spoken of her. Clients and lawyers alike loved her.

"So what happened to the Rover last night?"

"It blew up." Ben sighed.

"What do you mean, it blew up?"

"Peggy, look, the damn car blew up. I am not an automotive engineer."

"Well," she said turning to him, her brow furrowed, "I could have told you that when you bought the damn thing. But you wouldn't listen."

Ben let out an audible breath. "Yes, Peggy, I messed up. I shouldn't have ever bought the Rover. Can we please move on?"

"I'm just saying."

"I know you are just saying. Please don't say it anymore."

"My, my, aren't we a little cranky this morning?" Peggy grinned, attempting, as always, to bring Ben out of a funk.

"Sorry, Peggy, it was a tough night. That was the last thing I needed."

As they approached the traffic light at North Parkway, Peggy asked, "We are we going to do about Marco?"

"I would like to drive down to Texas and strangle the bastard right now."

Peggy laughed. "Hell, I know of about fifteen clients who would drive you down there and help you get the job done."

Ben turned to her, now serious. "I talked to The Sage last night, and he said we need to contact Sally Edwards at the DA's office and call the Board of Professional Responsibility. I will do that when I get back from motions. In the meantime, will you call the tech guys and get them to shut off Marco's access to our server and have his emails directed to my account? Make sure to get the ones from the past year. When you have time this morning, please go through all of them and flag any connected to the affected clients. Next, please start thinking of a way to organize notifying all the victims. I also think there is some fund with the State of Tennessee that may compensate them if we can show theft. See if you can find out about that online."

"Well," Peggy said, "that shouldn't take long."

"Peggy, I am sorry for this whole mess. I never should have let us get involved with that clown. I just made a poor choice, plain and simple."

"Hey, we will get through it. Take care of court today, and I got you covered here. By the way, how is that little sweetie Annie doing?"

Ben took off his sunglasses and rubbed his hand through his hair. "Peggy, I really don't know what we are going to do. No matter how many times it happens, it always breaks my heart. She looks into my eyes, and she is just begging for help, and I sit there knowing that I can't give it to her. I have never felt more helpless in my life. I would do anything to help her, but for the life of me, I cannot figure it out."

"Benji, you are all going to be okay. Just be patient and keep loving on her. I know it hurts."

"Thanks, Peggy."

When they arrived at their office, Ben went straight to his desk and pored over the motions. When Peggy had finished cleaning out the crime scene, otherwise known as the former office of Marco Alexopoulos, she showed Ben the huge garbage bag she had filled with empty bottles, pill boxes, and drug paraphernalia.

"Holy smokes!" Ben said. "I never saw the guy drink a drop."

"Well, judging by the bag, the man was no amateur."

"What's all that drug stuff?" Ben asked.

"The hell if I know. I have never seen anything like it. There was some kind of weird-looking pipe, lighters, and little burned spoons."

"Thanks for doing that, Peggy. Let me know what you hear from the tech folks."

Ben needed to focus on the task at hand. Pre-trial motions were not glamorous and are too mundane to be scenes in movies or television. They are long, tedious, and boring but of critical importance. Judge Jones was the gatekeeper of all evidence to be presented at trial, and this hearing determined what evidence the jury would hear or would not. A plaintiff's case could die in the pre-trial hearing if the trial judge gutted a plaintiff's best proof.

***

Just down the street, at One Commerce Square, Marston directed a trial team with efficiency and precision. For the past six weeks, three associates, a paralegal, and a nursing paralegal had prepared the case flawlessly. Every witness was known. All depositions had been cross-referenced on tape so clips could be accessed on a whim and a moment's notice during the courtroom examination of a witness. If one of Ben's witnesses even breathed a potential contradiction or slight inconsistency, the large video screen could blossom into a clip of the witness's deposition testimony. Every question Marston intended to ask a witness had already been pre-printed and vetted by the entire legal team.

Marston's organizational and logistic strengths were also his weaknesses. His intense anxiety about being caught off guard informed his entire trial presentation. In every case he had tried so far in his forty years, his methods had secured easy victories against outmanned and outgunned plaintiffs. Why change his strategy now?

If Marston's approach was like classical music, requiring precise discipline to execute every note precisely, Ben's approach to trial work was like Miles Davis's jazz. Ben prepared and knew the case, but he felt the preparation enabled him to riff at trial and explore new trains of thought and new lines of questioning he had previously not considered. An opportunity to create his own "Kind of Blue" masterpiece. Ben did not want to just pummel a witness with an anvil; he wanted to convert an adversary into a willing participant of his artistry.

Six months ago, Marston's team had conducted two complete mock trials with thirty-six potential jurors in each one, and then written a two-thousand-page analysis of every witness, claim, and question. In the weeks leading up to trial, defense experts and witnesses would endure at least five preparation and video sessions with Thornton Firm lawyers who would subject them to the harshest cross-examination possible in anticipation of any stone thrown by the plaintiff's side. In the month leading to trial, Marston read every medical record, deposition, question list, exhibit, and legal analysis at least three times. For the trial, he planned every suit, shirt, and tie for each day of the trial and hired chefs to prepare his breakfast, lunch, and dinner meals, which would need to be ready at precise times. Also, while the trial was happening, there would be, on standby, a team of messengers, movers, and trucks in a parking lot near the courthouse waiting to mobilize and move men and materials on a minute's notice.

During the trial, Marston's team carried into the court-room two entire paper copies of the file, laptops connected to servers holding any document that might be necessary, and two dedicated stand-alone hard drives. Marston's para-legal carried in two dry-erase boards and multiple packages of markers. Two crisp new legal pads with an assortment of colored pens would be placed at the table in front of his chair. Ben and Stephanie's more humble resources required a different approach. The two of them repeatedly reviewed and read medical records and depositions. While they prepared for witnesses in the weeks leading up to trial, Ben developed more of an outline than a script to use in the cross-exami-nation of defense witnesses, wanting to see the demographic of the jury before he committed to a strategic approach and wanting to hear the witnesses' words in open court in the context of a trial before choosing his approach. Ben's fearless nature was his biggest advantage over Marston. Ben had lost cases and noticed the sun came up the next day.

When Ben was in college, he played with Marc Perez, who would go on to become a successful PGA Tour player. Perez was one of the best clutch putters Ben had ever seen. When Ben asked Perez to share his secret, Perez was flippant: "I just don't give a fuck." It took Ben a year to understand what Perez meant. The only thing Perez could control was the process. Perez committed to the putt and trusted the process. The ball either went in or did not. The epiphany freed Ben's mind, allowing him to take risks and swing for the fences in trial.

After two hours prepping for the motions, Peggy drove Ben to court, dropping him off at the Washington and Second Street entrance where he would meet Stephanie. Marston and his team drove the five short blocks from their office to court in a caravan of rented black SUVs. The Shelby County Circuit Courthouse, built in 1909, covers a city block between 2nd and 3rd Street on the east and west and Adams and Washington on the north and south. It is a square grand neoclassical building featuring a long portico topped by a cornice supported by massive ionic columns. Courtrooms on four sides overlook a central courtyard planted with seasonal flowers. In the late 80s and early 90s, the county meticulously restored the building to its original grandeur with spectacular wood paneling trimmed in gorgeous marble. The classically picturesque courtrooms have been the site of many films including *The Firm*, *The Client*, *The Rainmaker*, *The People vs. Larry Flint*, and the television show *Bluff City Lawyers*. The elegant building contains nine divisions of circuit court, where the civil trials are held; three of chancery court, known as courts of equity, located on the main and third floors; and a basement level housing general sessions and probate that handle small claims, wills, and estates.

Criminal cases, from DUIs all the way to murder, were tried in a separate building across the street. 201 Poplar, set at a diagonal to the civil courthouse, is a disgustingly ugly brown high-rise with reprehensible 70s architecture, carpeted floors, and soulless fluorescent lighting.

The Honorable Jerome Jones presided over Ben's case. His Division VI courtroom was located on the north hall on the main floor with the pre-trial motions on the case of Landers v. Kirkwood set at ten on Friday morning. Upon entry, the courtroom's jury box covered the far side of the room. In the rear of the room were two rows of wooden pews for spectators behind a three-foot tall, wood paneled "bar" separating the spectator gallery from the attorneys, witness stand, and judge's bench. Just in front of the bar, there was a row of wooden chairs with black leather cushions for the plaintiff, defendant, and paralegals. In front of them, the lawyers shared a singular twenty-foot-long wooden table with a podium placed in the center to separate the two sides. Made of rich cherry, it faced the elevated judge's bench, with the round seal of the State of Tennessee prominently displayed. Between the bench and jury box stood the witness stand, a single leather-cushioned wooden chair with a long microphone to capture testimony. As counsel for the plaintiff, Ben and Stephanie were allowed to sit at the end of the table nearest the jury box and directly facing the witness stand.

Judge Jones was a sixty-year-old Black former medical malpractice plaintiff's lawyer who had ascended to the bench ten years ago. He was six foot seven, a former college basketball player, with salt-and-pepper hair and a close-cropped beard. The most respected judge in Shelby County, Jones was considered by both sides to be brilliant, prepared, and painstakingly fair. He had a reputation for patience in that lawyers needed to present cases in their own way but had an acute intolerance for drama or foolishness in his court.

Marston's team arrived long before the 10:00 a.m. start and set up the right side of the table with Marston's notebook containing the pleading and briefs, legal pads, pens, and a filled water glass so that Marston could stroll in carrying merely a single folio containing a legal pad and one antique Waterman fountain pen in his jacket. Marston dressed formally in a blue three-piece suit, white shirt, blue-and-red striped tie, and black Allen Edmonds lace-ups. Kip and Steve were both dressed in navy two-piece suits, white shirts, and conservative ties. His team of paralegals and assistants occupied the back wooden benches behind the bar. Marston's team sat with clenched jaws, nervously waiting to be called into action by the maestro.

Ben wore a summer tan suit, pink dress shirt, and blue tie with a wide brown belt and tobacco-colored Alden lace-ups. Stephanie always dressed impeccably, wearing a dark suit with a neutral-colored silk blouse and sensible heels. Never flashy, the only jewelry she wore was a wedding ring, a string of pearls, and diamond stud earrings.

The plaintiff and defendant, collectively known simply as "the parties," do not typically appear at these motions. Ben walked into the courtroom after Marston had been there a few minutes standing behind his space at the table fretting over the order of his objects. The counsel table area was tight as a submarine, which made it impossible to avoid contact with opponents. During today's motions and subsequent trial, Ben and Marston would never have more than six feet between them, close enough to perceive the other's distinctive aroma. Ben walked straight up to Kip and Steve, shook their hands, and greeted them with a warm hello. The two nodded but did not speak, worried to incur the wrath of Marston for fraternizing with the enemy. Ben walked by Marston close enough to touch him, but Marston never turned or acknowledged his presence in any way. Ben took his seat to the left of the podium and unpacked his briefcase, preparing himself for battle.

The Shelby County sheriff's deputy, who acted as bailiff, called the court to order.

"All rise, hear ye, hear ye, this honorable circuit court Division VI is hereby open for business, pursuant to adjournment. All persons give attention, and ye shall be heard. The Honorable Jerome Jones is presiding. No talking in the courtroom."

The already towering Judge Jones stepped up to his elevated bench, turned to face the courtroom, and lowered himself into his chair, resembling Zeus taking the throne on Mount Olympus.

Judge Jones instructed everyone to be seated. "For the record, we are here on the case of Landers v. Kirkwood, circuit court docket number CT-62305-12. Today, we are set for the parties Motions in Limine. Are counsel ready?"

Ben stood, "Yes, Your honor."

Marston followed suit. "We are ready, Your honor."

"Lawyers, I realize this is a highly contested case, with high stakes and a doctor's reputation at issue, and I also realize you two have a long history together." An insular and small group, the Memphis legal community kept very few secrets, and courthouse gossip regarding rivalries was coin of the realm.

"Let me tell you right now in now in no uncertain terms that I will not tolerate any foolishness. Gentlemen, this is playoff basketball. I am glad to let you push and shove and elbow, but let us keep the blows above the waist and below the neck. Mr. Jennings, you have been in my court many times and tried several cases. You are a fine trial attorney and I have nothing but respect for you and your abilities. I know you believe you are funny. But you really are not nearly as hilarious as you think you are. You are fine to display that thousand-watt smile and syrupy charm and good-natured remarks. But there is a line. So don't get your feelings hurt if I rein you in if you start getting a little too full of yourself."

Marston bowed his head and displayed a tinge of a smirk.

"Mr. Owens, the same goes for you. You have half the Red Army in here, and I know you are used to controlling every room you occupy. But please know this and know this well—this is my room, not yours, and I am in charge. When I rule, that is it. I do not want to hear any remarks to the jury about rulings. Do not address counsel, you address me. If it is anything more than a simple objection, you ask to approach the bench. I do not have to tell either of you lawyers how to try a case, and rest assured, you do not have to tell me either. Mr. Jennings, you represent the plaintiff, so we will consider your motions first."

Plaintiffs advanced few motions in such hearings. It is usually the defense who files dozens of ridiculous motions, essentially attempting to prevent the plaintiff from putting on any evidence at all. Ben's first three motions were handled with little fanfare. They were technical in nature, regarding specific documents to be used by experts and a motion to exclude any mention of insurance paying Sydney's medical bills. Next came the two motions that mattered most to Ben: limiting the number of defense experts who could be called and making sure those experts were limited to only testifying their opinions previously provided in the defense expert Rule 26 disclosures. This rule requires each side to provide a detailed description of the opinions offered by their experts so as not to surprise the opposing side with new theories that the opposition did not have the opportunity to prepare for in cross-examination. The colloquial phrase for this surprise attack behavior is "sandbagging," and it is not allowed. If no order is in place, an unscrupulous attorney can "ring the bell" by allowing the jury to hear new information of which the other side was never informed and then "apologize" for the "inadvertent mistake." Once the jury hears that improper testimony, there is no way to un-hear it or un-ring the bell. To protect his chances of success, Ben wanted a specific order requiring strict adherence to Rule 26 in place.

In the courtroom, it is required etiquette that one stands when addressing the judge and that the opponent remains seated while the other speaks. Ben rose first. "Your Honor, Plaintiff's Motion Number 4 is to limit defense experts to the Rule 26 disclosure. The rule is clear, and we notified Mr. Marston of choosing to not depose the twelve experts he identified. We have a right to rely on those Rule 26 disclosures, and no case or law requires us to dispose those experts. However, many experts you ultimately allow him to testify should be limited strictly to the Rule 26 disclosure he provided some time ago." Ben sat down.

Marston stood. "Judge, this is a highly complicated case, and the science is deeply technical. It is difficult to identify every opinion our experts may discuss during testimony. We, of course, used every reasonable effort in describing the testimony of these fine doctors our Rule 26 disclosures, but it is impossible to capture every word our experts may say, and we cannot be bound by Mr. Jennings' request to limit us in that way. It is overbroad and burdensome, and the court should not require it." Marston sat.

Ben sprang up. "Judge, look at the size of the group Mr. Owens has assembled. He has a lawyer in charge of filling water glasses. You can't tell me they don't have the resources to at least summarize the specific opinions of his experts and the factual basis for giving them. Nobody is saying he has to script the witnesses, even though we all know that precise script exists, but the rule requires Mr. Owens to provide full disclosure of his experts' testimony, and my client is entitled to rely on that rule."

Ben took his seat, and Marston began to rise again for another word. Judge Jones waved him down. "Be still, Mr. Owens, I have heard enough. You boys are veterans and know the rules. Mr. Marston, you travel at your own peril if you attempt to offer testimony that has not been disclosed. You do not have to have every word, but by God, every opinion and every basis must have been identified. If one of your experts offers testimony outside those bounds, I will welcome an objection from Mr. Jennings. And if the practice becomes rampant, I will consider excluding that expert. Next motion."

Ben breathed a sigh of relief but kept a completely straight face. Only amateurs showed emotion upon a successful ruling. Ben rose to address the next motion, "Judge, next is Motion Number 7 regarding limiting experts. Mr. Marston has identified eleven experts. Based on the disclosures, most of their opinions are similar. He should be limited to two experts. Anything after that would be cumulative and unfair to the plaintiff who cannot afford that many experts. The court has wide discretion on such matters and should limit these experts." Ben was hoping for a limit or three or four but was trying to give the judge a feeling he compromised if he allowed another.

Marston rose. "Your Honor, please!" he protested in mock indignation. "Dr. Kirkwood has been accused of terrible conduct, and his life and reputation are on the line. He has a constitutional right to defend himself, and we should be able to call anyone we choose if they have relevant testimony to offer the jury."

Ben jumped up. "Judge, come on! He can save us the sanctimony. There are no jurors or clients here. He knows this is ridiculous. We all know the Marston playbook. Identify ten experts, try to bleed the plaintiff of resources, or at worst, give your experts a tryout so you can see who will do best at trial. Neither is fair and the judge has province over this trial."

Marston countered, "Your Honor, I may have taught young Jennings all he knows, but I certainly did not teach him everything I know! I resent his implication and am personally outraged at the insinuation."

Judge Jones leaned forward and pointed at the lawyers. "Alright, here we go. Both of you sit down and let it rest. Mr. Owens, I have read your disclosures, and there is much redundancy. You are limited to three experts unless you can somehow prove me wrong. For now, my ruling is three defense experts with the addition of your own client testifying. Next motion."

Ben had completed his motions, and now, the defendant proceeded with his litany of motions. One of them was to prevent the use of the Reptile Theory. Lawyers who represent plaintiffs in personal injury actions now utilize an unofficial manual which describes how our brain stem acts in accordance with our evolutionary need to protect ourselves, our progeny, and our tribes. This essential book is known as the *The Reptile Theory*, and it compares the human brain's need to survive as the driver in making decisions, and not some aggrandized form of empathy or quest to carry out justice. This Reptile Theory is designed to circumvent the Golden Rule of trial law. This Golden Rule is not your Sunday school class's version of the Golden Rule. In the realm of civil trials, the Golden Rule is the absolute prohibition of asking a juror, "How would you like it if this happened to you or your family?" or something similar. And the reason you cannot ask a juror that question is because it is so damn effective the powers have labeled any such utterance grounds for a mistrial--and off with the offending party's head. Well, maybe not that last part, but they will certainly make you feel that way if you dare get close to the forbidden zone. Most of a civil trial is a lawyer trying get around the Golden Rule. This motion was a joke, but defense lawyers were so scared of the tactic that they constantly fought against it.

Ben could not resist. "Judge, defense motions can be consolidated into one motion that says, 'The defendant moves that the plaintiff not be allowed to offer any proof or evidence that in any way is negative to the defendant.'"

Before Marston could protest, Judge Jones waved his hands again.

"Ok, Mr. Jennings, there you go again with the funny man stuff. Save it for the bar this evening. I'm sure your buddies find you to be a scream. In regard to the so-called Reptile Theory motion, I am going to deny it as stated. But Mr. Jennings, that doesn't mean you have full rein to go too far. I will entertain motions on a specific basis once we begin."

The motions continued with no big losses on either side until Defense Motion Number 23, which had been squeezed in toward the end to portray it as a small matter.

Marston rose. "Judge, our next motion involves a document. It appears through an administrative error, the hospital submitted in discovery a protocol that was not officially in use and therefore should be excluded. Mr. Jennings was recently provided a copy of the one that was in place at the time of the events surrounding the alleged negligence. We certainly apologize for the mistake, but it would be reversible error in the court of appeals to allow the plaintiff to rely on a protocol that was not in use in the hospital at the time."

Even though he anticipated this, Ben seethed at the intellectual dishonesty that was likely a complete lie. His entire case was predicated on this protocol. If the protocol were excluded by Judge Jones, Ben would still have a case, but then it would amount to a battle of the experts. He counted on that document for his cross-examination of the defense experts. How could Ben and Stephanie refute that Dr. Kirkwood was negligent if he couldn't use the protocol as evidence that Dr. Kirkwood violated the rules of the hospital?

Ben attempted to be measured and hide his fury. "Judge, this is outrageous! We have litigated this case for three years and exchanged thousands of documents. Mr. Owens has a small army that handles every detail, and I mean every detail. It is hard to digest believing this was an inadvertent error."

Marston stood and interrupted. "Your Honor, this is unseemly! Counsel is accusing me of unethical conduct, and I take umbrage at the suggestion. In the old days, I would take the poor excuse for a lawyer out back and settle this once and for all."

"Sit down, Mr. Owens!" Judge Jones shouted. "This is enough and just what I told you two I was not going to tolerate. I will throw you both in jail and test me if you think I won't. Mr. Jennings, see if you can make your point in a less accusatory fashion."

Ben, who had remained on his feet, continued in a more subdued tone. "Judge, this protocol that Mr. Owens is attempting to exclude required Dr. Kirkwood to use radiologists to read x-rays and not himself. I have no way of knowing what happened with the hospital allegedly providing us with the wrong protocol, but there is zero chance this was an accident. The protocol is the key document to our case and proves beyond a shadow of a doubt that Dr. Kirkwood was negligent. It is pure sandbagging to wait until the eve of trial to tell us that the protocol we have been working with the entire time is the wrong one. It amounts to pure sandbagging, blatantly unfair and unconscionable."

"Do you want a continuance?" Judge Jones asked Ben.

"What good will that do, Your Honor?" Ben threw his pen down on the table. "The defendant's story will just get better with every day. Dr. Kirkwood's experts won't have to deal with answering the pesky question of how Dr. Kirkwood could have violated standing hospital protocol, and someone was not negligent. Alicia and Sydney Landers have waited a year for their day in court, and on the eve, defendants are coming through the back door trying to pull the rug out from under them. I object and believe they slept on their right to exclude this document."

"Mr. Owens, what do you have to say?" Judge Jones asked.

"Your Honor, it was the hospital's error not ours. Why should we be penalized for their error? I am glad to see if the hospital will provide a witness if the court wishes."

Judge Jones said, "Okay, here is what we are going to do. We have two weeks until trial. Mr. Owens, you are going to make available to Mr. Jennings the hospital witness, who can best testify as to why the alleged error was made. Mr. Jennings, we will revisit this motion after that deposition. Call my clerk, and I will set it specially either next week or the week after."

Ben had expected Marston to pull every trick in the book. Ben learned at Marston's knee and witnessed many instances of Marston stretching the line between aggressive lawyering and unethical conduct. Screaming and yelling in open court would do no good. The remaining motions were uneventful. Ben was going to have to return to the rock quarry and find some more weapons to use at trial. It was now 2:00 p.m. and he had not eaten in over twenty-four hours. It was time to get some grub and recharge.

CHAPTER 11

Ben walked out of court and turned his phone on to a blistering number of text messages and phone calls. He saw the number of the Range Rover guy, so first things first.

"Yo, Tommy, my man, what have you got for me?" Ben asked hopefully.

"Hey, Ben. Well, my friend, it does not look good."

"What is it now, a water pump?" Ben asked.

"I wish it were that easy," the service rep said.

"What? What is worse than a water pump?" Ben asked.

"The engine is gone, blown, dead, cracked block."

"You have to be kidding me!" Ben screamed. "I have 104,000 miles on the thing. How can that be?"

Tommy answered, "Well, I hate that it happened, but you know they did not make these so good five years ago."

"They made them well enough to charge me $90,000 for one."

"How much is a new engine?"

"Right around $34,000," Tommy said reluctantly.

"Right around $34,000," Ben replied incredulously. "What is the Blue Book value if I get the engine fixed."

Tommy answered, "I am not sure but guessing around $20,000."

"Wait! What? Tommy, I ain't no mathematician, but let's do the numbers together. I can pay you guys $34,000 to replace an engine so I can drive it out of your dealership and have it be worth $20,000! Am I missing anything, or am I just stupid? Forget that, I bought the damn car. That is evidence enough of my lack of intelligence."

Tommy attempted to recover. "Ben, I have a beautiful new one that is stickered at $125,000 and I can probably get it for you for $120,000."

Ben was incredulous. "So let me get this straight. I bought a $90,000 luxury car five years ago and drove it just over 100,000, and then it blew up, making it now virtually worthless. But now, through the generosity of Range Rover's heart, you are going to allow me the privilege of buying a brand-new Ranger Rover for the low, low price of $120,000."

"Well, Ben, we make them a lot better now than when you bought yours five years ago."

Ben was done. "Well, why didn't you tell me five years ago I was buying a piece of shit?"

The phone was quiet. Ben sighed. "See what you can get for that sack of shit and let me know. I will be by to get my stuff out of it, so leave it outside. And if anyone lays a hand on Scottie Cameron, I will sue you for everything you have."

"Who is Scottie Cameron, and why is he in your car?" Tommy tried.

Ben walked across the street from the courthouse to AAA Bail Bonds, which occupied the corner between the civil courthouse and 201 Poplar. He knew the office awaited him and had to make those phone calls to the DA and Board of Professional Responsibility, but he had to have an hour to decompress first with someone he felt completely comfortable with. He was going to see his childhood friend, Freddie "Fifty Feet" Franks, who owned the popular bail bond location with its convenient view of the exit of criminal court. The two had met the first week of tenth grade at Wooddale High School in the lower-middle-class section of Memphis suburbia that had an even split of Black and White residents. No one remembers what prompted the fracas on that day, but Ben and Freddie wound up tangling in the parking lot. After it was over, the two decided each had had enough of the other and would rather be friends than enemies.

To say they had been teenagers full of themselves would be an understatement. They were once caught after climbing out of a second-story window and crossing over the roof during class to win a bet with some classmates. A six-eight football coach stood on the ground looking up, demanding to know what the hell they were doing. Ben, the jokester of the two, attempted a little humor to lighten the load. "Coach, there was a beverage involved." The coach, unmoved and raging mad, forced them to run steps until they nearly needed a surgeon. When they could move no more, the coach said, "Boys, let me tell you something: Every morning you wake up, you are only fifty feet from the street!" Ben thought about it. Don't get too comfortable because whoever you are, you could be out on your ass any day.

For Freddie, the coach's pronouncement was an epiphany. It seemed to come straight from God through Moses and bellowed by the coach. From then on, that phrase became Freddie's mantra. Instead of saying goodbye, he would just point at whomever and say, "You are only fifty feet from the street." He became known as Fifty Feet Freddie. Freddie ran hilarious commercials advertising his bail bonds by proclaiming, "And remember, with AAA, you are only fifty feet from the street. And I don't care about your credit, I care about you!" as he pointed at the camera. Leave it to Freddie to flip the coach's meaning of the phrase and monetize a scolding.

***

In high school, Ben and Freddie got into endless scrapes with all kinds of people, but one always had the others' back. Ben was more of a hothead than Freddie, who seemed to have acquired a street wisdom at an early age. Freddie bailed Ben out of more jams than Ben could remember. On one occasion, an enraged Ben took a bat after a very large guy who had committed some serious breach of the man code. At that moment, Freddie, the only one who could possibly have laid hands on Ben and not been violently injured, came from behind, head ducked, grabbed Ben around the waist, and pulled him away. When Ben calmed down, he recognized that moment of near-violence as a turning point in his life and determined to get his head on straight from that point on.

Freddie played golf every bit as well as Ben did, without feeling the constraints of Ben's artistry bullshit. Freddie cared about putting a score on a card and, even more importantly, relieving an opponent of his cash. Unlike Ben, Freddie did not play tournament golf. Freddie felt it a waste. "Why would I give a shit about some damn trophy? I want some cash." Freddie's swing was not classic but amazingly reliable. People watched him swing on the range and could not get the bets down soon enough. A fool and his money are easily separated, and Freddie made sure to provide the method. In the parlance of the game, Freddie knew how to golf his ball, plain and simple.

A degenerate gambler, Freddie loved the hustle more than the game. The two played money games all over Memphis and the Mid-South, skipping those real jobs their classmates took. At school, Freddie and Ben were basketball and baseball stars, not wasting time with public school golf. Freddie, Joe Carrol, and Ben snuck onto Fox Meadows at night and Audubon on weekends. The Memphis area abounded with golf courses, and with golf came gambling. Every course had average golfers who believed they were one step away from the PGA Tour. Recognizing this, Ben and Freddie happily visited these courses and played to the egos of these fine fellows, looking for the proverbial "sucker at the poker table." Freddie often changed golf courses because he did not want to become too recognized—which would affect his ability to hustle. Immune to stress, Freddie flourished in the caldron and loved the juice he got making a $1,000 bet with only $20 in his pocket. Most people wilt under such strain but Freddie shined. Ben never met a more fearless man.

College finally separated the young men. Ben felt the pull of legitimacy in wanting a degree and potential career if golf did not work out. Freddie thought college was a hustle, and he was no mark. Ben went to college and law school while Freddie played golf and started his bail bond business. No matter how enmeshed in the establishment Ben became, Freddie reminded his old friend of where he came from anytime Ben got too full of himself. No matter their differences, they loved one another and would not tolerate any insult to the other.

They still played money games on the course together when they could find a willing opponent. Freddie accumulated significant wealth stacking cash from various hustles and golf games. Ben did not even want to know how much money Freddie had and where he hid it. Freddie's math skills were as good as any MIT grad and his mastery of numbers put him on the good side of most bets, sometimes even ensuring the outcome would not be a matter of chance. Freddie carried a wad of cash in his pocket and beautiful girls on his arm, and his bail bond office sometimes resembled a Hooters. Ben had been no saint, but Freddie would make Leo DiCaprio blush.

Ben crossed the street from the civil courthouse and walked into AAA Bail Bonds to see Freddie and one of his runners, Wally, who had washed up from New Orleans after Katrina, screaming at each other. Wally stormed out the door, almost hitting Ben in the face. Freddie sat leaning back in an office chair, looking very satisfied and decked out in a pressed cotton button down, spotless, creased blue jeans, and a pair of $2,000 Lucchese custom-designed ostrich leather boots. He was tall and lean with flowing brown hair, a square jaw, and Ray-Ban Aviators pushed on top of his head. Anyone within ten feet could smell the testosterone of this unabashedly masculine specimen. Part of his allure was that he made no apologies or offered any excuses for who he was.

"Benji!! What's the haps, my brother?" Freddie was the rare friend who still used Ben's boyhood nickname. "You look like shit. Have you not been laid lately?"

"What do you mean, I look like shit? This is a good suit."

"Yeah, but something ain't right with you. Don't bullshit me."

"What was all the commotion just now?" Ben said, changing the subject.

"I just took $1,200 off Wally. I bet him four-one that the next person out of 201 would be White." Freddie explained.

"That's a crazy bet. No way you win that bet."

"Needed to teach the boy a lesson." Freddie laughed. "I had Gretchen over here go across the street, pay six White folks to stand at the door blocking it, and at my text, send them on out."

All Ben could do was laugh. "Freddie, they don't make 'um like you anymore. You hungry?"

"Me? You don't even have to ask. How about six bones at the Cozy?" Freddie said.

"Let's go."

The Cozy Corner was a classic Memphis BBQ joint on North Parkway in a rundown strip center. It had been founded by the gregarious Raymond Robinson, who had famously greeted people at the door with open arms and a wide smile; his lovely wife Desiree and "Momma" once sat at the front table, requiring a hug and kiss as the price of entry. Raymond and Momma had passed, but Desiree and her family continued to run the beloved BBQ joint known for its ribs, sliced pork, bologna, and smoked Cornish hens. Locals of all classes and colors poured into the Memphis landmark daily to get a fix of God's BBQ ribs. Executives in shirts and ties stood shoulder to shoulder with construction workers in line. A special shorthand and cadence for ordering distinguished the locals from the tourists. Ben stepped up to the plate.

"Six bones hot, beans, slaw, sweet tea."

Freddie's turn. "Two bolognas, beans and potato salad, sweet tea." He stripped off a couple of twenties from a huge wad in his pocket to pick up the tab. The men took their number and drinks and headed to their customary back table, greeting other customers along the way in this biggest of small towns in America.

Ben gave Freddie a rundown on the last forty-eight hours, including the Range Rover.

Freddie adopted a pronounced country accent. "'Range Rover?' Is that one of them there English cars that all of you fancy boys drive?"

Ben, letting him have his fun, said, "Yeah, that's the one."

"Didn't you pay a fortune for that thing?"

"Yes, a small fortune."

"You know, I have heard of a way to make a small fortune owning a Range Rover."

Ben took the bait, "How, Freddie?"

"Start off with a Range Rover and a large fortune!" Freddie roared at his own joke.

"Hilarious," Ben said.

The plates of food arrived. Ribs at the Cozy were known as "country ribs," meaning they came on individual bones with large amounts of pork on each one. They oozed with BBQ sauce. A diner needed a loaf of napkins and a dry cleaner after eating a plate of those, but it was worth every stain. While they ate, Freddie regaled Ben with tails of romantic conquests and wagers won.

Freddie suddenly got serious and said, "I knew that Marco Alexopoulos was bad news. Something about him never seemed right to me. That son of a bitch needs a good ole-fashioned ass whipping."

"Pards, there is nothing I would like better, but that is not going to solve anything. He is in Texas in rehab, probably telling a counselor about his mamma issues. With rich guys like that, it is never their fault, and they never have to pay the tab. They always leave it to the regular guys to clean up the mess."

"Whatever you need, big man. I am here."

"Well, now that you mention it—do you have a car I can use until I figure out what to do next about mine?" Ben asked.

"Absolutely. In fact, I have just the car for you. So much better than that English piece of shit you have been posing in. Dashawn Taylor just skipped bail, and I had to execute on his car. It's in the parking lot by the building. You will love it. It is all yours."

"Thanks, brother, you are the man."

The two finished up at the Cozy Corner and headed back to Freddie's place. As they pulled up in Freddie's Cadillac sedan, Freddie gestured to a car parked in the second row. "Behold, my brother, the one and only Cadillac Escalade, American excellence at its best. No more socialist-commie cars for you, you liberal son of a bitch!"

The car came right out of "Pimp My Ride." A black Cadillac Escalade tricked out with gold trim, lift kit, performance sport wheels, blacked out windows, and curb feelers.

Ben looked up to the heavens as if he were going to get some help there.

"Are you kidding?" he yelled. "This thing with the Memphis trim package? I catch enough hell as it is and now this? Come on, dude, you have to have something better than this."

"Oh, Mr. High and Mighty Big Shot Lawyer. Have you forgotten where you come from?"

"I have certainly tried, but you make it extremely hard to forget."

"Come on, Benji, you will love it, the girls will love it, even those assholes at Choctaw Country Club will love it." Freddie reconsidered. "Strike the last one—those bastards don't love anything other than those pretentious S-class Benzes. I still don't know why they don't let me play there anymore."

"Oh, I don't know, Freddie, maybe when you took ten grand off the club president, felt up his wife, and then pissed in the swimming pool. I can't imagine what the problem was."

"Those bastards are so uptight. Fuck 'um if they can't take a joke."

"Thanks for the car. I will call you later."

"Hey, Benji, fifty feet, fifty feet."

Ben smiled to himself and thought it seemed even closer right now.

CHAPTER 12

There is never an off-period at the Thornton Firm. Even the easy days are hard and stressful. But trial mode is quite a different kettle of fish all together—especially this trial in particular. The trial team prepared everything conceivable that required preparing, yet that still was not near enough to please Marston. Marston conducted daily meetings with the trial team and screamed, yelled, and denigrated in every breath. Marston was always a nervous nelly when it came to trials. He ate sparingly for days and weeks at a time, and his already skeletal frame transformed into something of a walking corpse. He did not sleep and drank heavily at night, dashing off insane emails to the team, who did not know whether to respond or wait until the next day and see if he forgot about his drunken missive.

It was a quietly held secret among the Thornton Firm that Marston did not go to trial nearly as much as he had in previous years. Long ago, Marston had gone to many trials and made his bones winning cases thought impossible to win. For the last ten years, however, Marston had settled way more than he tried. Like his choice to drop out of law league basketball once his team had won, he wanted to quit while he was ahead without risking a loss. His self and public images centered on the perfection of his performance and his extraordinary ability as a trial lawyer. To lose a case would reveal him for the fraud he feared he was.

There had been some conflict with the insurance company as of late. Marston's bills were infamously huge, considering the resources he used on every case. This dedication won him the hearts of his doctor clients but the wrath of some of the bean counters who paid his bills. His pattern was to spend hundreds of thousands of dollars litigating cases and then, after most of the billing had been completed and the nut cutting arrived, settle the case. He did not seek settlement authority himself but maneuvered the doctor he was representing to demand that the company resolve the case. In the Tennessee physicians' insurance company, physicians had the power to initiate or refuse settlement discussions and to ultimately settle the case. Doctor's God complexes are well known, and their inflated egos make it extremely hard to secure agreement to settle. Adding insult to injury, a national database tracks and records all settlements and verdicts of $75,000 or more. Doctors abhorred placing themselves on what they considered the wall of shame. Any payout could endanger their standing among peers and hospitals and hinder their ability to seek employment at another group.

Marston pounded his doctors so hard during "trial prep" that the fear of taking the stand and suffering public humiliation often compelled them to beg Marston and the insurance company to settle. When a doctor asked to settle, Marston advised him or her to obtain private counsel who would perform the singular job of demanding the insurance company settle the case, thus removing Marston's fingerprints. Marston positioned himself as ever ready to go slay the beast and blame any settlement on the doctor. The insurance companies were on Marston's deception, but the doctors had the choice of counsel, thus tying the insurance company's hand.

In this case, a huge wrinkle arose. Marston's ego would not allow him to settle with Ben, yet losing to Ben made Marston crazy as a betsy bug. He had cut corners before and would do it again to secure a victory. Marston basked in the honor and integrity of being a member of the legal profession but when his ass was on the line, quickly abandoned his professional morals like a sinking ship.

Pre-trial motions signaled the beginning of the sprint to the finish. Every witness and contingency would be considered and planned for in granular detail. Every pleading, medical record, and document along with summaries would be placed in separate color-coded and labeled notebooks. The paralegals had the same information on their laptops as back-ups and even brought a printer with them to court, enabling Marston's team to have an office within the courtroom, allowing for any contingency. Marston and his team obsessed over question lists of opposition and their own witnesses. Kip and Steve, with the assistance of the tech department, prepared isolated video clips of a witness's sworn deposition testimony used in conjunction with the question lists to use as a cross-examination impeachment device. Any time one of Ben's witness deviated one ounce from their sworn deposition testimony, the video clip of the contradictory testimony would appear on the courtroom's video screen to discredit the witness.

There would be no sleep or relief for Marston's team over the next two weeks. They were exhausted and scared to death. Kip was the only one among them who had taken one to trial with Marston, so he acted as the lieutenant, advising them of their obligations and what to expect. Many cases had been prepped by teams, but the firm had taken only one case to verdict in the past five years.

While the lawyers and staff were at lunch in the conference room, all wearing the thousand-yard stare of the condemned, Marston burst in the room at exactly 3:00 p.m., energized.

Addressing the entire trial team, he began. "Alright guys, here is where we are: We have to get a Lutheran Hospital witness ready to go in three days who can testify about the protocol. She needs to say the protocol Ben wants to use was not in effect at the time of Sydney Landers. We need her to testify that the protocol we put in our motions is the one that was in effect, and she needs to say it was the hospital's mistake that Jennings got the protocol in the first place." Kip and Steve sat up straighter, their eyes getting bigger, knowing it was them who would have to execute this difficult request. "If we force Jennings to depose her, and she holds up, the protocol issue will be dead before the first day of trial. Time is of the essence, and I want this detail buttoned down and put to bed this week. Get this done with no excuses."

Kip steepled his hands, and Steve stroked his hair, neither looking at the other because they both knew that Marston's claim there was a new hospital protocol that made it acceptable for non-radiologist physicians to review x-rays for children with NEC was a complete fraud. The only protocol the hospital had ever had for treating premature infants with NEC is the one Ben and Stephanie had been working with for the past year. How could the team find a hospital witness to testify about something that did not exist?

Kip nervously asked, "Marston, do you have any idea of who we might get?"

Marston erupted. "That is what I am paying you all this goddamned money to do!"

There you had it. Marston had now put the two associates in a box. To succeed in the firm and their careers, they were being asked to concoct false proof and acquire a witness to support that lie. Forcing them to do it gave Marston insulation. If it went south, he had plausible deniability about the false testimony procured by Kip and Steve; he could sacrifice them to either the judge or Board of Professional Responsibility. And if the associates refused, they would lose their jobs at the Thornton Firm and struggle mightily to find another that would pay as well. Marston encouraged his associates to acquire wives, children, and big mortgages for this very purpose. Kip knew the score and would explain to Steve after the meeting.

"Marston," Kip answered confidently, "Steve and I will get this done."

"Good, see that you do. I want a report tomorrow."

The meeting continued and more projects were assigned. The paralegals and nurses were dismissed, leaving Kip and Steve.

Marston counseled, "Boys, I don't need to tell you how important this case is to this firm and to you personally. Our only option is victory. The insurance company could easily fire us if we get hit. That means we all crash. Don't let that happen. Now, get the hell out of here and handle this professionally and discreetly."

Kip and Steve walked back to Kip's office. Steve looked like he had seen a ghost. This was not Kip's first rodeo. Kip closed the door.

"Look, youngblood, it was only a matter of time until you were brought into something like this. This is your test. You will either make your bones, or you won't. This is the big leagues, and there is no room for errors or consciences."

"B-b-but Kip—" Steve stammered.

"Steve, stop. Don't say another word. Do you want to go home and explain to Judy why you are losing the house, the private school, and spring vacation?"

"Jesus, no." Steve agreed.

"Well, put your big-boy pants on and get with it. It we pull this off, Marston will owe us his life. If we help defeat Ben Jennings, he will be forever in debt to us. And then, my boy, you will be a made man and member of the club. A win like this is how you make partner. The protocol is our only weakness. If we eliminate that, we should be home free. Ben has got that one old codger expert, and we have the 1927 Yankees."

Steve, now reflective, pursed his lips. "When I went to law school, I never thought that I would be doing something like this."

Kip empathized. "Look, this is the sausage-making part of this business. We dress in these nice suits, work in these palatial offices, have staff catering to our every need. We live in nice houses and drive nice cars and take nice trips. Our kids go to great schools, and our families are proud of us."

Steve looked unconvinced. "It just feels so wrong."

Kip lost patience. "Come on! These damn plaintiffs' lawyers are full of shit, greedy bastards. You don't think they pull the same things on us if they can get away with it? Ben seems all preachy and good, but don't you think Marston sent him out to do wet work of his own?"

"You're right," Steve finally conceded. They stood up, gathered their materials, and headed to Kip's office to come up with a plan. Before they entered, Steve told Kip he needed five minutes to call his wife, and he would join him in his office.

"Hey, Lily, how is it going?"

"Oh, hey, honey, it's great. I was just about to pick the girls up at school and go home to start dinner and help them with their homework. How is your day going?"

Steve paused for just a second to gather himself. "It's just fine, sweetie, just fine."

"Steve, are you alright, honey? You sound like something is wrong. What is it?"

"Oh, it's really nothing." He paused. "It's just trial prep and a little stressful, but everything is great."

"You sure? Because you don't sound like everything is alright."

Steve smiled gently to himself, his voice now soft. "Ah, baby, it's all going to be great. I am just glad to hear your voice. After you pick up the girls, please call on the speaker phone so that I can talk to them."

"I will. And don't forget we are having dinner at the Jacobson's house Saturday night."

***

Steve went to Kip's office, where they outlined a strategy. Marston was friends with the chief hospital administrator. Kip would ask Marston to make a call and put the associates in touch with the CEO. Then, the CEO would select a vulnerable employee who could be manipulated into giving them the necessary testimony.

For the past few weeks, Steve noticed he had not been eating regularly and that, for some reason, his hair was falling out. There could be no margin for error in this game he was playing. He wondered if this was all worth it. He and Lily had been fighting more and more, and his social drinking had increased to professional drinking, consuming three or four cocktails every night just to take the edge off. Days turned into weeks, and weeks turned into years. He started asking himself the existential questions of life. Some young lawyers become so obsessed with competing and grabbing, they fail to realize their youths are sacrificed in the bargain.

CHAPTER 13

en's life was not getting any easier. He got to his South Main office just after 3:00 p.m. and walked in to find three separate groups of people demanding to see him and yelling and screaming at Peggy, who was doing her best to placate them. After reviewing the red files in Marco's office, Peggy had dutifully called each of them and told them of her and Ben's suspicions that Marco had likely stolen his clients' money.

Ben waded through the ten people who had gathered in the lobby, got to Peggy's desk, and turned and faced the room. "Folks, I am Ben Jennings, and I have, for the past two years and until today, been Marco Alexopoulos's partner. Yesterday, for the first time, I found out that he had likely stolen money from you and perhaps others."

A roar came up from the crowd.

"What the hell!" A man Ben would soon learn was Earnest Saulsberry was red-faced in blue jeans, a tee-shirt, and work boots.

From the other side of the crowd, a large man dressed in blue coveralls with the name "Pete" stenciled on his chest said, "You have got to be kidding me!"

A petite lady standing in the middle, whom Ben would later know as Martha Ferguson, pointed her finger at him. "What are you going to do about this? He is your partner. You are on the hook for this!"

Ben waived his palms down, asking for quiet. "I am as sorry as I can be, and I know sorry does not put money into your pockets. This situation is as new to me as it is you, and I am still sifting through details and learning enough to be able to give you honest answers. Yesterday afternoon, Peggy and I dug through the mess that is Marco's office and found a file cabinet we had no idea existed. It contained red file folders with your case information. Yesterday was the first time I knew any of you existed."

Ms. Ferguson shook her head as if trying to withhold curse words. Mr. Saulsberry appeared to be considering physical reprisal on the only lawyer in front of him. Ben raised his voice to quell the mumbled fury.

"First, as soon as I am through talking with you, I am going to contact the district attorney's office and tell Sally Edwards what I discovered about your cases and my ex-partner's criminal behavior. I'm going to be straight with you, and I promise you I will keep you informed. Peggy will give you each the number of the police to call, and I suggest you contact Ms. Edward's office as well and tell them everything you know. By tomorrow, I am confident they will have investigators who will want to speak to you. Also, if you don't mind, please talk to Peggy and give her your names and numbers and what cases Marco was working on for you. We are as in the dark as you are, but I promise I won't rest until we have answers.

"Once we have your information, we can work to prepare a list of the key things the investigators will need to learn—your case numbers, the dates of your hearings, that sort of thing. I am also about to contact the Tennessee Board of Professional Responsibility. They are the people who oversee lawyers and our licenses. I am about to draft my own complaint to them, and we will assist you to draft individual ones as well. His license will be suspended by the end of the month, and I can guarantee he will be disbarred. My understanding is they have a special fund that helps to compensate people whom their lawyers stole from."

"Sounds like this happens all the time," Saulsberry interjected.

"Sir, I am afraid it happens more than it should. One time is too many. I wish I had a better explanation, but let me assure you right now, the one thing you will not ever hear me do is defend the conduct of Marco Alexopoulos. What he did is criminal and shameful. You put your trust in him and he took advantage of you. I'm . . . I'm just so sorry. I know that doesn't help you now, but I am genuinely sorry.

"The board has a victim's claim form for you to fill out. Peggy will get you all copies of that before you leave. Also, in the coming days, I want to schedule individual appointments with each of you to learn all of the specifics of your situation. There may be some cases that have not settled. And on those, I will contact the opposing lawyers and make sure you get new counsel swiftly. I will draft affidavits that will help the police prosecute Alexopoulos. The simple truth is that he belongs in jail for a long time."

The crowd calmed, many unfolding their arms and looking each other as to how they took Ben's words. After looking down at a piece of paper handed to him by Peggy, Ben continued, "I know this will not help your feelings, but Marco stole a small fortune from me and our firm as well. The question is how to get the money back. Marco has run off to rehab, and I am pretty sure he has blown all the money he stole, but at this point, we are not certain of anything. There is a mechanism with the state that will reimburse you for at least part of your losses, but it will require each of you to participate."

"We trusted him," a middle-aged lady in a tracksuit said to no one in particular. She received various nods of affirmation.

"Look," Ben continued, "you already have our office number, and I am about to give you my personal cell phone number. We are not going to stop until we get justice for all of you. I cannot promise you will get every dime back, but I can promise you I will not sleep until Marco Alexopoulos pays for his crimes. By the first of next week, it is my plan to have each one of your claims documented and put in the hands of both the DA and Board of Professional Responsibility. Peggy and I will prepare a comprehensive spreadsheet and document everything that has happened. There is a chance for some of you whose cases have not yet been settled, and to that extent, we will make sure that your cases are properly taken care of."

For the moment, Ben had appeased the crowd and restored order. The unsinkable Peggy, whose magnetic personality charmed all who met her, began directing the crowd to the conference room and establishing order. Ben, finally able to get to his office, took off his coat, unpacked his briefcase, and pulled his phone out of his breast pocket. Ben saw that Annie had called him five times in the past ten minutes.

He stuck his head into the conference room and said, "Hey, folks, my daughter is ill, and I have to make a quick call. I will come right back in here."

Ben dialed Annie's cell phone, and she answered on the first ring. "Hey, punkin, how is it going?" He used his softest voice possible.

"Dad," Annie was crying. "I am just so sad, and I don't know what to do. I just want to go back to like I was before, and I just can't get there."

"Honey, it's going to be alright. I am so sorry you are going through this." Ben paced his office, running his free hand through his hair before deciding to look out the window.

"Can you come over and get me now?" she asked.

"Baby, I cannot come right now. But I will come as soon as I can. Where are you?"

"Oh, I am just walking down Union Avenue wandering around."

Ben resisted the urge to raise his voice. "Annie, please don't walk there. You know how bad that can get. Can you just walk back to your mom's, and I will come as quickly as I can?"

Annie was now crying so much she could not be understood. The only thing he could understand was "I am so, so sorry."

"Honey, have you had your medicine today?"

"No, I have decided I don't need the medicine. I am really good."

"Sweetie, look, you have to take the medicine. It's just like if you had high blood pressure or a low thyroid. It's just body chemistry. Taking medicine doesn't make you crazy. I know you think that, but it's just not so. Will you please go back to your mom's house and just trust me and take it?"

"I don't know. When will you be here?" she asked.

"As soon as I can get there. So please go home and wait for me on the steps, and I will do the best I can," Ben implored.

Ben quickly dialed Lisa. "Hey, have you talked to Annie?"

"Not in a couple of hours. I just got out of a business meeting. I am headed home around three." Lisa sounded worried. "What's up?"

"Lisa, she is wandering around the streets again and hasn't taken her medicine. This Marco thing is blowing up, and I am dealing with an angry crowd here in the office."

"I will go home as soon as I can," Lisa said.

"Thanks. And if you get there before me, tell Annie I am on my way."

Ben came back into the conference room. Peggy was handing out coffee, legal pads, and pens. There were fewer red faces, and the crowd seemed mildly placated. Ben addressed them.

"Now, let's just take our time and get this all down on paper. Mr. Anderson, Miss Emily, and Susan, you three come with me so that I can type up your statements. The others go with Peggy so she can get yours. I will gather them up and provide them to the DA and Board of Professional Responsibility."

"But when do we get our money?" Earnest Saulsberry yelled.

"I honestly don't know. I wish I did," Ben answered.

"How do we know you aren't involved as well?" Martha Ferguson asked.

Ben shook his head and grimaced. "First of all, you don't. I cannot ask you to trust me. I have to earn your trust, and I know it. But if I were in on the con, I would not have been the one to call you and tell you about it. I will sit here and answer all your questions and do the best I can. We will all speak to the police. I will do everything I can to support you. I wish I could tell you something better, but it seems like you have been lied to enough, and I don't want to add to it."

This answer seemed to calm the group down, and they began working with Peggy and him, painstakingly taking down all the information they could for the next two hours. At 4:30 p.m., Annie called again. Ben looked at the few who were left. "I'm really sorry. This is my daughter again. I will be right back." Ben walked out of his office to the back part of his space.

"Hey, Annie. How are you?" he asked.

"I just really need to see you." She was crying.

"I will be there in fifteen minutes, I promise."

Ben grabbed his jacket and announced to the remaining four people, "Folks, again, I am very sorry, and I will be back in the morning if any of you have any questions. I have to handle a family matter right now. Peggy will make sure we get all of your information. And if she hasn't already, she will give you my cell number."

Ben raced to the Escalade and sped to Central Gardens to see Annie. His heart raced and sweat poured off him. He put on Johnny Cash, playing the song "Hurt" to soothe himself and gather the patience he would need for a night with Annie. Ben arrived at his old house to find Annie waiting dutifully on the steps. Lisa was already home and waved to him from the front door. Annie looked as though she had not showered in days and held a set of keys and wad of tissues in one hand. She welcomed him with a big hug, and they held it for what seemed like a full minute. He wondered who needed the hug the most.

"How about some hoops at the gym?" Ben asked.

"Sounds great!" she exclaimed.

"Go get your brother, and we can grab a bite on the way."

Max banged out the front door, carrying his battered backpack and a basketball. They followed him down the steps to the sidewalk and the Escalade. He told Lisa where they were going. When Ben beeped the key to open the door, Max hooted.

"What the . . . !"

Annie laughed for the first time in a long time.

"Dad! Where is our Royal Motor Coach?"

"It died."

"Died?" Max looked astonished.

"The engine blew up last night and looks like it can't be fixed."

"Did you actually buy this car?" Max asked in disgust.

"No. Just a loaner from your Uncle Freddie. We will get another car."

"Can we get a Ferrari?" Max asked.

"No, more like a Toyota," Ben replied.

"Ah, come on dad, you need a car with some swag," Max protested.

"I need car that will start!"

Max raced to the front seat, and Annie crawled into the back. Max insisted on touching every button and lever in the car. He was so excited.

"Dad, this is like the cars the rappers drive."

Ben rolled his eyes. "Great, just great. Career goal, check. Now, I can die."

Ben drove just down the street to their school gym and used the key he got from coaching to get into the back door. Ben was not dressed for basketball, so he rebounded for the kids. They finally taunted him into a game of HORSE, which always brought out the laughter and competitiveness in them all. The gym was their cathedral where all problems went away. It was pure joy to launch jumpers and watch them arc and swish through the net. Max was an outstanding basketball player but had his dad's perfectionist streak. From the age of three, he could handle a ball like a magician. He had a natural shot and awed people who saw him play. He wanted to be in the gym every chance he could. In middle school, he became a star basketball player, but his temper often got the best of him on the court. Everyone thought him a prodigy except for Max himself. He saw only the shots he missed and the moves he failed to execute. It broke Ben's heart to see the trait he had passed down to his son.

Annie came out of her shell, and the three had a blast in the gym. After an hour, they went to Popeyes Chicken and loaded up on that yummy goodness, the kids devouring fried chicken, red beans, rice, and mashed potatoes. It was dark when they got back to Lisa's house, and she met them at the door.

"How is she?" Lisa asked.

"Well, full of fried chicken right now."

Lisa laughed. "I am glad you got her to eat."

Ben shook his head. "Me too. You just never know what's going to work. Tonight, it was basketball and fried chicken. Tomorrow—who knows?

***

The next day was Saturday. Ben grabbed a sausage, biscuit,

and Diet Coke from the Exxon at Third and Crump and went into the office to begin the hard work of drafting the board complaint on Marco. He spent the entire day preparing the complaint, gathering documents, and preparing affidavits for each of the individual victims. He called each person that could be identified as a victim and one by one went through the same story: what he knew, what he did not know, and what he intended to do to help.

He called the attorney general, Sally Edwards, on her cell phone and told her the situation. Sally could not believe what she heard. She told him she would have the white-collar prosecutor and investigator call him Monday morning to get the wheels rolling. Her office would jump on the investigation and get something done as soon as possible. Ben would file the board complaint first thing Monday, and Sally warned Ben that he would likely spend the better part of the day meeting with police and prosecutors.

"Sally, I can't thank you enough. I have a trial beginning in two weeks, so I am swamped, but I am at your folks' disposal whenever they need me."

"Ben, if you can just set aside Monday afternoon, that will get us started."

"Absolutely," Ben said. "That will give us enough time to finalize victims' statements and put together the documents you will need to prosecute."

"Jeez, Ben, I am so sorry this happened to you."

"Sally, does this happen very often?"

"More than you can imagine. Lawyers have these big escrow accounts, and it proves too big of a temptation for some to avoid."

"Thanks again for your help. If we could get your investigators to contact the individuals as well, it will go a long way in helping me establish some credibility with them."

"You got it, Ben. Hang in there and call me on my cell if you need anything else."

Ben spent the entire day going through files, emails, and the court docket, preparing a comprehensive spreadsheet on the level of Marco's theft. Ben had hoped it had been a couple of isolated events but soon realized the large scope of Marco's criminal activity. Like his old man, Marco ran a Ponzi scheme with his clients' money, but the clock had run out, as it always does.

Sunday, he was back in the office with a Danish and cup of coffee from Bluff City Coffee, preparing for the trial and still searching for some weakness in the defense case. After Friday's motions, Ben had deep concerns that Marston would get his ace-in-the-hole protocol kicked out of court, leaving him with a much thinner case. His dyslexia made it difficult to properly absorb the intensely complicated information, but to beat Marston, there could be no shortcuts.

Sunday night, he picked up Annie and Max for his week of custody. Even in the worst of times, those two made everything better. Annie had not bathed but appeared happy. They grabbed a pizza from Little Italy on Union Avenue and headed to the house where they could play basketball in the backyard. Annie sat on the porch swing while Max and Ben shot hoops. After a while, Ben and Max sat on a stone retaining wall to drink some Gatorade.

"Hey bud, I know all of the attention is focused on Annie, but I just want to know—how you are doing?"

Max looked down. He did not share feelings easily. "Dad, when is she going to be better? When can we all go back to being normal?"

Ben looked down and Max and put his hand on his shoulder. "Buddy, I wish I knew. I can't lie to you. I have never been through anything like this myself and am learning as we go. I can't tell you how much I appreciate you and how well you are handling this."

"Dad, she is just so weird. She scares me sometimes."

Ben turned his head and focused. "How so, son?"

"She just cries all the time and stays curled up in a ball. Then, she comes in my room all excited, and I don't really know what to say to her."

Ben took the ball from Max. "Little man. All I can say is you are a prince. One day, she is going to get better, I guarantee you. And she will remember how kind you have been to her and love you even more. I am sorry you are going through this. You know you can always call me if I am not around. And if you want to talk, I am here for you."

"I know you are, Dad."

They got Annie from the swing, and Ben made their favorite fettuccine alfredo with Velveeta cheese. They dined like kings and played video games the rest of the night. Ben put Max to bed and then went to Annie's room; the two sat on her bed for hours, neither speaking. After Annie fell asleep on his shoulder, he gently lay her down and covered her up for the night.

Monday morning came early for all, and Max, who got to pick the music, thought firing up Three 6 Mafia was the perfect accompaniment to the tricked-out Escalade. Max could not wait for his buddies to see his new pimpmobile. Annie was in the backseat. After dropping Max off at school, they met Ben's sister, Kimberly, who would take her to her to her house to homeschool her.

Ben walked into the office and had twenty minutes of calm, focused time before Earnest Saulsberry rolled in to ask when he could meet with the police. Ben spent twenty minutes telling him the same thing he already told him on Friday and assured Earnest that the police would be contacting him soon. The attorney general sent two prosecutors over to Ben's office for the entire afternoon, so Peggy and Ben had hurriedly gathered documents and a spreadsheet together for the prosecutors. Judging by their demeanor, the police investigators wanted to make certain Ben was not in on the plot before affording him any trust. Ben quickly dispensed any doubt by showing his bank account history for the past year.

After more than four hours with the police investigators, Ben left and picked up Max from basketball practice. When they arrived at Kim's house, Ben and Max were welcomed to the smell of steaks on the grill and Annie bathed, clean, and happy. Ben could not have made it without his sister's help and was so thankful that she treated his kids as if they were her own.

***

Tuesday morning, Kip Lane called from Marston's firm.

"What's up, Kip?" Ben mustered his friendliest voice. "How can I help you? Do you have a new document that shows Dr. Kirkwood was in Cancun when Sydney was almost killed?"

"And the top of the day to you, too, Ben. I am calling to tell you that the hospital has provided a witness to testify regarding the error in the protocol."

"You don't say."

"Yup, all a big misunderstanding. She is available on Thursday afternoon, but we must go to her house. It appears as though she is on medical leave."

"What? Did one of your guys have to kneecap her?"

"You are quite the funny guy, Ben. She lives in Holly Springs, Mississippi. I will email you the address. She is outside of subpoena, so this testimony will be used at trial."

"How convenient," Ben said, knowing Marston had likely "jimmied up" a witness who would unequivocally disavow the validity of the protocol, causing Judge Jones to exclude it from evidence. "You know, Kip, there are other ways of practicing law. I have heard you are a good guy. It does not have to be this way."

There was a brief pause. "I don't know what you are talking about, Ben."

"Partner, you keep telling yourself that. Understand, at some point, the music will stop, and you will be the one without the chair. I hope you have told Steve what he is in for. You are buying the ticket, better get ready for the ride."

With still a week and a half before trial, the remainder of Tuesday and all of Wednesday were blurs of phone calls interrupted by other phone calls, flurries of emails, additional calls with the prosecutors, and an hour on the phone with Sam Browne from the Board of Professional Responsibility, confirming the details of Ben's complaint and the various claims. Ben met with four additional clients of Marco's that Peggy had just discovered. They had no clue that Alexopoulos had robbed them blind, so Ben got the happy task of breaking the news that the money they had been counting on to cover medical bills, recovery, and unemployment had been stolen and was likely never coming back. Ben felt it akin to telling people they had been diagnosed with cancer. Lastly, Ben sent a certified letter to Alexopoulos telling him that he was formally fired from the firm and was never allowed back in the building. The letter was the first step for Ben in starting his new, Marco-free professional life, and it felt good. There was no telling how long it would take to clean up this mess, but step one would be to rid the office of any trace of the scourge of Marco Alexopoulos.

Ben grabbed tacos from Maciel's, and he and Peggy had their first quiet moment since the turmoil had begun.

"Peggy, I am so sorry I brought that clown into our office. It is all my fault, and I should have known better."

"Now, now, Benji." Peggy grabbed a packet of taco sauce. "Don't beat yourself up too bad. I thought he was a little strange but had no idea he was a sociopath. Looking back, all of his weird behaviors that we thought of as quirky were actually a lot more sinister."

Ben took a bite of his taco. "I should have seen it, and I didn't. If we hit this Landers case, I promise you will get a fat bonus for all of the stress."

Ben called Marco's brother, Nicholas, and told him Marco's office furniture would be placed on the curb if Nicholas did not send movers to get it by the end of the week. And now, he had a new witness with a new story to prepare for.

***

At the Thornton firm, Kip and Steve were trying to get their stories straight for the witness.

"So who even is she?" Steve asked.

Kip explained. "Three years ago, Marston bailed Joel Anderson, the hospital administrator, out of a, shall we say, quite embarrassing jam. Last week, Marston had me call in the chip. Joel found us an employee. Bethany McCandless worked in the administrative office and apparently was about to get canned for falsifying her time records. Joel cut a deal with McCandless. She helps us with this little matter in exchange for her issues at the hospital being forgotten."

"That sounds awfully convenient." Steve looked worried.

"Never underestimate the power and corruption of the hospitals. I have seen entire charts disappear and trouble-some records wiped clean. This is just a Tuesday morning for them. Shit, I bet they have a risk manager with a broom and mop whose only job it is to clean up messes just like these. The modern computer and printer are an amazing thing," Kip said, referring to the ability to change and alter trouble-some records.

"What is she going to say?"

"Her testimony is going to be that when the records were produced, she inadvertently placed the wrong protocol in the document drop. She will say that the one that was provided was merely a proposed protocol that had not yet been signed off on by the appropriate members of the medical community and, thus, not legally in force. She is terribly sorry for the confusion, but the protocol legally in place at the time of the incident did not have the section regarding responsibility for reading x-rays in the neonatal unit." Kip shrugged.

"It's just that easy, isn't it?" Steve asked.

"Buddy, nothing is easy. You just remember, you are in the big leagues with big stakes. Nobody is messing around with this case. You better make sure your mind is right. Partnership track is there for you."

"So, you keep telling me." Steve frowned, stood up, straightened his tie, pulled at his shirt, and walked out of Kip's office.

***

Thursday afternoon, Ben drove about an hour south of Memphis down Highway 78 to Holly Springs, Mississippi. Bethany McCandless lived in a small house out in the country with an old Ford in the dirt driveway. The living room was cramped and decked out with souvenir carved wooden figures from the swap meets held in Ripley. Bethany, who appeared to be in her early forties, was in a La-Z-Boy recliner with her casted leg propped up next to a wooden box labeled "Mators and Tators." She was short and dumpy and appeared to have donned her best yellow satin track suit for the occasion. When Ben arrived, he knocked on the door, and Steve answered, offering him a handshake. Kip was across the room with the court reporter and videographer.

Ben feigned good cheer. "Well, hello, folks. Looks like you have this show ready to go."

Kip walked over and shook Ben's hand. "Ben, this is Bethany McCandless. Ms. McCandless, this is Ben Jennings."

Ben waved across the room. "Nice to meet you, Ms. McCandless."

The walls were covered with family pictures and framed needlepoints of various versions of Ole Miss fandom. There was a framed needlepoint picture of Colonel Reb and photographs of Archie and Eli Manning at a game. Over the mantle, a snapshot of what appeared to be Ms. McCandless and the Ole Miss cheerleaders hung in the place of honor. A large, stuffed Colonel Reb sat in a corner with Landshark pillows on her red-and-blue plaid sofa covered in clear plastic.

Ben knew a fix when he met one. This was going to be tough. This witness would fall on her sword, and there would be no one to contradict her. It was too late to discover and investigate any contradictory proof. The judge would likely grant a continuance if Ben wanted time to look for other witnesses to refute Marston's claims, but Ben and Marston both knew that it would take another year to get back on the docket. By then, the hospital would have plenty of time to message the story. And Alicia and her daughter would have been on food stamps for another year, falling further into poverty. When you are fighting Goliath, you better make your shots count, and so, Ben made his count by choosing to not go for a continuance and finding another way to win the case.

Ben questioned Bethany as best he could. He had no information with which to impeach her testimony. She testified that the document production was all a big error. She testified that Marston's office requested the proper material and she inadvertently sent a protocol that had not been approved or implemented. She offered a lengthy narrative as to how protocols are proposed and passed through the hospital administration. She said that many people propose protocols, but few are implemented. She said that it was she who erroneously grabbed the wrong protocol in response to the discovery request, and she was so sorry for any misunderstanding or inconvenience it may have caused. When Ben pressed her about her recent leg injury, she offered that she had clumsily fallen on her steps and had been out of work the past few weeks recuperating.

The people assembled in that tiny room knew that every word spoken was a lie. Her injury was likely a guise to keep the fraud off of hospital grounds so they could deny complicity if the truth ever came out. No way on God's green earth did a protocol get misplaced. Hospitals protect protocols like nuclear codes. With only two weeks before trial, Marston had won a key round. It would take a miracle for Ben to win the case now.

CHAPTER 14

This would be the last weekend Ben would have with his kids before the trial. Lisa always handled them while he was in court. It could be a month before he had any quality time with them again. He needed their oxygen more than they needed his. In the South, Labor Day, if not the heat, marked the end of the summer. September temperatures would continue to spike in the nineties, but the humidity decreased ever so slightly, and the sun spent less and less time lording over its subjects.

Saturdays were for college football, but Friday nights were for the high school games. The biggest high school game on the Memphis calendar is CBHS v. MUS. Christian Brothers is the largest all-boys school in the state, consisting of students from all over the city whose parents are from all walks of life. There are doctors' and lawyers' kids there but also plumbers' and electricians' sons as well. CBHS admitted and gave financial aid to African American kids as part of its educational mission long before the other private schools did the same thing in order to improve athletic prowess. While it is a Catholic school, the boys are not required to be a member of that faith. The school prides itself on its sense of brotherhood and maintains a rich sporting history, with its students and alumni referring to each other simply as "Brothers' Boys."

Memphis University School, only a couple of miles away, exists as a completely different animal. MUS, as it is known, is academically one of the highest-ranked schools in Tennessee, producing National Merit Scholars and Ivy League admissions. The all-boys school caters to Memphis's elite and vanguard. It makes no bones about its standing and wealth, having assembled a modern campus that is the envy of many universities. While the CBHS kids drove old trucks and secondhand Chevy sedans, the MUS kids drove new BMWs, Porsches, and Jeeps. The two schools have been playing each other in football since 1894. To locals, the rivalry is known as "The Game."

The Game has far more significance than a sporting contest. At The Game, private school kids from all over the city gather for the largest adolescent outdoor social event of the year. Teenagers from twelve to eighteen cluster around the stadium in knots based on age and social standing. The boys run, jostle each other, and toss footballs, carrying on their own pick-up games here and there outside the stadium. For the girls, The Game was the place to see and be seen, where the social order for years to come would be determined. The competition among the girls was stronger than that on the football field. Tonight's game was played in MUS's gleaming, large stadium equipped with all the modern amenities, including a large video scoreboard, turf field, college lighting, a large press box, and plentiful concessions. MUS telecasted the game on its website, employing production values higher than those of the local television networks.

Annie had not been in formal school or to "The Game" in the past two years. She had not been in psychological shape to handle the social pressures and expectations attached to attendance. In her early teens, she loved to go and enjoyed acceptance among the other girls. But those same girls could be tough and cruel in their rejection of unwanted members of the pack. Annie talked all summer about going to The Game and getting reacquainted with friends she had not seen in so long. She thought that by going to The Game and socializing with her friends, she might prove herself ready to go back to school and pick up right where she had left off. Ben knew this to be folly and attempted to downplay and even avoid the subject of attending The Game. However, Annie would not be deterred and insisted she would go this Friday night and re-enter the world she had left.

Ben reluctantly gave in and agreed to take Annie and Max to The Game. Kickoff was at seven, so Ben knew he needed to get to Lisa's house early to pick them up. He had no idea what to expect with Annie, but he had a terrible feeling. At five-thirty, he called Lisa.

"Hey, Lisa, I planned on picking the kids up at six-fifteen for the game. How is Annie?"

"Well," Lisa paused. "Hard to say. She has been getting ready all day for this. She took a shower but had a set of car keys in her hand. She shaved one leg but not the other. She has put on and taken off makeup three times, and her room is littered with various outfits."

Ben took a deep breath. "Okay," he said. "Is there any way to talk her out of this thing?"

"No way, Ben. She is determined. This game has so much symbolic meaning to her. Annie thinks going will mean she is cured from whatever she has."

"Alright, then." Not knowing what else to do, Ben gave up. "Tell Annie and Max I will see them at six-fifteen."

Ben drove over to the house with dread in his heart and a pit in his stomach. He arrived at the appointed time and found Max sitting on the steps with a football in hand. He raced to the Escalade as soon as it pulled up.

"Hey, bud," Ben said as Max opened the door.

"Hey, Pop!" Max quickly buckled his seat belt and sat up straight. He wore gym shorts and a tee-shirt. "Who do you think will win tonight?"

"Son, I really don't have a clue. Did you ask Coach Cannon at school what he thought?"

"He says the Brothers are really good this year and have a good chance."

"Good for them," Ben said. "Hey, how is your sister doing in there?"

"Oh, Dad, you have no idea. She has been up and down all afternoon. I have been sitting out here for an hour just to avoid it."

Five minutes turned to ten and then to twenty. Ben and Max finally got out of the car and threw the football. Finally, at six-fifty, Annie walked out of the front door with Lisa behind her. Girls at these games dress nicely, but Annie had gone over the top in a tight, short skirt, a silk blouse, and high-heeled shoes. But it was her makeup that made the biggest impression. Annie's foundation was so thick it looked applied with a putty knife. Her eyeliner looked like it was drawn on with a black Sharpie. What could he say?

"Oh, Annie, you look absolutely beautiful tonight."

"Thanks, Padre, I am so excited."

The three climbed into the Escalade and headed across town to MUS. They walked to the front gate, and as soon as they were allowed in, Max took off to where he knew his buddies were hanging. Annie walked awkwardly on the high heels and stayed close to Ben's side. She did not speak, and her eyes looked unfocused. Ben tried to ease her into the experience.

"Hey, Annie. Why don't you come sit with me in the crowd a little while and keep me company?"

But Annie, determined to slay her demons, would not be dissuaded. "No, thanks. I am going to look for the girls." As Annie walked off, Ben reached to grab her arm to pull her back but stopped himself.

Ben followed Annie at a distance, ready to swoop in if it became unbearable for her but not so close that she would know he was near. He found a concrete pillar and lurked behind it, watching his fragile daughter bravely attempt to re-enter her social community.

It began so positively. Girls shrieked, jumped up, and hugged Annie, unseen in two years. Annie's face lit up like a candle at the reactions she received. They chattered and giggled for a minute or two. Then, one by one, the group of twelve girls gradually positioned themselves away from Annie, quietly, slowly, yet unmistakably separating her from the group. Soon, Annie was on the outside looking in, unfamiliar with the current gossip and inside jokes she'd missed during her exile.

Ben watched Annie's demeanor span from euphoria to grief over the course of ten agonizing minutes as she continued attempting to connect, only to be rebuked more and more overtly. Annie started obsessively twisting her hair with her fingers. She kept attempting to start conversations, only to be ignored. Then, her posture began to crumble slowly, and he saw her biting her lip to keep herself from crying. Some girls cut their eyes at Annie, while others raised their eyebrows and conspiratorially nodded their heads in her direction. But Annie would not move. She stood there and took the rebuke.

It tore into Ben's insides as though he had eaten glass. He did not fault the other girls. Their survival instincts aroused their own anxieties, causing them to worry they would catch whatever Annie had, as if it were a transmittable disease. While some of them were just mean, others were too young to be socially adept enough to work to include her, without a clear frame of reference from school. Annie made one last attempt to enter the conversation, and the rejection was more pronounced. The girls overtly turned away from Annie every time she attempted to address them. Ben could tell she was at the breaking point. He stepped out from behind the pillar. He quietly walked behind Annie and whispered into her ear.

"Hey, baby. I am really not feeling good. Do you mind if we go home early? I could really use your company tonight."

She was braver than he had ever been. She ate her pain without expression, but the excitement and hope had faded from her eyes, and he saw her despair growing. Ben fought his urge to just sit on the ground right there and sob.

"Sure, Dad."

Ben pulled out his cellphone and called his friend Bruce, whose son, Reese, was a good friend of Max's, and asked if he could give Max a ride home after the game.

Annie and Ben walked slowly to the car without a word, their arms around the other, each attempting to comfort the other's silent agony. At home, they changed into shorts and tee-shirts, sat on the sofa, and watched Annie's favorite movie, *The Notebook*. After thirty minutes, she fell asleep on his shoulder, leaving Ben alone with his thoughts. Ben wished he could find a way to take a vacation from himself.

***

The Gregorian Calendar is the international standard for the representation of dates and times. Americans mark the passage of time through this device but also through significant events such as Christmas, New Year's, Thanksgiving, and the Fourth of July. In the state of Mississippi, many mark time with six events that happen every fall near the small town of Oxford. Every year, the University of Mississippi, or Ole Miss as it is known, plays six home football games at Vaught-Hemmingway Stadium, located on its beautiful campus. In the South, college football is a religion. Nothing compares to the pageantry of southern college football or the excitement it engenders.

On Saturday, Ben's good friend Stevie LeBlanc invited him and the kids down to Oxford to attend the game between Ole Miss and Memphis. The game, marking the renewal of the old rivalry between Ole Miss and University of Memphis, observes a solemn rite of fall in the Mid-South.

Ole Miss has the dominant program and maintains a large advantage in the overall record of wins and losses. The pride of Mississippi, Ole Miss, is sometimes called the Harvard of the South, if only by its own alumni. Its huge athletic budget receives a giant payout every year from the Southeastern Conference for the enormous television revenue it generates. Ole Miss fans ridicule the University of Memphis, calling it "Tiger High" in derisive comparison to a high school and not a university. The University of Memphis teams had vastly improved in recent years, and the series between the two schools had now become actually competitive. Little brother Memphis carried a chip on its shoulder from all the years of insult and brought fight to the game.

The city of Memphis claimed graduates of all southern schools. On a fall day, drive through any neighborhood, and one will see the flags of Ole Miss, Mississippi State, Arkansas, Alabama, Auburn, Tennessee, and Memphis with a smattering of LSU and Vanderbilt flying from the porches of proud alumni. For three seasons of the year, these neighbors live in relative tranquility, attending events at the schools their children shared. But in the fall, the mood changes, and polite civil wars are waged over college football.

Ben and the kids got up early and headed over to Brother Junipers on the University of Memphis campus to load up on pancakes, eggs, biscuits, and gravy. Ben wore chinos, a blue oxford cloth shirt, brown belt, and camel colored Gucci loafers with no socks. Max and Annie wore khaki shorts with royal-blue polos and tennis shoes. Annie had her hair pulled back in a ponytail and had scrubbed off all the makeup from the night before. After breakfast, they jumped in the Escalade and headed south on I-55 toward Oxford, Mississippi to celebrate at one the most beautiful plots of land ever created.

The Grove, as it is known, is a ten-acre plot of freshly mown grass, situated in the center of the Ole Miss campus, blanketed with ancient oak trees whose high canopy provides shade and a picturesque outdoor cathedral for thousands of football fans to gather and celebrate. On game days, large party tents are placed in locations on a first-come basis, staked out the night before by well-paid students and private contractors.

Each tent is owned by a family or group who join in creating a unique atmosphere for ten to fifty guests. Some tents are elaborately decorated: tables covered with fine cloths, fresh floral center pieces around ornate silver candelabras, a fully stocked bar at one end, a big-screen TV broadcasting the football games of the day. Private caterers prepare feasts of fresh smoked game, roast beef, and gumbo served on china with silverware.

Other tents are humbler with butcher paper-covered tables topped with fresh crawfish boils, all the trimmings, an ice-cold keg of beer, and whiskey served in ubiquitous red Solo cups. In most tents, a kettle grill sits at one side with burgers, brats, and ribs, creating a magical aroma that wafts into the air, permeating the entire grove and hanging under the oak canopy like a ghostly fog. Families prepare traditional sides of potato and egg salad, Pimento cheese, fresh vegetables, grilled bacon-wrapped jalapenos, and the ever-present Rotel-and-guacamole dip. Everyone has a cold beer or cocktail in their left hand, freeing up the right to shake hands with old friends and new acquaintances.

Attendees take pride in their dress. Men wear dress slacks or chinos with dress shirts and well-polished loafers, usually with no socks. Mississippi women seem to defy age, looking twenty years younger than their birth certificates. Many say the torrid humidity prevents wrinkles. Others say plastic surgeons are pretty good, also. Women wear floral or white sundresses or white jeans with colorful blouses, some of them low-cut to show off enhancements. Some of the male students wear jeans and cowboy boots with white oxford button downs, while most Ole Miss men dress formally in dark dress slacks, white shirts, and red-and-blue striped ties. Young co-eds come attired as if they are attending a cocktail party, wearing short, slinky black dresses revealing more than their fathers would like. It is widely agreed, even among rivals, that on a college football Saturday, there are more beautiful women in those ten acres than in the entirety of most states. The children are dressed right out of a Vineyard Vines commercial, in colorful chino shorts, polo shirts, and custom belts with the hand stitched Ole Miss logo.

Together, it is a collective party made up of hundreds of smaller ones. People flow from tent to tent, catching up with friends, neighbors, and former classmates. The children run around with their friends and head to the outer perimeter to find a free space to run and throw a football. There are no more-hospitable people in the world than those from Ole Miss. They are warm, funny, and generous, despite their poor choice in schools. They welcome fans of rival schools, apart from LSU, and share their wonderful food, drink, stories, and good humor. A football Saturday in Oxford, Mississippi is a celebration of life at its finest.

At some point during the festivities, the Ole Miss band, playing rousing music, marches through the center of the sea of humanity; they're followed by the cheerleaders leading the Ole Miss football players, who make the "walk of champions" through the Grove on their way to the stadium for the day's game. Many a partygoer never actually makes it to the game, either too drunk or satisfied to leave their wonderful tents.

Stevie LeBlanc, a colleague and Ole Miss grad and zealot, had invited Ben and the kids to join game festivities each of the last three years. Stevie was a crucial part of the Ole Miss football program. He was its acting attorney, making many of the criminal charges filed against its players disappear. When any new coach is hired, Stevie is one of the first people added to their contacts list, knowing the importance of springing star football players, who often find their way to jail for an assortment of misdeeds.

Ben and the kids drove to Stevie's condo near the campus, and Stevie sent his private driver to pick them up and lead them directly to his tent. Annie, who appeared to have recovered from the night before, was happy to be on a road trip with her father and brother. Stevie rushed to them when they entered the tent.

"Yo, Maximus, my man! What is shaking, dog?"

Max grinned and ran up to the man he called Uncle Stevie and gave him a hug.

Stevie turned to Annie, "And who is this beauty? What's up, girl? Where have you been? I haven't seen you in forever." Annie ran up to Max and Stevie to join the hug.

Ben sidled up and gave Stevie a warm handshake. "Uncle Stevie, you Johnnies sure know how to put on a party." "Johnnies" was in reference to the nickname "Johnnie Rebels."

"If only we could make touchdowns as well as we do throwdowns! Come on in here and get some food. Max, you skinny little bastard, has your dad not been feeding you?" Stevie rubbed Max on the head.

For first timers, the Grove experience can be daunting with so much sensory overload, but Max and Annie soon relaxed and helped themselves to a wonderful buffet. Stevie, now standing alone next to Ben, adopted a more serious tone.

"How is Annie?"

Ben sighed. "Stevie, it's one day at a time. Yesterday wasn't so good, but today, we are having a ball. I cannot tell you how much I appreciate you having us down here. The kids are so excited. And truth is, I am too. This place is so special. Every time I come; I hate you guys less." Ben winked at Stevie, referring to the schools' rivalry.

After stuffing themselves with fried chicken and cheese dip, Stevie took Ben and the kids down to the Ole Miss sidelines to watch warm-ups. Stevie forced Ole Miss visors onto them just to upset their dad. Ben shook his head and laughed. "Uncle Stevie, you are always selling."

"You are damn right! I see Max as a starting point guard here in a few years."

Ben chuckled again. "Let's get him through high school first."

After warm-ups, the four took their seats on the forty-yard line and enjoyed one of the great spectacles of the south. Unfortunately, the scrappy but overmatched Tigers lost to the tenth-ranked Rebels twenty-four to three. The kids were disappointed, and Ben had to gently explain to them in the Escalade on the way home that there was a lifetime of pain awaiting any Tiger fan.

"Kids, you cannot appreciate the mountaintop if you haven't been in the lowest of valleys. When we do win, it is the sweetest taste in the world. Alabama fans have no idea."

Back home, the three cuddled up on the sofa and watched *Skyfall* until they fell asleep. When Ben felt the lowest, he called upon these moments to keep going.

CHAPTER 15

Monday morning. It was one week before trial, and Ben fell into depression mode. After the protocol disaster on Thursday that torpedoed his case, he had a week to find an alternative angle of attack. He called his expert witness, Dr. Bell, to confirm the details of trial attendance.

Dr. Bell, a prince of a man, had his limits.

"Ben, no offense, but you are going have to send me my money before I load up and head to Memphis. You owe me $10,000 from the deposition and another $20,000 for my trial testimony. I cannot afford to float you any more than that."

Ben sighed and looked to the ceiling as if an answer hung in the rafters. "Doc, I completely understand and will have the money wired to you by Friday." Ben tried to convince himself it was true.

Marco had cleaned out their firm's expense account, leaving Ben without money to fund the case. Ben was flat broke. He had already tapped his savings and reserves. He had not settled a case in months, and his cash flow dwindled to next to nothing. Now, his car blew up, office rent and the mortgage on his house was due, and of course, Peggy had to be paid. Ben had only one option.

He picked up Freddie, and they headed for lunch at the BBQ shop on Madison Avenue, founded by one of the all-time great pit masters, Frank Vernon, and now run by his son, Eric. Freddie and Ben shared a combo plate of smoked sausage and BBQ bologna. Ben ordered the chopped pork sandwich on Texas toast and a side of Eric's famous BBQ spaghetti. Freddie locked in on some of Frank's world-famous glazed ribs, potato salad, and baked beans.

"Freddie, I need $30,000 to get my expert to town, and I am all tapped out. I have never asked you for money, but I am desperate."

"Benji Bear, why didn't you say so earlier? You are my guy. I always have your back. I know you want to forget me with all of those suck up blue bloods you run around with. But you and I both know at the end of the day where you come from. And it ain't the blues," Freddie said, referring to the blue bloods. "Look," he continued, "not a problem. We can hit my safe on the way back, or just send me the wiring instructions, and I will get your guy the money. I am happy to help. And when I get my hands on Marco Alexopoulos, that boy is going to wish he never laid his hands on your money."

Ben could not believe how easy that was. "Wow, Freddie, you are a lifesaver. I cannot tell you how much I appreciate this. I owe you big time."

"Well, now that you mention it . . ." Freddie had a gleam in his eye.

"What?"

"I have been trying to get you out to play those big-shot stockbrokers at Southwind in a little four-ball match for a few dollars. They want to play Thursday, but I told them I would have to ask you." Freddie licked BBQ sauce off his fingers.

"Freddie, I don't have the money to pay my rent or experts. How can I play in a money game?"

"Benji Bear, that there is the beauty of this whole thing. I will front the money for the match, and if we win, your tab is clear, and there is no need to pay me back. If we lose, well, I am going to need that 30k back."

What choice did Ben have? "How much are we playing for?"

"Not your concern, big man. Your only concern is fairways and greens." Freddie reached over with his fork and helped himself to some of Ben's spaghetti.

"I guess I'm in, then," Ben said, knowing he was out of options.

"Well, great, its settled. Southwind at one on Thursday. Get there early and loosen up. Make sure you sleep with Scottie Cameron Wednesday night. And how about sending some of that spaghetti across to papa?"

***

Friday, Ben and Stephanie would be preparing Alicia for her testimony, and Ben planned to spend the weekend perfecting his question outlines for Dr. Kirkwood and Marston's experts. Ben still needed to finalize his opening statement, likely the most important part of the trial. The clock was crushing him, and his head was splitting from the pressure. He had so much to get done and now had to spend half a day playing competitive golf for Lord-knows-how-much money.

Ben was a successful college golfer, but his career stopped there. In Ben's senior year, his father suffered a fatal heart attack. Ben put aside his golf dreams to take care of his mother and her chronic arthritis and high blood pressure. Planning on a career on the circuit, he had majored in history, a subject unlikely to provide employment. Most history majors head to law school, so Ben took the plunge even though he barely knew a lawyer and had no real idea what they did. When he began law school, Ben moved home to help his mom, taking care of household chores and chipping in financially when he could. Fortunately, Ben's law school entrance exam scores afforded him a scholarship at the University of Memphis Law School.

Ben poured himself into law school but was hampered by his substandard Memphis public school education. As a product of bussing, he had attended schools with kids who could barely read. Recognizing his gifts, schools placed him in programs where they emphasized creativity over basic reading and writing skills. In college, he played catch-up trying to teach himself the rudiments of language and grammar that were taken for granted by his more affluent classmates. His dyslexia exposed a real weakness; Ben took twice as long to digest written materials. If they had only had audiobooks in the 90s, life would have been so much simpler.

Law school presented more of a challenge and was where he first encountered the subtle political moves of the monied class. During his formative years, everything was fists and frontal assault. Now, he found himself thrust in a world where nuance and well-placed cuts from a sharp tongue were the coin of the realm. For the first time, the person insulting Ben had a smile on his face. It had taken hours of refection to realize the chap in his class that he spoke to had insulted him. Before law school, no one had ever asked him what his father did for a living. Ben's real wake-up call came when he tried flirting with the girl who sat beside him in "Constitutional Law." He asked her what she did the previous weekend, and when she responded that she had been at the family cottage in Martha's Vineyard, Ben realized just how poor he had been. Ben competed in sports all his life but never academically. He found himself ill-prepared for the questions regarding grades and "Law Review," which he had not known existed. Ben had only known one lawyer his entire life, and he was a probate lawyer who went to their church. He felt as though his classmates were speaking a foreign language when discussing summer clerkships in Dallas, Atlanta, and Nashville. *How in the world did one go about doing that?* he thought to himself. Most of the other students were well-connected with parents who were lawyers, doctors, and business owners. Ben just knew the starters at the municipal golf courses.

He paid his way through law school by clerking at the notorious Henry "Fats" Feldstein's office. He made extra money playing money games with Freddie at Windyke Country Club, where Freddie had ingratiated himself with the club pro by giving him a cut of their winnings, who, in turn, set them up with monied opponents. Ben's golfing prowess also proved to be a professional asset, allowing him to network with clients and lawyers and hang with judges who loved a scratch player on their scramble team at the Bar Association golf tournament.

Part of the hustle with Freddie necessitated Ben's intentionally understated golf dress and kit. He infamously showed up late to money matches to give opponents a false sense of confidence, appearing in shorts and sandals with his old green-and-yellow Ping golf bag held together by grey duct tape. Still, any golfer with a modicum of experience could look in Ben's bag, see his ancient Australian tour blades with nickel-sized blemishes in the sweet spots, and know this was not an average weekend hacker. Ben wielded a golf club like Van Gogh handled a paint brush: equal parts magic and artistry. It wasn't only the look of his swing but the satisfying click of efficient energy transfer it made upon contact—and not the cluttered noise from the glancing blow of a less proficient player. Avid golfers can close their eyes and know the quality of a player by the sound their club makes at impact. One can fake the clothes, clubs, bag, and shoes, but cannot replicate that transcendent sound that only comes when players have mastered their craft. However, Ben's swing of beauty acted as a blessing and a curse. Many players get caught up in the visual aesthetics of their swing to the detriment of lower scores. Chasing a beautiful swing sometimes leads to a case of style over substance. If Ben's timing were off, the beautiful fluidity of his move could be difficult to tame.

There are two types of golfers: mechanical and feel. The mechanical guys focus on repetition, multiple swing thoughts, club position and grip, and often become successful, consistent players. But mechanical players do not create art.

The feel player paints a picture with every shot. A short-left pin over a bunker requires a high-soft draw where the ball travels right to left around the bunker, its trajectory causing the ball to land softly and run out gently to the hole. A back right pin may necessitate a low fade, with the ball traveling left to right, to impart more roll to allow the ball a better chance of getting near the hole. Ben was a feel player. He obsessed over sound, ball flight, and trajectory, fanatically chasing the perfectly executed shot. He could post incredibly low rounds with ease and fluidity that took his opponents' breath away. He also had a tendency to obsess over shots that were effective but not struck as precisely as he had intended. The adage that the hardest part of the game lies in the six-inch space between your ears applied to Ben. He had enough game for the PGA Tour but lacked the emotional stability to accept the inherent imperfections of the game and swings of good and bad days. Ben never liked the good shots as much as he hated the bad ones. He could shoot the easiest sixty-four you have ever seen and, the next day, hit three drives out of bounds in a row, reaching for the proper shot impervious to the score, obsessing instead on trajectory and ball flight. His moral code demanded chasing the dragon of a proper shot and rejecting any compromise for the sake of score. To that end, nobody had the authority or license to offer praise. Mediocrity was maddening.

Golf was not a game but an obsession that must be played correctly or not at all and had led to fits of temper, depression, and ecstasy. He had once lost a college tournament by a single stroke and threw his clubs into the lake at the eighteenth hole, only to retrieve them the next day. His obsessions created extreme highs and painful lows. He fought perfectionist tendencies and could be merciless on himself for even small infractions.

On Thursday, the match was to begin at 1:00 p.m. at the TPC Southwind, located in eastern part of Shelby County in the wealthy suburb of Germantown. Southwind was a gated subdivision with large houses lining both the course and surrounding area. The PGA makes an annual stop at Southwind, and the course challenges even the best pros. Built in the 80s on an old farm site, it had now matured beautifully with trees, Zoysia fairways, and Champion Bermuda greens. Freddie and Ben played the course many times but never had Ben played for so much money. He left downtown early to make the forty-minute drive in time to loosen up on the range. At the security gate, the guard gave him a skeptical look. The Escalade was not the type of vehicle they usually raised the security arm for to allow admittance. After a chat and call to the pro shop, Ben was allowed passage. For this game, with this much money on the line, Ben dispensed with his overly casual act and wore appropriate clothes and spikes and used his regular bag. In the past years, he had relented and upgraded his irons to TaylorMade; the latest TaylorMade driver gave him at least twenty more yards off the tee than his old one.

Their opponents were wealthy local stockbrokers who made Southwind their home course but also kept memberships at the exclusive Jack Nicklaus-designed Spring Creek Ranch. Trey Johnson and Chett Evans were both in their mid-thirties, lean and tan with full heads of hair, perfectly coiffed with generous amounts of product. Freddie had bailed Trey out of a couple of DUI charges, and they got to know each other. Trey and Chett were no virgins to money games. As stockbrokers, they gambled for a living. Both were accomplished golfers: Chett won the Club Championship twice; Trey, once. Guys like that attracted Freddie like a moth to a flame.

Ben hit balls at the end of the range as Trey and Chett used the middle. At about ten minutes to one, Freddie "Fifty Feet" Franks arrived in all his glory. He dressed like he was going straight to Beale Street after the match: pressed slacks, new golf shirt, alligator skin golf shoes and belt, and the ever-present Ray-Ban Aviators. Two adult dancers he knew through work accompanied him, dressed in short shorts and tee-shirts two sizes too small.

Ben shook his head and laughed. Freddie went up to Trey and Chett with a big smile and open arms.

"Fellas, what's the haps? How are you feeling? You both look a little heavy to me. I am thinking you boys need to lose a ton of cash today and slim those fat pockets of yours."

What can you do with Freddie? Trey and Chett had to laugh and greeted him warmly.

"Hey, Freddie," Trey said. "Just make sure you have your cash. We are about to teach you some manners today."

Freddie snorted. "Why try, my mother gave up years ago. Hey, I want you to meet our caddies, Crystal and Tiffany."

Trey and Chett got a full and approving look at the girls. Freddie made his way down to Ben, who was going through his bag hitting crisp shots that floated like angels.

"What's with the girls, Freddie?" Ben asked.

"Ah, my lovely friends here. They are our caddies. And more importantly, a big distraction to those two hard legs. How are you hitting them, boss?"

"I am hitting them fine. How much are we playing for?" Ben said.

"You leave the bets to me, big man. I have it covered. By the way, Picasso, you aren't painting a canvass today, you are painting a house. So save the artistry bullshit for the pricks at Choctaw."

Ben feigned ignorance. "What are you talking about?"

"We are playing money golf, so I need your head square and straight, you dig?"

"I got ya."

"And oh, here are two sleeves of the balls for this game. My gift to you." Freddie handed Ben Titleist balls with distinctive red dots on them.

"What's with the balls?" Ben asked.

"Don't worry, big man, those are special. I had the priest pray over them."

"Freddie, I am not pulling any shit today."

"Don't worry, pards, you won't have to. We have this in the bag," Freddie assured him.

Four-ball, a match play format with two-man teams—Ben and Freddie versus Chett and Trey—meant that the lowest score per team counted on each hole. If one guy made a four, it did not matter if his partner made ten; the four was all that mattered.

Freddie, a veteran money-match player, lost a fortune a year ago when one of his balls went out of bounds by two yards. It drove him crazy that he had not considered and planned for that contingency before the match. For this game, it just so happened that the girls and a golf course worker were carrying around a few balls matching Ben's. Freddie knew that Ben would never go for any such scheme, so Freddie had to execute his contingency plan covertly.

The golfers and girls drove their carts to the first tee, which at Southwind, offered a challenging uphill par 4 dogleg right. A dedicated drink cart and young lady followed along with one of the course workers in a separate cart.

"What's with the gallery?" Chett asked.

"Nothing worse than an unquenched thirst on a golf course. I want to make sure we have all the provisions we need to stay hydrated. Our health comes first," Freddie insisted as he lit up a cigar and palmed a beer. "Men's tees?"

On a course like Southwind, there could be five or six different tee boxes defined with different colored tee markers. But on any golf course, when someone says men's tees, they are referring to the back tees, or "tips"—the furthest point from each hole. The men's tees were plenty long at TPC Southwind, stretching out to over 7,200 yards.

What followed was a round for the ages. All four golfers brought their "A" games and played sizzling golf. The first two holes were halved with birdies, and on the par 5 third hole, Ben sank a side hill thirty-footer for eagle, giving the boys a one-up lead. Chett and Trey tied the match on the 196-yard par 3 fourth hole with a beautiful shot to eight feet to the left pin tucked just over the water, which Chett converted to a birdie.

The fifth hole plays as a 485-yard par 4 for the tournament and a 525-yard par 5 for members. In four-ball, par does not matter because the object of the game is scoring better than your opponent whether it is a three or a five. Freddie and Trey both made outstanding fours to keep the match all square. The sixth and seventh were hard par 4s, which they all parred sparing any blood on those holes. Coming back toward the clubhouse is the getable par 3 eighth hole measuring at 178 yards. The left-handed Ben hit a beautiful high draw to a front right pin tucked just over the bunker and made the only birdie in the group.

As they approached the ninth hole, they noticed several more carts had joined the gallery. Word had gotten out about the level of golf being played, and rumors percolated of enormous stakes being wagered. Ben did not like the ninth because of its right-to-left downhill swing, which always presented him with his hardest tee shot on the course. Being left-handed, it was more difficult to execute the precise high draw than the right handers who could control cuts to the bottom of the hill. Ben went straight through the fairway into the high rough while the others had 8 and 9-irons to a green protected by water. Ben made his first mistake of the day shooting for the left back pin. He caught a flier and went over the green leaving him an impossible up and down resulting in bogey. Freddie hit the center of the green, and Chett and Trey were both inside him. But Freddie being Freddie rolled in an implausible thirty-footer that left his opponents shaken. Neither made their birdie putts, and Freddie and Ben took a two-shot lead to the tenth.

By now, a full-fledged gallery with a convoy of carts followed at a respectful distance. All four men made par, and they headed to par 3 island eleventh with Ben and Freddie still two up. While only 162 yards long, the surrounding water has been the grave for many a professional's golf ball. Freddie played first and hit it over the green into the water, leaving him in his pocket. Forced to play safe, Ben hit one into the center of the green. Chett seized the advantage and hit a beautiful cut to ten feet. Ben missed, and Chett converted and cut the lead to one.

The twelfth hole is a short par 4 around a lake, offering risk/reward options for the players. Nobody took the bait and hit 3-irons and 3-woods off the tee. This time, Trey hit it tight, giving him an almost "give-me" birdie. Ben and Freddie only managed a par, taking the match to the thirteenth hole all tied up. The group all parred thirteen and headed to the difficult par 3, fourteenth hole, which stretched out to 239 yards over water. Chett hit his tee shot into the water, causing Trey to play safely left of the green. Freddie sizzled one to the middle of the green, but it rolled off the back edge. Ben carved a beautiful draw over the water and eight feet from the hole for perhaps the best shot anyone had hit all day. Trey and Freddie got up and down for par leaving the birdie putt for Ben. He hit a beautiful putt that looked perfect but dove at the edge and at the last second, causing the ball to do a 180-degree horseshoe around the hole before lipping out.

Fifteen is a short par 4 that requires two precise shots. Each player hit 3-woods into the fairway, leaving wedge approaches. All four hit the green; it would be a putting contest. Freddie and Trey sunk their putts, halving the hole with birdies. For a Thursday afternoon round of golf, the crowd of carts was huge. No spectator uttered a word, and the golfers appeared to not notice anyone watching.

Sixteen is a very getable par 5, and it would likely take a birdie just to half the hole. The three other players all hit sound drives down the right side of the fairway. Ben, trying to get extra yards, blocked his shot well left toward the trees and out-of-bounds left. Ben asked if he should hit a provisional, and Freddie quickly cut him off.

"Oh, no, pards. No way that ball is OB. We will find it easy," Freddie said for all to hear. At that point, Freddie motioned the girls and the course worker who had been quietly following all day. The girls rode their cart alongside Trey and Chett, who were suddenly wishing to get to know them better. The course worker quietly rode down the tree line well in front of the group. When Ben arrived, the worker, who had not spoken to him all day said, "Here it is. Are you playing a ProV1 with a red dot?"

Ben walked up to the ball lying perfectly with a clear shot to the green and looked closely.

"That is not my ball," he said, clearly shaking up the man. This is where Ben and Freddie's philosophies diverged. To Freddie, golf was a means to gamble and hustle. He liked it fine, he was good at it and made good money playing, but that was it. To Ben, golf was a sacred game that carried religious edicts that he would never violate. Cheating in such a fashion amounted to an unpardonable sin. He would quit the game before he would cheat. Many non-golfers do not understand the slavish devotion to the rules that some golfers practice, but those rules were a metaphor for life. You can learn everything you needed to know about a man's character in an eighteen-hole round of golf.

Ben continued to look and finally found the ball just a yard inside the out-of-bounds marker, in a tall but thinnish rough under the line of trees that protects the left side. Freddie hit his shot just short of the green, Chett went to the back of the green for an easy two putt birdie, and Trey fell just short right in a grassy bunker. Ben cut off the distance to the hole considerably by going left but left himself at least seventy-five-yards of trees to go under before reaching the fairway. He hooded a 3-iron and put it back in his stance he had opened slightly. With a mighty blast, Ben hit a stinger that never went above ten feet traversing under the trees and then, almost if on a string, made a left-hand turn and headed straight toward the green. The ball landed about fifty yards from the green and rolled to within three feet of the cup. The up-to-now quiet gallery erupted with cheers and screams dispensing any pretense of golf etiquette. The shot so shook Trey and Chett, neither could get up and down, and Ben picked up a conceded eagle. Ben and Freddie went to seventeen one hole up, but both hit into trouble off the tee. Ben hit another miraculous shot from the trees, but it landed just short and into a bunker. Freddie hit his short of the green. Neither man could get up and down for par, ceding their lead to the opponents who both two-putted for pars.

They walked to the tee box at eighteen with the match all square. The winners of this hole would take home the cash, and the losers would have their feelings hurt and pockets emptied. The crowd that began as a couple of guys in a golf cart had now swollen. Every golf cart owned by Southwind was occupied by members who heard about the match and prolific scores being shot. Carts of spectators covered the right side of the eighteenth hole stretching for a view of the match. The 18th hole at Southwind is a challenging 453-yard risk/reward hole that doglegs left around a large lake. One can take driver and cut off a huge chunk of yardage, but it is serious gamble and risks a double bogey if unsuccessful. The safe play is a 3-wood or long iron straight with a longer second shot to the green. It plays easier during tournament week as players can bail out right and have the hospitality tent used as a backstop.

Chett and Trey had the honor, and both took out 3-woods and striped them down the right side of the fairway, just inside the rough. Freddie hit next--and right off the club could tell the shot was dicey. His natural flight was a draw, and this turned into more of a hook. There is an old saying that you can talk to a fade, but a hook will not listen. As the ball crested at the dogleg, it was perilously close to the water, but maybe he would get lucky. The ball hit solid ground and, for the slightest of moments, Ben and Freddie breathed a sigh of relief. It would be a short-lived respite as the ball took a sharp bounce to the left and splashed into the water.

"Fuck!!!" Freddie yelled with the guttural scream of a Viking.

Ben was now trying to decide between driver and 3-wood. Freddie noticed the indecision and immediately piped up, "Oh, no, you don't Benji. This is not the time. Three-wood down the right side, and the worse we make is par."

"Yeah, I hear you, but driver is the proper play." Ben reasoned. Ben was a left-handed player, and so, he figured he could hit a big cut that shaped around the lake.

"Benji, I told you, not today. Hit the goddamned 3-wood. Don't fuck this up!"

Ben was torn.

"I think I can hit this driver perfectly around it."

"You son of a bitch, there is one hundred grand riding on this hole, save the art for another day, or I will throw you in this lake myself."

"Oh, shit, a hundred grand. Jesus, Freddie, are you out of your mind?"

Ben thought he was going to throw up. He had known there was big money on the line but had no idea how much. His mouth felt like cotton, and his heart raced. This was far worse pressure than tournament golf. He pulled his 3-wood, stood over the shot, and told himself to trust the process.

He took a few more seconds than usual and breathed deeply, trying to slow his fear. Ben hit a perfect 3-wood shaped nicely down the right-side landing perfectly in the center of fairway 185 yards from the front left pin.

Chett had 205 yards to the front left pin, which was known as a sucker pin because of its slope to the nearby lake. Chett took no chances and hit a 4-iron to the middle of the green, which would allow Trey to take a shot at the pin. Trey had 190 to the pin and decided to hit a 5-iron draw attacking that flag. Trey's shot was spectacular off the club, soaring toward the middle of the green and then turning gently to the left with a soft draw. But at the apex, a gust of wind seemed to hit it and push it further than desired. The ball landed just over the pin, and the draw and wind did not let it stop. The ball slowly rolled down the bank and descended into a watery grave. Trey could not move. He stood there staring in disbelief as if he waited long enough, the ball would come back. It did not.

Jacked up, Ben knew the adrenaline would add distance to the shot. He usually hit a 6-iron from 185 but would go down to a 7. He would rather hit a full shot with a 7 than try to hold back with a 6. When he struck the shot, Ben did not have to look; he knew. He had hit millions of golf balls in his life, and he could tell by impact where the shot would go. It was perfect. The ball started at the right side of the green, and then, a little butter cut pushed it to the center where it landed and took a hop toward the hole. From the fairway it looked to be four feet, but as they got to the green, it measured more like twelve.

With Freddie and Trey in their pockets, the match came down to Ben and Chett. Chett looked at a makeable twenty-foot side hill putt. However, he could not be too aggressive because a three putt would allow Ben, who had an easy two putt from twelve feet, to win. With hundreds of golfers now watching, Chett measured his putt from all sides and then stepped up and stroked it. The ball tracked the hole the entire way and looked to be dead center, but the break toward the water at the last second caused it to hit the right lip and spin out. The crowd went crazy. The one-foot tap in was conceded by Ben, who now had the stage.

Ben took a deep breath. He thought of the money, the trial, and his golf career that had never happened. For once, Freddie was dead silent, leaving his man to contemplate those demons present in all men. Everyone who has ever played the game has scar tissue from missed putts under pressure. Before he hit the putt, Ben straightened up and smiled to himself the smile of the damned. Only men who have seen the fires of hell understand that look. What could anyone do to him that had not already been done. He had his ass kicked by the best and lived to tell the tale. Ben gripped Scottie Cameron like a fragile bird, stood over the putt, and applied that Da Vinci brush stroke of his. He had rolled millions of these putts, and this one was no different. The ball did not know how much was at stake. The Titleist tumbled effortlessly off the blade, creating a precise roll, making the writing look like one continuous line as it rotated perfectly. There was never a doubt. Ben turned and walked away from the putt knowing he had done everything in his power to make it, and now, it was up to the golf gods. The ball dove over the edge center cut into the darkness like there was no other place it could go.

Pandemonium erupted around the hole. Grown men and women screamed and laughed at the guy who had just turned away from a huge money putt without bothering to watch the result. Freddie jumped into the air and screamed as loud as Ben ever heard. Freddie ran over to his life-long buddy and jumped into his arms, followed by Tiffany and Crystal, who made it one big group hug on the eighteenth hole at Southwind.

With that birdie, Ben carded a sixty-four. Freddie shot sixty-eight and Chett and Trey both sixty-sevens. It was perhaps the best money game ever played in a city that had seen its share. Trey and Chett were gracious in defeat. Chett shook Ben's hand and clapped Freddie on the back. "It was worth a hundred grand to be part of that round of golf."

Freddie left them befuddled with his standard, "Fifty feet from the street, boys."

Freddie and Ben headed to the parking lot with the loot and smiles from ear to ear. As Ben put his clubs into the Escalade, he looked up to see Freddie quietly making the rounds to the course worker and the girls, scratching off several bills for each and placing them in their hands.

"Freddie, I wish you had not pulled that with the girls and guy in the cart. You know I don't roll like that."

"That is why I didn't tell you, Benji Bear. Look, we see this whole thing differently. This is a hustle to me and not a religious experience. I lost a ton of dough with other guys pulling the same thing on me, and I was determined to never be a mark again. And by God, I haven't been!" Freddie exclaimed.

Freddie handed Ben $20,000.

"What's this for?" Ben asked.

"Forget about the $30,000 I loaned you and use this to take care of Annie and Max and those clients of yours. You are my brother. I am so proud of you. You do it the right way. I do not understand it, but we each have our demons to answer to."

"Losing $200,000 would have left a mark, even on you."

"Hundred grand, hell. I didn't have any two hundred grand." Freddie had an ear-to-ear grin.

"Wait!! What? What do you mean, you didn't have the two hundred grand?" Ben asked.

"I had fifty and the titles to the cars. It would have been dicey had we lost. At the very least, it would have been an Uber ride," Freddie said.

"You son of a bitch! Are you serious! Why didn't you tell me?"

"Never a doubt. I had all the confidence in the world. You had enough pressure. I figured you didn't need any more," Freddie said.

"Jesus, Mary, and Joseph," Ben mumbled as he got in the Escalade. Then, Freddie motioned him to roll down the window.

"What?" Ben asked.

"Fifty feet, my man. Don't ever forget, fifty feet."

CHAPTER 16

No one at the Thornton Firm played golf. The trial team worked around the clock, checking and rechecking every detail. The tech team engaged with Kip, Steve, and the paralegals to ensure their presentation would be seamless. Marston's opening statement would be a synchronized symphony of oration mixed precisely with medical records, visual aids, and PowerPoint slides in a presentation worthy of a Madison Avenue ad campaign. Marston's demands for perfection as they prepared made everyone's life a living hell. Kip and Steve again questioned their decisions to go to law school. Being a soldier in the Thornton Law Firm was not all it was cracked up to be.

Marston drove himself harder than any of the troops. Never in his career had he faced such competing emotions. Every trial was life or death, but this one meant much more. In his mind, a loss would not just end his career but his life because he could not bear to face the world if defeated by Ben Jennings. The jury would answer the referendum on the worthiness of Marston Owens' life.

As much as his staff hated Marston, his personal suffering and torture seemed worse than theirs and they had some sympathy for the man. He called six meetings a day; one of them had been about the color of pens to be used for notes taken during trial. The work had been done, but no one could relax, leave, eat, or breathe, else they be chastised for not caring enough. The mood was tense and the nerves, brittle.

Meanwhile, on Friday morning, Ben went to the bank, deposited the cash, and immediately wired Dr. Bell his fee. Peggy was still dealing with the fallout from the Alexopoulos fiasco, with clients calling and coming by unannounced. His fellow lawyers had all heard the news about Marco and bombarded Ben with text and calls to get every juicy bit. Ben needed to prepare for trial but also wanted to preserve whatever part of his reputation remained, so he felt the need to be transparent and get his story out. It was also cathartic to tell a few courtroom buddies the real story and hear their outrage. Ben needed that support. Now, if he could just pull off a big win with this Landers case, the narrative in the legal community would change and put the focus on Ben's success and not on the debacle of Marco Alexopoulos.

Before the trial began on Monday morning, Ben had to get away where he could think. Trial lawyers prepare for cases in different ways. However, one common factor is that the case never leaves their heads. In those weeks leading up to trial, thoughts of every detail occupy every available brain cell. Whether its driving, showering, running, or working, the trial owns all the bandwidth of a lawyer's brain. Instead of walking around the office mindlessly, Ben liked to get away somewhere private and allow his subconscious to feed his conscious brain. His best ideas had come from allowing his mind to metabolize information into cogent concepts. Ben had to simplify the case and create simple themes everyone could understand and empathize with.

***

Years before, Ben had bought a Fay Jones-designed cottage, "Stoneflower," located in the Eden Isle development in Heber Springs, Arkansas on Greer's Ferry Lake. Built in 1965, it was a tiny 1,600-square-foot oasis with one bedroom in a tree house setting. Greer's Ferry Lake is of Arkansas's five largest lakes, located about three hours west of Memphis and an hour north of Little Rock, nestled in the Ozark foothills between Clinton and Heber Springs. Beautiful rock formations and hills surround the stunningly crystal-clear water. Its atmosphere is distinctly White trash meets the Catskills. Many retirees call it home and enjoy the Red Apple Inn and accompanying golf course, walking around in Bermuda shorts and white knee-high socks.

Ben quickly stuffed a duffle bag and made the three-hour trip through the winding roads of eastern Arkansas. Ben unpacked the Escalade, unloaded his laptop and trial file in the cottage, and headed straight for the marina to launch his Cobalt speed boat. He raced it at high-speed, traversing the lake and burning adrenaline to make room so calm could take over his thought process. After an hour of putting the boat through its paces, Ben settled down in a nice cove, surrounded by huge boulders. Labor Day had passed, and Ben practically owned the lake, the boat now sitting on glass-smooth water. He cut the engine, dropped anchor, and popped open a Diet Coke. He splayed out on the back cushion and processed the entire case, resting on his back staring at the cloudless ski. The dyslexia might make Ben struggle to see words and numbers, but the order of proof, voir dire, opening statement, and elements of trial naturally assimilated into a coherent presentation in his mind. Preparing for trial is like an architect designing a house. It is not done one room at a time but in unison, with all the elements eventually coming together to form the whole.

After an hour, while he was thinking about the cross-examination of Dr. Kirkwood, it hit him. It had been right in front of his nose all along, and he had never seen it. It was not an obscure document or deposition testimony. The essence of the case stared him right in the eye, and he had missed it. Ironically, Ben's dyslexia had helped him discover the answer. Ben battled all his life with decoding techniques for reading that regular people took for granted. He fought reading; he hated reading; but he knew reading unlocked the keys to life. Now, the decoding techniques he had longed to be able to use opened the entire case. Ben screamed a shout of joy, thrilled for the answer, and then dove into the cold lake for a rigorous swim. Armed with this ammunition, Ben could not get into court soon enough.

After the swim and diving off the rocks a few times, Ben raced back to the dock and headed quickly over to the cottage to crank up the laptop. He was right! There it was. By presenting one document, one deposition, and the defense expert disclosures, Ben believed the case could be won. The information was straightforward and simple but executing its delivery would take all the courage and guile he could muster. Ben had to thread the needle perfectly to make it work. If he exposed his play too early and tipped his hand, Marston would pounce just as he had with the protocols and blunt the force of the spear. Ben knew he had to go against all conventional strategy and take the biggest gamble of his career to pull off this move. It scared him to death, but he had no choice. He had to be an artist in that court and not a mechanic.

Ben spent Friday night and all day Saturday at Stoneflower, bolstered by the excitement of his discovery. Ben loved to cook and had become an accomplished amateur chef, but Saturday night would be his go-to pregame meal, spaghetti. In college, he lived on Ragu sauce and vermicelli noodles, developing creative but inexpensive ways to enhance the flavors. Cooking became a spiritual endeavor. Chopping, cutting, and stirring were meditative states. The olive oil coated the pan; he let the chopped onion sweat before adding the minced garlic; that simmered until it was time to add the San Marzano tomatoes, which made any meal delicious. Then, the red pepper flakes, oregano, salt, and black pepper were added with just a touch of sugar to offset the acidity of the tomatoes. Ben added the rind of a bar of Parmesan Reggiano to the tomato sauce to allow it to better coat the noodles. After the noodles were cooked, the sauce was added, and the two finished together in perfect harmony. The chef's kiss of flaked Parmesan Reggiano and fresh basil from Ben's backyard created a symphony of taste and the security of comfort food. Smell and taste are two of the most sensitive connections to our memories, and this meal never failed to take Ben to a place of complete calm, remembering his past days of little money and simple ingredients.

Ben drove back early Sunday morning, cranking up Jason Isbell and Johnny Cash, enjoying the ride with his windows down. He met Stephanie, Alicia, and Sydney, who had just turned two, at his office where they would spend several hours prepping Alicia for the trial and her testimony. Alicia and Stephanie took turns holding and engaging with Sydney, who was having a bad day. Ben, no stranger to babies, took a turn walking Sydney around the office in his arms singing her James Taylor songs.

Ben did not like to script the testimony of the plaintiff. He did not want the jury to doubt the sincerity of the testimony because it sounded overly rehearsed. Paradoxically, Alicia would sound more believable if her answers sounded a bit disjointed rather than perfectly synchronized. Ben and Stephanie worked up an outline to cover and general points to make. Stephanie prepared Alicia for cross-examination. As the examiner, Ben put himself in the shoes of the jury and asked questions he thought a juror would want to know the answers to. Ben initiated potential cross-examination questions in his direct exam to steal the thunder from the defense counsel and allow the witness to explain a potentially troublesome issue to a friendly face. Right before Alicia would take the stand in the real courtroom, Stephanie would tell Ben which, of all the topics they practiced, had worked best and then give him the question to finish on.

"Ben," Stephanie's eyes were earnest. "She is going to absolutely destroy them with the last answer."

Ben's trust for Stephanie allowed him to proceed with preparations, despite not knowing exactly what Alicia would say. Just as in golf, Ben played by feel and sound and wanted that last shot to be real and not rehearsed. The more practiced the answer was, the more mechanical it became. It would be missing the pure sound of a perfect 8-iron. Ben would trust that last shot and not think about it.

It didn't get dark until after eight. The trial started in the morning, and as they say in the South, the hay was in the barn. Ben debated between taking a long walk in the old woods of Overton Park and putting at Galloway. He needed to find a place of peace to gather his thoughts. Galloway won out because there was a good chance that The Sage would show up, and he could use a little pep talk. He was correct. Twenty minutes after Ben started rolling putts with Scottie Cameron, The Sage appeared, as he always had.

"Got anything going this week?" he asked, attempting to elicit a rise from Ben.

"Just a little contested matter set in Division 6," Ben replied with lawyerly understatement, never looking up from his putter.

"How do you feel about it?" The Sage asked seriously.

Ben turned around now and faced his mentor. "I feel like I have about an 80 percent chance of getting my ass kicked and 20 percent of just losing." There was doubt in Ben's voice. "Homey, I just don't know if I am cut out for this. As much as I need the money, damn it, I want to help Alicia and Sydney. They are good people and did not deserve this. Kirkwood and Marston know that. Any other lawyer but Marston would have settled this thing a long time ago. But he will do anything to win this case, ethically or not. Last week, he concocted a witness to knock out the protocol that put his guy in a noose. I have one more arrow in my quiver but am worried that if I tip it too early, Marston will come up with one of his shady moves to neutralize it." Ben threw down three balls and began to putt them. "Every time I get ready for one of these, I ask myself, why I do it? It is just so painful. You put in every bit of emotional capital you have and set yourself up to be crushed. Losing this case will devastate me. I have lost cases before, but to lose this case to Marston, I don't know if I could come back. I just can't lie to you, boss. This is Alicia and Sydney's only chance to get the resources they need . . . and the justice they deserve. I am just not sure I am the man that can do it."

The Sage took the putter from Ben's hands. "Get your chin up, big fella, and stop feeling sorry for yourself," The Sage chided. The two men walked over to the stone wall adjacent to the putting green and sat down.

"Look," he continued, "no one is better prepared to beat Marston than you. I know I am a sarcastic asshole most of the time and love making fun of you plaintiffs' lawyers, but what you do is important. It's important not only to Alicia and Sydney but to our community and way of life. Nobody needs to get too much power. And despite my usual annoyance with you guys, I must admit that our community would be less without you. If the doctors and hospitals were not held accountable, think of what kind of treatment the public would get. The corporate bean counters would reduce medicine into a pure profit animal with no guardrails to curtail their greedy impulses."

The Sage turned and put his hand on Ben's shoulder. "Ben, you have read Marston's playbook. Hell, you helped write it. What makes Marston tick is control and power. He has his team, his loaded teleprompter, and every single detail and contingency mapped out. You cannot beat him at his game, so don't try. Attack him with chaos. Surprise and misdirection. He expects linear progression because that is how he and most successful trial lawyers are wired."

Ben rubbed his hand through his hair, leaned back and looked at the sky, and drew a deep breath.

"Let me tell you a story," The Sage said. "Do you remember King Leonidas from Sparta?"

"Of course," Ben replied. "He led the 300 Spartans at the Battle of Thermopylae. They took on Xerxes' huge Persian army. The Spartans knew they would not survive but had to hold off the Persians for as long as they could so that the remaining Greeks would have time to prepare their defenses. They knowingly and willingly sacrificed their own lives for the greater good of their own city-state."

"Exactly, and I thought you went to public school," The Sage chuckled. "Leonidas's speech to his soldiers was amazing. Do you remember it?"

"No, I don't. Please tell me." Ben drank a bottle of water, eyes locked in on The Sage.

"He told them that this is a moment in which man feels the gods as close as his own breath. 'What unknowable mercy spared us this day? What clemency of the divine has turned the enemy's spear one handbreadth from our throat and driven it fatally into the breast of the beloved comrade at our side? Why are we still here above the earth, we who are no better, no braver, who reverenced heaven no more than these our brothers whom the gods have dispatched to hell?'"

Ben nodded to Sage. "I have always loved that story, but what does that have to do with the trial tomorrow?"

The Sage stood and faced Ben. "Leonidas was reflecting that lady fortune and skill have an equal say in the outcome. Before gunpowder, all killing was of necessity done hand to hand. For a Spartan warrior to slay his enemy, he had to get so close that there was an equal chance that the enemy's sword would kill him. This produced the virtue of valor and honor which was prized as much as victory. Ben, you have committed to action. You have committed to the battle. The virtue of taking on Marston's army alone is more of a virtue than an actual victory. In my book, you are heroic because you will step in the arena, bare and naked, ready to do battle against overwhelming odds.

"Ben, you are one of the few. You are a man of action. You have devoted yourself to a worthy cause. Like Teddy Roosevelt said, 'who at the best knows in the end the triumph of high achievement, and who at the worst, if he fails, at least fails while daring greatly, so that his place shall never be with those cold and timid souls who neither know victory nor defeat.' Ben, trust the process. Trust your instincts. Create chaos. And in the end, get close enough to Marston that you can drive the knife into this throat like the goddamned Spartan you are! Get so close you can hear and feel the breath and life leave that sorry son of a bitch."

The Sage walked off without another word. Ben remained on the wall, left to his thoughts and Scottie Cameron.

CHAPTER 17

Monday, day one of trial, came on a hot, cloudless day. Ben had been up since 4:00 a.m., and Marston never went to sleep; preparations were complete, so it was hours of restless energy for the lawyers, waiting to burst through the starting gate. Court began at 10:00 a.m.

Ben had lost count of the cases he had tried in his career but knew he got nervous in every single one until the first shot was fired. Then, all the nerves vanished, and his instinctive competitive nature took over. Ben used the time to wrestle with himself over what to wear. Some schools of thought say that plaintiffs' lawyers should dress humbly and almost look poor. Stories abound of rich plaintiffs' lawyers wearing shoddy clothes and driving a twenty-year-old pickup truck to court as props for trial. They put on wrinkled khakis and an old blue sports coat with beat-up loafers. Ben refused the artifice. Even the poorest kids have one nice Sunday outfit. Growing up, though, Ben did not, and when he showed up at homecoming in junior high, his classmates taunted him for his unfashionable suit and beat-up shoes. Childhood insults live with men for the rest of their lives. The sting hurt so bad that when he was able to, Ben bought the nicest clothes he could find. Ben dressed for court in a Brooks Brothers navy suit, white shirt and Stefano Ricci dark purple tie, brown belt, and chestnut Alden lace-ups. He chose his prized Cartier Tank with a brown alligator strap. Looking good, feeling good.

The first day of trial would likely be used up in just selecting the jury, but Ben needed to be prepared for opening statement if it went quicker than expected. Judge Jones ran a tight court room and did not allow wasted time or inefficient lawyers. Ben finally gave up on sleep, put on his suit, and headed to his office, where he sat at his desk and practiced his deep breathing, going over his voir dire questions again.

Marston's troops jumped into action, organizing and readying what had already been done a dozen times, and the man himself would not utter one word in the courtroom that had not been scripted. The Thornton runners loaded up the trial materials and headed to the courthouse. The tech staff waited outside the door for the court clerk to arrive at 8:00 a.m. to begin setting up their mini studio.

Ben and Stephanie met Alicia and Sydney at the courthouse. Sydney used a specially constructed wheelchair, and the four of them took the tight elevator to the second floor.

"Alicia, just when I think you cannot be more beautiful, you top yourself."

Alicia looked down with a sheepish grin. "Ah, Ben, you are too sweet."

"What am I, chopped liver?" Stephanie teased.

"Stephanie, it goes without saying that you are always a paragon of class and grace. Forgive me for not pointing it out sooner."

The three of them smiled.

Ben turned back toward Alicia. "How is Sydney?"

The elevator doors opened, and they walked out. "She had a tough night. Hopefully, she will sleep a lot today."

As they walked together down marble staircases, Ben said, "Alicia, Judge Jones will be very sympathetic to you. If Sydney starts fussing or needs to eat, just tap me on the shoulder, and I will either get you or all of us a break so you can manage. The jury will be very sympathetic to your plight. In fact, watching you handle Sydney for two weeks will bring home what you have to do every day of your life."

Ben and Stephanie walked into the courtroom together, leaving Alicia and Sydney on a wooden bench just outside.

Lawyers set up camp in their allocated seats the courtroom, organizing their materials, documents, exhibits, and visual aids. The counsel tables in Shelby County are long rectangular ancient heavy oak separated by a wooden podium set in the center. When addressing the judge, protocol dictates that lawyers stand or, if it's more than a brief comment, move to the podium equipped with a microphone. Custom dictates the plaintiff's counsel sits on the side adjacent to the jury and directly across from the witness box on Judge Jones' right. Judge Jones' court clerk occupies the left side, and the court reporter resides just in front of the court clerk.

Ben entered the courtroom around 9:30 a.m., bringing his laptop, notes, and Rules of Civil Procedure, at the ready for any obscure objection that may come his way. Alicia and Sydney remained outside in the hall until court convened because Sydney was two years old and needed to move around. Sydney could not walk and occupied a wheelchair when she was not in Alicia's lap. Her cerebral palsy was distinctive in her anatomy, her arms irregularly shaped with limited movement, her head tilted unnaturally as she made noises uncommon for a two-year-old. She could not speak but possessed a warm smile. Therapy greatly improved her ability to use her arms and legs in small ways, but she would never have any kind of normal life. Sydney required intensive twenty-four-hour care with a specialty bed, a wheelchair, and living space that could accommodate her wheelchair both inside and out. Alicia's uncle constructed a makeshift ramp to help ease the wheelchair into the house.

Kip and Steve arrived a few minutes later and exchanged handshakes and greetings with Ben and Stephanie. Marston appeared in a three-piece charcoal suit, white shirt, red-and-blue striped tie, and black lace-up shoes shined to a gloss. Some rules are unbreakable; Southern lawyers shake hands and greet opponents. To do otherwise would erode the very underpinnings of accepted culture. The two met in front of the podium, which acts as Switzerland during the trial, shook hands, and looked each other in the eye.

"Good morning, Marston."

"Good morning, Ben. I hope you had a restful night last night," Marston responded without any hint of sarcasm.

"Slept like a baby," Ben said. "Do we have any preliminary matters we need to discuss?"

"None that I am aware of." Marston's tone was sharp.

There is a strange silence and tension in a courtroom before a big jury trial. The participating lawyers do not speak, and lawyers who have brief business with the court prior to trial give the combatants a wide berth. A handful of lawyers stood in the back of the room, waiting to make quick announcements or enter orders when Judge Jones took the bench.

The bailiff asked Marston and Ben if they were ready. Each gave the thumbs up. The door from Judge Jones' chambers opened, and he climbed to the elevated bench. He instructed the bailiff to open court. In a booming voice, the bailiff, Marcus Cochran, demanded, "All rise!" There was shuffle of chairs and feet as lawyers, jurors, technicians, and assistants stood. "Hear ye, hear ye, Division 6 of the Shelby County Circuit Court is now open for business, and all who have business before this court shall be heard. The Honorable Judge Jerome Jones is presiding."

Judge Jones nodded to the courtroom. "You may be seated."

For about five minutes, other lawyers present for other cases are first allowed to address administrative matters before the Judge, enter orders, and make announcements; in the meantime, Ben and Marston sat passively in their chairs at the counsel table.

"Mr. Jennings, is the plaintiff ready to proceed?" Judge Jones asks.

"Yes, Your Honor, ready for the plaintiff," Ben responded. "Judge, Ms. Landers and Sydney are outside. May I go escort them in?"

"You may. Mr. Marston, is the defense ready to proceed?"

"Yes, sir. Indeed, we are," Marston replied firmly.

Ben went out in the hall and came back shortly, holding the door so Alicia could wheel Sydney into the courtroom.

After they were settled, Judge Jones took control of the courtroom and explained to the litigants that the prospective jury panel will start with forty candidates so that a jury of twelve plus two alternates can be chosen. Judge Jones instructed the clerk to go across the street to the jury commissioner's office and return with forty potential jurors. The clerk complied, and the game was on. It took an hour to get the jurors as the jury commissioner had to provide jurors for every trial in the nine divisions of circuit court and eight of criminal court. Depending on the day, there could be several trials also demanding jurors.

After thirty minutes, the clerk appeared with a list of the forty perspective jurors' names, addresses, occupations, and spouses. Ben took the list, photographed it with his phone, and shot it back to Peggy, who scoured social media for clues to potential biases and prejudices. Marston's jury consultant and assistant immediately started typing on their computers in a more sophisticated process of evaluating the same thing.

The process of picking a jury is called *voir dire*, the literal translation from Latin being "to say what is true." Ben learned a trick from Fats Feldstein: memorize all the juror names before addressing them. He had about fifteen minutes to get the juror names and begin his questioning. This was a dicey move because, if he got it wrong, he would lose credibility early, but if he got it right, the jury would think he has magic powers. The odds were so against Ben in this case, he had to pull out all the stops. Safe would not win this trial for him. The Lord hates a coward.

Jury selection immediately demonstrated the difference in styles between the two lawyers. Ben was comfortable in a courtroom and around jurors. He moved around the entire courtroom and asked jurors about their high schools and talked freely about Tiger basketball and the current prized recruit. He knew the companies they worked for and the people with whom they went to school. He knew the most important thing in jury selection is getting the prospective jurors to talk and reveal who they are, what they think, and how they are likely to feel about the case. They are often nervous, not happy about being there, and unlikely to offer the very personal details Ben needed to know that could make the difference in picking the right juror.

"Ladies and gentlemen, believe it or not, I have served on jury duty. I sat over there in that cattle call with a thousand of your closest friends waiting to see if I got called. Part of you wants nothing to do with it, but the other part of you is a little competitive and wants to get selected. Then, once you are selected, the anxiety comes about what if it's a murder trial. What if I do the wrong thing. I answered the same questions I am asking you. Maybe the only thing in this trial that Mr. Owens and I can agree on is that neither of us is naturally nosey. We do not wish to pry into your personal lives, but this case is of utmost importance to both sides. I don't believe any of you would be intentionally biased to one side, but all of our life experiences make us predisposed to certain beliefs. It does not make any of those beliefs right or wrong. It just means either side may think some experience may make you less likely to appreciate the position they are taking in this trial. What you are doing is one of the greatest acts of patriotism you can perform outside the military. It is citizens like you who allow our system of democracy and justice to survive."

Marston took the opposite approach. By the time his turn arrived, Judge Jones and Ben had already asked every pertinent question. His time in front of them was shorter and focused on inserting defense positions in the form of questions to see how prospective jurors react. Marston's commanding height, voice, and age gave him an effective natural authority. Ben was the friend they wanted to drink with, and Marston was the school principal who ran the courtroom.

The forty-person jury panel took seats in the jury box and benches behind "the bar" where spectators sat. During jury selection, no spectators were allowed because the court lacked sufficient space for both the prospective panel and people unessential to the case. Judge Jones took charge, introducing himself, the lawyers, and the litigants and described the process of selection. He spoke to each juror, asking them their job, spouse, occupation, and whether they had ever been involved in a lawsuit themselves. Stephanie took crucial notes Ben would use when making selection decisions. While Judge Jones questioned the jury, Ben made eye contact with each potential juror, focusing on remembering their names. It is extremely stressful to memorize forty people that quickly, but his listening skills (developed long ago to blunt his dyslexia) gave him a huge advantage.

Judge Jones took over thirty minutes to ask his questions. Then, it was Ben's turn, and first impressions were everything. Making it look natural was the key. Ben carried no notes. He walked up and down the panel, speaking randomly to people, calling each by name and, in most cases, remembering their jobs and spouse's names. Ben often used this little parlor trick during jury selection, because it would invariably set up a key exchange with a witness later during the trial when there was a question of whose memory to believe. At those moments, Ben looks at the jury and says: "I don't know, Mr. Jones, you may be right because my memory isn't so good," and the jurors laugh out loud, knowing what Ben had done in jury selection. The witness's lack of awareness of the inside joke gave Ben an advantage.

Ben's questioning of the panel was exceptional and a masterclass of how to connect with jurors. He employed the "I'll show you mine if you show me yours" routine espoused by the great Gerry Spence, a member of the American Trial Lawyer Hall of Fame who never lost a criminal case no matter which side he was on. This move required Ben to open up about his own life and experiences, turning the exercise of probing personal questions during jury selection from an annoying intrusion into an almost-pleasant exchange with a funny man. He loved to describe his own public-school education, causing defense lawyers to groan, but which always received a double take from Black jurors, who could not believe this suited-up White lawyer had gone to the same schools as they had.

Ben utilized the Reptile Theory technique, asking jurors about safety rules at work. He walked directly to a potential juror he knew worked in a factory.

"Sir, are there safety rules at your factory?"

"Yes, sir. Absolutely." The man leaned forward.

"And if the safety rules are not followed, what can happen?" Ben asked.

"Someone could die."

"In your job, are safety rules important for the health and well-being of the workers?" Ben probed.

The juror leaned forward. "Sir, we would be lost without them."

These questions set up the jury to compare simple safety rules with the conduct of the doctor. It would be much easier to understand a doctor's conduct in those terms rather than the abstract esoteric explanation the defense would likely provide. All jurors embrace issues like safety.

Lawyers who represent plaintiffs in personal injury actions now utilize an unofficial manual which describes how our brain stem acts in accordance with our evolutionary need to protect ourselves, our progeny, and our tribes. This essential book is known as the "Reptile Theory," and it compares the human brain's need to survive as the driver in making decisions—and not an aggrandized form of empathy or quest to carry out justice. This Reptile Theory explains why humans act this way and is designed to circumvent the Golden Rule of trial law. This Golden Rule is not your Sunday school class's version of the Golden Rule. In the realm of civil trials, the Golden Rule is the absolute prohibition of asking a juror, "How would you like it if this happened to you or your family?" or something to that effect. And the reason you cannot ask a juror that question is because it is so damn effective that the powers that be have labeled any such utterance grounds for a mistrial--and off with the offending party's head. Well, maybe not that last part, but they will certainly make you feel that way if you dare get close to the forbidden zone. Most of a civil trial involves the plaintiff's lawyer trying get around the Golden Rule. It takes a lot of chalance to look nonchalant. A plaintiff's entire presentation and every word, diagram, and picture are coordinated to have a specific effect on a particular demographic of juror. There are not just Republican jurors, old jurors, or liberal jurors. They will all be represented, and every one of them brings different life experiences, prejudices, and beliefs to a trial. Some are auditory learners, and others are visual learners. Good lawyers must present seamlessly and without notes so they can maintain eye contact with jurors and witnesses. The production takes a tremendous amount of effort to look calm, cool, collected, and yes, nonchalant. A plaintiff's lawyer uses every tool at his disposal to distill complex medicine and legal concepts down to a narrative that the average citizen at the bus stop can understand. On the other hand, the army of high-paid, well-educated, experienced, and overly funded defense lawyers with a seven person "trial team" do everything they can to complicate every issue and make the case so confusing that a jury will throw up their hands and take the easy course, which means ruling for the defendant. Tennessee is one of the most conservative states in the country, and jurors do not like plaintiff's cases, unless of course, one of their family is a victim, at which point they become the converted. Tennessee is a death penalty state, and the law requires a jury to decide whether one of its citizens lives or dies. However, when it comes to an insurance company or corporation's money, Tennessee has decided to put artificial limits on the authority of that same set of citizens.

Back when Ben and Marston tried cases together, Marston always let Ben handle jury selection. Now, Marston watched from the other side and felt the pain he knew other lawyers must have felt trying to counter a lawyer who displayed such command and genuine connection to jurors. Marston hated jury selection because it was the aspect of a trial that was the least controllable.

Marston gathered his notes, stood up, and walked to the lectern. He took a deep breath, looked down at his notes, introduced himself, and asked Dr. Kirkwood to stand up. Marston told the jury about Dr. Kirkwood's education, training, experience, and overall excellence, then addressed the jury.

"Do you agree that there are two sides to every story?" Several nodded affirmatively.

"Since the plaintiff goes first, will you agree to hear our side before making any judgments?

"Will you agree that it's the evidence that comes from that witness stand that matters and not what the lawyers say?

"Do you agree that just because something bad happened to a patient, it does not mean Dr. Kirkwood was negligent?"

Most of the jury nodded their heads. His presentation concluded twenty minutes later. Marston had all the information he needed but wanted to plant the defense seeds in the jury's mind. Marston calculated Ben's only advantage at this trial was jury selection. He reckoned that by the end of the trial, they may want to go to dinner with Ben, but only after they found on behalf of the defendant.

Judge Jones recessed for lunch, allowing everyone an hour and a half. Marston's team adjourned to the third-floor library conference room where they could spread out. Ben hustled down the long hallway and grabbed sandwiches for the group at the snack bar. They crammed into the court room and reviewed Stephanie's notes and the texts sent by Peggy about the social media posts of the prospective panel. Stephanie and Ben's worst argument as colleagues had occurred during jury selection in a previous trial. Stephanie saw many things through the prism of race and demanded that a Black nurse be kept on the jury panel because both the plaintiff and Stephanie were Black. Ben argued that the Black nurse would be loyal to the doctor and nurse defendant because of their shared profession. Ben and Stephanie butted heads and argued for ten minutes before Ben finally relented, not wanting to be considered a racist. The nurse remained on the jury and ultimately pushed what was a pro-plaintiff jury all the way to a defense verdict. Ben would never again make the same mistake of allowing anyone to override his judgment in selecting a jury or make him feel like a racist for removing a Black juror.

Picking a jury is far more art than science. Some jurors favor one side or the other, but most are difficult to discern. There are sweeping generalities with plenty of anecdotal evidence, but there are also always exceptions. Lawyers who think Black jurors as monolithic in their thinking make a mistake. While Black females tend to be liberal and plaintiff-friendly, Black Southern men tend to be conservative in civil trials unless they have a cause to stand behind. Whites in the city tend to be liberal and plaintiff-friendly, and Southern Whites from the suburbs lean far-right and pro-establishment.

Marston's team rode in the caravan of SUVs back to the office where the team of lawyers and jury consultants settled in the large conference room, dissecting the panel looking for the twelve who would most likely be in their favor. While they debated, roast chicken, steamed vegetables, and fingerling potatoes were served on fine china. The team ran Lexus/Nexus searches, combed social media, and created individual juror profiles. Each side possessed four peremptory challenges used to strike four jurors for any reason except for race. If Judge Jones or the opposition believed the prospective juror was challenged for race, the lawyer accused must articulate an independent basis for striking the juror. It is called a Batson charge based on the US Supreme Court case of that name. Prior to exercising their peremptory strikes, challenges for cause are made. Before using up those valuable peremptory strikes, lawyers use "cause" strikes to eliminate troublesome jurors. Cause challenges can be a juror admitting a bias to one side or the other, or perhaps, their mother was killed by medical negligence, and thus, they don't feel they could be fair and impartial. Many times, jurors have family members in the medical field and admit to a distaste for plaintiffs' lawyers and medical malpractice lawsuits. There is no limit to cause challenges. Often, cause can be an obvious bias wherein the trial judge believes that the juror cannot be fair and impartial to one side or the other. The whole process is a chess game to see who can shape the jury in their client's favor.

Court resumed at 1:30 p.m. because of the late morning session. The two teams argued cause challenges for thirty minutes with five perspective jurors let go for reasons ranging from having family involved in a medical malpractice case to personal medical problems to acknowledging they could not be fair for one reason or another. For the next forty-five minutes, the parties played cat and mouse with their four peremptory challenges plus one extra peremptory challenge for the two alternates.

Late in the afternoon, they had completed the selection. The jury pleased Ben, who had only a few concerns. In final, the jury composition of fourteen citizens of Shelby County divided into two categories: eight Black individuals (five women, three men) and six White individuals (four women, two men). While seemingly anachronistic to speak in such base racial terms, in Memphis, most everything comes down to race; one can act like it does not, but race matters. People see almost every question through their personal prism of shared experience that, in a southern city with a history of prejudice, comes down to race. Even so, there are many examples of Shelby County jurors working together across racial lines in reaching a unanimous verdict as required by state law.

For the next thirty minutes, Judge Jones gave the panel preliminary instructions about their duties. They were not allowed to speak to any of the lawyers, parties, or the judge. They must not perform any independent research about the trial or attempt in any way to engage in an independent investigation. Since it was the first day, Judge Jones dismissed the jurors early and ordered them to return at 9:00 a.m. the following day ready to start.

CHAPTER 18

Opening statement is perhaps the most critical part of any jury trial. Closing arguments grab all the glamour, but research reveals that most jurors formulate strong impressions of a case during opening and subsequently view the proof through a lens that confirms their initial impressions. If it were a case about likeability, Ben would win in a landslide. However, a lawyer's likeability matters far less than that of the client and case. Lawyers have license to be arrogant and rude because jurors expect the stereotypes to be true.

An effective opening statement needs to set out a roadmap for the proof the plaintiff expects to prove. Early on, a plaintiff's lawyer should set out the short "rule" he believes applies to this case and explain in concise terms the reason for suing and what they seek to gain. More importantly, it needs to be in story form to engage the jurors. While Ben had the advantage of going first, he also had the burden of proof, which evened the playing field. A lawyer is not allowed to argue in opening statement but simply inform the jury of what the lawyer believes the proof will show. Lawyers blur this line every day, and opposing counsel rarely interrupts an opponent's opening with a legal objection for fear the jury will find them rude. Each side pushes the line, and when objected to, a guilty advocate feigns horror and outrage at the indignation of the interruption.

"Mr. Jennings, are you ready to make your opening remarks?" Judge Jones asked.

"Yes, Your Honor." Ben replied. Stephanie looked at his checklist on the table in front of him, touched his arm, and whispered, "You got this."

Ben stood up, buttoned his jacket, and turned toward the jury, making sure to take his time. He made a good impression during voir dire, but the mood then had been much more congenial to elicit honest responses from prospective jurors. He laughed and joked with prospective jurors to relax them and get them to open up. Now, it was soliloquy not conversation, and he needed to focus them on the case. Many times, cases are won based on who told the best stories. The facts were the facts, but the jury would see them first through the lens of the lawyers.

"Ladies and gentlemen, along with Stephanie Mann, it's my honor to represent and be the voice for Ms. Alicia and young Sydney Landers." Ben walked down the rail, making eye contact with each juror. "We believe the rule of this case is this: If a doctor takes on a medical task, he is required to perform that task up to the same standards as other reasonable doctors in this community would." Ben said this to establish a "rule" to help simplify the case in a simple sentence in anticipation of Marston's presentation to make it complicated. "Now, you ask, why are we suing Dr. Kirkwood? We are suing Dr. Kirkwood because we believe that he undertook a reading of vital x-rays of Sydney Landers and, by failing to do so properly, caused an anoxic brain injury. Now, Sydney suffers from cerebral palsy that but for Dr. Kirkwood's negligence would not have occurred." Ben always buttressed these two concepts—the rule of the case and the reason for the suit—to frame the case in a simple fashion before the complex facts were explained. He felt it gave the jury a foundation to work from and ordered his presentation. He also knew that jurors were inherently suspicious of lawyers, so he wanted to establish a clear, concise reason for the lawsuit to build credibility before he delivered the facts of the case.

Next, Ben grabbed their attention as a grandmother may when talking to her grandchildren: "I would like to tell you a story." Many of the jurors leaned forward, ready to hear the case they had been chosen to decide. "Two years ago, Alicia Landers had just finished college at Mississippi Valley State and was preparing for law school when she found out that she and her long-time boyfriend were expecting a baby. As you can imagine, this came as a surprise, and Alicia had crucial decisions to make. Alicia prayed on the matter intensely and decided that being a mother is the most important thing a woman could do. She was working as a law clerk for a local law firm and decided she would put off law school until her child was old enough to make that practical. She went to all the prenatal visits and took good care of herself during pregnancy. However, as many of you know, around her thirty-second week of pregnancy, she went into early labor. Fortunately, Sydney, despite being very premature, was born healthy in all other respects. But because of her low weight, the hospital wisely kept her in the neonatal unit to make sure she was well taken care of." Ben paused, stepped back, and looked at Alicia, causing the jury to follow his gaze. "After several weeks, Sydney was progressing nicely, but then, doctors noticed she was not having sufficient bowel movements. This is a concerning event because there is a well-known condition in premature babies like Sydney known as NEC. NEC stands for necrotizing enterocolitis. We will just stick with NEC, if that's okay with you. NEC means Sydney's tummy was not moving the food through her body, which means it could build up and cause a puncture in her digestive tract. This becomes very dangerous because that digested food contains a lot of bacteria that should not be outside of her intestines. A baby that small could become septic very quickly and die or, as in Sydney's case, suffer cardiorespiratory failure. During cardiorespiratory failure, Sydney's brain failed to receive vital oxygen for over eight minutes, which led to her current condition known as cerebral palsy." Ben walked to the counsel table and took a drink of water from a glass.

"Your job at the end of this trial will be to decide if Dr. Kirkwood met the standard of care. And a simple way of describing the standard of care is what a reasonable physician of his expertise would do in like or similar circumstances. Our expert proof will show that the standard of care for doctors requires them to order and have x-rays read in this situation very often. They are known as serial x-rays. Dr. Kirkwood did, in fact, order serial x-rays, and the hospital did, in fact, perform those x-rays properly. However, where we believe Dr. Kirkwood failed young Sydney is that he did not read those x-rays accurately and missed the evidence before his eyes that she had a hole in her intestine. Had he done his job, a surgeon would have immediately been called and corrective surgery performed. Further, the proof will be that the hospital had specialized radiologists on staff trained specifically to read these x-rays and make the proper diagnosis. Even though not trained as a radiologist, Dr. Kirkwood believed that he, a neonatologist, was as qualified to read those x-rays as were those special radiologists. Our expert, who is the leader in the field, will testify that if you are going to take on that task, you are required to do it properly. Dr. Kirkwood failed in his duty to Sydney Landers." Ben had the jury focused on every word. While Stephanie swiveled in her chair, Alicia bravely held Sydney, who slept peacefully after some fussy moments during jury selection the day before. Kip and Steve furiously wrote down every word Ben said. Marston turned in his chair facing Ben and the jury, expressionless, straight as a statue.

Ben told the jury what witnesses and proof they should expect to hear. To steal thunder from the defense, he told the jury what he expected Marston's proof would be and why it should be discounted.

"The defendant will put on three different experts and Dr. Kirkwood himself. Judge Jones will later tell you that this not a numbers game. Just because the defense has more resources at their disposal and can afford more experts than Sydney, it doesn't mean they are right. It is not fair for you to go into the jury room and make your decision based on who had the most experts. Please listen carefully to all of the experts."

Ben wanted to drop an Easter egg for the jury. His experience told him that many jurors liked to figure things out for themselves and play amateur sleuth. "I urge you to listen and watch carefully." Ben pointed to his temple with his right index finger. "We will not be putting a lot of medical records before you, but the ones we do are of utmost importance. Please be vigilant and pay attention to what Dr. Kirkwood said in his medical record and not what he says on the witness stand after having a team of lawyers prepare him for his testimony."

Ben walked right to the line with that statement and likely a bit over, but Marston hated to object to another lawyer's opening. Marston moved to the edge of his seat as if to rise, and Ben changed the subject, figuring he had gone far enough. An opening should grab a jury's attention, but it would be a tactical error to use all the ammunition early. A good lawyer needed to always keep some of his powder dry.

Lastly, Ben struck where Marston could not defend—damages.

"Ladies and gentlemen," Ben turned back, his left arm directing the jury's view to Alicia and Sydney. "This sweet little girl's life and her mother's life have been irreparably harmed by the callous negligence of Dr. Kirkwood. Had Dr. Kirkwood done his job the way he was supposed to, Alicia would be finishing law school right about now. And Sydney?" Ben tailed off and paused to let the question sink in. Sydney was two years old but had the mental acuity of an infant.

Ben looked at Sydney, smiled warmly, and looked back at the jury with angst. "Folks, God bless this little girl, it will only get worse. The doctors will tell you that Sydney will never develop mentally like other children. She will grow to be just as tall but will never do the things that other children do. She will be confined to a wheelchair for the rest of her life. She will have a feeding tube for the rest of her life. Sydney will never get to be like other children, and Alicia will never get to be like other moms. No band-aid or pill can fix what Dr. Kirkwood did to her."

Ben walked to the center of the rail, a mere four feet from the first row of jurors. "In our system of justice, we can't extract an eye for an eye. It would be chaos if we did. All you can award is money damages. I wish you could just fix her and give this mother and daughter back their lives, but that is not possible. As Southerners, we are raised that is impolite to speak of money or to sue someone who made a mistake. But you have taken a solemn oath to follow the law, and we are asking for justice under that law. I am not asking any of you for a gift or charity.

"Folks, at the end of this trial, I will come right back where I am standing now. And when I do, I expect the proof to have been laid before you just as I have described. I will look you in the eyes without blinking and ask you for a substantial amount of money that Sydney and Alicia are entitled to under the law of our state. I urge you to give them the justice that the facts demonstrate and the law demands."

Ben held his position and stared at the jury. He needed to communicate his commitment to his position. He had boxed Marston in on damages. If Marston attempted to minimize this horrific situation, he would be seen as cold and callous. Now, any efforts from Marston asserting that Sydney was born in her condition would be fraught with peril.

Ben released his gaze, pivoted to his chair, and quietly sat down. Judge Jones wasted no time giving the floor to Marston. "Mr. Owens, you have the floor, sir."

Marston stood up and buttoned his coat, his six feet, four inches appearing even taller because of his thin, almost-gaunt frame. His brown hair was painstakingly barbered, his shoes glistened, his red-and-blue striped tie was elegantly knotted. Everything in his bearing conveyed power and authority. When he stood up, even the jurors straightened to adjust their posture as if their junior high school principal had walked in. Team scurried quietly and professionally behind him, readying the video to ensure his opening statement would be a seamless narrative. Marston had expected that Ben would strike an emotional chord with the jury. He had witnessed Ben's charisma firsthand many times, even harnessing Ben's natural connection with people for Marston's own purposes. Ben had been the only lawyer who had tried cases with Marston and been given the privilege of speaking to the jury.

Marston approached the jury, making piercing eye contact. To his credit, Marston Owens III knew who he was and refused to fake congeniality like so many other attorneys did in the courtrooms. His strength was raw power. When he started, he threw a curve.

"Ladies and gentlemen, I listened to Mr. Jennings' opening statement with great interest, and although we are going to disagree about most things in this trial, there is one thing we will not disagree on: This is a human tragedy. If you are not sympathetic to Sydney and Ms. Landers, you are not human. Ms. Landers is a lovely lady. I have had the privilege of being around her, and she is a genuinely nice lady. Sydney, even with her challenges, radiates goodness. I am so sorry this happened to them, as is Dr. Kirkland. If you thought I was going to get up in front of you and say anything bad about those two, you will be sorely disappointed." Marston's move was the mark of a skilled veteran. He knew from Alicia's deposition that the jury would be sympathetic, so why not agree with the inevitable and gain credibility with the jury? He could show both he and Dr. Kirkwood were human and caring without conceding ground on negligence. Marston carried an iPad in his right hand and looked down after completing a thought.

"However, and I say this just as earnestly and hope you hear me: What happened to them is not Dr. Kirkwood's fault. Humans want to assign fault and cause whenever something tragic occurs. We find random events unsettling and need to find an explanation for them so we can try to convince ourselves that we can avoid tragedy in our own lives. Dr. Kirkwood did not wake up one morning and decide he would harm a baby. Quite to the contrary, this man has spent his entire career and life's work saving the lives of countless babies for scores of grateful families. Dr. Kirkwood is a hero and did not depart from the standard of care in his treatment of Sydney. Further, he bears Ms. Landers no ill will for bringing this suit because he recognizes our climate of trial lawyers being in our faces twenty-four hours a day looking for cases to bring."

With that statement, Marston declared they were playing by Texas rules. He had taken Ben's opening digs without rebuke and demonstrated he was more than able to spar with extra-judicial jabs such as the personal one thrust at Ben. Ben had to take it. He had started down that road, and it would appear petty to whine now when his opponent struck back. He could have objected but Judge Jones would have, in all probability, invoked the gander rule, which is not codified but utilized in every court in the land: "What is good for the goose is good for the gander." A lawyer cannot take a position or make inappropriate statements only to criticize his opponent when he or she returns the favor.

Marston wowed the jury with science and technology. His staff choreographed the presentation like a ballet. He showed statistics on NEC and how dangerous it was to infants. Marston covered Dr. Kirkwood's impressive resume and those of the three medical experts who would later explain to the jury how Dr. Kirkwood was a leader in the field. Marston concluded where he began. He walked back to his side of the counsel table, sat the iPad down, turned, and slowly walked back to face the jury.

"Ladies and gentlemen, you can be sympathetic to this family and follow your oath. Doing as the law requires does not require you to remove your personal feelings of sympathy. But to discharge your oath, as even Judge Jones will instruct, you cannot and should not allow any sympathy to affect how you consider the proof in this case. And the proof, the science, and the overwhelming opinions of some of the most respected experts in this country absolutely require you to find in favor of Dr. Kirkwood."

Marston turned on his heel in confident self-assuredness, strode back to his seat, unbuttoned his jacket, and sat like a king taking his throne. If they had not previously realized it, the members of the jury now knew that their jobs would not be easy. Two heavyweights laid out compelling cases for their clients. After Ben's opening, most of the jurors were convinced of the piety of his case. An hour later, their heads hurt, and anxiety levels rose, knowing their task would be one of the biggest of their lives.

CHAPTER 19

After opening, Judge Jones adjourned court until 2:00 p.m., when Ben would put on his first witness. During the break, Stephanie grabbed sandwiches, and Ben went to the hall and fired up his phone. He saw forty emails and at least fifteen texts. Annie had texted him six times, progressively sounding more desperate. Ben told her ahead of time that he would be in trial for the next two weeks, but she didn't seem to understand the demands it put on him.

Annie's texts were followed by ones from Max, who rarely texted, asking Ben to come by the house and help with Annie. Lisa was stuck at work, and Kimberly had dropped Annie at home an hour before. The other handful of texts were from Marco's clients wanting to know the status of their cases. Ben called Peggy at the office to check his first line of defense.

"Peggy, hey, how is it going back at the ranch?"

"Ben, we keep getting more and more calls. I have been going through Marco's email, and you won't believe it."

"Oh no, what?"

"Prostitutes."

"What do you mean, prostitutes?"

"Apparently, our boy Marco is like a sailor with one in every port. There are emails from girls all over the Southeast, and you can tell by their names and the way they talk, they ain't amateurs."

Ben couldn't help but laugh. "You have to be kidding."

"Benji Bear, I wish I were. Now, all I can think of is getting home and taking a hot shower."

Ben walked down the back hallway and took the stairs on the way out of the building. "That boy- Jeez Louise. We learn something new every day."

"And none of it good. I just can't believe I was in the same office with him for two years."

"Shit. You are telling me." Ben looked at his watch. "Hey, but seriously, Peggy, thanks for all you are doing. I would be dead without you. Please know I appreciate you."

"Ahh, you promised it would never be boring, but I had no idea we would be investigating a major criminal from our own office."

"I definitely didn't have that on my bingo card either."

Ben texted Stephanie and told her he would be back in time for court. He raced to the Escalade and sped toward Midtown. He hit a donut shop drive-thru for a bag of treats for the kids. On the ten-minute ride, he returned every call he could fit in and told the police and FBI his trial situation. He would gladly meet with them after court or early in the morning. As he pulled up to the house, he saw Max and Annie sitting on the front steps. Annie's head was between her knees.

He got out of the car. "Max, my man," he said, tousling the boy's hair. "You are a lifesaver. I know you didn't sign up for this, but little man, right now, you are holding this team together, and I very much appreciate it."

"So. Decide to take a pass on school today?" he asked Annie.

Max rolled his eyes, and the two exchanged knowing looks acknowledging the real issue.

Annie refused to lift her head, but managed to speak, "Hey, Dad, thanks for coming by. Do you want to go to the park?"

"Sweetie, there is nothing I would rather do, but I am in a trial, and the judge would likely not understand," Ben replied. "But I did bring you guys donuts. How about a little sugar high to get you through the afternoon?"

Annie did not answer but instead burst into tears and moaned the cry of pain. Ben would have sold his soul to free her of this but maddeningly felt his efforts were futile. Time and patience were all that worked.

"How about a quick game of horse in the backyard?" Ben asked.

Annie did not respond and kept weeping. Ben handed the donuts to Max who happily dug into the sweet treats. The three sat quietly for thirty minutes, and Annie never looked up. Ben put his arm around her and spoke softly to her. He knew he had to be back in court soon. This was one of those times he just wanted to quit it all.

"Honey, I have to leave now."

"Please don't leave, Dad. Just stay a little longer," she begged.

"Baby, I can't. I have to go back to court. They are all waiting on me," he said.

She lifted her head and put it on his shoulder and squeezed him as though her life depended on it.

"I am so sorry, Dad. Thanks for coming. I am fine. I will be fine."

"I know you will be, honey. I promise this is going to get better. It has to." Ben looked at Max. "Bud, you are my guy. I need you to take my place here and do the best you can. I will come back as soon as I can. You can also call your mom. I know she will be home soon."

Max didn't speak but just nodded a knowing look they had shared many times. Ben jumped into his car. Fifteen minutes until his first witness. Taylor Swift's "Soon You'll Get Better" describing her mother's battle with cancer and John Mellencamp's "Troubled Man" came on his 500-song playlist on shuffle, and he teared up as he had done so many times after leaving his children. His stomach churned and head pounded. Ben carried so much guilt from the divorce and felt like he had ruined his kids. They were the two kindest souls he knew, but both seemed to feel things deeper than the other kids. Max, the virtuoso basketball player, followed in his dad's perfectionist steps and waged war on himself for any perceived mistake. Ben hoped Max could hold it together long enough for Annie to get back in shape. Ben parked illegally in an alley and raced back to court just in time to call Alicia's sister, Sherry Landers, as his first witness. Sherry had regal posture, a classical profile, and intelligent eyes that missed nothing. She took the stand proudly, looking directly in the jurors' eyes on the approach. Stephanie handed him an outline she prepared. Ben placed it on the lectern and began.

Ben's questioning was not extensive. From his perspective, it was a simple case, and he wanted to put his proof on and move along. Strategically, he would put Sherry on first and close with Alicia. He needed the jury to learn the story from Sherry but wanted Alicia's emotional testimony to be the last thing the jury heard before he rested. Ben, Stephanie, and Alicia decided not to put Alicia's mother on the stand because they were worried she would not stand up to the pressure. She had a history of drug problems and minor brushes with the law. Ben did not want the White conservatives to have any ammunition to marginalize this family.

Sherry engaged the jury, and she and Ben shared a relaxed rapport. She told of the family's history and Alicia's excitement of having a child. Ben wanted the first witness to be easy and not subject to much cross-examination. While not exciting, Sherry offered a window into the lives of Sydney and Alicia and delivered a much-needed narrative for the jury to understand who the plaintiff was as a person. They were not wealthy but were simple working-class folks trying their best. Not the most articulate witness,

Sherry made up for her lack of communication skills with an earnest and kind presentation that resonated with the jury. Marston wisely offered no cross. He had nothing to gain, and the real battles were yet to come.

For the next hour, Ben put on the videotaped deposition of Sydney's treating physician, Dr. Amy Ketchings, explaining Sydney's condition and the cause. She explained in detail how the lack of oxygen to Sydney's brain caused a cascade of events that created the condition Sydney now faced. Sydney would never develop into a functioning child or adult. She would be stuck with the awareness of a small child in the body of an adult. Sydney would be wheelchair-bound for life and need around-the-clock care. Sydney would never be able to eat without a feeding tube. Dr. Ketchings explained the benefits and rewards of physical therapy and other forms of assistance that would improve Sydney's limited quality of life.

No local doctor would criticize a colleague. It was unheard of in the city. For all their sanctimony about honor, dignity, and self-policing, physicians maintained the most close-knit, self-protecting group in the state. To testify locally against one of their own would amount to career suicide. In a business that relies on referrals, such testimony would mean kissing your practice goodbye. So Dr. Ketchings was not there to offer standard of care proof but evidence of Sydney's medical bills—at the moment, over $280,000 and mounting. She provided objective details of Sydney's diagnosis and permanent prognosis. Neither were good.

On cross-examination, Marston needed to make a few points.

"Doctor Ketchings, you are not here to offer any criticism of Dr. Kirkwood?" he asked.

"No, sir."

"You do not specialize as a neonatologist?"

"Correct."

"Doctor Ketchings, do you know Dr. Kirkwood?" Marston asked, knowing the next exchange had been bargained for with the doctor's lawyers. He would never ask a question for which he did not already know the answer. Old school dogma believed this rule absolute.

"Why, yes, I know him."

"What is Dr. Kirkwood's reputation within the Memphis medical community?" he continued.

"It is excellent. He is a fine doctor," she allowed.

"Thank you. No more questions." Marston looked smug.

Ben could not leave it on this note and felt he had to ask at least one follow-up on redirect.

"Dr. Ketchings, again, you are a pediatrician, correct?"

"Yes."

"And as a pediatrician, you rely in large part on referrals for your patients?"

"Yes."

"And the biggest source of referrals to your office comes from either the OB/GYN or the neonatologist?" He continued.

"Yes, that is correct."

"In fact, Dr. Ketchings, Dr. Kirkwood referred Sydney Landers to you for your care?"

"Yes, I believe so."

"No more questions." Ben concluded.

That concluded the first day of proof. Little blood drawn from either side. Ben's philosophy was to make the proof tight and succinct. In years past, juries sat for hours listening to lengthy debates and arguments, ably focusing on every word and nuance. Today's juries were Twitter juries capable of thinking only in 280 characters or less. They needed quick, concise information and would lose attention if the subject lasted too long. This posed a real dilemma for trial lawyers who had large amounts of evidence to communicate to juries with the attention spans of gnats.

Tomorrow morning would be uneventful testimony from the principal of Sydney's special school narrating a day-in-the-life video, and a life-care planner explaining to the jury the actual costs of providing for Sydney for the rest of her life. Then, Ben would call Dr. Kirkwood to the stand and follow up with his expert, Dr. Martin Bell, later in the afternoon or the first thing on Thursday. Prior to his deposition in St. Louis, they spent three hours having dinner at Charlie Gitto's and going over the case. This time, Ben met him at the Madison Hotel, and they spent an hour in the lobby going through his expected testimony and the crucial cross-examination of Dr. Kirkwood.

Bell, an old-world gentleman, radiated intelligence and kindness. People wished he were their grandfather. Barely five-feet-six in shoes, he was a tiny, round man with beautiful grey hair combed back to reveal an intelligent face. He spoke confidently but never with arrogance. He possessed the self-assuredness of a man of accomplishment, who did not need to prove his worth with boasts or condescension. They arranged for Bell to be present in the back of the courtroom when Ben called Dr. Kirkwood to testify so that when Dr. Bell followed, he could comment precisely on Dr. Kirkwood's testimony.

Ben picked up the kids and headed over to Madison Avenue to grab a Huey burger. Huey's was perennially voted Memphis's best hamburger for good reason. Its success had spawned several locations, but this was the original hole-in-the-wall location founded by the famous Thomas Boggs, a former drummer for the band The Box Topps. It was dark and dank with a ceiling full of toothpicks shot from the straws of customers. People sat close and tight, ball games on the surrounding big-screen TVs. On Sunday nights, live Memphis music blasts through the small joint, bringing back a bygone era.

They walked in and saw Boggs' daughter, Lauren McHugh Robinson, who, along with her two other sisters, ran this now-very large business empire. Lauren's children attended the same school as Max and Annie, so it felt like going to a friend's house when you ate at Huey's. The three sat down and immediately broke into conversation. Annie was excited to be at dinner with Ben and Max, referring to the three as "the squad." Max wanted to passionately discuss the big college football games of the week. They laughed and giggled as they devoured their burgers. It was just that way with Annie. She would have long periods of absolute joy and contentedness that made Ben's heart soar. He had learned that he had to enjoy every minute of her good periods. For someone like Annie, a permanent fix was a naïve notion. Instead, he needed to live in the present and accept this good night with grace and appreciation. He knew he would never give up on that wonderful child.

Dinners like these were imperative during a trial. They evened Ben out and allowed him to decompress and put things in perspective. Nothing calmed him more than debating Max on whether Michael Jordan or LeBron James was the goat or discussing the cultural significance of the Kardashians with Annie. After this respite, a challenge lay ahead. Tomorrow, he would take on Dr. Kirkwood, and the jury would expect a show. Ben had to figure out how to give them one.

CHAPTER 20

The next two days would be crucial to this trial. Mistakes meant losing. Ironically, the courtroom was the most peaceful place in Ben's life right now. The morning started off calmly. Principal James Carter of the Shriner's School in Memphis provided live narration of a professionally produced video that captured a day in the life of Sydney Landers. The video team had been at Alicia's house when Sydney awoke and documented the process required to get Sydney up and ready for a day at school. Alicia made Herculean efforts every morning of every day to take care of her special needs child.

It started before dawn. Alicia got up at 5:30 a.m. every weekday morning and rushed to dress herself. Then, at 5:50 a.m., she began the ritual of waking Sydney, changing her diapers, and feeding her through her PEG tube. She bathed her and dressed her. Some days were easier than others, depending on Sydney's mood when she awoke. Sometimes, Sydney's crankiness made it a challenge of wills to accomplish even the simplest of activities. Unlike other children, Sydney, was physically unable to assist in helping her mother in these tasks because she lacked the basic ability to control her muscles. Alicia put together all the food and medicine she would need for the day, placed Sydney in her carrier, and strolled her down to the street. Alicia tried to get outside ten minutes before the bus was scheduled to arrive so that she had time to talk and sing to Sydney, connecting in whatever way she could before leaving for the day.

The bus came to pick Sydney up at 7:00 a.m. for her special Shriner's School. Alicia raced off to a downtown law firm, where she worked as a secretary, to arrive by 7:30 a.m., starting early so that she could leave at 2:45 p.m. to meet Sydney when the bus dropped her back home at 3:30 p.m. Then, Alicia spent the next two hours interacting with Sydney: reading, singing, and watching *Sesame Street*. Sydney smiled when her favorite character, Elmo, appeared. They repeated this routine every single day. Alicia did not complain but instead took pride in her daughter, her job, and her will to prevail.

Some of the jurors were moved to tears as Ben walked Mr. Carter through the video—seeing the warm environment that welcomed and nurtured children with a variety of physical and mental challenges—and they asked questions about the kinds of treatments Sydney received at the school. The video showed Sydney's physical therapy to increase her muscle movement as well as teachers interacting with her, hoping to promote any gain possible. Ben knew he walked a razor-thin line when pointing out the challenges Alicia and Sydney faced. He had to show adversity and pain to move a jury to find in Alicia's favor and award real damages. But he had to avoid pandering, looking melodramatic, and even desensitizing a jury by overplaying his hand. If they saw too much, by the end of the case, the tragedy and horror would wear off. The video struck the right note, and Ben dismissed Mr. Carter as soon as he was able to. Marston asked no questions of Principal Carter.

Julie Jacobs took the witness stand next. Julie was a professional life-care planner whose job consisted of taking medical records, physician orders, and therapy needs prescribed by various professionals to formulate a comprehensive plan for the care and treatment of patients throughout their lives—and then attach those needs to an actual cost. Julie had spoken to Sydney's physicians, therapists, and teachers and spent extensive time with Alicia and Sydney. She presented detailed findings and conclusions, taking over two hours to describe in scrupulous detail what Sydney would require and how expensive it would be.

Ben knew the risk of boring the jury but also knew if he were to get the type of money this case deserved, he needed concrete proof of both injury and need that would stand up on appeal. Juries were famous for awarding damages in an attempt to retroactively fix a situation as opposed to penalizing a bad actor. Ben wanted both. From past experience, he knew there would be at least two, if not more, women on the jury taking detailed notes that, in deliberation, could be used by the jury to substantiate a large award.

Marston, a seasoned pro who had cross-examined many life-care planners, knew very well what worked and what did not in this situation. He wanted to shave some money off the claim but did not want to appear callous to the family and this little girl. Marston spent twenty minutes questioning Julie about selected details. Occasionally, he raised one eyebrow dramatically like a father considering a child's college tuition bill. He played to the conservatives on the jury, hoping that if they did rule for Alicia and Sydney, those jurors would help temper the amount.

The proof came in beautifully from the life-care planner, and Marston had not laid a glove on her. Ben had successfully established the nuts and bolts of his case. Details like medical care and long-term economics were not exciting and never make the movies, but in real trials, they are crucial elements to any major tort case.

Judge Jones adjourned court for lunch. Ben had an hour to get his mind ready for his next witness. There would be no room for error. He did not dare look at his phone. He knew it was selfish, but he had to be completely focused on the task at hand.

A professional gladiatorial confrontation was looming: Ben and Dr. Kirkwood. Years ago, it was unconventional for a plaintiff's lawyer like Ben to call as a witness the defendant.

Ben debunked this theory many times. Dr. Kirkwood is highly educated, and his counsel wanted to demonstrate Dr. Kirkwood's knowledge and expertise by asking him open-ended, friendly questions that would allow Dr. Kirkwood to wax on about his education and accomplishments. If Ben waited for Marston to call Dr. Kirkwood, Marston would frame the entire examination, spending the initial hour allowing the doctor to impress and charm the jury. In that situation, Ben would have to undo all the goodwill established by Marston on his direct examination and walk a thinner line in challenging Dr. Kirkwood.

However, if Ben called Dr. Kirkwood first, Ben could go after the doctor, expose his weaknesses, and score big points creating a negative first impression on the jury. Then, when Dr. Kirkwood's friendly lawyer, Marston, followed up, the jury would see Dr. Kirkwood through a different lens. Ben always called the defendant doctor as part of his case-in-chief. The other benefit of this strategy was having Ben's expert in the courtroom—Dr. Bell, sitting in the back—taking notes and preparing to dispute any misstatements made by Dr. Kirkwood. This kept Dr. Kirkwood in check and made him less likely to exaggerate or misstate the medicine.

Judge Jones called the court to order and instructed the bailiff to collect the jury. Sometimes, after the lunch, the jury's focus waned, but today, they would witness the fight they wanted to see.

"Mr. Jennings, call your next witness," Judge Jones ordered.

Ben stood up and looked at the jury. "Plaintiff calls Dr. Kirkwood to the stand," he said formally. The jury perked, surprised at Ben calling Dr. Kirkwood. Dr. Kirkwood was not shocked. Marston prepared him extensively for this eventuality. Dr. Kirkwood stood up, walked confidently around Ben and in front of the jury box, stopped, looked at the bailiff, and took the oath. Dr. Kirkwood unbuttoned his jacket and took his seat, adjusting the stem microphone to his height of just under six feet. Dr. Kirkwood looked younger than his years with wavy blond hair and boyish features. He wore a grey suit, a blue button-down shirt, and a specialty tie of puzzle pieces in support of children with autism. He looked at the jury with self-assurance and smiled.

"Good afternoon, Dr. Kirkwood," Ben said courteously. He knew he did not have license to attack Dr. Kirkwood before he had earned it. Doctors enjoyed elevated status and being aggressive with him too early would turn off jurors.

"Good afternoon, Mr. Jennings." Dr. Kirkwood smiled, demonstrating civility but not familiarity. Dr. Kirkwood felt prepared because Marston knew almost every move in Ben's bag. Days ago, in Marston's office, Kip used a script drafted by Marston to brutally cross-examine Dr. Kirkwood, readying him for what awaited. With the other witnesses on direct, Ben stood behind the jury box to focus the jury on the witnesses and their answers. Now, crossing Dr. Kirkwood, he moved closer toward the witness to focus the jury on himself. Ben did not want the examination to linger but needed it to last long enough to score points. Ben did not have to win this skirmish, but he certainly could not afford to lose. He held the advantage of asking the questions. Dr. Kirkwood possessed the advantage of medical expertise.

Ben went through the basics of Dr. Kirkwood's educational background to steal thunder from Marston. Ben downplayed the doctor's resume so that Marston would look silly and rehearsed during his examination if he tried to repeat the same questions to give Kirkwood a chance to play up his accomplishments. Ben covered Dr. Kirkwood's background, holding Dr. Kirkwood's resume in his hand.

"Dr. Kirkwood, we have gone through your education and training. But one thing we have not covered is radiology. Dr. Kirkwood, what is a radiologist?"

Dr. Kirkwood turned toward the jury as he was taught and said, "A radiologist is a physician trained to read and interpret various radiographic studies."

"You say radiographic studies," Ben said. "Would that include what are known as x-rays?"

"Yes," Dr. Kirkwood said.

"So you are telling these ladies and gentlemen of the jury that there is an entire specialty of reading x-rays called radiology?"

"Yes."

Ben sat the resume down on his table. "And at Lutheran Hospital, when Sydney Landers was being treated, were there radiologists working there?"

"Yes."

"Were those same radiologists available twenty-four hours a day?"

"Yes."

"If you so wished, you could request a radiologist to read x-rays of your patients?"

"Yes." Dr. Kirkwood saw where this going and turned to the jury to answer this question. "But one was not necessary in the case of Sydney because I was equally as qualified to read her x-rays."

"Wait a second." Ben pointed his index finger into the air. "You are telling us that you, Dr. Kirkwood, a neonatologist, is able to read x-rays as well as the physicians whose specific training and only job is to read them?"

"I am saying," Dr. Kirkwood was now a little more defiant, this time staring at Ben, "that I was perfectly able to read the x-rays I ordered for Sydney Landers."

Ben opened his jacket and put one hand in his pocket. "You say that, but really, with all due respect, you were not perfectly able to read Sydney's x-rays."

"I disagree. There is a real question as to whether or not the x-rays showed free air."

"Oh, really?" Ben raised his eyebrows and scratched his head. "You see, I don't see it that way. And the reason I don't see it that way is that there was, in fact, free air in Sydney Landers, indicating a perforated intestine."

Dr. Kirkwood again turned to the jury and calmly answered, "Mr. Jennings, it is easy to say that in hindsight, but in real time, the x-rays did not appear to show free air."

"But here is what I know." Ben waved his finger. "X-rays were taken, correct?"

"Yes."

"Within an hour, Sydney became septic and suffered cardiopulmonary arrest?" Ben nodded.

"Yes, that is true, but I still say the x-rays did not show it," Dr. Kirkwood defied.

"But we certainly know, in hindsight, that there was free air."

"Perhaps, Mr. Jennings, but it was not shown."

Ben looked at Dr. Kirkwood quizzically. "Well, that is funny, because the same radiologists that you refused to consult with later read the same x-rays and described, and I quote, the 'presence of free air.'"

"That was their opinion," Dr. Kirkwood said sternly.

"And that opinion was validated by the results?"

"Again, hindsight is 20/20."

"They looked at the same x-rays as you did, so had you given them a chance, they would have seen the free air in real time?" Ben reasoned.

"Objection! Calls for speculation!" Marston quickly stood up.

"Not really," Ben said, turning to Marston. "It only calls for observation."

"Lawyers approach!" Judge Jones said firmly.

The two lawyers circled around opposite ends of the counsel table and met at the bench, both lawyers leaning in to hear the whispers of Judge Jones. The court reporter had an earpiece with a speaker at the bench to allow her to make a record of the conversation. At the sidebar out of the jury's hearing, Jones admonished Ben in a stern whisper. "Don't start with the shenanigans Mr. Jennings. Mr. Owens, your objection is overruled."

The lawyers resumed their places. Ben needed to let the jury know he won the objection. It was petty, but what the hell. He feigned annoyance at being disturbed during his questioning.

"As I was saying before being interrupted, Dr. Kirkwood, if the radiologist had the x-rays at the time you saw them, they would have seen the same free air they later saw after the horses were out of the barn?"

"We have no way of knowing that." Dr. Kirkwood said. But the question hit him hard, and he knew he looked bad. Ben had scored points with the jury. Ben went back to his seat. Stephanie handed him the one record that had been dictated by Dr. Kirkwood.

"Yes, we do!" Ben raised his voice. "Because an x-ray is like a snapshot, frozen in time, correct?"

"Yes," conceded Dr. Kirkwood.

"So the same x-ray you reviewed and the x-ray they reviewed was the exact same snapshot of Sydney's intestines?"

"Yes."

Ben stood no more than eight feet away. "As I understand your previous testimony, Dr. Kirkwood, this is the only record you dictated relative to the day Sydney's anoxic event occurred?"

"That is correct," Dr. Kirkwood answered.

"As such, you have no other memory of the events surrounding that day?"

"That is correct."

"And just to make sure I am clear: It was you who ordered the serial x-rays for Sydney Landers."

"Yes."

"And it was you who decided when, where, and how they would be done?"

"Yes, and those instructions completely complied with the standard of care."

"Oh, did they?" Ben turned to look at him, baiting him.

"Yes, they did," Dr. Kirkwood said defiantly.

Ben spent a few minutes going over the record drafted by Kirkwood and made sure to lock him into his testimony so that he could use it later against Marston's experts. Then, Ben gambled a little bit. He asked a question that he did not know the answer to. But he believed he could take Dr. Kirkwood's answer in a positive direction no matter what the response.

"Dr. Kirkwood, after Sydney suffered her cardiopulmonary event, she was transported just across the street to undergo corrective surgery to repair her bowel. Is that correct?"

"I believe so," Dr. Kirkwood answered, now a little nervous because this had not been covered in his discovery deposition or trial preparation.

"So when you went to check on Sydney after the surgery, how was she doing?"

"Sir, I am not sure what you are talking about," Dr. Kirkwood was genuinely confused.

Ben followed up. "Well, I am sure you walked across the street to check on your patient, didn't you?"

"She was no longer my patient," Dr. Kirkwood said.

"What?" Ben cocked his head sideways.

The jurors exchanged stunned glances with each other.

Ben stopped, let that soak in, and made sure the jury had time to process the answer. After a pause, Ben asked thoughtfully, "You mean to tell me that this little girl, who had all of these problems that you attempted to treat for three weeks, suffered a terrible event that resulted in an emergency surgery, and you did not walk the hundred yards necessary to check on her?"

"She was no longer my patient. I saw no reason to do anything," Dr. Kirkwood said coldly.

No matter how much a witness is prepared, pressure situations bring out the real person sooner or later. More than a few jurors looked surprised by Dr. Kirkwood's indifference. The doctor could smile and grin all he wanted, but that exchange alone spoke volumes about Dr. Robert Kirkwood. Ben stood still, just staring at Dr. Kirkwood. He could spend another hour splitting hairs about the minutiae of medicine, but he wanted to leave the jury with this lasting impression. Additional questions would only give Dr. Kirkwood a chance to redeem himself.

"Your Honor," Ben said, "I pass the witness." And he sat down.

Marston rose. "Your Honor, may we have a brief break to set up for our examination of Dr. Kirkwood?"

Marston did not need time to set up his well-oiled machine but instead wanted a ten-minute pause for the jury to hopefully forget what his client had just said and to calibrate his examination. Ben had taken an unconventional approach to cross Kirkwood. Most practitioners would take a full day grinding over every detail ad nauseum in an ego-gratifying exercise to demonstrate to the jury their comprehensive knowledge of medicine. But Ben used The Sage's advice, employing surprise and misdirection. His examination of Dr. Kirkwood took less than forty-five minutes. The jury had no idea how long these things usually took. Lawyers had been known to take five hours in such an examination. This brief examination now set the bar for the rest of the trial. If Marston took a long time with Dr. Bell, he risked annoying the jury with what then might appear as wasting their time. Marston's team had size and bulk as strengths, but its weakness was an inability to adjust tactics in response to changing conditions. Ben had thrown them for a loop, and Marston couldn't lumber into an effective response fast enough. To Marston, to shift tactics mid-stream and diverge from the playbook was untenable. Marston would not shorten his examination time or change his question list but instead stick to the script that served him so well in every other trial.

Marston began his examination as if Dr. Kirkwood had just taken the stand. The two danced in sync with a PowerPoint video show displaying Dr. Kirkwood's education, accomplishments, publications, and association with professional societies. It excluded nothing, even including several pictures of his age-appropriate Barbie wife, and perfectly scrubbed teenaged children, his daughter in an angelic white dress and son in classic khakis and a blue button-down shirt. The American dream on full display before the jury who suddenly hated their own less-than-perfect lives. This move would fail in class-resentful England, but because America is the land of aspiration, the jury admired an accomplished man. This also put a face on the family that would suffer if Dr. Kirkwood were blamed by the jury.

Dr. Kirkwood took over the video screen, using a laser pointer and turning the courtroom into a classroom to demonstrate his incredible intelligence and command of medicine. Dr. Kirkwood explained NEC and why it was so dangerous.

"Dr. Kirkwood," began Marston, "are you familiar with the recognized standard of care for neonatologists in this community?"

Kirkwood turned to the jury and said confidently, "Yes, I am."

Marston continued. "Did you comply with that standard of care in your treatment of Sydney Landers?"

"Yes, I most certainly did."

"Dr. Kirkwood, please explain to the jury how you complied."

Kirkwood turned to the jury, steepled his hands, and raised his brow. "I care about all of my patients. I work night and day to make sure they are given the best care possible. I have examined thousands of x-rays and have the requisite experience and knowledge to make appropriate interpretations. I ordered the correct x-rays. I also ordered hundreds of other appropriate treatments for Sydney Landers. I spent two weeks looking after that little girl as though she were my own. It is a crying shame what happened to her, but it was not my fault. Just because a bad outcome happens does not mean the doctor was negligent. I used my best medical judgment. To be brought before you and accused of medical negligence is an outrage, and I take exception to it."

Marston paused to let Kirkwood's well-scripted answer seep into the jury's consciousness. Then, he said quietly, "That is all I have of this witness." Marston unbuttoned his suit jacket, placed his notes and pen down purposefully, and took his seat.

"Mr. Jennings, any redirect?" asked Judge Jones.

"Briefly, Your Honor, please." Ben stuck to his strategy of being short and sweet. "Dr. Kirkwood, just a couple of questions. They call for true or false answers. I would appreciate you answering in that fashion. If you need to explain, I am more than happy to have you do so after you have answered the question. The radiologist, who later read the x-ray that you had ordered and reviewed, stated there was free air present on that x-ray?"

"Yes. But like I said, I don't agree there was free air present on the x-ray."

Ben looked disapprovingly. "Doctor, we can do this the easy way or hard way. True or false. I realize you disagree, but the radiologist—educated, trained, and paid to review x-rays—testified that when he reviewed the x-ray, he saw free air?"

Exasperated, Kirkwood replied, "True."

"And we know, yes, in hindsight, that there was, in fact, a perforation in Sydney's bowel at the time you read her x-ray and found no free air?"

"Hindsight is 20/20," Kirkwood retorted.

Ben scolded, "Dr. Kirkwood, true or false? If you are having difficulty answering the question, you are free to ask either Judge Jones or Mr. Owens if you need to answer it. I can save you the time and tell you that you, indeed, have to answer the question."

Dr. Kirkwood sighed. "True."

"Further," Ben continued, "had that radiologist seen and reviewed that x-ray and reported free air, the standard of care would have required you to immediately make a surgical consultation to make needed repairs on Sydney's bowel?"

"True."

"And had she received that surgical intervention, more likely than not she would not have suffered the cardiopulmonary arrest she did several hours later that led to her cerebral palsy?" Ben pressed.

"I don't want to speculate about what would have happened."

"Neither does Ms. Landers, but that is all she is left with."

"Objection!" Marston bellowed.

"I withdraw the question, Judge. The jury will make their own judgments," Ben said as he sat down in disgust.

Judge Jones said, "Lawyers, it's 3:30 p.m., who do you plan on calling next?"

"We intend to call Dr. Bell as our expert," Ben responded.

"How long do you anticipate his direct taking?"

"Hard to say, Judge, but I believe I should be able to get close by 5:00 p.m.," Ben answered.

Judge Jones spoke to the courtroom, "Ladies and gentlemen, we are now going to take our afternoon break. Be back here in fifteen minutes."

This was going to work out just right. Ben wanted the jury to leave for the day immediately after his direct examination of Dr. Bell. They would eat dinner and sleep thinking of Dr. Bell's supportive testimony without corruption from Marston's cross. The only negative would be that Marston would have the night to perfect his cross-examination. Ben saw this as a minimal risk because Marston's internal teleprompter was locked and loaded with his cross-exam script written a month ago. Little would change.

CHAPTER 21

"Mr. Jennings, call your next witness."

"The plaintiff calls Dr. Martin Bell."

Dr. Martin Bell took the oath and assumed his position on the witness stand. Tennessee's arcane medical malpractice law requires a potential expert to jump through multiple hoops prior to offering opinions. Jurors roll their eyes at the endless required foundational questions, but failure to comply results in the exclusion of the witness. Tennessee is one of the few states that has a contiguous state rule requiring any expert witness to come from Tennessee or a state that physically touches the state of Tennessee. Very few Tennessee physicians will testify within the state on behalf of plaintiffs, making the pool of potential available experts who will speak against another doctor extremely small. Next is the locality rule. In Tennessee, a doctor must demonstrate specific knowledge of the locality in which he is testifying, so examination must ascertain the doctor's familiarity with the community, leading to hours and hours of deposition testimony about the composition of the city council, the location of the Delta gates at the airport, and the specific number of Black kids enrolled in Shelby County schools. Rafts of Tennessee cases exclude world renowned experts for failure to know the precise population of Memphis, Tennessee. This is just one of the many Tennessee protectionist statutes bought and paid for by the medical and pharmaceutical lobby.

After a twenty-minute tango of Dr. Bell answering innocuous questions such as the number of beds at Lutheran Hospital, specialties afforded at the hospital, and curriculum offered at the University of Tennessee College of Health

Sciences, the undisputedly competent Dr. Martin Bell was allowed to discuss Sydney Landers' care and treatment. Dr. Bell gave his own description of NEC, its causes and treatments.

"Dr. Bell, are there different stages of NEC?" asked Ben.

"Yes. There are three different stages of NEC," Dr. Bell answered and described these stages to the jury in great detail.

"Dr. Bell, you seem very familiar with the staging of NEC. How did that come about?"

"Because I am the one who developed it," Dr. Bell said.

"Excuse me?" Ben turned, put his hand behind his ear, and feigned needing to hear this answer again.

"Yes. Back in the 70s, I was dealing with NEC patients and decided the categorization needed to be bolstered. So I studied and researched and continued working with patients until we came up with a staging system to better treat the children."

Ben walked around the counsel table, and Stephanie handed him a printed document. He read it and put it back down. "Was that criteria accepted by other physicians in the country?" Ben asked.

"Actually, the world," Dr. Bell responded. "The Bell criteria is the accepted method for staging NEC cases around the world."

"Does that mean it was named after you?"

Dr. Bell looked somewhat embarrassed and answered, "Yes, as a matter of fact it is."

Ben summarized. "So the criteria for staging and treating NEC was developed by you, named after you, and is now accepted worldwide as the preferred diagnosis for the condition known as NEC?"

"Yes."

"Dr. Bell, would it help you to better explain NEC to the jury with some visual aids?"

"Yes, it would."

Stephanie, already prepared, hit several keys on her laptop, and a diagram appeared on the video screen.

"Dr. Bell, please tell the jury what we are seeing on the screen."

Dr. Bell spent the next ten minutes using a laser pointer and several diagrams to explain NEC and its various stages.

Ben continued, "Based on that, this may seem like a stupid question, but Tennessee law requires me to ask it. Dr. Bell, are you familiar with the standard of care for the diagnosis and treatment of the condition known as NEC?"

Bell gave his warm grandfatherly smile as if indulging a child. "Yes, Mr. Jennings, I believe I am."

"Dr. Bell, do you have an opinion as to whether Dr. Kirkwood complied with the standard of care for the diagnosis and treatment of the condition known as NEC in this community?"

"Yes. I believe that Dr. Kirkwood failed to comply with the standard of care."

Ben went back to the table and exchanged the printed document for a legal pad with handwriting on it. He pulled his black Monteblanc rollerball pen out of his jacket and removed the top. "Doctor, please explain to the jury the basis of your opinions."

Dr. Bell smiled formally and turned to the jury. "Dr. Kirkwood fell below the standard of care because he missed the free air on the x-rays. He is a neonatologist and not a radiologist. Radiologists go through lengthy education and training. Lutheran Hospital keeps a team of radiologists on call and on site for the purpose of reading x-rays just like those of Sydney Landers."

Ben asked, "You heard Dr. Kirkwood claim to have the competence to also read the x-rays. Do you have a response to that?"

Dr. Bell dropped his head and frowned before looking up to the jury. "Well, Dr. Kirkwood may claim to have the knowledge, training, and experience to read such x-rays, but we have proof that this is not the case. And the proof is that Dr. Kirkwood missed the free air present in Sydney Landers, which was later seen by a radiologist who clearly observed free air. I guess my point is that if you are going to undertake a task that is outside of your specialty, you better darn well do it correctly, or there is going to be a big problem. It appears to me that Dr. Kirkwood's arrogance got the best of him. One of the many benefits of large hospitals like Lutheran is the various disciplines at your disposal. The radiologist was right there and could have read it, but Dr. Kirkwood's hubris overrode his judgment."

"Dr. Bell, I direct your attention back to the video screen where Ms. Mann has kindly put up an x-ray. Have you seen this before?"

"Yes. It is the x-ray taken of Sydney Landers." Dr. Bell used the laser pointer. "This section here is Sydney's small intestine. And here—" Dr. Bell moved the pointer slightly "—is where the free air can be seen."

"And once again, what is the significance of seeing this 'free air'?"

Dr. Bell turned toward the jury. "The significance is that it means Sydney had a hole in her intestine and needed surgery immediately."

"Did that surgery happen immediately as required?"

"No."

"Dr. Bell, do you believe Dr. Kirkwood was negligent?"

"Yes, I think he was negligent in not asking a radiologist to read the film and compounded that error in failing to identify the free air. It's the very reason you call a radiologist."

Ben signaled Stephanie to turn of the video screen, and then turned back to Dr. Bell.

"Is it your opinion that Dr. Kirkwood's negligence caused her anoxic brain injury?"

"Absolutely!" Dr. Bell responded emphatically. "The reason the serial x-rays are performed is to provide a constant vigilance to guard against the sepsis that can cause cardiopulmonary arrest. The records show she was deprived of oxygen for approximately six minutes, which without a doubt caused her cerebral palsy."

Ben looked down at this legal pad. "Dr. Bell, what do you say to someone who claims that perhaps Sydney was born with brain damage and that there is no way to connect the arrest to the brain injury?"

Dr. Bell again turned to the jury. "I would say they are not very smart or informed. It is a ridiculous claim. There is absolutely zero evidence of any prenatal issues, and my review of the birth records also record a completely normal birth. I am completely confident Sydney's brain injury was caused by Dr. Kirkwood's failure to one, consult with a radiologist; two, properly read the x-ray once he decided to do it alone; and three, get a timely surgical consult."

Ben used his pen to point at the witness. "Dr. Bell, how do you know that a surgical consult would have resulted in a different outcome?"

"Because, Mr. Jennings, just as the hospital had radiologists on call, they also had general surgeons available as well. Again, this is a major metropolitan hospital that plans for events just like this. Time was of the essence. Had the surgeon had that extra two or three hours prior to her arrest, he would have more likely than not corrected the problem in her bowel."

"Dr. Bell, have you ever encountered a patient such as Sydney?"

"Yes," Dr. Bell said, "Many, many times. And as soon as free air is identified, it is all hands on deck. It is an emergent situation that requires immediate attention. The bottom line is Dr. Kirkwood failed Sydney Landers."

Ben handed Dr. Bell a stack of medical bills pre-marked as exhibits and signaled Stephanie to display pictures of them on the screen.

"Dr. Bell, have you reviewed these medical bills?"

"Yes, I have."

"Are these charges in line with like or similar medical charges in this community?"

"Yes, I believe they are."

"Dr. Bell, what is the total of the medical bills incurred by Alicia Landers for the care and treatment of Sydney after she suffered her cardiopulmonary arrest?"

"$285,102.00."

Several jurors hurriedly scribbled the number down in their notebooks. It was a good sign but by no means a guarantee. Early in his career, Ben had been fooled into drawing too many conclusions by observing when jurors took notes. Ben wrapped it up.

"Dr. Bell, have all of the opinions you expressed today been based on a reasonable degree of medical certainty?"

"Yes, they most certainly have."

As it was approaching 5:00 p.m., Judge Jones adjourned for the day. Marston wouldn't get his cross of Bell until tomorrow. Ben and Stephanie exchanged knowing glances while collecting their papers. The day had gone as well as possible. Dr. Bell made a solid and convincing witness. His charming, grandfatherly disposition clearly won over some jurors. Ben pulled in a deep breath and exhaled, releasing the stress of the day. He turned around and looked at Alicia and Sydney, who were looking right at him. Ben knelt down to the little girl and put his finger in her hand. She couldn't quite grasp it but gave him a smile. His eyes moved to Alicia. Her weary face showed the pain of the past two years. The stress of being in a fishbowl all day with twelve sets of eyes on her took some getting used to.

"Alicia, you are doing great." Ben put his hand on her shoulder. "Tomorrow afternoon, it's your turn to testify. I have no doubt you will be great."

"Ben, I am so nervous. I don't want to mess up this case."

"You won't, Alicia. Just be yourself and tell the truth. The facts are on our side. This is your chance to tell your story, and I am confident they will love you."

Alicia stood up, and Stephanie took Sydney so that Alicia could get her things together. For Ben, it had been a solid day of proof, but tomorrow would challenge whether Dr. Bell could hold up. Many a brilliant expert on direct has folded like a cheap suit once exposed to the bright lights of cross-examination.

Tomorrow, Marston would bring the heat. He would do everything in his power to discredit Dr. Bell. Since Dr. Bell's opinions were hard to dispute, Marston would likely make it personal and attempt to goad Dr. Bell into some misstatements. After Dr. Bell, Alicia Landers would take center stage.

CHAPTER 22

When they returned to the office from court, Kip and Steve worked on the motion for directed verdict that would follow Ben's proof and scoured the research service, Westlaw, for every potential loophole that might be used to convince Judge Jones to dismiss the case on a technicality. A motion for directed verdict is a motion submitted by the defendants at the close of the plaintiff's case-in-chief, asking the judge to dismiss the case because the plaintiff failed to prove an essential element required to even allow the jury to consider the case. Granting such motions was exceedingly rare, but defense lawyers took every chance they could to take the case out of the jury's hands.

This was Steve's first trial, and he showed signs that it may be his last. Steve had spent no meaningful time with his wife and their young children for weeks, causing extra strain at the house. He found himself on LinkedIn looking for potential openings at less competitive firms. Besides, if they lost this trial, Marston would be looking for a scapegoat to fire, and Steve was low man.

The veteran Kip smelled partnership, and his ambition overcame any physical discomfort the job presented. He reached for the elusive golden ticket that he believed would change his life. Many times, it takes lawyers ten years of practice to realize the juice was not worth the squeeze. Kip was on his eighth year and could smell partnership.

***

Marston relied on the statistic that 80 percent of all

Tennessee jury trials against doctors and hospitals resulted in defense verdicts. But if he was honest with himself, he had never faced an opponent as skilled as Ben who also had such a meritorious case. Marston tossed and turned. Sleep was difficult with no relief in sight. He wanted nothing more than to drink whiskey and pop a few of those happy pills.

Instead, he ran over tomorrow's cross in his mind, rehearsing to himself what he would say to Dr. Bell. Marston's standard bag of tricks for experts consisted of discrediting not the actual opinions but the man himself. Dr. Bell posed big problems for Marston because not only was he the preeminent authority on the subject of NEC, but the man demonstrated a kind, grandfatherly presence. The jury would not take kindly to Marston attacking Wilford Brimley or Santa Claus, and Bell looked like both. Marston debated between using the short-bomb storm-cross or a drawn-out affair, stretched to dilute the sharp, crisp testimony presented yesterday. In the end, Marston was a slave to habit and would not diverge from a well-oiled game plan.

Marston also readied himself for the subsequent cross of Alicia Landers, which would be fraught with peril. She held her head like royalty, and the male jurors would feel smitten and protective. The questions were whether her haunting good looks would turn off the jury and if she could connect with the mothers of the group. Alicia's deposition testimony impressed him, and he knew he traveled in a minefield when he faced cross-examining her.

***

The new day dawned, and Marston now had a crack at his most important cross. Thinking ahead, he knew he would have a difficult time getting Bell to diverge from his opinions, but Marston needed to give the jury the illusion of contradiction or lack of credibility. Marston planned on following the defense lawyer's playbook by asking a bunch of questions not related to the fact or opinions of the case, such as how much he was being paid, what Ben told him about the case, and when he formulated his opinions. Plaintiff's lawyers call that "focusing on the margins" because it has nothing to do with the substance of the case. It is meant to distract the jury by implying that Dr. Bell was paid to give certain opinions as opposed to being paid for his time. The jury had now settled into a routine and adjusted to their hurry-up-and-wait lives. Some of the jurors had started to dress better after spending hours each day in a room with lawyers and staff dressing to the nines.

After court opened, Judge Jones began: "Good morning ladies and gentlemen. We will start today with the defense cross-examination of Dr. Bell. Dr. Bell, will you please take the stand?"

The small and elderly man with a spry step dutifully made his way around the counsel table and took his seat on the witness stand. He held a manila folder in his lap with his handwritten notes. Judge Jones turned to Marston. "Mr. Owens, you may proceed."

Marston rose from his chair, his long, tall frame creating a sharp contrast with the short, round Bell. Marston wanted to set the tone early by attempting to make Dr. Bell uncomfortable.

"Dr. Bell, you are from all the way up in St. Louis. Do you know how many neonatologists are right here in Memphis?"

"No, I don't," Bell responded simply.

"I can tell you that not one of them has come to this stand and criticized Dr. Kirkwood."

"I am sure you are right," Bell answered.

"I am sure I am right also," Marston said as he moved to the lectern. "Besides, you are getting paid handsomely for your opinions."

"Sir, I am being paid for my time and not my opinions."

"I am right because those Memphis neonatologists know Dr. Kirkwood was not negligent."

"I would not say that. More likely he is friends with them all," Dr. Bell chirped back. Dr. Bell was not an easy victim to bully.

"Right," Marston said sarcastically. "How much did Mr. Jennings have to pay you to get you down here these last two days?"

"Mr. Jennings paid me $30,000 for some of my past time, my trial preparation, and my time testifying today."

"Whew," Marston almost whistled as he spoke. "That is some good cash when you can get it. Do you think he would have paid you $30,000 if your opinion had been that Dr. Kirkwood had done everything right?"

"Objection," Ben stood up. "Your Honor, this is inappropriate, and Mr. Owens knows it."

Without waiting for a response, Judge Jones said, "Sustained. Move on, Mr. Owens."

But it was the question that mattered and not the answer. Marston could go on forever with snippy questions designed to cast doubt about Dr. Bell's credibility.

"Dr. Bell, you have never practiced at Lutheran Hospital, have you?"

"No, sir."

"You have never practiced in Memphis?"

"No, I have not."

"Dr. Bell, you would agree with me that experts disagree all the time?"

"On certain matters, yes."

"You agree that Dr. Kirkwood should have ordered the x-rays?"

"Yes."

"You don't know how many x-rays Dr. Kirkwood has reviewed?"

"No, but whatever the number, it certainly was not enough to read this one correctly."

"Doctor, you certainly don't require perfection from a physician do you?"

"No, I expect competence," Dr. Bell said firmly.

"Do you now?" Marston said sarcastically. "Dr. Bell, have you ever made a mistake?"

"I am sure I have."

"And you didn't get dragged down to court for it, did you?" Marston raised his eyebrows.

"No, but I also did not give a little girl permanent brain damage." Dr. Bell refused to concede ground. Marston would not be deterred. He switched gears to his medical hat and went over the statistics for children born with NEC, the death rate, and the danger of the condition. Bell conceded the risk of the condition and difficulty of the treatment.

"Dr. Bell, everything is clear in hindsight?" Marston walked toward the jury box, iPad in hand.

"Yes, I would say it is," Dr. Bell answered.

"But as an expert, you cannot say what should be done in hindsight. You must use judgment from real time, and you were not there in real time."

"Mr. Owens, only Dr. Kirkwood was there in real time. There would be no such thing as a lawsuit if experts had to be present while the events were happening. It is a ridiculous statement. But had I been there, I most certainly would have availed myself of the trained radiologists." Dr. Bell was a pro and would not be intimidated.

"How much time does it take to get a consult from a radiologist at Lutheran Hospital?" Marston asked.

"I don't know precisely," Bell said.

"You don't know generally either, do you?"

"I know there were radiologists on call, and I know how long it takes in my hospital. I also know that even a little extra time would have saved Sydney Landers from going into cardiopulmonary arrest." This was not Dr. Bell's first rodeo, and he would not back down.

Marston would not back down either. "Dr. Bell, is it easy, coming from the ivory tower and criticizing a man in hindsight?"

"I would not say it's easy, and I wish it had not been necessary."

"But you agree with me, Dr. Bell, that just because a bad result occurs does not mean a doctor departed from the standard of care?"

"Yes," Bell responded.

"And you yourself have had patients who have suffered bad outcomes, have you not?"

"I certainly have."

"You have had patients even die on your watch, haven't you?"

"Regrettably, yes," Dr. Bell conceded.

"And for all of those bad outcomes and deaths, you do not consider yourself to have departed from the standard of care one single time in all of those occasions?"

"Correct. I did not deviate from the standard of care."

"But today, after having been paid $30,000 for your efforts, you dare to tell this fine jury that Dr. Kirkwood departed from the standard of care for this bad outcome?"

"Again, sir. I was paid for my time and not my opinions. And—"

Marston interrupted. "I have heard enough."

"May I finish my answer please, Mr. Owens?"

Judge Jones interrupted. "Yes, Dr. Bell, please finish your answer."

Dr. Bell turned to the jury. "Thank you, Your Honor. I would not have agreed to testify against Dr. Kirkwood had I not been completely convinced that he failed Sydney Landers and departed from the standard of care. I take my oath and my career very seriously and would never dare to cheapen it by selling my opinions. I am offended by your suggestion and resent the implication."

Marston had been hurt by the answer and, in a rare lapse of discipline, could not resist the lawyer comeback. "Dr. Bell, you will know when I offend you, and it will be neither implied or suggested. I am through with this witness, Your Honor."

Dr. Bell had performed wonderfully, and Ben had to make the quick decision of whether or not to redirect to clean up some the points made on cross. However, the end of cross would leave an indelible impression and he did not want to spoil it. The mechanical lawyer would redirect for fifteen minutes, the artist chose to sit down.

"No more questions from the plaintiff. Thank you, Dr. Bell."

CHAPTER 23

N ow, it was time for the star of the show. No matter how well Ben and Stephanie did, trials ultimately come down to the plaintiff and whether the jury likes and believes them. Along with her stunning looks, Alicia carried herself with a moving, quiet dignity. She had been dealt a terrible hand with Sydney but had handled herself with grace. The jury had watched her interact with her special needs daughter with a gentle, motherly hand all week. Marston would have his hands full on cross. Whatever the outcome of the trial, it would be hard to criticize this lady.

Before Alicia could testify, the issue of where to put Sydney during that time needed to be resolved. Alicia had held her in her lap during the entire trial and had no outside help. Finally, after lengthy discussion, Judge Jones determined that instead of taking the witness stand, Alicia would be permitted to testify from the chair she had occupied during the week. This arrangement benefited the case because it subtly reminded juries just how difficult even the most rudimentary of activities became with a special needs' child. Further, the jury's eyes would be on both Alicia and Sydney during her entire testimony.

Now, the conventional order of attorney and witness was reversed: Ben, next to the witness box and Alicia, behind the counsel table holding Sydney. The jury had watched Alicia for four days, but this was the first time they would hear her speak. Her voice was clear, crisp, and articulate but not forced or pretentious. She came from a neighborhood that did not emphasize diction, yet she had managed to teach herself, while not drawing the ire of her friends.

Ben and Alicia went through the basics, covering her childhood and education at Trezvant and then Mississippi Valley. She told the jury of her dreams and wishes and how Sydney had put them on hold. She did not complain or act resentful for the burden thrust upon her. Alicia testified that she hoped to someday become a lawyer herself and dreamed of providing a better life for Sydney and herself. Alicia described her relationship with Sydney's father and managed to not appear bitter. She was even hopeful that they could someday make their relationship work. Ben laid the foundation, and now, it was time for Alicia to talk about what happened after she gave birth to Sydney.

"Alicia, now tell the jury about your stay in the hospital."

Alicia looked down at Sydney and then back at the jury. "It was all so surreal. I delivered prematurely, and I didn't know what to expect. The delivery went fine. Then, the doctor told me told me they needed to keep Sydney in the hospital until she gained weight."

"So did you stay?"

"Well, they discharged me the second day, so I went home without my baby. That was so strange. But I went to the hospital every single day to see her and be with her. They let me hold her and rock her. They were very kind."

"When did you meet Dr. Kirkwood?" Ben asked.

"He was one of the neonatologists who took care of her," Alicia smiled. "Before Sydney, I had no idea what a neonatologist was. Boy, do I now." She switched Sydney to her other arm. "Dr. Kirkwood told us they needed to get weight on Sydney but that he was worried about NEC. Of course, I had no idea what that was. It was all so scary. But I kept coming every day to make sure my baby was okay."

"Alicia, now, I want to direct you to the day Sydney suffered her cardiopulmonary arrest. How did you find out?"

"Well, I walked into the neonatology unit like I always did, and one of the nurses met me at the door and looked really upset. She told me that something happened to Sydney. I lost my breath. She was doing so great; I didn't know what it was."

"Then what happened?"

Alicia took a deep breath and appeared to physically brace herself in her chair. "Dr. Kirkwood came and told me that Sydney had arrested and that they had saved her. He said they needed to send her across the street to the children's hospital to have surgery on her intestine. And then, he walked off."

"Did he say anything else?" Ben looked at Dr. Kirkwood to draw the jury in his direction.

"No. I never saw him again."

"Did he ever come across the street or call you and ask how Sydney was doing?"

"No, never. We got handed off to a whole different set of doctors who worked really hard to get Sydney better."

Ben grabbed his notepad for a second and put it back down. "After surgery, how did you feel?"

"I thought we were out of the woods. The surgery went fine, and Sydney was alive."

Alicia talked about the day Sydney was released from the hospital and was finally able to be taken home.

"Alicia, what was it like to be a new mom?"

Alicia smiled. "I loved it. It was great. Sydney was home, and we could start our life. I was so happy."

"When did things change?"

"After a few months, I noticed that she was not progressing like other kids. I had been around nieces and nephews and could tell something was different. Then, her pediatrician started expressing concerns and told me she believed Sydney may have some brain damage from the heart attack, or whatever it is called."

Alicia explained that she took Sydney to a specialist who diagnosed Sydney with cerebral palsy, because of the loss of blood to her brain during the cardiopulmonary event.

"Alicia, based on your discussions with the specialist, what is your understanding of Sydney's diagnosis and future?"

Alicia looked down and gathered herself. "Mr. Jennings, it's not good. Sydney has cerebral palsy, which is a fancy term for permanent brain damage. She will never walk, talk, or eat food like a regular human being. She will need twenty-four-hour care for the rest of her life. Someone has to get this food"—Alicia reached in her bag and pulled out an eight-ounce plastic container and showed it to the jury—"and put it into her feeding tube and make sure that tube is clean. Sydney will be wheelchair-bound for the rest of her life and never do anything that normal kids do." She took a couple of breaths, trying to hold back her emotion. "My little girl will never have any kind of normal life, and it breaks my heart for her. And to find out this could have been avoided . . . well, it just hurts my soul, is the most Christian thing I can say."

Alicia told the jury that, during her few quiet times, she researched ways she might help make her life and the life of her daughter better. In the past year, she found the Shriner's School and enrolled Sydney. Alicia discussed the treatments and therapies that could enhance Sydney's life if they had the money to pay for them.

"Alicia, what is Sydney's level of awareness?"

Alicia smiled warmly. "Mr. Jennings, she knows her mother. She smiles at me and cries at me. But the way she looks at me. I just know that sweet little thing inside of her just wants to get out." Several women on the jury dabbed their eyes. "But Sydney is strong-willed. She will get into one of her moods and fuss and shout for no reason. It's like she knows what happened to her and sometimes can't help being angry."

Then came the moment of truth. Ben and Alicia had discussed most of her testimony, but not the very last part.

Before they went into court that morning, Stephanie told Ben the last question to ask. Stephanie spent so much time with Sydney, the two had become like sisters. Stephanie's stoic exterior concealed a soft heart. She wanted to help Alicia and Sydney. Stephanie spent endless hours the past two years counseling and being a friend to Alicia.

Most lawyers would never agree to ask a critical witness a question they did not know the answer to, but Ben trusted Stephanie and knew she would not lead him astray. It was against conventional wisdom, but Ben wanted his interactions with Alicia to be authentic. It was the artist versus the mechanic. Jurors sensed inauthenticity a mile away, so he wanted Alicia's testimony to feel like a discussion among friends rather than a rehearsed narrative that might come across as false.

Ben walked around in the space between the witness box and counsel table, taking a moment to draw the jury's attention. Sydney stirred and made gurgling noises. Alicia slowly rocked her. Ben allowed a moment for Alicia to appease Sydney.

"Ms. Landers," Ben started, "you have waited for years to have your day in court. Today is it. In hearing your testimony today, I can only imagine you what have gone through. Now, as we are here in front of this jury—do you have any fears for Sydney's and your future that you would like to express to them?"

Alicia swallowed, looked down at Sydney to gather herself, then lifted her head, projecting strength, and began.

"Mr. Jennings, I am from nothing. I grew up poor in North Memphis and fought for everything I got. I tried to do everything right, even though I did not always succeed. I did not use drugs or commit crimes like most of my neighborhood. I read books and studied my lessons. I managed a scholarship to college and went there and gave my best efforts. I met a guy down there that I believed I would spend the rest of my life with.

"When I was a senior, we made a mistake and got pregnant. It was not planned. I take the blame for that. But I cannot be sorry, because my lapse brought me this beautiful little girl who is now my entire life. We had a terrible break, and I am fighting every day to do the best I can for her. I don't ask for charity but only a chance. I willingly devote my life to Sydney and view it as the honor of my life. It looks like I will never be a lawyer as I dreamed, but I will be the best damn mother that ever existed. I love this little girl like no one has ever loved a child. We only have each other, and every day, we do our best. We don't always accomplish our best, but by God, we sure try.

"In the end, all parents want better for their children. Like everyone else, I wanted a better life for my kids. I wanted them to go to school, go to college, get married, and have kids. But I know Sydney will never go to school, she will never walk down the aisle to get married, she will never have the joy of motherhood. I must live with the fact that I will not do better for my child, and it hurts. It hurts terribly."

Alicia paused again, attempting to gather herself. Several women on the jury wiped their eyes with tissues, and a few men rubbed their faces. Up until now, her voice had been even and calm. But having been bottled up since Sydney's birth, Alicia could no longer hold the emotions in. Her chin quivered and tears ran down her face. She made a little noise that only the front row of the jury could hear. She closed her eyes tightly and clinched her jaw. Then, Alicia opened her eyes, turned to the jury, and spoke again. "But when I think about Sydney—when I think about this beautiful sweet little helpless creature—it destroys me. We have no one else. If something were to happen to me, what will happen to her? In those quiet nights alone, I tremble thinking about who would take care of her. I live my life in fear. And not fear for me. I fear Sydney being left alone and not understanding what is happening to her. I fear her not getting care, treatment, or even more importantly--love."

This calm, cool woman began to wail.

"Who will take care of my baby? Who will love her? Who will tuck her into bed and wake her up in the morning? Will someone make sure she has her stuffed animal or play the television program that makes her laugh?"

Hearing her mother's elevated voice, Sydney began fussing. Alicia took a moment to calm herself and then looked her little girl in the eye to reassure her. It was all that was needed. "So you see, I constantly worry that something will happen to me and nobody—nobody will be there to take of her like I do. She is a helpless, defenseless little angel, and what will happen to her without me?" Alicia turned her face up to Judge Jones. Her cheeks were wet. "Your Honor, I apologize for going on like this, but it is just so hard. Please forgive me."

Judge Jones quietly nodded. Ben stood motionless. He had tears streaming down his face as did most everyone else in the courtroom. The deputy turned his head, the court clerk covered her face, and the court reporter wept tears onto her transcription device. Judge Jones looked down and appeared clearly moved. The women on Marston's team looked the other way lest their humanity be observed. For what seemed like thirty full seconds, Ben Jennings did not speak or move. Then, he simply and humbly walked back to his chair, sat down, and put his face in his hands.

Even Judge Jones had to wait a moment to gather himself. The entire courtroom lay still, everyone left to their private thoughts. Finally, Judge Jones spoke softly.

"Mr. Owens, would you like to cross?"

Marston stood up quietly and slowly and responded, "Your Honor, please, may we approach?"

Ben had no idea why Marston would want to approach the judge at this point. What in the world would he ask?

The court reporter put on her headphones, and once Ben, Marston, and Judge Jones were inches apart, Marston whispered, "Your Honor, I move for a mistrial. There is no way this jury can be fair after this emotional display. Her testimony will be too prejudicial, and Dr. Kirkwood would be deprived of a fair trial."

Judge Jones quickly turned his head sideways like that of a curious dog trying to decipher what Marston was asking. But before Ben could respond, Judge Jones said, "Mr. Owens, proof is supposed to be prejudicial. If it is not, I do not see what purpose it has. The entire point of Mr. Jennings putting on a case is to introduce proof that would make a jury see your client's conduct in a prejudicial light. Otherwise, it is likely irrelevant. Of course, there is a standard of it being unfairly prejudicial, and in this case, there is nothing unfair about her testimony. Sir, your motion for mistrial is denied."

Ben walked back to his seat and sat down. Marston took longer to get back to his place, contemplating his next move. What the hell could he ask of Alicia now that would not make the jury hate him? His only play would be to get her off the stand as quickly as he could and hope the weekend would cause the jury to forget. He looked down at his prepared question list on the iPad and uncharacteristically abandoned it. Marston calmly looked up and said, "No questions of Ms. Landers, Your Honor."

Ben stood up, looked at the jury and then back to Judge Jones. "Plaintiff rests, Your Honor."

CHAPTER 24

J udge Jones dismissed the jury for the weekend and told them to be back on Monday. Marston weakly argued his motion for directed verdict, and after brief discussion, it was denied. Shelby County Circuit Court hears motions and domestic cases on Fridays, so the case had a long weekend off. Alicia's testimony had shredded everyone's emotions. For Ben, it had worked out perfectly that her voice was the last the jury would hear for next three days.

Ben was happy to have Friday off from trial. He checked his phone and saw that his girlfriend, Alexis Thompson, was in town. Alexis, the daughter of a prominent Memphis doctor, spent two years at Ole Miss before she determined there were much better ways to monetize her stunning looks than to marry the son of a rich Mississippi Delta planter. She was now an Instagram model/influencer with over a million followers, and she made hundreds of thousands of dollars promoting hotels, resorts, and beauty products on her account. As an accomplished golfer, Alexis was paid handsomely to make appearances at corporate golf events, where she charmed with her looks, personality, and swing. When Ben returned her call, Alexis told him she had just returned home from a month of island hopping in the South Pacific, posting picturesque scenes that convinced Instagram follower Bob from Cincinnati that if he just went to the Four Seasons in Bali, he, too, could have a girl like Alexis. When she not hocking a resort, she was posting pictures of the latest, greatest beauty products, giving average women around the world the illusion it would make them look like Alexis, who happened to have won the genetic lottery.

Their relationship worked because she knew Ben was not the jealous type and, with work, kids, and golf, had plenty to occupy him while she was away eight months a year. While not classically educated, Alexis was no dummy and, like many girls with her gifts, found out early how to open doors with just a smile. She knew her looks would not last forever, so she saved all the money she could and planned a future off the road. Her rapier wit surprised people because Southern girls that pretty usually never had to think.

They had met when Alexis needed help with a creep who was stalking her, and a friend recommended Ben. Ben got a court-ordered restraining order to restrain the pervert. Next, he put Freddie on the job, which likely had a more persuasive effect on the gentleman. After that, Ben helped Alexis negotiate contracts with various customers and got her business properly papered. Their common love of golf forged the bond.

Ben pulled up to her South Bluffs condo. It had spectacular views of the Mississippi. She opened the door and took his breath away. Ben had been around a lot of beautiful women and had dated Alexis for the better part of year. But after a month of not seeing her, he forgot just how stunning she was. She was blonde with blue eyes Ben could drown in and was a leggy five-seven. She wore a body-conscious, closely cut black linen sheath with a keyhole neckline, tapered to accentuate her perfect proportions. Her golden-brown tan from a month in the islands contrasted with her Hollywood Pepsodent smile. She threw her arms around him and kissed him passionately. All he could manage was, "Wow, you sure know how to greet a man."

"Benji, I have missed you so much," she said.

"Really?"

"Well, maybe just a little." She winked at him.

"I guess all of those five-star resorts make you long for the glitz and glamour of good ole Mempho."

"Not exactly. But truthfully, it really is good to be home. I know you make fun of what I do, but it does actually get tiring after a while. The resorts are all amazing, but they seem to run together after a while."

"What do you say we go to McEwen's, grab a proper meal, and come back and watch the sunset?"

"Best offer I have had in a month."

"Oh, I doubt that." Ben teased. "I cannot imagine how many billionaires have hounded you."

"You know those guys aren't my style, but damn do they have some nice boats."

They walked down the steps to his car, and she looked confused.

"Where is the Rover?" she asked.

"About that," he grimaced. "It kind of blew up a couple of weeks ago, and I am in this little rig for the time being."

"Get the hell out of here. Are you messing with me? Is this an episode of *Punk'd*?"

"I wish it were."

"You must be pimping on the side to supplement your income."

"Busted," he said. "Do you know how much I could get for a date with you?"

"Brother, they cannot afford me."

"Don't I know it." He shook his head. "Actually, Freddie hooked me up. It was from one of his customers who won't be needing it for a while."

"That Freddie," she said. "That boy is one of a kind. I am just glad he is on our side."

"Freddie is ride or die. I wouldn't have made it without him." Ben said.

As they got into the Escalade and Ben turned on the car, Taylor Swift came on the speaker. Alexis started laughing.

"Really, Taylor Swift?"

"One of the greatest American songwriters." Ben was completely serious.

Laughing, she mocked him. "I get that. I am just wondering which one of us is the twenty-five-year-old girl and which one is the guy in his forties."

"Hey, let me put it in terms you can understand. Taylor Swift has 140 million followers on Instagram, writes all her own music, and is worth a gazillion dollars."

"Oh, I know who she is and love her too. It just cracks me up that your old ass listens to Taylor Swift."

"Hey, Taylor Swift is one of the most important voices in our country, and I will die on that hill."

"Okay, okay. You do not have to get so testy about it, Aristotle. You are definitely a different cat than all the others."

"I don't know if that is a good or bad thing."

"Yeah, me neither."

Alexis was the first woman Ben had dated since his divorce who made him laugh. Obviously, he was first attracted to her beauty, but the laughter kept it interesting. She would not let him get by with his customary bullshit. The fact that she knew golf better than 99 percent of men made her even sexier. When they arrived at the restaurant, Ben got out and handed his keys to the regular valet, Johnny, who greeted him with a look of abject horror and then a smile.

"Yo, Mr. Ben. Look at you, finally getting down with the cause."

"Yeah, yeah, funny man," Ben replied.

Alexis piped up, unable to resist. "I told him I wouldn't go out with him unless he traded that awful Range Rover for something classy like this."

Johnny and Alexis shared a good laugh, and Ben shook his head. "New car" was on the top of the list if he won this trial. All the comedy about the Escalade was starting to annoy him.

They entered the restaurant to see Bert running the place. Luckily, it was not crowded this Thursday night. Bert offered Ben his regular table in the bar next to local lawyer Max Shelton's table, where he held court at lunch every weekday. Brad the bartender quickly came over, and they ordered Negronis and appetizers.

"How is Tiger, by the way?"

"Oh, he is great. In November, I am going to help him open the new course he designed near Branson, Missouri."

"How many strokes does he give you?"

"Four a side."

"Do you ever stop to think what a cool life you lead?" Ben asked.

"Yes, all the time. But I have made my breaks. I know I started with some advantages, but no one has given me this." She sounded defensive.

"Hey, hey, I get it. You are a badass. I am impressed. When I grow up, I want to be just like you," Ben said.

Alexis rolled her eyes. "You and growing up are two things that will likely never meet. By the way, how is your swing?"

"The swing is actually fine. Freddie and I played a little money game a couple of weeks ago, and I thought I was going to lose my shirt."

"What did you shoot?"

"A sweet little 64, and it took all of it to win. Had to make a screamer on eighteen."

"Jeez. And yet, you are still driving the Escalade with the Memphis package! Couldn't you upgrade after that payday?" She teased.

"But for my expert requiring thirty large, yes. Unfortunately, Team Jennings badly needs a W in this trial."

"How is it going?"

"Well, you always feel good after your proof. But we'll see after Marston puts on his cadre of perfect grey-haired experts. Alicia did great today. I don't see how anyone could not be sympathetic toward her. But in this political climate, people are not empathetic like they used to be. Instead of people, jurors see plaintiffs as belonging either to their tribe or the enemy one. I have to figure out a way to bridge that gap and get them together."

"Benji," she answered, "you got this. You could sell snow to the Eskimos. Trust your gut and don't be shy about showing emotion. I know you always keep that stiff upper lip, but you cannot go halfway. You have to be that child's voice."

"Look at you," Ben responded. "You sound almost like a liberal."

"Hey!" Alexis looked in mock scorn. "Don't tell any of those guys on the PGA Tour, or they may blackball me."

"Oh, those are good guys. They just want to protect their money. I am not mad at them for that," Ben shrugged. "Everyone is trying to get through it the best way they can. Speaking for guys, at the end of the day, all we want is to take care of our family, eat a hotdog, drink a beer, and enjoy a ballgame. We are very simple beasts."

"Yeah, right," Alexis countered. "There is nothing simple about you, so you can dispense with the good ole country boy routine around me. You have more stuff going on in your head than any ten other guys. You may fool the others with the "oh shucks" routine, but don't forget who you are talking to."

"Right back at you, Miss Instagram. Do you really think any of those million guys who follow you have any idea who you really are? The sad thing is that if they did, they would love you even more."

"Look at you, Mr. Charmer," she said. "You are trying to get lucky tonight."

"Darling," Ben said. "I am already past lucky and just holding on for the ride."

Alexis was one of the few who read him like a book. Wearing one's heart on one's sleeve in the South quickly exposed a guy to mockery from other men. Luckily, the waiter delivered the blackened catfish, sweet potatoes, collard greens, and black-eyed peas in the nick of time.

"You can't get this in Bali!" Ben crowed.

"No, you can't," she agreed.

After a bottle of wine and bread pudding with whiskey sauce, they returned to their relaxed rhythms. When they got back to Alexis's condo, she excused herself. Ben grabbed a nice bottle of Cabernet and two glasses and headed to her balcony as the sun, almost finished for the day, glistened on the Mississippi River and painted the Arkansas sky. Alexis came from behind him wearing nothing but her official Ole Miss red jersey with the name Manning and the number "18" on the back. She straddled his lap, put her arms around his neck, and kissed him passionately.

"Well, hotty toddy, gosh almighty!" Ben said, repeating the beginning of the famous Ole Miss cheer.

"I heard we kicked your ass while I was gone." She couldn't resist.

"You know us Memphis boys. We are lovers not fighters."

"Well, lawyer, you are going to have to prove that claim," she said with a wicked grin.

"Who am I to deny an order of the court?"

***

Ben slept better than he had in a month. The litmus test for a man's feelings about a woman occurs after the act of sexual congress. If he truly wants to remain, it means the attraction is more than physical. Ben not only wanted to linger; he feared his feelings would not be reciprocated. Alexis was the first woman to make him feel slightly insecure and very happy.

He stared at her while she slept, taking in her essence like a great painting. It was hard to believe she was real. Finally, he got up, and ran down to Bluff City Coffee on Main Street for pastries and hot coffee, bringing them back to Alexis's balcony, enjoying the morning. The fog hung over the Mississippi like a gentle white blanket. It was an unseasonably cool morning, and Ben enjoyed the welcome sound of peace. He thought of the line from R.M. Drake: "She slept with wolves without fear, for the wolves knew a lion was among them." With Alexis, his anxieties quieted to a dull roar. He always wondered if he could give himself fully to another person. And if he were honest with himself—would that person even welcome the offering? She finally joined him, this time wearing his dress shirt.

"I just love how your shirts smell," she said.

"I just wish I looked as good as you in one of them."

He handed her coffee and a pastry, and she sat quietly beside him.

"We aren't leaving this condo today," she proclaimed.

"I wish," he said. "But I need to get some work done, and then we can have lunch."

"I hope I am here when you get back," she teased. "You better make it worth my while to wait. You know there is some billionaire waiting by the phone right now."

"On second thought, I think work can wait for another hour," Ben said as he took her hand and led her back inside.

CHAPTER 25

The Thornton Firm employees received no such respite. Marston's manic behavior jumped off the scales now. Kip, Steve, and the trial team got emails throughout the night, and if they didn't respond quickly, they risked a full Marston meltdown. Marston knew he had three of the best experts in the country, but he was used to having all the cards in his favor. Alicia's testimony had devastated the defense, and the jury's demonstration of emotion struck fear down to his brain stem. He wanted to settle so bad he could taste it, but he had already spent a million dollars of the insurance company's money and to cave now would destroy his reputation with them.

Steve melted under the pressure. His wife screamed at him for not coming home. Kip, also feeling the heat, fussed at the staff for imagined failures. Steve swore to himself he would never do this again. The money and prestige were not worth this physical and emotional toll. His body and brain ached. He thought of how Abraham Lincoln once compared how he felt to the story of a sixteen-year-old boy who stubbed his toe: too old to cry, too hurt to laugh. At this point, Steve did not care about the outcome of the trial—just as long as it ended.

Kip had the advantage of experience here, but even he had never seen Marston in such a state. They had tried several cases together but never one as strong as this or with an opponent so capable. Ben Jennings was the first lawyer Kip had seen to not blink under the withering pressure of Marston's dominance. Ben seemed to derive some devilish delight in pushing Marston's buttons and poking the bear with a sharp stick. Kip even admired the guy. Ben had balls.

Kip knew that for Ben, this case would amount to amazing triumph or spectacular defeat. Kip also felt the jealousy of the second son who remained loyal while his father loved the older prodigal, despite his betrayal. It pained Kip to know that no matter how hard he worked, he could never fill the shoes of Ben Jennings for Marston. As he witnessed Ben's courtroom performance, all illusions Kip had before the trial about his own abilities washed away. To the inexperienced and untrained eye, Ben Jennings appeared to be the precocious, smart-assed kid who once charmed teachers and now charmed juries. Ben made it look easy. However, Kip knew the talent and work required to pull off such a show against the likes of Marston Owens in front of a jury with huge money on the line. This trial broke Kip of any hope that someday he could sit at the grown-up table of trial lawyers.

Ben rolled into the office Friday around two with the distinctive affect of a man who had a good night. Peggy, who had been doggedly manning the office, the phones, and the Alexopoulos complaints solo while Ben was in trial, could not decide whether to laugh or cuss him out. As he walked in the door, she gave him one look and knew where he had been.

"Hey, Mr. Big Shot walking in here with a shit-eating grin while Rome burns." She sounded like a schoolteacher scolding a child.

Ben looked at her, unable to hide his smile, and spread his arms out wide with his hands up. "Peggy, in my defense—" He looked up to the corner of his eyes as if thinking and finally said, "I have none." Ben let out a belly laugh. "And I am not even sorry!"

What could she do with this fool? How could she even stay angry? Ben was maddening this way. She continued in her authoritative tone. "All right, big fella, now that the pipes are clean, do you think we can maybe put out some of these fires blazing around us?"

Ben happily responded, "I am all yours. Your wish is my command."

The two went to Ben's office and sat down around a mound of files and messages to be returned. Three more Alexopoulos victims had appeared, and clients and lawyers from Marco's other forty cases had demanded status, deposition dates, and requests to set various motions. The smile quickly evaporated from Ben's face as the two went through the mound of paper, triaging priorities and formulating strategies to manage the storm. Ben decided to call the victims first and make sure they were completely informed. He sent emails to his opposing counsels, most of whom were understanding about a colleague in a big trial. He asked Peggy to contact the University of Memphis law school a few blocks away on Front Street to see if they could get a student to come in and help with the research and writing needed to manage the pending legal motions facing imminent deadlines.

Peggy stood up to leave. Almost as an afterthought, she said, "By the way, Marco called me today."

"Marco who?" Ben squinted his eyes in disbelief.

"Alexopoulos."

"Are you kidding? Did you talk to him? What did he say?" Ben almost spit out the words.

Peggy was calm. "You know Marco, same old stuff. He was working that bullshit syrupy fake Southern gentlemen thing he fails so badly at. Then, he announced that he found the Lord and was on the road to recovery."

"How many times did he mention the Lord?"

"At least twenty-four," Peggy deadpanned.

"The Lord is not going to bail his ass out! I would love to get my hands on him," Ben was now angry. "Did you tell him the gig was up? That he was to never come here again?"

"I told him," she said, "But you know a conman always thinks he will get his way if he just keeps trying."

"I will see him in hell. The Supreme Court has suspended him. What does he say about that?" Ben asked.

"Oh, yeah," Peggy said as she pulled through his stack of papers. "Here's his response to the Board of Responsibility. It appears this is all a big mistake that he will clear up once he has completed his treatment."

Ben was enraged. "That son of a bitch left me with this office and a dozen people from whom he has stolen at least a million bucks. He lied, cheated, and stole from them, from me, and from everyone else. And instead of remorse, that malignant narcissist is sitting on his sorry behind in rehab blaming everyone else for his problems."

Peggy waived her hands at Ben, "Easy, fella. I almost didn't tell you. Nothing we can do right now. Let's get through this trial, and then, we can handle his sorry ass."

"You are right," Ben said as he quickly calmed down. "It is just so raw. If we lose this case, we are ruined. And we are ruined because Marco Alexopoulos is a sociopathic thief who thinks only of himself. His actions were pure greed. We make a good living here, honestly. And my dumb ass. I thought his crazy expensive lifestyle was because he had inherited a bunch of money from his dad. I had no idea it was because he was a thief. How did I miss that?"

"We both missed it, Ben," Peggy said. "I had no idea either. He was always a strange bird, but whoever thought he was Bernie Madoff?"

Ben called the three new victims and spent over an hour telling them his now-practiced narrative about what he believed happened and what potential remedies for the clients may work. He listened to them vent and patiently apologized for what they were going through. A little of his soul left his body with each call. Ben came from nothing. He prided himself on integrity, and now, he was connected to a major criminal who had stolen from people when they were at their most vulnerable.

Marco Alexopoulos was the face of evil dressed up in a Zegna suit. He hid in plain sight, blatantly stealing from people who trusted him and could least afford it. A hot place in hell waited for guys like Marco. Ben wanted to arrange that meeting.

CHAPTER 26

Monday morning came and brought the first day of defense proof. Marston's case would likely take two full days of court, depending on the length of cross-examinations. Marston's direct testimony with each witness usually took an hour or two. Some lawyers spent hours, if not days, crossing an opposing expert. Ben thought it a waste of time because many on the jury lacked the education to appreciate the esoteric points being made.

Marston called Dr. Matthew Stevens to the stand. A board-certified neonatologist, Dr. Stevens trained at Duke and Emery Medical Center, where he now held the position of chief of neonatology. He had authored multiple peer-reviewed articles and published extensively on several subjects, including NEC. Dr. Stephens had delivered the keynote speech at several international neonatal conferences and consulted with the National Institute of Health.

Dr. Stevens and Marston danced through an array of photographs, slides, and graphs educating the jury further on the subject they had already heard so much about. Dr. Stevens did a good job of explaining the defense position. Educated and credentialed, Dr. Stevens fell a bit on the dry side. He had the jury's attention, but at some point, Marston wondered, would they tune out such a highly technical discussion? Marston's strategy was not to educate the jury but to impress them with the fancy degrees and backgrounds of his experts to make the jury feel special for having had these great men speak to them. He effectively used this strategy his entire career and saw no reason to change now. After two hours, Marston passed the witness to Ben. He looked at Ben and then the jury as if to say, "Good luck with that."

Ben did not want to spend an hour battling over minutiae with Dr. Stevens. He had two more experts to cross and fighting over esoteric points would not move the jury in Ben's direction. He needed to sublimate his ego and approach the witness from an oblique angle. Ben saved his big gun for his last witness and intended to spar over the medicine with Marston's second expert. Ben did not want to be repetitive. Further, the jury needed a show. They watched enough movies and television and expected something special. Ben took The Sage's advice and went for the misdirection. Ben rose to his feet without notes, buttoned his jacket, and walked toward the witness, commanding the floor with a confident bearing.

"Hello, Dr. Stevens. How are you today?" Ben said in his most courtly Southern manners.

"Just fine, thanks," Dr. Stevens responded curtly.

"Well, you look like a nice fella."

"My wife thinks so," Dr. Stevens responded sarcastically, drawing laughter from some of the jury.

"Dr. Stevens, I expect you believe Dr. Kirkwood was not negligent don't you?"

"Yes, that's my belief," Dr. Stevens answered sincerely.

"And you want the jury to believe it, don't you?"

"Yes."

Ben continued in a more pronounced folksy tone. "In fact, that's your purpose being here. To kind of convince the folks on the jury that Dr. Kirkwood was not negligent."

"I am not sure what you mean."

"That is why you came here. To convince these people Dr. Kirkwood was not negligent," Ben repeated patiently and courtly, like the perfect Southern gentlemen.

"I will provide the facts on our side," Dr. Stevens said, beginning to act uncomfortable with the direction of questioning. He had not been warned about this. Marston started to squirm in his chair, weighing whether or not to object.

He wanted to maintain a calm confidence so the jury would not perceive any weakness.

"Didn't you want to convince the jury that Dr. Kirkwood wasn't negligent?" Ben repeated the question.

"Mr. Owens will take care of that," Dr. Stevens said, now irritated.

"Don't you want to answer the question?" Ben said in a rhythm. After a silence, Ben continued. "It's all right if you don't want to answer the question. I will ask you another question. If you wanted to convince the jury that Dr. Kirkwood was not negligent, there are certain ways a fellow could do it."

"I am not sure what you mean," Stevens answered.

"Certain techniques," Ben said.

"You are more familiar with that than I am, Mr. Jennings."

"Well, I don't know about that," Ben countered. "I never did have a coach to tell me how to testify. Did you have a coach to help you know how to testify here today?"

"Briefly, we did, yes." Dr. Stevens conceded.

Ben knew he had him. "Oh, did the coach kind of practice your testimony so that you could convince the jury that Dr. Kirkwood was not negligent?"

"No, we didn't get into details like that," Stevens said.

"Was it a 'he' coach or a 'she' coach?"

"It was a lady," Stevens said.

"Did you kind of go over how you would act on the witness stand?"

"It was a general session we had."

"Just a little session about how to testify?" Ben asked in mock inquisitiveness.

"Yes."

"She was called a witness consultant. The woman who worked with you?" Ben asked.

"Yes, she was."

"And it was her idea that to tell the ladies and gentlemen of the jury the truth, you had to get coached, is that right?" Ben continued.

"I don't believe I had to be coached, no," Dr. Stevens responded defiantly.

"Really?" Ben tilted his head looking at the jury who were now in on his point. "But you WERE coached. Somebody must have believed you needed coaching." The jury spontaneously roared with laughter. Marston was stuck. He could do nothing now.

Ben continued. "Well, sir, let me ask you a question. I don't mean to be personal, but a minute ago you mentioned your wife. Do you have to be coached when you go home to explain things to the wife? I mean, do you hire a coach to decide what to tell momma?" The jury grinned ear to ear, enjoying the theatre and watching this highly credentialed doctor succumb to the good-ole-boy treatment.

"I have never done that, no," Dr. Stevens answered soberly.

"Do you hire a coach when you want to tell the facts and the truth to the boss?"

"That all comes with experience." Stevens tried to get out of the box but could not figure a way.

"Wait a minute. Could I get you to answer the question? Do you hire a coach to help you tell the truth to the boss?" Ben pressed.

"No. I never have."

Ben raised his voice. "Have you at any other time in your life ever had a coach to help you explain anything in the world other than today when you testified that Dr. Kirkwood was not negligent?"

"I have never hired a coach," Stevens said.

"No, you haven't, have you? Not until today. No more questions, Your Honor."

Dr. Stevens sat stunned. He had prepared for hours with coaches, lawyers, and staff, going over medical records, literature, and other depositions. What just happened? Ben Jennings had not asked one single question about the merits of the case, yet he felt somehow like he had been bested. The jury had laughed at Stevens' testimony. They laughed at him. After two hours on the stand with Marston, the cross had lasted less than a few minutes, Ben had embarrassed him, and Stevens could not figure out how it happened. Marston had nothing with which to follow up. He was forced to dismiss the witness.

One down, two to go. After the lunch break, Marston called Dr. Jack Martin, the neonatologist who filled the local slot on the dance card of defense experts. Dr. Martin, a native Memphian, went to the University of Tennessee at Knoxville for undergrad and then UT Memphis for medical school. He performed both his internship and residency in Memphis.

Marston played the hometown card and went through Martin's entire career and knowledge of Memphis. Dr. Martin testified that Dr. Kirkwood possessed an impeccable reputation and occupied a place as a pillar in the community. Marston spent an hour covering Dr. Martin's education, training, publications, and accomplishments saving babies' lives. Marston pulled out a similar slideshow reiterating the care and treatment provided to Sydney. An adage among trial lawyers is to make sure the jury hears every important point at least three times. Marston sledge-hammered competence, training, and dedication. Dr. Martin also emphasized that bad outcomes can and do happen in the absence of negligence. This was the jury's third medical expert; they could pass a medical school exam on NEC. The defense did not care if they bored the jury. In fact, jury fatigue could even help the defense if the jury were so worn down they made a quick decision in deliberations just to get out of there. The defense goal was to overload the jury with so much information, they would capitulate and simply throw up their hands when it was time to decide.

After two hours with Stephens on the stand, Marston finally passed the witness. Judge Jones gave the jury, who was clearly fighting to stay awake, a fifteen-minute afternoon break.

Ben was committed to his strategy of saving his big guns for the last expert. He would use little time to examine Dr. Martin. It killed him not to blow Dr. Stephens and Dr. Martin out of the water, but he had to wait. If he burned his powder now, Marston would cover the mistake with the last expert and have him explain away the damaging cross, muting the powerful effect if dropped on the very last witness. Ben had to hold his cards to the end.

"Good afternoon, Dr. Martin."

"Good afternoon, Mr. Jennings."

"I know that we have never met, and I have never had an opportunity to ask you any questions. There are really only a few things I need to cover. First, have you ever testified as an expert in court like this?"

"Yes, I have. Six other times."

"And of those six other times, how many were on behalf of the injured party?"

"Well, none."

"So you have only testified on behalf of doctors?"

"That is correct," Martin said.

"You have taken the oath seven times now, and not a single time have you ever taken the witness stand and told a jury like these fine folks that a doctor departed from the standard of care."

Dr. Martin could see how this sounded. "Well, yes, it just happened to work out that way."

Ben pressed. "So tell the jury how many times you have given a deposition, signed an affidavit, testified in public or even at the country club, or even said out loud that one of your fellow doctors did anything wrong."

Dr. Martin did not answer. Ben waited to let that sink into the jury and continued.

"I will help you out, Dr. Martin. The answer is none. Zero. Zilch. Nada. You have never, ever publicly criticized a single fellow physician for any reason, have you?"

Dr. Martin shifted in his seat; his confidence eroded in the stares of the jury. "No," he said.

"Do you mean to tell this jury that doctors are infallible?" Ben asked.

"Of course not," Dr. Martin answered.

"So you have no problem finding the time to interrupt your busy practice to come down here and speak on behalf of your buddy, old Dr. Bob Kirkwood, but somehow have never found a way to speak on behalf of someone injured by a negligent doctor?"

Dr. Martin did not speak.

"Dr. Martin, do you have an answer?"

"I have already answered," Martin said curtly.

"Oh, you have, have you?" Ben boomed. "I certainly did not hear you. But based on your other answers I am going to take that as a no."

"That is correct," Dr. Martin finally said.

"But the truth is you have seen and borne witness to other doctors making mistakes that had dire consequences, haven't you?"

"I cannot say offhand, but I am sure mistakes have happened that have hurt people. Mr. Jennings. Doctors are humans, and we all make mistakes," Dr. Martin said, trying to gain the high ground. But Ben jumped on this answer.

"Exactly!" he snapped quickly. "We all do. I bet even you have made mistakes."

"Yes, I am sure I have," Dr. Martin conceded.

"And the point is not whether anyone makes a mistake. The point is that mistakes have consequences."

"Yes, they do," Dr. Martin said.

"Dr. Martin, are you a conservative or one of those liberal types?"

"Objection!" Marston yelled as he jumped to his feet.

Without waiting for grounds or a reply, Judge Jones said, "Sustained. Come on, Mr. Jennings, get to your point. I cannot see any relevance to that line of questioning."

"Thank you, Your Honor, I will rephrase my question. Dr. Martin, the reason I asked you that question is that when I watch TV and read the news reports, one of the things I always hear is that conservatives emphasize accountability. Do you believe in accountability?"

"Of course, I do," Dr. Martin responded.

"So if someone makes a mistake, they should be held accountable?" Ben asked.

Dr. Martin anticipated where Ben was going. "Yes, of course, but in this particular case, Dr. Kirkwood did not depart from the standard of care."

"I see," Ben said. "So let me just ask you a couple of yes or no questions. You are welcome to explain, but I think Judge Jones will require you to first answer the question before explaining. If you don't believe me, you can ask him."

Martin did not move.

Ben continued. "Sydney Landers had NEC?"

"Yes."

"Sydney Landers developed a perforated intestine?"

"Yes."

"As a result of that, she developed sepsis?"

"Correct."

"As a result of the sepsis, she suffered an anoxic event?"

"That is likely, yes."

"As a result of the anoxic event, she now has cerebral palsy and permanent brain damage?"

"I am not sure the brain damage was caused by Dr. Kirkwood."

"That is not what I asked you, Dr. Martin. You agree she has permanent brain damage and cerebral palsy."

"Yes."

"And can you point to this jury one shred of evidence that links that brain damage to anything other than the anoxic event caused by the sepsis caused by the perforated intestine caused by the NEC?"

"No," he conceded.

"Dr. Kirkwood did not diagnose her condition in time to prevent her anoxic event?"

"He did not, but he certainly complied with the standard of care by ordering the serial x-rays and various treatments and therapies. Bad things can happen without someone making mistakes."

Ben shot back. "On that, we can agree, but can we also agree that bad things can also happen when someone does make a mistake and does depart from the standard of care?"

"Yes," Dr. Martin said quietly, having to concede the point.

Ben sat down. Marston did not offer a redirect.

Marston knew he and Ben were playing a game of chicken, and it vexed him to wonder what Ben had in store for the next day and the final expert witness. No way would Ben dance around another expert with his little circus show. Surely, Ben would confront the substantive medical issues. If Ben never did, Marston could murder him in closing for not challenging the medicine. The thought gave Marston a glimmer of hope he might salvage a victory in the case. But Ben was no fool. Why had he crossed this expert like this? It did not add up. He began wondering what he could be missing. Marston hated that he did not understand people and what made them tick.

CHAPTER 27

en knew that Marston saved his best expert to close his show. On the lake that day in Heber Springs, Ben had discovered a huge discrepancy in Dr. Kirkwood's single medical record. It had stared him in the face the entire time he had reviewed the medical records, and he had not noticed before. More importantly, Stephanie never noticed. For once in his life, he thanked God for dyslexia. His intense visualization of that document finally opened his eyes. His bigger question was whether Marston also recognized the discrepancy and was deliberately avoiding the topic. If so, Marston was gambling on Ben failing to see it. Ben wanted Marston to keep thinking he had no clue. If Ben brought it up during his case or during the defense expert's testimony, Marston would know Ben was onto it and have an opportunity to counteract the damaging proof. This way, waiting patiently until the final expert was called, Ben held his cards close and gambled that he had the best hand.

Dr. Jonathan Cook was perfect in every way a defense team wants an expert to be. A man with confidence and authority, Dr. Cook, now in his late fifties, wore his salt-and-pepper hair cut short with a straight military part. At about six feet, he dressed immaculately, with a high shine on his black lace-ups. He walked across the room confidently with a distinctive military gait as though he owned the space. He looked Judge Jones in the eye and nodded. After being sworn in, he looked toward the jury and gave them a confident smile.

Marston practiced this examination with Dr. Cook ten times, and the two were prepared to dance like Fred

Astaire and Ginger Rogers. Marston quickly established that Dr. Cook attended West Point, reached the rank of lieutenant colonel in the Army, served two tours in Iraq and Afghanistan, and was awarded the Silver Star. Dr. Cook attended Harvard Medical School and completed a fellowship at Mayo Clinic. Dr. Cook decided to be a neonatologist after his young daughter died unexpectedly six weeks after birth. He devoted the remainder of his career to caring for young children who could not take care of themselves. Dr. Cook held the title of chief neonatologist at Vanderbilt Hospital in Nashville, Tennessee. The jury leaned forward, with elbows on knees, chins in hands, to hear every word from this American hero.

Dr. Cook went through NEC: its causes, its treatments, and the difficulties associated with the condition. He looked the jury in the eye with each answer, giving confident explanations and demonstrating a mastery of the subject. Marston then put Dr. Kirkwood's note on the screen.

"Dr. Cook, now, I want to direct you to the note we have just put up on the screen. Do you recognize it?"

Dr. Cook put on his wire-framed glasses, raised his head, and thoughtfully examined the record before answering.

"Yes, I do. It is the medical progress note authored by Dr. Kirkwood."

Marston nodded in acquiescence and asked, "Dr. Cook, can you explain that record to the ladies and gentlemen of the jury?"

Dr. Cook looked at Marston then the jury and confidently asserted, "Yes, I can." He continued, "This note records the actions taken by Dr. Kirkwood in his efforts to treat Sydney Landers. As you can see, Dr. Kirkwood had examined Sydney, determined correctly that she had the potential for bowel perforation, which in simple terms means she had a hole in her bowel. And the reason this is so critical is that when that happens, dangerous gastric contents leak out and find their way into the bloodstream. When that happens, a little baby like Sydney can get septic and have serious consequences, including death."

"Doctor—please go on."

Dr. Cook took a sip of water from a glass sitting on a ledge inside the witness box and continued. "The standard of care for physicians such as Dr. Kirkwood would be to order a series of x-rays that would show what is known as free air. Free air would indicate a hole in the bowel and the need for immediate surgery. Dr. Kirkwood ordered these x-rays, and they were appropriately taken every four hours."

Marston asked, "Did that treatment by Dr. Kirkwood comply with the standard of care for a community like Memphis, Shelby County, Tennessee?"

Dr. Cook looked straight into the jury's eyes and said, "It absolutely did. Dr. Kirkwood did a wonderful job taking care of this little baby, and it is just a shame what happened. However, it was in no way his fault."

Marston attempted to steal Ben's thunder and blunt the force of Ben's attack.

"Dr. Cook, it has been alleged by the plaintiff that Dr. Kirkwood should have allowed the radiologist to review the x-rays because they are better trained to read them. What do you have to say about that?"

Dr. Cook almost barked a response. "That is a bunch of hogwash! Dr. Kirkwood is a highly trained and experienced physician and is as qualified to read those x-rays as any radiologist. He is completely able and within the standard of care to rely on his education, training, and knowledge to read that x-ray and complied with the standard of care by doing so."

"Dr. Cook, some have testified that upon reviewal, the 6:00 a.m. x-ray did, in fact, show at least some evidence of free air in Sydney. If the jury chooses to believe that claim, would it affect your opinion as to whether or not Dr. Kirkwood complied with the standard of care?"

Dr. Cook looked defiantly into the jurors' eyes, "Absolutely not! Even if the x-ray shows a small amount, which I don't necessarily agree that it did, Dr. Kirkwood discharged his duty by examining and reviewing the x-ray to the best of his ability. Doctors do not nor cannot guarantee perfect outcomes. Bad outcomes happen through no negligence of the physician. This is a very sad situation but let me be absolutely clear. Dr. Kirkwood did not depart from the standard of care of this community. He did a fine job and should be applauded instead of sued by one of these guys." Dr. Cook pointed derisively toward Ben.

Marston smiled thinly and nodded his head ever so slightly. "Dr. Cook, now that you have reviewed the records, heard the testimony of Dr. Kirkwood, and reviewed the transcript of plaintiff's expert, do you have an opinion to a reasonable degree of medical certainty about whether or not Dr. Kirkwood complied with the standard of care as it relates to his treatment of Sydney Landers?"

Dr. Cook looked at Marston and then stared straight at the jury, "Yes, and my opinion is that he absolutely complied with the standard of care. Dr. Kirkwood is an exceptional physician who saves lives, and his treatment not only met the standard of care—it meets the gold standard for doctors."

Marston stood still and quiet for a moment to let that sink into the jury and obtain the desired dramatic effect. He looked down at his notes and then faced Judge Jones.

"Your Honor, please, I believe those are all the questions I have of Dr. Cook. I pass the witness to Mr. Jennings."

Marston sat down, pleased with his powerful witness. For the first time in a long time, Marston believed he would win this case outright.

Now, Ben had to deliver. Marston had not addressed the crucial conflict Ben had spotted in the record—either through ignorance, which was unlikely, or by calculation, figuring that Ben had missed it. Ben's cross had to be short enough to make the point stand out and add drama at the same time. When challenging a confident witness like Dr. Cook, Ben knew to go with Dr. Cook's energy and not against it.

Judge Jones asked, "Mr. Jennings, are you ready to cross, or do you need a break first?"

Ben adopted a low-key, "ah shucks" tone. "Well, Judge, I guess now is as good a time as ever. I don't have too many questions for the good doctor."

The jury knew better and felt in on the joke. They sensed Ben Jennings had something up his sleeve, and they could not wait to hear it. But first, Ben had to set the trap tight before he could pull the string. Any mistake, and the brilliant Dr. Cook would blunt the sting.

"Good afternoon, Dr. Cook," Ben began.

"Good afternoon," Dr. Cook responded in a firm, authoritative tone.

"We have never met, but somehow I get the feeling that you don't like me very much."

Dr. Cook, a self-respecting man from West Point, took an aggressive approach. "Sir, it has nothing to do with like or dislike. I am bothered by people like you who sue fine doctors like Dr. Kirkwood who have spent their careers helping save lives."

Ben kept his tone low. "So I take it you never feel it is appropriate for anyone to sue another doctor?"

Dr. Cook snapped back, "I didn't say that. It's just there are so many frivolous lawsuits out there; I get angry."

Ben nodded. "So I guess you believe the doctors should be both judge and jury when someone is unhappy with another doctor's conduct? Leave it to you guys?"

"Honestly, yes, that would be a better system."

"But you, yourself, have never, ever testified in a courtroom that another doctor was negligent?"

"Correct."

Ben continued, "You have taken the stand many times to tell jurors just like these fine folks that a doctor did nothing wrong?"

"I have testified several times on behalf of doctors, if I believed them to have not been negligent."

"Right," Ben crossed one arm and used the other to hold his chin. "So you are telling us that you have never once reviewed a chart where you believed a doctor was negligent?"

"No, that's not true. And you are trying to put words in my mouth. I have seen charts where a doctor fell below the standard of care."

"But not once, not one time, have you, Dr. Cook, ever seen fit to testify in court under oath that a fellow doctor fell below the standard of care?"

Dr. Cook did not answer. Marston stayed seated, not wanting the jury to think his witness needed protecting. If this all Ben had, Marston would win this case. After Dr. Martin, Marston had prepped Dr. Cook on this potential line of questioning from Ben. Ben knew Cook would have been prepped and used this opening to give Dr. Cook a false sense of security that the questioning would go just like Dr. Martin's, whose transcript he had undoubtedly read this morning. Ben walked around the counsel table and stood behind Stephanie. "Because who, of course, would be best at defending doctors but other doctors?"

"Objection!" Marston had enough.

"Sustained," Judge Jones said.

Ben's eyes never left Dr. Cook. First, he had to lay the groundwork.

"Dr. Cook, you will agree with me that Dr. Kirkwood's only memory of this patient was through the single record he authored?"

"Yes," Dr. Cook answered.

"Further, this is the only record, so this one document is the sum total of his treatment of little Sydney over there?"

"Yes," Dr. Cook agreed.

"Doctor, you spoke to Mr. Owens about the standard of care, but you also talked about the gold standard. What is the gold standard?"

"It's not a formal standard. I just meant that by saying 'gold standard,' Dr. Kirkwood not only met but exceeded the standard of care."

"I see. And as we sit here right now, you stick by that testimony, under oath?"

"I do," Dr. Cook answered emphatically, turning his head to the jury.

"Doctor, you testified with Mr. Owens that the serial x-rays ordered by Dr. Kirkwood complied with the standard of care to determine if Sydney Landers had free air in her bowel?"

"Yes," Dr. Cook replied.

Ben walked back just beside the rail to the jury box and faced Dr. Cook square on. "And there are different types of x-rays a doctor can order based on the position of the patient and the views one would want to see?" Ben asked.

"Yes." Cook was almost dismissive.

"For example, the best set of x-rays to detect free air in a patient with NEC would be the LLD type, right, Dr. Cook?"

"Why, yes, of course. The LLD x-rays, which stands for left lateral decubitus, is the gold standard to detect free air," Dr. Cook explained.

"And what position does the LLD place the child?" Ben asked.

"Well, in a left lateral decubitus x-ray, the patient would lie on her left side to get the best view." Dr. Cook was now enjoying teaching the jury.

Ben continued, "And not only is the LLD the gold standard, it would certainly also be the standard of care for diagnosing free air in a child like Sydney Landers."

"Yes, absolutely it is," Dr. Cook said confidently.

"In fact," Ben turned to the jury, "the LLD or left lateral decubitus x-ray is the only way a physician could really detect free air in a patient like Sydney."

"Yes," Dr. Cook answered, almost annoyed by the obvious nature of the question.

Ben took a moment, rubbed his chin, and walked around for a moment to let it all soak in with the jury. Then, he continued as though he was through with that subject and going to another.

"So let's talk about that one record of Dr. Kirkwood. Can someone put that record back on the screen?"

Marston's tech assistant dutifully placed the document on the projector.

"Dr. Cook, you testified that this record is the only record of Dr. Kirkwood and the only evidence of his treatment and memory of the patient."

"Yes," Dr. Cook said, annoyed by having to repeat himself.

"Dr. Cook, if you would be so kind, could you please indulge me and read for the jury the one sentence in the record that mentions the x-rays ordered and reviewed by Dr. Kirkwood?"

It was then that Dr. Cook knew he was in trouble. Marston lost blood flow in his face and turned white as a ghost as he and Dr. Cook realized for the first time the mistake. Marston's gamble turned up snake eyes. Dr. Cook paused but finally, seeing no way out, dutifully complied.

"It says, 'No free air seen in serial KUB x-rays,'" he read with a dour look.

"And if you please," Ben said in his most polite voice, "tell the ladies and gentlemen what KUB x-rays are."

"KUB stands for kidney, ureter, and bladder."

Ben would milk this for all its glory. He walked by Marston, putting his hand over his mouth, and whispering words only Marston could hear. "Pards, this one is going to hurt bad. You probably want to write it down with your red pen."

Ben would figuratively kill him face to face and up close like the Greeks at Thermopylae. Marston sat motionless, attempting to maintain a straight face, feeling the entire courtroom's eyes upon him. Ben walked to the back corner of the courtroom, causing every juror's eye to follow him. At the lake, Ben's dyslexia had forced him to focus so hard on the medical record that the conflict of the x-ray's three letter abbreviations set off the light in his head. Ben, forty feet from the witness stand, elevated his voice and asked, "So Dr. Carter, this would explain why Dr. Kirkwood did not see any free air in Sydney?" Dr. Cook did not answer. Ben continued. "In fact, in his very own words, and the only words we have, Dr. Kirkwood admits to us and the entire world that he ordered the wrong x-rays!"

The trap was sprung, and the witness knew he had been caught. The once-supremely confident expert now looked down to his lap, searching for some way out of this hole but knew it was helpless. He mumbled something inaudible.

"Doctor, I did not hear the answer."

Finally, Dr. Cook spoke. "Yes, as the note reflects, he ordered the KUB x-rays and not the LLDs."

Then, Ben, in a thunderous voice bordering on a scream: "HE ORDERED THE WRONG X-RAYS, DIDN'T HE?"

The jury gasped; the oxygen left the room. Dead silence held. Finally, defeated, Dr. Cook could only answer in a soft tone, "Yes."

"And the only reason the radiologist noticed the free air on the wrong x-ray is because they are specifically trained to see it?"

Dr. Cook tilted his head downward. "Yes."

Ben had drawn blood and would finish him off. "So based on your own testimony a few minutes ago that the LLD x-rays were the standard of care, you now admit by ordering the KUB x-rays, Dr. Kirkwood departed not only from your gold standard but from the standard of care for which you have testified to for the past hour and a half?"

Marston jumped up and shouted, "Objection!"

Judge Jones quickly barked, "Overruled!"

Dr. Cook still did not answer. Ben kept on. "Dr. Cook, either you can answer, or we can let Judge Jones make you answer."

Finally, Dr. Cook relented, "Yes, if that record is correct, Dr. Kirkwood departed from the standard of care."

The jury, now motionless, mouths agape, sat shocked at the sudden turn of events. Ben wanted desperately to look at the jury, to take in this moment, but discipline prevailed over vanity. Dr. Cook, confident and convincing in his defense of Dr. Kirkwood, had turned 180 degrees and was now forced to admit Dr. Kirkwood had been negligent. Ben stood motionless, again letting the weight of the testimony sink in. But at the last second, he just could not resist.

"Dr. Cook, look on the bright side. You can check off your list that you have now testified in court under oath that another doctor was negligent. That wasn't so hard, was it?"

"Objection," Marston said firmly.

Judge Jones looked at Ben in the way an annoyed teacher looks at the kid who had gotten a little full of himself. Ben raised his hand to the judge, apologized with his eyes, and said sheepishly, "Withdrawn."

Marston still could not move. Ben walked back to him, leaned down, and whispered caustically in his ear, as Marston had done to so many. "Did you even prepare for this case?"

On his way back to his seat, Ben said to no one in particular, "I am through with this guy."

CHAPTER 28

S ilence engulfed the courtroom. Adrenaline flowed through Ben's body as he tried to calm down from the battle. Marston sat motionless, retaining his ever-present dignity. Kip and Steve did not look up, like two men avoiding the sun during an eclipse. Stephanie held Ben's arm in affirmation of the destruction of Marston's best witness. Dr. Kirkwood sat still, attempting to calculate the cost of this turn of events. The jurors' expressions ranged from surprise to delight at witnessing blood from the gladiators' battle. Marston had not been gambling. He had missed it. Hidden in plain sight, and he and his entire team had just flat missed it. Whether Marston ultimately won or lost this trial, this mistake would inform the rest of his career. Everyone made mistakes. Marston did not. He felt as though he had been stripped naked for all the world to see, exposing a lifetime of insecurities held at bay by extreme overcompensation.

Judge Jones even paused a minute to gather himself and then asked, "Mr. Owens, do you have additional witnesses or proof?"

Marston stood with great solemnity and responded, "No, Your Honor, the defense rests."

Judge Jones looked to Ben. "Any rebuttal proof, Mr. Jennings?"

Ben stood. "No, Your Honor."

Judge Jones continued, "Ladies and gentlemen, that concludes the proof of this case. You are dismissed for the day. Please be back at 9:00 a.m. for jury charges and closing statements. I hope you have a restful evening."

After the jury left the courtroom, the lawyers remained seated, silent, and motionless, alone with their thoughts. Judge Jones spoke again. "Mr. Marston, do you have any motions you wish to have heard?"

"Your Honor, we would like to renew our motion for directed verdict," Marston said.

"Denied, Mr. Owens. I have completed the juror charges and passed them to you earlier. Does anyone have any issues? If not, I will read the charges to the jury at nine in the morning, and you can do closing after that. Any further issues before we adjourn court?"

"No, sir," Ben said.

"No, Your Honor," Marston replied.

Judge Jones adjourned the court, and the lawyers gathered their belongings. Despite the victory today, this case was still a long way from over. Jurors side with doctors 80 percent of the time in Tennessee courts, so closing would be crucial. There would be no rest for either side.

Marston spoke to no one, stood up, and walked out of the courtroom, followed by the gaggle of lawyers, paralegals, and jury consultants. When they all returned to the office, the silence continued. Marston went into his office and shut the door. Kip and Steve were left not knowing whether to stay or leave. Steve went to Kip's office and finally broke the silence.

"What the hell was that?"

"That was the sound of us losing our jobs," Kip responded.

"How could we have missed that?" Steve asked.

"Steve," Kip continued, "there are a thousand ways to make a mistake every day in our business. We walk the tightrope and get down our knees every night and pray that we don't make a mistake like we did today. But if you practice long enough, it is going to happen. Today, it just happened to be catastrophic."

"What's going to happen now?" Steve asked.

"Well, Marston is a professional. He will show up to court and be ready in the morning, but don't underestimate the gravity of today. Even if we win, Marston will never be the same. To my knowledge, he has never had a witness flipped like today. Even if we are lucky enough to win, our lives will never be the same."

"So what do we do now other than update our resumes?" Steve asked.

"We sit here, and we prepare. We will be here until Marston tells us otherwise or until he leaves. This is new territory, so I don't have any experience from which to draw."

Steve ran his hands through his hair and held them on the back of his head. "Jesus Christ, I knew it would be hard, but nothing prepared me for this."

***

Marston sat in his chair, sipping a drink, looking out over the Mississippi River and its vast landscape to the west. He had waged so many battles with others and himself. His forced self-discipline compelled him to prepare for closing, but his self-loathing demanded pity. Why did this happen to me? Why did it have to be Ben Jennings? How could he be so stupid to have missed the record and allow a guy who could barely read outmaneuver him on the documents, of all things? He expected Ben, with his down-home colloquial language that the masses found endearing, to be good with jurors and witnesses. Marston thought Ben to be a carnival barker who played parlor tricks in a courtroom. Ben was not the skilled, polished attorney Marston was. But now, this carnival barker had bested the best lawyer in the state.

Marston called Dr. Kirkwood to discuss the situation, explaining that there was a chance they could lose. While he still felt their case was strong, Marston felt an obligation to ask Kirkwood if he had changed his mind and now wanted to settle. Marston felt conflicted. A settlement would make the pain go away and keep his record perfect. But it would still mean that he had been beaten by Ben, and that would be intolerable. Marston and Dr. Kirkwood agonized for over an hour, discussing every scenario. Dr. Kirkwood decided to stay put and let the jury decide. He was a proud man and could not bear for a settlement be associated with his name.

Tonight, Marston thought about Robert Thornton and, for the first time, was glad his old mentor was not alive. Marston could not have abided the shame of his mentor. In his home study, Marston sat alone in a leather club chair with a crystal tumbler of scotch and stared out a window at his backyard garden. Marston knew he had to gather himself for closing. The war was far from over, and despite the debacle with Dr. Cook, they had a good jury with several conservatives, who usually sided with doctors. Statistics favored the defense. At the very least, he could perhaps convince a couple jurors to hold out and secure a hung jury. A hung jury would be a defense win.

After several drinks, he paced the floors of his study and went over the case in his head, regrouping for the battle the next day. He still could not speak to Kip and Steve. It was partly out of anger at them but mostly from embarrassment of his own failing. Marston could not even tell his wife for fear that she would think less of him. He was above all else a fighter and would not give in to his feelings. There was work to be done. Kip and Steve finally left the office at midnight, still not having spoken to their boss. At 3:30 a.m., they received emailed instructions for the next day.

***

Ben walked out of the courthouse like he was on air. Lawyers rarely experience a cross-examination like he did today.

However, no matter what the stakes, Ben never danced in the end zone. He knew what it felt like to be on the bad side of a beating. He would wait until a victory was secured. One of the worst scoldings he ever received as a child was when he did a touchdown dance in a sixth-grade football game. Ben's father did not wait until after the game but sought him out on the sideline and ripped him apart in front of his teammates. "We don't do that!" his father said. "Act like you have been there before and not like some clown in a circus."

The rebuke stung Ben to the core and he would never forget the lesson. For now, he had business to attend to. He would be up late preparing and needed to focus. Ben went by Phuong Long, the Vietnamese restaurant on Cleveland Avenue, and devoured one of their signature bowls of pho with a couple of egg rolls. He called Alexis and talked to her, reliving the dramatic events of the day. She lifted him up. "Benji, I am so proud of you. I have been thinking of nothing else all day. I lit candles all over the place to send you good energy."

Ben laughed. "Baby, that is much appreciated. I need all the good energy I can get."

"Hey, when you win this thing, how about a little trip down to New Orleans to hit up the French Quarter?"

"Oh, now you are talking. I can taste the gumbo and shrimp etouffee from Coop's right now."

They hung up. It made him feel warm inside to have someone again to genuinely share his life with. He changed out of his suit and put on shorts and a tee-shirt to prepare for closing as he always did: going for a walk. The tenacious summer heat had somewhat abated and was now an almost frigid 82 degrees. It was early September, and the sun was still up past 7:00 p.m.. Ben took to the dirt paths in the old woods of Overton Park and let the trial flow through his conscience and subconscious. Overton Park is the only urban old-growth forest in the Southeast and represents a thousand-year-old ecosystem, with some trees older than two hundred years. In the 50s and 60s, the federal government attempted to construct an interstate through its center. A group of concerned citizens fought all the way to the US Supreme Court and won a landmark decision, saving the park. Today, the only break in Interstate 40 between the Atlantic and Pacific Oceans is this beautiful plot of land in the center of Memphis, Tennessee.

Ben walked the ancient dirt paths, allowing the case to marinate in his brain. He wanted to distill simple concepts that would speak to the jurors in terms they could understand. Real life closing statements differ from the ones seen in movies and television, because in reality, there is so much information to distill and communicate. His usual closing lasted between forty-five minutes to an hour, and he had a standard sequence he used. Because the plaintiff has the burden of proof, Ben would go first before Marston and then offer a rebuttal after Marston finished his remarks. A good lawyer wants to end his primary closing on a high note but saves the fire for the end of rebuttal, right before the jury deliberates.

Research demonstrated that by closing, most jurors have already made up their minds, and those jurors opposed to your case are unlikely to change. Therefore, the best advocates for Ben's case were the jurors that already sided with him. Ben knew he needed to arm them with soundbites of ten words or fewer that they could then use to convince fellow jurors once deliberations began. He also needed to combine visuals and simple concepts to easily communicate to jurors of various degrees of education, age, and life experience. Unlike a politician, Ben needed more than 50 percent of the vote. He needed all of it. Marston only needed one holdout for a hung jury, known as a defense win. Ben could not allow that holdout to exist.

For most jurors, this would be the first time they would ever experience a group dynamic with strangers in which they would be required to communicate and discuss their opinions. They also had to disagree in a civil manner. Hopefully, they would not become intimidated by someone more experienced in the group or by a bully who might try to hijack the deliberations. Ben had participated in many mock trials where the jury deliberations were observed on close-circuit camera and saw the effect of a dominant personality.

Ben structured a closing like a symphony, conducting emotions up and down and finishing with a crescendo. Spectators watching Ben close came away thinking the whole thing was simple and natural and off the cuff. Nothing could be further from the truth, but it amounted to a compliment because Ben wanted the jury to feel as though he and they had just had a nice conversation, not like he had just delivered a carefully written and planned speech. Like Churchill, Ben had spent a life preparing for impromptu remarks. He would draw on those skills while making his rebuttal after Marston's closing. Then, Ben would urge the jury to action and do it with artistry drawn from the moment, not planned in a formula.

***

Defense closings are much different from those of the plaintiff's side. Marston would spend his time speaking in medical terminology and extolling the testimony of clients and experts who had spent a lifetime saving lives. His demeanor would be formal, precise, and authoritative, attempting to influence the group dynamic to gravitate to status quo and authoritative conservatives. It was a lot easier for a jury to say no than affirmatively return a large financial verdict against a man they had shared a room with for two weeks (and whose family pictures they had seen).

Marston would emphasize Dr. Kirkwood's education, authority, and knowledge and appeal to the insecurities of jurors by forcefully presenting his case as if there were no other way to look at the circumstances. There would be a flurry of medical records, timelines, statistics, and medical literature. When he finished, the jurors would be traitors to the country and doctors everywhere if they dared enter a verdict against dear ole Dr. Kirkwood.

Ben counted heavily on the impact Alicia and Sydney had during Alicia's testimony. Her words had been devastating and impactful. The men on the jury could not help feeling paternal toward them both. Alicia's plight had to garner real sympathy from the women. It helped Ben that Kirkwood was White and not Black. A Shelby County jury had never ruled against a Black male doctor, as far as Ben knew. Ben had to convince the jury that the Memphis tribe would be better served by rebuking Dr. Kirkwood's negligent behavior to protect the remaining herd.

Neither lawyer got a full night's sleep. Ben nodded off for a few hours around midnight but rose at 3:00 a.m. and headed to the office. Sitting at his desk in the middle of the night, Ben recognized the beauty in the process and struggle. He never felt more alive than during a jury trial. Yes, it was agonizing, but by God, his heightened senses tingling through his body as he competed for the highest stakes brought an irreplicable euphoria. Later that morning, Ben would take the fight to Marston and let the chips fall where they may.

CHAPTER 29

Before he flipped Cook in the stand, Ben had prepared himself to lose the case. It is a psychological device employed to protect the core of a lawyer's soul. It does not work, but there are no atheists in a fox hole. Nor are there any in a courtroom. Every trial lawyer who takes on Goliath possesses the romantic hope that, even in the face of overwhelming odds, justice and the jury will see the righteousness of his cause and reward him accordingly. Most would never admit it, but they all feel an irrational hope that they will catch lightning in a bottle and get that one big hit.

Ben sat still, his hands steepled, staring at the table. Ben did not use notes, preferring to make eye contact with each juror. His heart raced like a thoroughbred at the gate who is eager to run. He took one deep breath. Then two.

"Mr. Jennings, the floor is yours. Please proceed with your closing remarks."

Ben did not look up at the judge and sat transfixed for seconds that seemed like an hour to the expectant jurors. Was he going to speak? Ben rose quietly, thoughtfully, and walked to the jury box, where he had stood a thousand times. He walked side to side looking each juror in the eye, peering into their souls. Finally, he spoke.

"Ladies and gentlemen, when you retire to the jury room in a little while, you are going to have two jobs." Ben always started with this line; it got the jurors' attention. He knew they would value information to help with their deliberations. It set up his goal of arming the favorable jurors with ammunition to convince the others to join their side. "The first job is to decide how you feel about the case. The second is to convince the others why you feel the way you do. In the next little while, I hope to provide you with the information you need to accomplish that duty. You have been attentive during this trial, and my goal is to not be repetitive with information you clearly already have. But I do ask your indulgence, because this is the only day in court for Sydney and Ms. Landers, and they have waited for years for this opportunity. Ms. Mann and I have been honored to speak on their behalf, and we hope we have done them justice."

Ben spent the next twenty minutes delivering crisp sentences chronicling the case in simple terms that all could understand. He carefully added words such as "responsibility" and "accountability," appealing to the conservatives, and "justice" for the liberals. He emphasized the testimony of the defense expert who admitted that Kirkwood had read the wrong x-ray and thus, by his own witness's words, was negligent.

Ben spent half of his time addressing damages. Ben used a dry-erase board and wrote as he spoke. It would have been easier to pre-print a visual aid, but Ben believed the act of writing in front of the jury garnered their complete attention to see what he would write. The trick in arguing damages was that he had to ask for a lot without offending the more conservative jurors but still leave room for the more generous folks to negotiate during deliberations.

In the last portion of his initial closing, Ben used a visual aid of a blown-up image of a jury verdict form. The form was technical and could be confusing, so it was crucial for the jury to understand exactly what it meant and how to complete it. Abundant stories circulated of jurors thinking they had indicated one verdict on the form and then discovering they had marked the opposite. Ben meticulously walked through the form and explained why it should be answered in support of Sydney and Ms. Landers.

Ben then told the jury, "Moral excellence comes about as a result of habit. We become just by doing just acts, temperate by doing temperate acts, and brave by doing brave acts. Ladies and gentlemen, you have a chance to demonstrate both bravery and justice in your work here. I pray you return a verdict that justice demands, and the facts dictate. Thank you."

"Thank you, Mr. Jennings," Judge Jones said. "Mr. Owens, the jury is yours." Marston nodded to Judge Jones and rose to his feet, determined but not hurried. He buttoned his jacket and walked purposely across the courtroom. His fear of omitting a key fact forced him to use notes while his audio-visual team displayed key medical records and statistics. Marston profusely thanked the jurors for their time and attention and extolled that jury service was the most patriotic thing a person could do outside serving in the military. He quickly turned on the charm and eloquence learned from years on his feet before juries and careful study of the greats. Marston was the ultimate professional at the height of his powers.

He immediately downplayed his last expert's testimony and attributed it to Ben Jennings' attempt at lawyer tricks to misconstrue the proof. He told of Dr. Kirkwood's spotless career and record of helping children in the community.

Then, after bringing the thunder for forty minutes, he threw a changeup. Marston put down his notes and turned off the video screens. He, too, knew his away around a courtroom and would be damned if he was upstaged by Ben Jennings. Marston put his hands in his pockets, looked down in an almost humble posture, and finally looked up pensively to the jury.

"Folks, if you don't feel bad for Alicia and Sydney Landers, you don't have a heart. It would be inhuman to not mourn for what they have gone through and will continue to deal with in the future. Dr. Kirkwood is very sympathetic to what happened. I would be less than candid if I did not confess to spending countless hours thinking of those nice people. But you have taken an oath. And that oath is to follow the law. I took an oath. And that oath was to follow the law. Dr. Bob Kirkwood did not depart from the standard of care in his treatment of Sydney. He did everything he was supposed to. Doctors cannot guarantee results. Bad things happen to good people. And just because we are all sympathetic to their plight, does not mean that you can find in their favor because you feel sorry for them. Judge Jones will charge that you are not allowed to let sympathy enter into your deliberations. I know how difficult it will be but to discharge your oath, you must. You have sworn to do so. We have heard a lot about their lives and how they were affected. But Dr. Kirkwood's life has been affected as well. He has spent the last year attempting to defend himself from being wrongfully accused. I urge you to do your duty and find in favor of Dr. Kirkwood."

Marston enthralled the jury with his powerful presence and ringing baritone. Marston did not have the personality to force men to like him but had the charisma to make them follow him. But the jury maintained a poker face, refusing to tip its hand on their feelings.

***

It was Ben's turn to rebut. He needed to immediately blunt the force of Marston's strong closing and get the jury back where Ben needed it to be. The jury had given its full attention for the past hour and a half, so Ben needed to hit hard and hit quick.

Ben rapidly addressed every issue raised by Marston and swatted them away as though they were flies. He spent five full minutes projecting his voice, raising his tone, and emphasizing the cadence of his words, attempting to break Marston's spell. And then he pumped the brakes. The time had come to inspire and move them to action. He stood only feet away, erect with arms outstretched, imploring them into action.

"Ladies and gentlemen, so many times we feel lost. We don't know what to do. We start to doubt our institutions, and we doubt ourselves. We become overwhelmed and want to give up. 'What can I do?' you ask yourself. If we believe in justice, if we want justice, all we must do is *act* with justice, for it is in our hearts. Today, you are the law. You will decide this case, each and every one of you. Mr. Owens spoke to you about your duty. Your duty above all else is to reach a just verdict. The only just verdict is on behalf of Alicia and Sydney Landers.

"Let me tell you a story. There was an old Chinese gentleman who was considered the elder wise man of the village. The people revered him and went to him for advice and counsel. A young man, jealous of the man's position, wanted to expose him as a fraud and embarrass him before the others. So during a town meeting, the young man approached the elder and said, 'I have a bird in my hands. If you are so wise, tell me if it is dead or alive.' The wise man knew the dilemma. If he said the bird was alive, the boy would crush the bird. If he said it was dead, he would simply release the bird. The old man looked at the boy and said, 'My son, the answer is in your hands.'"

Ben looked at the jury and opened his hands. "Ladies and gentlemen, it has been the honor of my life to be the voice of Alicia and Sydney Landers. I have spent a lifetime speaking for those who cannot speak for themselves. I pray that my words have been adequate to convince you of the justice of their case. I have said all I can. You are now the voice of Sydney Landers. What will you say for her?"

Ben stood still, quiet, looking at twelve people who were clearly drained from the emotional journey on which these lawyers had taken them. Ben turned and walked quietly to his chair. He sat, knowing he had given his last full measure for this cause.

CHAPTER 30

J
udge Jones read the law to the jury. It is a thirty-minute process in which the jury is given complex, lengthy, and confusing instructions. Often, jurors become daunted by the deluge of information and are tempted to check the first box in favor of the defendant and quit. It took real strength to find in favor of a plaintiff, and Ben hoped he and Stephanie had done enough to make that happen.

Now that the jury had the case, the waiting began. There was never any way to tell how long a jury would take to decide a case and reach a verdict. Only one thing was certain. If the jury came back quickly, nine times out of ten it meant a defense verdict. Ben had enjoyed many of those as a defense lawyer, and now realized how much pain it must have caused his plaintiff opponents.

Lawyers utilize many strategies for killing those waiting hours. Sometimes, it takes days for a jury to decide a major tort case. At the very least, lead counsel was required to remain in the courthouse in the event the jury had a question or returned a verdict. Judge Jones would not indulge holding up the case waiting for a lawyer to come from their office. Some lawyers bring laptops and sit in the library, feigning to work on other cases. Others bring books. Court reporters bring transcripts from other depositions and use the time to edit. Ben made no pretense. He took turns sitting on the bench outside the courtroom and walking circles around the square configuration of the courthouse. Lawyers walked by and nodded, but the climate is like that on a major league bench when a pitcher is working on a no-hitter. They avoid eye contact and conversation all together.

As day one of jury deliberations extended into day two, Marston moved for mistrial, claiming the jury was hung and could not decide. Ben could not believe it was taking the jury this long. This case was clear. What could be the problem? Judge Jones denied Marston's motion. Judge Jones, a veteran of plaintiff's practice, knew the time, money, and sweat that went into a case like this and would not shortchange Alicia Landers' opportunity to have her case decided.

***

The deliberations started well enough. Tom Johnson, a fifty-five-year-old Black postal worker, was elected foreman. The jury's initial vote was nine for the plaintiff and three for the defendant. By the end of the third day, it was eleven–one for Sydney and Alicia, with the one hold-out being James Binkley, a thirty-year-old White man with tattoos and long red hair. Binkley had been especially strident during the deliberations, refusing to engage in discussion or assert a basis for his position, and it appeared he would single-handedly hang this jury.

The law affords juries wide latitude to deliberate and rarely invades its providence, except in exigent circumstances such as physical fights, which are not uncommon in Shelby County juror deliberations. On day three, Ben went into the dark place. All trial lawyers know it. It is screaming noise in your head that will not go away. It is doubt, pity, anger, frustration, and helplessness. Ben had poured his heart out in other cases before, thinking he had won, only to lose. Now, he had just tried the best plaintiff case of his career, and he believed there could be no doubt. If he could not win with his best effort, then maybe he was in the wrong business. Maybe he needed to find something else to do. Maybe he was not good enough to play with the big boys. Maybe he had deluded himself this whole time. Maybe he was just not good enough to handle a big case like this. If he lost this case, he would be broke, which would likely make the career decision for him. He would have to go hat in hand to another firm and humbly ask for a job. The prospect crushed his soul.

Marston kept his distance from Ben and everyone else by hibernating in the courthouse's third-floor library, pretending to work but processing the same demons as Ben. Marston faced his own dark place; some trial lawyers feel a loss as a jury's rejection of them as people. Twelve people lived with you for two weeks, heard everything you had to say, and rejected you summarily. Colleagues are quick to tell their fallen brothers that they did not make the facts of the case, and the result is not, in fact, an indictment of them personally, but it sure feels like it is. Fellow plaintiffs' lawyers thank their brothers-in-arms for joining the fight, because by taking up the plaintiff's side, they advance the interests of justice. Still, in the end, nothing moves the jury's decision off the shoulders of the lawyer who tried the case.

On the morning of day three, voices were raised in the jury room and heard out in the hall by some of the lawyers. The jury took a break to allow everyone to cool down. About an hour later, the deputy told the lawyers the jury had a question. This is common. Many times, the jury wants a break, an exhibit, or a clarification. Other times, they just want to quit. Ben suspected the jurors were about to ask Judge Jones to let them declare an impasse. As Ben walked the halls, Stephanie sat on a bench in the hall, reviewing medical records from another case. Alicia sat nearby, quietly trying to entertain Sydney. Marston sat alone in the third-floor library. Steve walked upstairs to notify him of the judge's request.

Ben staggered into the courtroom, feeling defeated. Dejected, he sat down at the counsel table with his head in his hands, not bothering to even look at Judge Jones. He never glanced the five feet to his right to see Marston, who was ready to throw up his hands and just quit, himself. The pain was too much to endure. Maybe he could be a bail bondsman with Freddie. The jury remained in their room. It was only the lawyers.

Judge Jones interrupted those thoughts. "The jury has a question. No, wait. The jury has a request."

Something in Judge Jones' tone caused Ben to lift his head.

Judge Jones said, "The jury has asked for a calculator."

Ben's heart burst. He screamed to himself, *What!!! Are you kidding?* Marston's head dropped to his hands. Whatever the amount, Ben knew he had won. He did it. He put it over the goal line. He gave Marston Owens III the first loss of his storied career. Ben began to believe that maybe he did have what it took to be a trial lawyer. Ben turned to Alicia. She whispered, "What does this mean?"

"It means, my dear, those good folks are going to take care of you and Sydney."

"How do you know?"

"Juries do not ask for calculators if they are finding for the defendant. Calculators mean damages, and damages mean a win. And if they need a calculator, it is likely a number with a lot of zeroes."

Alicia closed her eyes and leaned back in her chair, then opened her eyes to look toward the heavens. Judge Jones sent a calculator back with the bailiff. Ben walked down the hall, went into the bathroom, and when he was sure no one was looking, punched the air and defiantly said to the empty room, "Yes!"

***

Thirty minutes later, the deputy told the lawyers they had a verdict. Any lawyer who tells you they do not feel complete terror after hearing that phrase is either a liar or has never tried a jury case worth anything. Standing in the hallway outside of the courtroom, Ben squeezed Stephanie's right hand with both of his, and they looked into each other's eyes like two people who had shared a foxhole and survived. Alicia was just visible at the end of the hallway, pushing Sydney in her wheelchair. Stephanie waved her over, and they walked into the courtroom together. Stephanie and Ben took their seats behind the table, and Alicia settled in with Sydney.

Judge Jones solemnly reviewed the verdict form and then turned to the jury and calmly asked if this was their verdict. The foreman stood and said, "Yes."

Judge Jones asked, "What is that verdict, sir?"

Foreman Tom Johnson stood and read from a sheet of paper. The other jurors looked at the parties. "We, the jury, in the above-styled matter, do find by a preponderance of the evidence that Dr. Robert Kirkwood deviated from the standard of care in his treatment of Sydney Landers."

Ben closed his eyes and made fists with his hands. Stephanie, always stoic, began writing the finding, readying herself for the numbers. Alicia's mouth started trembling and tears physically shot from her eyes, but she stifled any audible noise for fear of upsetting Judge Jones. Several women on the jury smiled, and one went so far as to put her hands together in front of her as if she were praying. Marston sat rigid and unmoving, refusing to break eye contact with the jury, as if that was part of his punishment. Kip and Steve bowed their heads. Steve appeared to wretch as if preventing himself from throwing up.

The jury was not through. How much money had they awarded Alicia and Sydney? Judge Jones turned back to the jury foreman. "Sir, did the jury find that Alicia and Sydney Landers were damaged by Dr. Kirkwood's negligence?"

"Yes, sir." The foreman nodded.

Judge Jones inclined his head. "And what were those damages?"

Now, Ben grabbed his pen and turned to a fresh page on a legal pad. Stephanie had already been writing. The foreman continued: "For non-economic damages, item number one. Physical pain and suffering, past: $2 million. Permanent impairment: $2 million. Loss of capacity for the enjoyment of life, past: $2 million. Loss of capacity for the enjoyment of life, present: $2 million. Section two, economic damages. Medical care and services: $ 285,102.00. Future medical care services: $2 million. Total damages: $12,285,102."

Judge Jones asked the remaining jurors, "Is this your verdict?"

The jurors all nodded their heads and in unison said, "Yes."

The judge spoke directly to them. "Ladies and gentlemen of the jury. Thank you for your service. You are now discharged and free to go. Mr. Jennings, please draft an order. This court is adjourned."

The jury dutifully marched from their box into the jury room to collect their belongings. Ben sat motionless and quiet, staring at the numbers he had just written on his legal pad. Stephanie rose and turned to Alicia, who shrieked with joy. The two embraced with little Sydney in the center of the euphoric hug. Finally, Ben gathered himself, still speechless, stood up, and embraced Alicia and Sydney. Alicia put her head on his shoulder. "Ben, I knew you could do it. Thank you. Thank you."

Ben, choked up and unable to get words out, turned to Stephanie and hugged her tight. He held on to the hug and did not want to let go. No words passed between them. They looked each other for a long moment, both knowing how inadequate words would be.

In an act akin to execution, Marston, who waited patiently as the plaintiff's team hugged, turned to Ben, offered his hand, looked him in the eye, and said quietly, "Congratulations."

Ben took his hand and returned his gaze. "Thank you."

In some strange way, Marston meant it. His personal feelings for Ben went deep. Even in his despair, he felt a perverse joy in the success of his protégé. Ben shook hands with Kip and Steve, remembering all too well what it felt like to be them in this moment. They walked out of the courtroom and thanked the jurors, who had gathered their things and were standing in the hall. Ben wanted to ask the jurors what had taken them so damn long but did not dare ask.

***

As Ben and Stephanie stood in the hall talking to jurors as they exited their deliberation room, Marston walked out of the courtroom alone. He carried nothing in his hands and bowed his head politely at the jurors as he strode away. Kip and Steve remained in the courtroom and assisted the defense team packing up their things. Soon, other bailiffs and lawyers from around the courthouse came offering congratulations and cheers. Ben hugged Alicia and Sydney, and they cried all over again. Alicia looked as though she had been walking through the desert and had finally been offered water just before she died of thirst. The understated Stephanie was ebullient.

"You're damn right!" Stephanie shouted.

Ben leaned back and grinned, having never heard the proper Stephanie curse. Alicia laughed heartily for the first time in two years. "I will drink to that!"

Ben laughed loudly. "Look at you guys. I think a party is in order."

Alicia's sister, who had been there all day helping Alicia, picked up Sydney and raised her over her head in an act of triumph. "Baby girl, you are going to be all right."

Stephanie looked at Ben. "How about a drink, lawyer? I think you have earned one."

"Yes, I have. But I will have to take a rain check on that. And you are buying."

They all laughed. Alicia and her sister pushed Sydney between them, and Stephanie pushed the button for the elevator. As the door slid shut, Ben stood alone in the hallway for a long minute. Finally, he took a deep breath, smiled to himself, and walked through the courthouse like Sinatra through the Sands Hotel in 1964. He was going to soak in this baby.

CHAPTER 31

Ten years ago, Ben and his close friends started an informal club known as the Lunch Crew. They gathered three or four times a week to talk smack and argue sports and politics, never taking themselves too seriously. Ben figured the lunch group had saved him a half a million dollars in therapy bills over the years. Anytime he could shake free, he gulped in the air of laughs and chops busting over a wonderful lunch at the under-the-radar haunts of Memphis. Every weekday morning, the unofficial head of the Lunch Crew, attorney Robert "Rob-O" Verstappen, sent out an email notifying the group of the chosen restaurant of the day along with faux derogatory stories about where the missing members are likely to be. Some days, the location goes up for debate, but Rob-O, as Godfather, makes the final call.

There was Warren, the poet whose day job happened to be a lawyer. Dr. Mo was a semi-retired neurosurgeon and gentleman car racer who spent summers in Europe attacking the world's great tracks and restaurants. Rossie Vaught practiced law when he was not in a high-stakes card game. David Apple, a hotel wonk, had long hair that made him look like either an aging rock star or a terrorist. Charles Clein was a retired chef with a master's in international politics from Harvard and was the group's resource on geo-political matters and 60s and 70s music. Mikey C, an arch conservative, was a real-estate lawyer and developer who provided political fire and brimstone and possessed a home arsenal of weaponry that would be the envy of many small countries. There was also a mysterious international man of mystery known as Graflin, the closest thing in Memphis to James

Bond. Graflin had been a celebrated international DJ of tech house music with a huge following in Germany. He had homes in Memphis, New Orleans, and Naples, Florida. The group's leader and godfather, Rob-O, ran the unruly bunch with an iron fist. Rob-O was a powerful brass plate lawyer by day and obsessed Porsche race car driver by weekend. His car always seemed faster than the others of his class, creating an aura of suspicion about rules compliance, but his driving skills were unquestioned.

Their meetings rotated among restaurants all over Memphis, except for Mondays and Fridays, which were religiously booked. Rob-O, being a man of habit and order, insisted on some level of predictability. Mondays were held at Bangkok-Alley on Brookhaven Circle, where the events of the weekend were discussed and analyzed. Rob-O set strong guidelines forbidding discussion of certain incendiary political topics that had previously caused disharmony among the group. Fridays were convened at the Rendezvous Restaurant, located in a downtown alley. The Rendezvous is Memphis' most famous BBQ restaurant (whether it's the best is disputed). It serves dinner every night but is only open for lunch on Fridays—except for ribs, which can be obtained on any day. On Fridays, "The Vous" serves complimentary red beans and rice, and the crew always orders the Rendezvous special of sausage, ham, cheese, and banana peppers. Then, the Crew devours slabs of ribs, shoulder sandwiches, and BBQ shrimp.

The trial had caused Ben to miss the Lunch Crew for the past few weeks, and he was seriously homesick for his boys. Lunch began every day at 11:26:32, and it was already approaching noon. Rob-O, who kept in close contact with Ben and knew the battle his friend had been in, would make an exception today. The boys all knew Ben was waiting on a jury and were ready to celebrate or commiserate, however the blade fell. As a sign of support, Rob-O uncharacteristically answered his phone when Ben called.

"Rob-O, what are we having today?"

"Benji, what the hell, you are late. Rules are rules."

"Mighty harsh, my friend. Motion for an exception."

"It better be good. How do you plead?" Rob-O the lawyer responded with a staccato delivery.

"Godfather, I just laid a twelve-million-dollar lick on the one and only Marston Owens III."

"Shut up!" Rob-O screamed. "No shit?"

"I shat you not, my friend. We are going to need to switch from sweet tea to cold beer. And I want two red beans and a large slab. Order me up. I am walking that way."

"Done."

***

If Ben had felt like Sinatra at the courthouse, he felt like Julius Caesar walking down the steps to the Rendezvous' iconic dining room, with its huge wooden bar, sports and Memphis memorabilia-covered walls and ceilings, and checkered tablecloths. Shouts came from the back of the front room. It appeared the boys had already finished the first pitcher. When Ben arrived, the Lunch Crew went crazy, and Ben regaled his buddies with every detail of the trial with extra emphasis on the coup de grâce on Marston. Ben ate like a Viking, devouring the ribs and red beans and rice as if he had not eaten in a week, washing them down with the best ice-cold draft beer he had ever tasted. Ben felt twenty pounds lighter, and the realization came to him. There was no one else he would have rather celebrated with than these crazy guys who were like brothers.

They laughed and talked way too loudly, frightening away other diners as many of their topics were not suitable for mixed or younger audiences. The greatest joy of this band of misfits was their insistence of being a First Amendment zone where any view could be expressed. But just because the view could be expressed did not preclude it from being heckled mercilessly if it defied logic or common sense.

After the hoopla died down, Ben expressed real thoughts about the entire affair.

"Boys, I am scared I won't be able to hold on to this verdict. When the money gets this big, it gets the attention of a lot of people with agendas not so aligned with mine."

"Don't even think about that right now," Rob-O barked. "Today, we eat, drink, and be merry, for tomorrow, we die."

"Now, you are coming over to my side," Graflin said.

Rob-O got down to important matters. "We need to decide about a new car. What ya thinking about?

"Maybe a Porsche." Ben pursed his lips and pronounced the car manufacturer with a single syllable.

"Well, not if you cannot pronounce it properly," Rob-O said. "It's Pors-sha."

Ben fervently nodded his head. "Ohh, right, Poorrr—sssshhhaaaa."

Warren Douglas, always able to crystalize the thoughts of the table, spoke. "Boys, as the great poet Tom Petty once observed, 'The bad nights take forever, and the good nights don't seem to last.' Let's drink some more cold beer and worry about that tomorrow, for today, my good man Benji, you are among the Gods, and it is there you shall remain until you are not."

Beers were raised and glasses clinked.

***

After the beers and ribs, Ben had another stop. He walked the short distance to The Sage's downtown office building and headed up to the penthouse. With a big smile, he told the receptionist, "Judy, I need to see homey right now! Tell him it's Babe freaking Ruth!"

The receptionist grinned, buzzed The Sage, and announced Ben. She told him that The Sage had been expecting him. Ben walked into The Sage's huge corner office with his hands in the air and smiling from ear to ear.

"Did you win?" The Sage said in mock confusion. The Sage had already heard the news.

"I went down there, didn't I? Came back with the shield."

The Sage, who never gave an inch and was always the first to take the starch out of anyone that full of himself, could only smile. He would give the man his due. He walked around from his prodigious desk, sat in the facing chair, and motioned for Ben to sit next to him.

"Benji, that is a hell of a verdict. Now, tell me all about it." He sounded like a proud father.

The Sage was the man from whom Ben most craved approval. Ben enjoyed celebrating with the boys, but he needed The Sage. He told The Sage everything. The Sage occasionally interrupted to gain additional details. The two giggled like schoolgirls. In the South, a boy is not a man until his father tells him he is. Ben's father had never bestowed that affirmation before he died, and it left an unresolved sting and self-doubt in him. When he was through telling the story, The Sage suddenly became serious and looked Ben squarely in the eye. "Ben, you overcame a lot to get that victory, and you earned it. I am so proud of you. I don't know if you father ever told you, but I am here to say you that you are a goddamned man."

It hit Ben like a brick. He did not see that coming. Suddenly and uncontrollably, tears came streaming out, and he began sobbing in a way he had not since his childhood. He became embarrassed because he could not control the tears. All the emotions he had bottled up—Annie's illness, his fears about Max, Marco's betrayal, his own self-doubt, even the crumbling of his marriage and family— came to the surface at once. The display was so overwhelming that even the stoic former Marine Sage had tears running down his own face. The Sage wanted to put his arm around Ben, but The Sage but was not capable of that type of intimacy. So the two just sat quietly for a while as Ben regained control. Ben stood up, embarrassed and still trembling from emotion. "Thanks, homey, for everything you have done for me. I would not be here without you."

The Sage stood up. "You are welcome. And yes, you would. Ben, you have all it takes. You just need to trust yourself. You did something today that very few lawyers have ever done. Getting a big verdict in a medical malpractice case against a lawyer like Marston doesn't happen. Soak it in and let yourself enjoy it. Right now, you feel as good as a man can feel."

Ben walked out of The Sage's office and past Judy, embarrassed by the clear evidence he had been crying. She looked at him quizzically, seeing him for the first time as someone other than the cocksure comedian with a ready quip.

He walked to his office, taking, and making calls in rapid succession to his brother-in-arms, fellow injury attorneys across the city. Keith Carlton, Bryan Smith, Edward Martindale, Jeff Boyd, Les Jones, and Jeff Rosenblum all called with congratulations and real understanding of what Ben had just pulled off. As he was hanging up the phone, Freddie swaggered into the office in his boots, jeans, and Ray-Bans like Wyatt Earp storming through Tombstone.

"BENJI BEAR!" he boomed, extending the words, "MY BOY! Now that is what I am talking about. Shit, son, first time you have ever made me want to be a lawyer. For that kind of money, that is quite the hustle. Maybe we can get you a lift kit on the Escalade. We definitely need to get you into some proper boots."

Ben just laughed at his lifelong friend. Ben stood up and met him with a hug.

"Hang on, boy," Freddie mocked him. "As good as I know I look, I am not ready to switch teams. But I certainly appreciate the sentiment." They smiled. "What the hell, boy? Does a man have to die of thirst before you offer him a proper drink?"

Ben laughed. "Pards, we are pulling out the single malt eighteen-year-old scotch for this one."

"Look at you, Mr. Fancy Pants. Hit a big lick and now drinking the foreign stuff. Now, you are too good for a little Tennessee whiskey or Kentucky straight bourbon. I guess that is what you big-shot Range Rover guys drink. But wait, you are finally driving a fine American automobile."

Ben smiled. "Yes, we are having a proper scotch, and you will like it."

"Well, just twist my arm, then. You don't have to be an asshole about it."

The two sat in Ben's office enjoying the scotch and each other's company. Peggy came in and shared a cocktail with the boys. Freddie rambled on about his latest gambling wins, his new hot girlfriend, and the next big thing. Ben sat, sipped, and smiled, enjoying every word. He could listen to Freddie all night.

Freddie's batteries finally ran down, and he headed off. Ben got in the Escalade and drove to Lisa's house. He pulled up, jumped out, and hustled to the front door. Max answered.

"Hey, little man, go grab your sister. We are going to celebrate!"

"Celebrate what?"

Ben grinned. "Your ole man just hit a big lick down at the courthouse, and the squad is going to party."

Instead of going to get Annie, Max yelled from the front door. "Annie, come on, Dad won his case, and we are going to party!"

Lisa appeared at the door. "What's up, Slick? Did I hear something about a big jury verdict?"

Ben put his hands out, palms down, and looked sheepishly at Lisa. "Well, kind of."

Lisa winked. "Looks like a raise of child support."

"Thanks," he said wryly.

Just then, Annie ran down the steps and jumped into Ben's arms. "Hey, Daddio, what happened?"

"We won."

"Really? That is so awesome. You are the best lawyer in the world. I knew you would win."

Ben put Max and Annie under each arm, and the three walked as one to the Escalade. They cranked up the stereo with Gwen Stefani's "I'm Just a Girl," and Annie and Ben sang while Max played the imaginary drums in the backseat. They headed to El Toro Loco on Poplar, sat on the patio, and feasted on fajitas, cheese dip, and guacamole. They gorged, laughed, and joked for an hour. He drove them back to Lisa's house and pulled into the driveway.

Annie reached over to hug him. "Dad, we are so proud of you. You are the best."

Ben closed his eyes and smiled. "Thank you, sweetie. I love you guys."

Ben rolled back to his office, grabbed the scotch, and walked two blocks west down Nettleton toward the Butler Steps, which sat high on the bluff above the river. He stared at the river, enjoying the reflections of the lighted bridges glistening on the water. This was the first moment he had to himself to process everything that had happened. People would look at him differently now, but he was the same guy he would have been had he lost. He thought about the old saying, "Success has a thousand fathers, and failure is an orphan." For some reason, his mind raced to the ancient Roman warriors who had returned from the wars. They rode in chariots adorned in gold and were cheered by adoring citizens. Their families would follow them, but there would be a lowly servant in each chariot beside the heroes who would speak into their ears, "All glory is fleeting."

Ben walked the few blocks to Alexis's condo, carrying the remainder of the scotch.

"Well, hello, sailor," she said. "Looks like today was really good or really bad."

"Oh, it was good, my dear. As good as it gets."

"Well, get your ass in this house, pour us up a few fingers, and tell me all about it!"

He allowed himself to enjoy the victory that night. But the morning would be different. He knew that it was one thing to hook the big fish but another to get it in the boat. Marston would bring the wrath of God and all available resources to work to overturn the verdict and erase the loss. Ben knew the battle to cash that check would not be easy.

CHAPTER 32

Ben slept the sleep of the dead. Ben was always the first one up, so he felt disoriented when Alexis woke him up with breakfast in bed.

"What time is it?" he asked.

"Almost noon, cowboy. You have not moved. I enjoyed sitting here watching you sleep. You look like a sweet little boy."

Ben was embarrassed to be so vulnerable.

"What time did we go to bed last night?"

"Late. You got a bit overserved," she informed him. "I have never seen you like that."

"What? Tipsy?" Ben asked.

Alexis leaned over and gently kissed his forehead and brushed his hair back with her hand. "No, you got very sentimental and very emotional. You were talking about your father and wishing he were still alive. You talked about all the conversations you two did not have, and you started weeping."

Ben flushed. "Jeez, I am really sorry. I did not mean to put that on you."

"Not at all," she said. "The more I think I know you, the less I do. You put up such a front sometimes. I had no idea all of that was under there."

"Well, if you tell anyone, I will kill you."

"Your secret is safe with me." Alexis grabbed a croissant off the tray, took a bite, and sipped fresh orange juice. "You know, you don't always have to be the tough guy. Sometimes, it's okay to let others in."

"That's bullshit," he shot back. "No woman wants some weepy, weak-ass dude. They want a real man who gives them security. I don't buy that Hallmark movie stuff. I guarantee you saw me crying last night and thought less of me."

Alexis shook her head with a disapproving look. "Ben, for being so smart, you can really be stupid. Yes, we want security. We want to know our men can take care of us and provide. I know, I know, twenty-first century, but yes, some evolution is engrained. But that does not mean we don't want a human. Crying when you are happy or even sad is cool. But crying when facing the lion is not. That is being a big pussy. And you are right, no woman wants to be with a big wuss. Yesterday, you slayed a lion. Nobody, and I mean nobody, thinks you are not a man. Yes, having money can be attractive, but it's not the money. It's the competence it represents. Competence, my dear boy, is sexy." She grabbed a big strawberry. "So shut the hell up, eat your breakfast, and take me back to bed or lose me forever!"

***

That afternoon, he picked up Annie and Max and headed to the gym. He underplayed the victory to them because he never wanted them to be too vested in his work. Being a trial lawyer gave anxiety to the bravest of souls, and he did not want to make his kids ride the roller coaster which was his career. They would be with him for the next week, and he could not wait to catch up.

Sunday, they made Sloppy Joe's together and played football in the yard. He thought about Annie and what he could do to make her future more secure. Marco would soon be back from rehab, and he wondered how in the world that mess would play out. Ben also deliberated introduction his kids to Alexis. He had not introduced them to a woman since his divorce from their mother: he did not want the kids to get to know a woman unless he was really serious about her. Ben wanted Alexis to know these wonderful kids and for them to meet this amazing woman.

***

Ben rolled into the office Monday morning around nine. The first day back after a weeks-long emotional battle is always strange. It felt like a surreal out-of-body experience to simply sit at his desk and go through snail mail and emails and prioritize calls to return. Ben welcomed the calm.

All of that ended by ten. Into the office walked Steven Burks, unannounced, demanding to see Ben. Ben had known Steve for years as a casual acquaintance and fellow lawyer. Steve had a bit of reputation about town for dating his divorce clients and employing sketchy and sometimes unethical methods that others resisted. He had a rakish charm that appealed to the seedier element but disgusted the establishment. The open floor plan of Ben's office made it almost impossible to hide. Ben could hear Peggy attempting to shoo Steve away. Ben sighed, stood up, and walked over. "Hey, Steve, what's going on?"

"Hey, Ben. I was just in the neighborhood and thought I would drop by. Do you have a minute to talk?"

"Sure. Is my ex-wife about to hit me up again? Let me lock my wallet up before we go into my office." Ben was only half-kidding.

Steve wore a shiny suit, flash print tie, and abundant product in his jet-black hair. The two sat down. "What's on your mind, Steve?"

"First, I have to congratulate you on that victory last week. Everyone downtown is buzzing about it. That is amazing to put a lick on Marston Owens like that."

"Thanks, Steve. I appreciate that but am confident you didn't drive down to South Main to give me a high-five."

344 🩴 HOLES IN THE SOLES OF HIS GUCCI LOAFERS

"Well, the thing is . . ." Steven looked sheepish. "I was talking to Marco Alexopoulos last night, and we were discussing your deal with him."

Ben sensed a rat. "What deal?"

"He says you two have a partnership deal where you split everything fifty-fifty. I wanted to let you know I am going to represent him in getting his share of anything you recover from that verdict."

Ben gave Steve a crooked smile. "You have to be kidding me. That son of a bitch raped, robbed, and pillaged this entire community. He stole hundreds of thousands, if not millions of dollars, from needy clients and our business. And you have the nerve to come here with your hand out for a cut of this case?"

"Hey, man," Steve put his palms up. "This isn't personal. Somebody was going to do it. You guys have an agreement."

"Where in our agreement does it say that he is allowed to steal money from clients and me?" Ben snapped.

"I am sure he will be reasonable. You know he is in rehab trying to get his life together. He is trying to heal himself. I am sure there is a deal to be cut," Steve assured him.

"Yes, there is a deal to be cut. Over my dead body! I will see both of you in hell before I voluntarily give that piece of shit a dime. Steve, I knew your standards were low but had no idea they were this low. I have defended you to others who talk about how despicable you are. Between you and Marco, it is clear my judgment of character is extremely flawed."

But Steven Burks was shameless. In fact, his nickname was Shameless Stevie Burks.

"Ben, I know it is raw right now, but he is coming after part of that verdict one way or another. Besides, Marco told me you had been in on some of the alleged improprieties. He says you are just throwing him under the bus because he is in rehab and cannot defend himself."

Ben jumped up and started yelling. "That's it! Get the hell of my office before I put my foot up your ass! I am telling you right now you will regret this."

Shameless Stevie was not the least bit affected. He rose to his feet. "When you calm down, give me a call. There is plenty of money. We can all get our beaks wet."

"You greedy bastard!" Ben yelled. "You disgusting piece of garbage. You make me sick. Get out of here before I kick your ass."

Steve saw Ben was serious and quickly made his way out.

Ben's fury overcame him. He picked up a paper-weight and cocked his arm as if about to throw it. Those greedy bastards. Shameless Stevie gave all lawyers their bad reputations.

CHAPTER 33

The Thornton Firm rose to Def Com 4. Marston had not come into the office or contacted anyone on staff since the verdict. His wife, Rebecca, contacted his two partners, Jack Martin and Tommy Crenshaw, as well as his old friend, The Sage. She was home with him and on suicide watch, believing it could be the end for Marston's sanity. Since the trial, he had gone full tilt, mixing booze with pills, waiving a pistol around, and making threats. Jack and Tommy, who were partners in name only, could do little to cover for Marston now; they'd spent years of partnership being granted very little actual decision-making power. The Thornton Firm was Marston Owens; he occupied the office of president, was managing partner, and headed the compensation committee of exactly one: him.

Only The Sage had a chance of reaching Marston. Rebecca and The Sage met at the Starbucks in Midtown to develop a strategy for talking Marston off the ledge. Rebecca, now in her forties, was a lovely, if plain, woman who honed her figure with a rigorous daily regimen of exercise. When married to a volatile man like Marston, there were two approaches of survival. One was to be a dutiful, subservient wife who was seen and not heard. The other was to be an independently strong, confident person who would not be intimidated by his desire to dominate. Rachel was the latter. To her friends and Marston's colleagues, she was known as Saint Rebecca. Although quiet, Rebecca carried an undeniable strength. She lived her own life and truth. She allowed Marston to indulge in his obsessions but did not cower in fear from his abuse. He respected her for her unwillingness to back down. Rebecca and Ben were the only two people who refused to let Marston dominate them.

The Sage occupied a different slot in Marston's life. The Sage was a full fifteen years older than Marston and from a different generation. Marston generally was very deferential. The Sage and Mr. Thornton had been contemporaries, both seeing the undeniable talent of this comet of a young man that was Marston in his youth. While Mr. Thornton was a father figure to Marston from the time he was thirteen, The Sage became a close uncle. The two were introduced through Thornton who, as a personal favor, asked The Sage to introduce Marston to medical malpractice defense and assist in getting him his early clients. In the beginning, The Sage threw business—conflicts and downstream defendants—Marston's way so the young lawyer could learn at the feet of an experienced elder and develop his own name in the business. The two remained close until Marston, previously respectful, began to forget who had provided his golden ticket. In a pattern familiar to many fathers and sons, Marston's narcissism and need to win at all costs affected his memory of the uncle figure who had provided the ladder that Marston climbed. After amassing victories and success, he believed he needed The Sage less and became passive aggressive and competitive. Marston used people and discarded them after they were of no more use to him. This allowed his narrative of being self-made to go unchallenged. Despite Marston's outward performance of deference, he worked toward dethroning The Sage's hold on being the best civil trial lawyer in the city.

Rachel was unaware of this nuance and wrongfully believed The Sage would be the anecdote to Marston's current self-sabotage. She was unaware that The Sage knew Marston better than Marston knew himself and could accurately predict every move Marston would make before he made one. Also, The Sage had a mean streak and took quiet delight in Ben's crushing defeat of The Sage's former protégé, who had forgotten from whence he came. It was hard to feel sympathetic toward a man as arrogant as Marston.

"Rebecca, so good to see you. I am sorry it's under these circumstances," The Sage said.

"Thanks so much for coming. I didn't know who to turn to," she said.

"How is he doing today?" The Sage asked.

She looked up in the air and breathed out deeply. "It's a roller coaster ride. He has not been sober since he came home Thursday night. He goes through various manic stages between rage and depression."

"Will he talk to you?"

"You know Marston. He goes from ranting like a lunatic to sobbing uncontrollably. He has only had three other events like this in his life: when his father died, when Mr. Thornton died, and when Ben left him. I was not around for his father. Marston was only thirteen. His mother told me stories at length. His father's death shattered him and made him feel like he had to be the man of the house. He did not cry and stood like a sentry at the funeral, refusing to speak. He never dealt with his grief. Thank God for Mr. Thornton, who practically raised him from that point. Mr. Thornton's death had its own baggage. Luckily, he had gotten old and had been sick for a long time. Marston had time to prepare, but afterward, he went into a deep funk, drank too much, and used pills. And then there was Ben Jennings. That one is a complete head scratcher. Marston had some kind of weird obsession and fascination with him. Don't get me wrong, Ben is amazing and all, but this was strange. I think Ben was the son he never had. Ben has the personality and gift with people that always alluded Marston. Marston compensates for his lack of people skills with a command of books, language, and knowledge."

The Sage nodded. "But will he talk to me?"

"He has all of these unresolved issues of grief. He masks them with alcohol and pills. This trial is going to be the death of him. He is humiliated. He does not feel like he can leave the house or show his face. He made his name as a winner, and his sense of self was destroyed last week."

"Rebecca," The Sage said, "we all lose cases. Anyone who has tried real lawsuits against real lawyers lose cases. Show me an undefeated trial lawyer, and I will show you a trial lawyer that has never tried a hard case. He has got to snap out this. He has to buck up and go back to work."

Rebecca agreed. "The biggest problem is that the case is not over. Will it settle? Will they file motions? Will they appeal? He must face Ben as a defeated man. He must face his office, his partners, and his clients, and the bloom is now off the rose."

"Jeez." The Sage shook his head. "He is a legend in his own mind. Do not get me wrong, he is great at what he does. But he has been playing in a fixed dice game for years. We have all the resources, money, and law on our side. The game is completely slanted in our favor. Yes, we must be good at what we do. But we have a cookbook. Marston has a staff that loads the teleprompter for him. Juries side with us 80 percent of the time. We look like prosecutors with great records because we get to choose what cases to try. He got caught between a rock and a hard place and had to try a tough case against a good lawyer. Come on! It's time for Marston to grow up and be a man, for Christ's sakes."

Rebecca took in a big breath and blew it out. "If you say that to Marston, he will shoot you and then put the gun on himself."

The Sage was having none it. "I fought in the jungle against the Viet Cong and lived to tell about it. I am not going to let the likes of Marston Owens take me down. Look, I am just going to go over there and tell him straight. I should have done it years ago. I let him get too big for his britches."

Rebecca touched him on the arm. There were tears in her eyes. "I sure hope you are right but am very worried you are wrong." The Sage followed Rebecca to the Owens' home a few miles away. He walked in the door behind her. Marston was nowhere to be found. They both feared the worse until they spotted him in the backyard sitting in the garden. The Sage told Rebecca he wanted to go it alone.

When he saw The Sage approach, Marston's distressed face changed and became vacant. He looked horrible. He had not shaved or bathed in four days and clearly hadn't changed clothes either. He had a tumbler in his hand and a bottle of scotch on the table beside him. He was drunk.

"What the hell are you doing here? Did you come to gloat?" Marston demanded without greeting.

"I heard you were throwing a garden party. I just wanted some free booze," The Sage joked. "Why in the hell would I come to gloat? It happens to the best of us."

"Fuck you! You have never gotten hit like I just did," Marston barked, the alcohol eliminating Marston's usual cool.

The Sage, an old war horse, was not shocked or moved by the language. He pointed to his chest in mock protest. "Fuck me?" he asked. "You arrogant son of a bitch. Who do you think you are? Maybe we can convert the garden party into a pity party."

"What do you want from me?" Marston asked. "Why are you even here? I didn't invite your old ass."

The Sage answered him. "I want you to man up and handle your goddamned business. This is what we signed up for. So you lost. Who gives a damn? Nobody doubts your abilities. Some guys take it as a badge of honor to get hit big. To them, it demonstrates they handle the big cases. This business is Russian roulette. Sooner or later, your number comes up. Hell, do you think I was a better soldier in Vietnam than my buddies who were killed? No!

"I got lucky. Life is not fair. You are a grown-ass man. What do you think Mr. Thornton would make out of this? What would he tell you?"

Marston looked down at his shoes. "He would be embarrassed."

"And he would tell you to man up and get on with it."

"I know you like him more than me," Marston said, sounding like a petulant sibling.

"Like who?" The Sage asked.

"You know damn well. You have always loved Ben. Think I don't know how close you two are?" Scotch sloshed out of Marston's glass.

The Sage furrowed his brow in disbelief. "Marston, what, are we in fifth grade? Yes, I like Ben. I like you too. Give me a break. Get yourself together, man. If you can't get yourself together, someone is going to have to step in. Do you need to take a trip to take the cure?"

Marston became even more angry. "What? Are you threatening me?"

"No. I am just telling you to get your shit together and take care of your business. If you want a friend, get a dog. You know the stakes in this game we play. If you can't handle it, get out. Otherwise, show some backbone."

The Sage did not wait for a reply. He turned abruptly and walked out of the backyard. Marston sat stunned. No one talked to him like that. Now, he was even more angry. He would show the damn "Sage" who he was and dance on Ben Jennings' grave when he was finished with him. He had more arrows in his quiver, and he would show them both who the trial lawyer was.

CHAPTER 34

The next day, as if nothing had ever happened, Marston Owens III walked into the Thornton Law Firm wearing a fresh suit, clean white shirt, red tie, and a swagger. The office had been in chaos since the verdict, causing most employees to update their resumes. Marston greeted his staff and colleagues politely, if not graciously. He had his assistant call Kip, Steve, and the entire trial team to his office for a meeting.

The beleaguered staff quickly made their way down the hall but were reluctant to make eye contact with their boss. He had always been mercurial, and now, he seemed to have regained his old sense of determination and focus. He addressed them all.

"Guys, we had a bad result last week. One that I hope to never relive. But this game is far from over. Today, we start the fight to get back. We should have the transcript ready. I want a motion for new trial on my desk ready to file by Monday. Kip, I need you to take the lead and bring in two more associates to help with the writing. You and Steve will have some other duties which I will describe to you in more detail in a minute. I want no stone unturned, and our brief need to be a comprehensive work of art. No excuses will be tolerated. The rest of you get busy. Kip and Steve, I want to speak to you privately."

The staff left as quick as they could. Nobody wanted any more face time with Marston than necessary. Kip and Steve sheepishly moved their way from the back of the cavernous office to the two side chairs facing his immaculate desk.

Marston addressed them. "First of all, you two made career-ending mistakes in this trial. At some point in the very near future, we will discuss how it was you missed the key component in the only document our client drafted and let that sniveling little dyslexic outmaneuver us. Frankly, I am not sure if you guys can come back from it. However, the next two weeks will likely determine your legal career."

Kip and Steve sat frozen and expressionless, staring dead into Marston's eyes, afraid to look away. To show any sign of discord, fear, or disagreement would lead to an epic explosion. They knew how musical chairs was played. They would take the fall for missing the x-rays, despite Marston sharing in their negligence. "Kip, you know Steve Burks. He left me an email and said he was representing Marco Alexopoulos and may have some information for us. He wants to work together. You cannot trust his greasy ass as far as you can throw it, but we just may have to get down into the mud with him. Call him and find out what he has on Jennings." Marston turned to the junior associate. "Steve, it is my strong belief that there was some juror misconduct. I want you to contact Steve Binkley. Do you know what a quotient verdict is?"

"Yes," Steve answered weakly. "How do you know there was juror misconduct?" he asked. Steve looked down, knowing the question should not have been asked.

"Because I am goddamned clairvoyant!" Marston snapped. "Contact Binkley and get him to sign an affidavit swearing the jury entered an improper quotient verdict and put undue pressure on Binkley to find for the plaintiff."

An illegal quotient verdict is one in which all twelve jurors agree in advance to be bound by the averages of the twelve individual amounts submitted by jurors. The key component is if an agreement was made in advance of submitting the numbers to be bound by those numbers. Jurors can use the average of each one of their feelings on damages as a tool in coming to a consensus but must ultimately independently agree to the value and not be bound by a number they did not know in advance. For example, if the jurors agreed in advance to be bound by the average of the twelve jurors' submissions, and one juror wrote down a billion dollars, this would pervert the system. Therefore, even if used as a tool, after the average number is revealed, the twelve jurors must all then independently agree before placing it on the verdict form.

"If you cannot handle it, I am confident I can get someone who can. Are we clear?"

"Yes," the two spoke in unison.

"Any questions?" asked Marston.

"No," Kip said.

"Good," Marston said. "Do this like your careers depend on it, because they do. Now, get the hell out of here and do not speak to me until you have something good to tell me."

Marston had the ability to deal thunder blows. The young lawyers jumped up and scurried out with Steve following Kip to his office. He shut the door behind him but still felt the need to whisper. Steve was frenetic now.

"What in the hell is that? How does he know there was juror misconduct? And how does he know Binkley is the one?"

Kip shook his head. "Stevie, you are all in now. Don't ask questions you don't want to know the answer to. You are a smart guy. You know damn well the answer to your question. So spare me answering it."

Steve was wild-eyed. "Kip, we can lose our licenses over this. This is illegal. We can't do this. I did not sign up for this."

Kip put his hand up to stop him. "Cut with the Mary Poppins shit. You knew exactly what you were signing up for. You went with the highest offer you could get. Don't go acting like Mother Theresa now. It's time you paid the price for admission. If you feel guilty, go say a couple of Hail Mary's and get on with it. You are in deep now. Do you think you can get out of this shit show without any stink? Who do you think will be left without a chair if the music stops? It's you, youngblood. So suck it up and get going."

Steve froze with disbelief. He knew he wore the golden handcuffs. He knew his wife would not tolerate a loss of income. More importantly, he knew he could not take on Marston Owens and win. He would be the fall guy if their endeavor failed.

***

Wednesday, Ben attempted to dig out from under the mountain of messages and work that awaited him. The buzz of the verdict had been replaced by the stress of keeping the office open. If he could hang on to the verdict, Ben's financial woes were over. But what if he could not make it that long? An appeal could take a year or more to conclude. While the money would be put aside in a bond, he still had to figure out how to hang around long enough to collect it. He had to successfully defend Marston's appeal. But first, he had to survive the motion for new trial. Such a motion is presented by the losing party as a precursor to any appeal. It sets out all the alleged legal errors in the case and states the basis for either a reversal or new trial. In Tennessee, the judge must act as the thirteenth juror and independently weigh the evidence and certify that the verdict of the jury was also his verdict. When this much money is on the line, crazy things start happening.

Ben was now flat-ass broke. Pride would not allow him to go back to Freddie. Ben had to weather this storm alone. He started digging through his files, looking for friendly defense lawyers and low-hanging fruit that would provide new, easy, fast settlements. He and Peggy went down their file list, making calls and sending emails to opposing lawyers. In the middle of plowing their way through the list, Ben's cell phone rang. While that was not unusual, the caller certainly was. The iPhone identified the caller as none other than Marston Owens, who had not called Ben once in the ten years since he had left Thornton. Ben showed the caller ID screen to Peggy, who raised her eyebrows. He touched the screen. "Hello."

Without identifying himself, Marston demanded, "Ben. Meet me at Court Square at 2:00 p.m. today."

Surprised, Ben quietly said, "Okay." And that was it. The phone went dead.

Ben looked at Peggy. "What the hell?"

"Who knows, maybe he wants to pay you," Peggy said optimistically.

"Yeah, right. Not going to happen. Over his dead body. But beggars can't be choosers. He has the money. I guess I have to go listen to what he says."

***

Historic Court Square is the center of downtown Memphis and has been a gathering place since the city was founded in 1819. On most days, it is occupied by food trucks, downtown workers, and homeless people. Ben arrived five minutes early to the small square designed around an old, decorative fountain. There was a gazebo off to the side where bands played during warm months. Marston stood by the fountain, waiting for him. The two neither shook hands nor exchanged a greeting.

Marston got right to his point. "I have received two million dollars authority to settle the case."

"But my verdict is over twelve million," Ben said, almost confused.

"Look, two million is a lot of money for both you and your client, and you need to take it," Marston said firmly.

"Marston, I cannot justify that kind of discount. You are going to have to get at least ten," Ben countered.

"Ten, my ass," Marston barked. "Look, I made you. Everything you are is because of me. I took you off the streets and mentored you, gave you a shot when no one else would. You had been fired by Fats Feldstein. I treated you like my own. I introduced you to this world and, without me, you would have never been in this club. You are a good lawyer because I made you one. Without me, you would be trolling 201 Poplar for DUI clients."

Ben focused his eyes into a squint. "Marston, just like in the trial, you have made a crucial error. I am not a great lawyer because of you. I am a great lawyer in spite of you. My tab to you is paid in full. I helped you win a lot of cases, and you have a ton of money to show for it. So just like you taught me, this is not personal, it's business. Although, on second thought, it is kind of personal."

Marston's eyes bulged with anger. "I did not want to do this, but you are giving me no choice. Stevie Burks came to see me yesterday. He told me you are up to your neck in the same stuff as your disgraced partner, Marco Alexopoulos. He says you were stealing money right alongside him. I would like to keep this away from the Board of Professional Responsibility, but you are leaving me no choice. It will be hard to handle an appeal if you don't have a license."

Ben shook his head in disbelief. "Just when I think you can't go any lower, you surprise me. Do you ever get sick of being you? I mean, at what point did you lose every ounce of morality you had? When did you just completely sell your soul? I will see you in hell."

Ben turned without another word and walked away.

CHAPTER 35

Ben was too furious to think straight. He had spent so much time working to win the case, he had failed to consider what might happen if he did. He needed to speak with his inner circle immediately before this entire train went off the rails. Ben called Rob-O and Warren and demanded an emergency war council meeting the next day.

Located on Lamar Avenue just west of McLean stood a smallish cinder-block building that had either been bombed or severely wounded. The neighborhood along that corridor is one of the poorest in the state of Tennessee. Most buildings are boarded up or completely gutted. Sprinkled with liquor stores, shade tree mechanics, and maybe a Dollar Tree, the area has a decidedly dangerous yet sad atmosphere. It once was one of the most thriving Black sections in Memphis, but despite their humble circumstances, the people in that area of town remained a proud bunch. Yes, crime was rampant and drug use high, but underneath that stood a group of hard-working blue-collar Black folks who took pride in what they did. In this humble and simple location, Payne's BBQ served the best BBQ pork sandwich in the world.

Many first timers must be convinced and sometimes cajoled into leaving their car and walking into the restaurant. They think someone is playing a joke on them. How could this place serve the food you claim it does? However, as they enter this sanctuary of pork, their noses dispense with any fears they may have entertained. A restaurant that is the "best" conjures visions of gleaming décor, sparking glass, and beautiful china. Garden patios, elegant dining rooms with fresh flowers, and an obsequious maître d'. And yet, at the risk of sacrilege, the humble BBQ is the culinary equivalent of the manger where Jesus was born. No five-star restaurant in the world serves a more perfect dish than the pork sandwich at Payne's BBQ.

Inside is a square room, maybe twenty by thirty feet, with around ten mismatched tables and chairs, most of which have been stressed to the point of failure. There is no waitstaff. Hungry patrons stand in line at a window to order from a man who is putting sandwiches together while he takes orders. The kitchen behind him looks like that of a poor apartment dwelling, and the stove appears to have been salvaged from a torn-down house fifty years prior.

There are very few menu items and even fewer extras. There are canned Cokes and bottled water from a forty-year-old fridge. It may be the only place within Memphis city limits that does not serve sweet tea. But the sandwich. The sandwich is the Mona Lisa of sandwiches. The pit master is an artist, a prodigy, a goddamned virtuoso. It is impossible for anyone not personally blessed by the gods to produce that miracle combination of tastes and textures as does the man who works that pit.

Part of the sandwich's beauty is its simplicity. Only three chords make up the song which awaits diners. First, there is a large quantity of perfectly slow-smoked chopped pork with a generous portion of bark—the charred, black, crunchy outside of the shoulder that holds the smoky flavor and provides the texture and taste that contrasts with the warm, succulent meat. It is topped with a sauce comprised of Memphis tomatoes and North Carolina vinegar, combining in a savory combination of tanginess and gentle heat. The third but equally important element of this symphony of flavor is a yellow, finely chopped, and juicy slaw that harmoniously marries the three to form the most delicious culinary combination ever created.

Sublime baked beans topped with yet more pulled pork is the only side. Anything else would be superfluous and disturb the music that is the main course. The sandwich is best eaten inside, lest the time spent traveling to another location spoil the perfect balance of flavors. Juices can render the bun soggy. In sum, it is perfection. Of all hills Ben Jennings would die on, a Payne's BBQ sandwich is likely the highest. When the Lunch Crew dines at Payne's, they also get a couple of BBQ bologna sandwiches with the same slaw and sauce combo—not because they are hungry, but because of the sadness they would feel if they did not get a taste of that delicious morsel after the pilgrimage. In any other place, the bologna sandwich would be a superstar. But at Payne's, it is merely a very talented supporting character.

Rob-O, Warren, and Ben ordered their food and sat down on unstable chairs at one of the old wooden tables.

Rob jumped right in. "What is this big emergency of yours? Did you get one of those Instagram models pregnant? Did they catch you trolling the high schools for new talent?"

Ben sighed. "Everyone has to be a wise guy. Save it for your next Netflix special, how about."

Rob chided. "Come on big fella. Just jokes. I would have thought a newly made millionaire would have a much better sense of humor."

"That is just the problem," Ben said. "I am not quite the millionaire yet. In fact, I am dead broke."

"Is he going to pay you your money?" Warren asked.

"Not without a fight," Ben replied. "That is what brings me to my brain trust. Well, my brain trust couldn't make it today, so that is what brings me to you two."

Rob chimed in. "Now, now, Benji. No sense getting cranky. We are going to get this whole thing figured out. Tell us all about it."

Ben began. "Freaking Shameless Stevie Burks came to my office Monday to shake me down on behalf of Marco, claiming

I was involved in his tsunami of theft. I almost stuck my foot up his ass when I kicked him out of my office. Marston called me and we met, and he offered me two million. And if I don't take the two million, he is joining forces with Burks to bring ethical charges against me with the board. And there is no telling what he has in store for his motion for new trial. I can only imagine what he is capable of."

"Ain't that some shit?" Warren shook his head.

"Yeah, a big pile of it," Ben said. "And I have to make something happen before he runs out the clock on me."

"The good news," Rob said, "is that if this goes up on appeal, he will have to bond the entire amount of the judgment plus ten percent interest. That is the best card you have. I knew the lawyer who got the billion-dollar verdict on the Exxon Valdez case, and he sat in his office smoking cigars waiting for that ship to come in."

"What do you mean?" Ben asked.

"Well, he got a billion-dollar verdict that was up on appeal and would take a few years to resolve. Exxon had to post a bond so that if they lost their appeal, the plaintiffs could quickly turn the bond into cash. That guy's partners were all going to retire on that case many times over, so they were more than glad to let their star litigator take a knee until the appeal concluded."

Ben shook his head. "If I only had a bunch of fat cat partners to fund me while I waited, I would love to do that. But my former partner is down in Texas in a bath robe, drinking spiced tea trying to figure out how to stay out of the hoosegow. What did Mark Twain say? 'A lie can travel around the world and back again while the truth is lacing up its boots.'"

"Have you thought about taking the two million?" Warren asked.

"Yup. But I just cannot do that. Forget my fee—once we recover the expenses I advanced, that little girl would not have near enough to get what she needs."

"It is a whole lot more than zero," Rob added soberly.

Ben rubbed his neck. "Yeah, tell me about it. If they had offered that pre-trial, I would have had a tough time turning it down. But there is something about having life-changing money for everyone. Reasonable accountants can't go out to the Serengeti and kill an elephant, but they sure know how to divide it up when someone else does."

"I hate to say it, but you need to seriously consider the two million," Rob said.

Warren jumped in. "That is just a first offer. I think Judge Jones is going to be on your side. I think you can squeeze Marston for more. I just worry if Marston had someone on that jury. If so, he did not pay him enough for a hung jury, but he may have paid him enough for some kind of crazy affidavit alleging juror misconduct."

Rob nodded. "Let's sit tight and work on that motion for new trial. I got you covered on some cash in the meantime. I can wait on that new Porsche I was about to get. The motion will be heard in a couple of weeks max so it will happen quick. Then, the clock is on him to put up a bond for the appeal amount, assuming Judge Jones does not lose his mind in the meantime."

"Well," Warren said, "without the shadows, we couldn't see the light."

"What the hell does that mean?" asked Ben.

Warren smiled patiently. "It means your light will expose their darkness. You can't out-dirty those guys. They are wired for it, and you are not. We must expose them. Don't let Burks' extortion stay in the dark. Go on the offense with the truth and watch the lies scurry away."

Warren and Rob convinced Ben he had to combat Marston and Burks head-on. Energized, he raced to the office. First, he dashed off a letter to the Tennessee Board of Professional Responsibility:

Dear Counsel,

This letter is sent, pursuant to my duty as an officer of the court and licensed attorney, to report unethical conduct. Monday, Steven Burks came to my office and threatened to report me to this body unless I agreed to provide him and his client Marco Alexopoulos potential funds received from a recent jury verdict. He claims that I worked in concert with Mr. Alexopoulos to illegally steal funds from clients. I attached herein all of my banking information and, by this letter, authorize you to take whatever steps you deem necessary to analyze every aspect of my current and past financial history. Further, I stand ready to answer any and all questions you may have concerning these slanderous allegations made by Mr. Burks.

Sincerely,
Ben Jennings, BPR #13989
cc: Steven Burks, Marco Alexopoulos

***

Next, it was time to bring in Freddie. Ben took the Escalade over to Freddie's office with a box of Gibson's donuts. He walked through the door, and Freddie started in on him. "Benji, my boy! Now that you are rich, I thought you would forget about me. Look at you rolling up bearing gifts. Did you get me some of those cream-filled little gems?"

Ben popped open the top of the box. "Of course! The only thing you like better than cream-filled donuts are French onion dip and Fritos."

"You know me well, paisan. Hey, how about a little game of golf on Friday? I met these guys from Mississippi who seem anxious to be separated from their wallets."

"I wish," Ben said. "But I actually have a job for you, and I need you badly."

"Of course you do. I am sure you want me to go to Choctaw Country Club and please some of those old bags."

"Not quite."

"Or maybe spend the week with little Max and teach him how to be a man?"

Ben smiled. "As tempting as that is, I had something else in mind."

"Okay, I'll bite. What is it?"

"I think Marston is going to pull some crazy shit in his motion for new trial. One thing I am guessing is that he will try to get at least one juror to allege misconduct, or what is called a quotient verdict."

Ben explained what a quotient verdict was and what kinds of allegations he anticipated Marston making. Ben told Freddie of his suspicions about Juror Binkley. Ben hadn't interviewed the jurors specifically, but he recalled in the hallway many of them complaining about Binkley. They shook their heads and said he had been a pain in their asses. In all the excitement of the verdict, Ben did not take the time to get more specifics from the jurors, who were clearly ready to return to their lives. Ben's plan was to draft affidavits from the eleven remaining jurors and then have Freddie talk to Mr. Binkley.

Freddie rubbed his chin and looked up as if calculating. "Benji. You know I love you, but this little errand is going to cost you two money games of my choosing. And a date with that hot friend of your little Instagram model."

Ben grinned. "Deal! And if we are successful, I will throw in a slightly used Escalade."

"Ahh," Freddie said, "you deride this fine American engineering, but I assure you the joke is on you. One day, you will admit that beautiful Cadillac Escalade was the best car you ever drove. And I will be there to hear it. I think we can get some spinners for it."

***

By Friday afternoon, Freddie had signed affidavits affirming the sanctity of the deliberations from eleven of the twelve jurors. To a one, the jurors in one way or another questioned Binkley and whether he had a separate agenda. There was something shady about that guy. The jurors told Freddie that they agreed on the verdict on the first day, but Binkley was the one hold-out. Worse, Binkley refused to even discuss the case or offer any reasons for his opinion. Reluctantly, one juror admitted that Juror Craig Flowers may have had a private and candid conversation with Binkley that brought him over on that last day. Freddie called Ben to give him the good news.

"Benji, eleven out of twelve is pretty damn good. I have not been able to run down that Binkley character."

"Freddie, you are the best. Did you talk to the jurors about Binkley?"

"Funny you ask. Every one of them thought something was very off about him. He would not even deliberate until Juror Flowers apparently threatened to kick his ass."

This confirmed Ben's worst fears. He knew from the past that Marston knew no bounds. It did not surprise Ben that Marston potentially paid off this redneck. Ben came up with a plan.

"Freddie, you have to find Binkley and get him on tape. I don't want to know how you do it, but I need him on tape. I am going to break Marston Owens from sucking eggs."

"All right, but this is really going to cost you," Freddie warned.

"How about a Sara Lee poundcake and a two-liter Coca-Cola?" Ben referred to their formative years and horrible dietary choices.

"Now you are talking homeboy. Singing my music, Benji Bear."

CHAPTER 36

The Thornton Firm was abuzz with the flurry of activity. A team of lawyers and paralegals spent the week assembling a lengthy brief challenging the validity of the verdict. The page count came in at fifty-four pages, replete with allegations of error of the court and misconduct on the part of Ben Jennings. They claimed Ben was inappropriately and unprofessionally overdramatic and caused the jury to act with passion and prejudice as opposed to assessing the clear facts and law. They claimed that Dr. Bell, while the foremost authority on NEC, was still for some reason not competent to testify in Shelby County. They attached case law and voluminous appendices of their contentions of error. Their final allegation was juror misconduct and an illegal quotient verdict. In support of this contention was the affidavit of Juror James Binkley. The affidavit said that the jury had used an average of their individual numbers to arrive at a final number.

Ben had a week to respond to the defense motion. He recruited two third-year law students to assist. They locked themselves in Ben's office, split up the sections, and attacked them one at a time. Take-out Chinese food, cold beer, and hot coffee flowed through the office, fueling long days and nights. Ben, Stephanie, and two law students took on the full might of the Thornton Firm.

Ben pounded Marston with eleven juror affidavits to combat Binkley's. Once again, Ben gambled and kept the ace in his pocket. Just like the medical record, Ben did not want to give Marston time to fix the harm Ben had planned. He risked Judge Jones not allowing the evidence that Marston had attempted to fix the jury, but it was so strong that the chance was low. Ben got his response filed on the Friday deadline. Judge Jones had a week to review before oral argument the following Friday.

The week felt like a month. Both camps were unusually quiet, calculating next moves. Motions for new trial were not often granted, and the appellate courts favor the sanctity of the jury. Judge Jones could leave the verdict in place, grant a new trial, or completely reverse the jury's award in what is known as a judgment notwithstanding the verdict. The former two were not rare, but it would be a stretch to reverse the case altogether. Ben's nervous energy pulsed through him, making it impossible for him to think of anything other than the trial. He paced the floor, obsessing over every nuance of the briefs and steadying himself for the battle. This would be quite different from a jury trial. There would be no clowning around, and his charm would not affect the result. The biggest issue to be decided would be the allegations set forth in Juror James Binkley's affidavit.

Down the street at the Thornton Firm, an uneasy quiet covered the office like a winter blanket. Lawyers and staff walked around in hushed tones, updating resumes, and whispering gossip. Marston's personality had perceptively changed again. Now, he seemed detached from the world, going through the paces without commitment. He continued to bark orders and reply sarcastically to impertinent questions, but now he was acting like Marston instead of being Marston. Kip and Steve distanced themselves from each other, both feeling out the loyalty of the other. Steve successfully got Juror Binkley to sign the affidavit and knew Kip had leverage on Binkley and Steve should either of them ever find a conscience.

Friday came on a blustery, rainy day, promising the fall to come. There would still be hot days, but ones in the high nineties had now passed. The day was cool yet humid, causing the strange sensation of feeling cold while sweating. Judge Jones specially set the motion at 2:00 p.m. so that the courtroom would likely be empty and not full of nosey lawyers anxious to see blood. Without a jury and the accompanying trial team, the courtroom took on a more relaxed feel, yet paradoxically, the stakes involved made the tension palpable. Motion hearings are polite and formal affairs with neither side allowed to interrupt the other. Since it was Marston's motion, he had the burden and would go first; Ben's response would follow. Marston would be allowed additional time to rebut. Generally, lawyers do not raise their voices and conduct themselves more academically than people are accustomed to seeing during a trial. Time would tell if this hearing played out according to norm.

Motions like this were up in Marston's wheelhouse. Erudite and academic, Marston possessed a greater command of the English language than any lawyer in the city. A student of history, he prefaced his remarks with a brief history of the jury system and Tennessee's own constitution. He emphasized the judge's role as the thirteenth juror.

Then, he changed gears and went after Ben personally in the most professional way. "Your Honor, it pains me to say this, especially because I raised this young man, but Ben Jennings acted inappropriately throughout this trial. His conduct eroded the dignity of the bar and profession. We have a history of separation of church and state, yet he saw fit to raise the specter of religion and the Lord. Mr. Jennings inappropriately appealed to the emotions of the jury, which clearly corresponds to their runaway verdict so outside the bounds of reasonableness. Further, Mr. Jennings' antics were more suited for a circus than a court of law. Based on his conduct alone, this court should grant a new trial and sanction Mr. Jennings."

Marston spent the next thirty minutes systematically covering the various legal grounds outlined in their brief, giving reasoned and cogent arguments as to why the verdict should not stand. He urged Judge Jones in his role as thirteenth juror to set aside the verdict and, at the least, reduce the judgment to a reasonable amount. He told him that the jury system was not meant as a mechanism to redistribute wealth but as an apparatus to right wrongs. Marston saved what he believed his best argument for the end when he addressed the alleged juror misconduct.

"The only thing worse than Mr. Jennings' conduct was that of the jury. The court has been provided with the affidavit of Juror James Binkley. I have never heard of such behavior among jurors. Mr. Binkley's life was threatened. He was verbally abused and violence was intimated against him."

Marston raised his voice and began a pronounced Southern accent. "Your Honor, this is just unseemly and outside any rational confines for juror behavior. Further, as outlined in our brief, the jury returned an illegal quotient verdict, which we all know is grounds for immediate mistrial. In all my years, I have never seen such misconduct from another lawyer and jury. This court is duty-bound to correct this grave error and set aside the verdict and, at the very minimum, provide a new trial to Dr. Robert Kirkwood, who is the victim of this lawless chicanery."

Marston sat down.

Ben had made up his mind days ago that he would remain professional, no matter what Marston said. No matter how much Marston goaded him, he would not resort to his public-school beginnings and street fight history. He was a distinguished lawyer and had risen above his youthful emotions and aggressive behavior. He, too, was a distinguished member of the Memphis bar and would acquit himself in such a fashion, no matter what.

The famous poet Mike Tyson once said that all plans go out the window the first time you get punched in the nose.

Ben rose to his feet, buttoned his jacket, collected his notes, and slowly moved to the podium.

He began softly. "Your Honor, may it please the court. Yes, Mr. Owens did teach me a few things about the practice of law and specifically medical malpractice. And the first thing was that when we went to court, we put our big-boy pants on. I have just listened to forty-five minutes of a defeated man sniveling like a five-year-old who had his ball taken!"

Marston shot to his feet and yelled, "Objection, Your Honor! How dare he speak like that in this courtroom or any other place!"

Judge Jones was clearly not amused. "Mr. Jennings, really? That is what you are leading with? You have a twelve-million-dollar verdict, and you want to talk like you are in the playground at grade school? Objection sustained."

But Ben refused to be bowed. The courage and determination it took to get such a verdict came from those beatings on the playground. Growing up, Ben had been beat up, kicked, cut, and slammed, but something inside him made him keep coming back.

"Your Honor," Ben continued, "you see, here is the deal: When Ms. Mann brought this case to me, we did not have anything. We took this poor woman and her severely injured child and pored over medical records trying to determine what happened. Then, we consulted several experts, costing thousands of dollars. And that was just the start. We filed suit, and lo and behold, the great Marston Owens got assigned the case. For the past year, we have fought the equivalent of the Red Army and asked for no quarter and given none in return. We spent days in depositions, fought every legal motion, and took whatever they threw at us. And do you know why? Because Marston Owens did not owe me a quarter. If he chose to resolve the case pre-trial, that was his opportunity because he who has the gold makes the rules. Mr. Owens made the decision to not resolve this case before trial. He and his client made the decision to take their chances with a Shelby County jury. And do you know what? Their chances were 80 percent that they would get a defense verdict. It was a good risk to take mathematically because they did not owe me anything.

"But—and I say 'but' with emphasis—I brought my case down to this room and put on my proof in front of twelve strangers and knew I had to get all twelve to agree before I could get a dime. Again, we took on the Thornton Firm, its resources, Ivy League experts, jury consultants, and trial coaches. And guess what? That jury came back and said we were right, and he was wrong. I played by every rule the game has offered. Not my rules, the establishment's rules. The honored members of the bar's rules. And now, they do owe me a quarter. In fact, they owe me a bunch of quarters. In fact, they owe me about fifty million of them.

"You have never seen Mr. Owens down here crying and whining for a break. And the reason why is that he never needed one before. His career was born on third base. Always had the numbers. Always had the resources and the ability to steamroll an opponent. He rolled the dice and came up snake eyes. So please forgive me if I don't shed a tear for his pleas for pity for his client."

Ben then went through his response, meticulously covering each point in Marston's brief. He demonstrated his ability to be eloquent and even polished in his legal arguments quoting from memory case citations and quotes. After speaking for thirty minutes on the various issues, it was time for him to finish Marston Owens off once and for all.

"This brings me to the final issue before the court, and that is the alleged juror misconduct. As everyone in this community knows, Mr. Owens and I have a history. And that history has informed the approach I have taken throughout this case. Many of his lessons were helpful and productive.

However, some of his tactics—how shall I say this—were not exactly kosher with the Marquess of Queensberry Rules for the practice of law. Perhaps it was negligent of me, but I previously opted to not address what I believe are ethical failings on Mr. Owens part. But today, listening to his sheer audacity and hypocrisy regarding this case and Juror Binkley, I have no choice but to address these head-on."

Ben paused for the stunned and silent courtroom to catch their breath. Marston sat still as a statue but internally was about to implode. Ben reached into his pocket and pulled out a jump drive and held it up to the court. "Your Honor, if I may, I have brought my laptop, and I can connect with the court's video screen. I have a video affidavit of Juror James Binkley that I would like to play."

Marston sprung to his feet. "Your Honor, objection! This is improper. We were not given notice of this. We were not provided a copy of this. He cannot show this video without our review."

Judge Jones looked at Ben. "What do you have to say about that, counsel?"

Ben replied, "What I have to say is due to the abject corruption on the part of Mr. Owens, we were given no other option but to play it in front of this court to protect the safety of Mr. Binkley and the video. Further, this is rebuttal argument to the allegations he brought up in his brief, and the rules of discovery do not apply. After the verdict, we are no longer under obligations from this court's discovery order during the pendency of this case."

Judge Jones, now very curious, agreed with Ben. "I am going to allow it. There is no jury here. Mr. Owens, if there needs to be additional information gathered, we can discuss later. But for now, let's see the tape."

Ben powered up the laptop, which was now connected to the large courtroom monitor. The screen showed the face of James Binkley in what appeared to be his home. He was being questioned by an unidentified man, who likely wore blue jeans and cowboy boots.

"Can you state your name?" the questioner asked.

"My name is James Binkley?

"Sir, are you here on your own accord?"

"Yes."

"Have I threatened or coerced you into your testimony now?"

"No."

"Do you swear that what you are about to say is the whole truth and nothing but the truth, so help you God?"

"Yes."

The questioner began. "During the trial of Landers v. Kirkwood, were you approached by any of the lawyers or trial team?"

"Yes. The day after we were selected, Mr. Kip Lane came to my house and offered me $50,000 if I would vote in favor of Dr. Kirkwood in the trial."

An audible gasp came over the court. Kip Lane's face turned bright red as he looked straight down.

"Did he pay you any of the money?"

"He gave me $10,000 and promised me the remaining $40,000 after the trial."

"Did you take Dr. Kirkwood's position during juror deliberations?"

Binkley answered, "I couldn't really take his position, so to speak, because I really did not understand it. From what I heard, he seemed guilty as hell. So the only thing I could do is vote 'no' and not say anything."

"How did that work out?"

"It was horrible. The worst thing I ever did. Those other jurors were yelling and screaming at me, and I did not have anything to say in return. I held out almost three days, and then, I finally caved. I knew what I was doing was wrong, and I felt so bad for that little girl. I don't want to go to hell for doing this, so I finally gave in. I never meant to hurt anyone. I needed the money so bad. But this just was not worth it. I thought I could do it, but then Ms. Landers just broke my heart talking. I feel real bad, and I am sorry."

The screen went black. Ben stood up and said, "Your Honor, I don't really have anything to add unless you have some questions."

Marston sat motionless, as did Kip, Steve, and their paralegal. Judge Jones sat quietly for a full five minutes, contemplating his next words. Marston stood to speak, and Judge Jones waved him to sit. Finally, in a measured tone, he spoke.

"In this matter, the court has read the briefs. I have listened to the arguments of counsel. Regarding defendant's motion for new trial, I find it not well taken and denied. If an appeal is taken, I will require a bond of the amount of the verdict plus ten percent interest for a year to be placed in the bosom of the court.

"Now, I would be remiss if I did not address the video-taped affidavit offered by the plaintiff. While it is irregular, I know nothing in the rules that prevents me from considering it. To say I am deeply troubled would be an understatement. Mr. Owens, Mr. Lane, I believe at this point you should retain private counsel as Mr. Binkley's allegations constitute multiple crimes alleged to have been committed by you. It is also my duty to notify the Tennessee Board of Professional Responsibility and notify them of this conduct, because if true, it represents a breach of the highest level. Mr. Owens, I believe it be in your best interests not to speak again until you have consulted counsel."

Judge Jones noticed Stevie Burks in the back of the courtroom. Apparently, he had been there since the start of the hearing but had gone unnoticed until now because of the abject focus of the parties on the motion and subsequent video. Judge Jones took measure and then asked, "Mr.

Burks, do you have business with this court, or are you just a spectator?"

Burks stood up and said, "Your Honor, a little bit of both. You see, I represent Marco Alexopoulos, and we believe he is entitled to a portion of the attorney fee in this case."

Judge Jones rubbed his chin. "Really? And may I ask under what theory?"

"Well, sir," Burks began, "Mr. Alexopoulos was partners with Mr. Jennings when this case began and continued until recently."

"Did he perform any work on the case?" Judge Jones asked.

"Not that I am aware of, but we would certainly like a hearing to sort that out."

"I see," Judge Jones said. He turned to Ben. "Mr. Jennings, I assume you and Ms. Mann have a contingency fee contract with Ms. Landers. Is that correct?"

Ben rose and quietly said, "Yes, sir."

Judge Jones lifted a paper in his hand. "It's funny you bring that up today, Mr. Burks, because today, I received this notice from the Tennessee Supreme Court instructing me that Mr. Alexopoulos has been suspended from the practice of law. Do you have any information to the contrary?"

Burks stammered. "Well, um, no, sir, but he tells me that he is confident that he will be absolved of all charges and resume his practice very soon."

Judge Jones had a curious expression on his face. "I am sure he said that. In fact, I recall his brother telling me the same thing before his disbarment became final."

Then Judge Jones pulled out a small green spiral book and opened it. "I am very familiar with Rule 1.5 of the Tennessee Supreme Court as it relates to contingency fee contracts, and I think it's pretty clear that the first step in being eligible for an attorney's fee requires one to actually be a licensed practicing lawyer. And based on this document here, Mr. Alexopoulos does not enjoy that status. So while it is indeed premature, and the defendant still has appellate recourse, it is my initial opinion that Mr. Alexopoulos is not entitled to any attorney fee whatsoever in this case in the event Mr. Jennings and Ms. Mann are fortunate enough to receive one. Further, based on what I have read and heard, Mr. Alexopoulos should be focusing on both his sobriety and likely criminal charges."

The red-faced Burks sat down quickly without a peep. Judge Jones turned his attention back to the parties. "Do I have anything else left to resolve today?"

Ben stood up. "Not that I know of, Judge."

No one from Marston's team moved or spoke. Marston was expressionless and as still as a statue.

"Alright, then," Judge Jones said. "I want to see the parties back here Monday morning at 10:00 a.m. so that we can discuss what further actions are necessary. Court adjourned."

With that, Judge Jones stood up, turned, and left the bench without another word. For some reason, Ben did not feel like celebrating or gloating. He had just witnessed the destruction of Marston Owens III, who had incredible talent and ability but had given in to his worst impulses. His need for success and affirmation at any cost clearly came from a dark place of which he was not self-aware. Quiet hung over the room, except for the muted sounds of men gathering their things and moving to the door. Ben and Marston did not speak or make eye contact. This event would be talked about in Memphis legal circles for years. Never had a lawyer of Marston's position and prowess fallen so quickly and decisively.

CHAPTER 37

Ben's head spun. In all his years, he never experienced what he had in the past two hours. He was so stunned he did not have a real grasp on his emotions. The result could not have been better, but the human carnage he just witnessed—and caused—was brutal. No doubt Marston had it coming. Still, Ben was shaken to his core with the reality of the events. This much money could bring out the worst in people, and Marston and his team had fallen into the trap.

Ben called Freddie. "Hey, bud, where are you?"

Freddie said, "I just dug into a platter of hot wings and cold beer at the Bayou. I am sitting on the patio. Come join me, and I will buy you a beer."

"I will be there in ten." Ben hung up.

The Bayou Bar & Grill was an old dive at Overton Square in Midtown that specialized in New Orleans-style food. It does not compare to the real thing, but it is the best imitation in Memphis, except for the exceptional Owen Brennan's in East Memphis. As Ben approached, he could see Freddie holding court with two young, nice-looking girls who were giving him their devoted attention.

"Yo, my brother from another mother!" Freddie exclaimed. "What's the happs?"

Ben sat down in the empty seat at the four-top and shook his head. "You won't believe it when I tell you."

Freddie bid the girls good-bye, knowing this was likely going to be a long night.

Ben went right to it. "Man, I had to use that video of Binkley. Wow, you nailed it! You saved my bacon. How did you get him to let you record him?"

Freddie turned his head and smirked, "Benji Bear, you know you do not want to know the answer to that question. All I can say is that Mr. Binkley had a shock of conscience and change of heart. Fortunately, I was present and able to accommodate and record his act of penance for his very bad behavior. He doesn't have any visible scars." Freddie winked.

"My God. Freddie, it was crazy."

"Tell your rabbi everything, my son. I am all ears," Freddie said.

Ben did not spare a detail. The two ate three dozen wings and drank at least six beers each. Freddie could always bring Ben around, and it felt good to decompress. Freddie's outward appearance clothed a complex, intelligent guy. Most were misled by those things, believing he was a simple man. Freddie's dress, actions, and demeanor were all a shield to disguise the complex, emotionally intelligent, intellectually curious, and sharp-witted real man. Ben may have been the only man in the world who knew the real Freddie and was not about to give up his secret.

They left the Bayou around ten. After six beers, Ben did not want to press his luck and called an Uber. Freddie scoffed but Ben insisted. The Uber dropped Ben off at the front of his house. As he walked down the walkway toward the front door, out of the shadows stepped a man. Ben almost jumped out of his shoes.

"Wooo, now!" he yelled and raised his hands.

As the man came into focus, Ben realized it was Marston. He was drunk and disheveled, his tie knot hanging halfway down his shirt and usually perfect hair splayed all over his head.

Ben was shocked. "What the hell are you doing here, man? We have nothing to talk about."

"Oh, yes, we do, you son of a bitch," Marston hissed. "We have much to discuss."

Ben kept his distance, stepping back when Marston move in his direction.

"I made you!" Marston said, the words coming from deep in his gut. "You ungrateful, little bitch! I made you."

"You did not make shit, Marston," Ben said evenly. "Screw you, you silver-spoon son of a bitch. The Sage made you. Mr. Thornton made you. Yet your ego and narcissism give you the false impression you are self-made. Today demonstrated that you are the emperor with no clothes. Stripped naked to your bare, bullshit tricks. What makes you effective is a total lack of conscience. But you forget. I read your book. I watched you and learned what I didn't want to be."

Marston sneered. "Yeah, Mr. Goody Two-Shoes. Little pretty boy everyone likes. You can't spell cat, but I took you in and raised you like you were my son. You were the only one. Never have I let anyone in, but I did you. And the thanks I got in return was disloyalty and betrayal."

Ben shook his head. "I left you because you cheat. I left you because you are a liar and a crook dressed up in Brooks Brothers suits. I left you because I knew it would end badly, and I knew if I stayed, I would lose what was left of my soul."

Marston staggered. "You and your little poor-ass public-school bullshit. You walk around with that goddamned chip on your shoulder because you had it a little tough. You don't know what tough is. People have always liked you. Everything comes easy to you. You don't worry, you don't sweat, because Ben Jennings always wins the day and gets the girl. You have no idea what real struggle is. You look at people with positions and money and think that is success. By the way, how did you know about Binkley?"

Ben looked into Marston's red and bleary eyes. "Because you are you. I knew you would never play by the rules. You always have to put your thumb on the scales. You cannot help yourself. Your insecurity does not allow you to play it straight. I sat in the weeds and waited, knowing what you would do. And with Dr. Cook, you underestimated me; you never believed that I could break a medical expert without your help. Well, I got news for you. I can. And I did."

Marston's hands and shoulders shook. "Have you ever wondered if you could kick my ass?"

Ben chuckled. "You mean physically? You are asking me if I have ever wondered whether I could physically kick your ass?"

Marston jutted out his chin. "Yes, goddamn it! Have you ever wondered if you could kick my ass?"

In complete calm, Ben said, "No, Marston, I have not ever wondered if I could kick your ass." He paused, "I have always *known* I could kick your ass."

Marston lifted a shaking arm. Ben realized that all along, Marston had been holding a 9mm Glock 43 pistol at his side. He aimed the pistol at Ben. "If I am going down, we are going down together."

Ben had just enough beer in his system to mute a sensible response to a pointed gun.

Instead of fear, he felt anger. "Marston, you are not shooting anyone. You don't have the stones. So take your sorry ass home and sleep it off."

"You don't think so?" Marston yelled.

"No, I don't think so," Ben said.

Marston put the gun under his chin and his trembling finger reached for the trigger.

"Marston, you are not going to shoot yourself. Your arrogance is so caught up in your damn legacy, you don't want it tarnished. I have no doubt you will get out of this little mess you are in by throwing Kip and Steve under the bus. No, you will one day have the grand funeral you've always envisioned, with the judges and lawyers of Memphis marching down the aisle in your honor, giving speeches about dignity and commitment to the rule of law. Your exemplary pro-bono record will be extolled, and they will build a statue in your honor. Oh, no, you have been thinking about that retirement dinner and funeral way too long. You will not besmirch your legacy with an ugly bullet to the brain."

Marston dropped the gun to his side and bowed his head. He began to weep. Marston sat down on the front steps and cried as though he had held it in for the past forty years. Ben walked over, sat by him quietly, and let him purge his soul. Finally, after what seemed like five minutes, Marston spoke again.

"Ben, I am sorry. I am man who cannot be redeemed. After my father died, I chased his memory. I thought that if I were successful, I would vindicate his memory. Mr. Thornton was so good to me, but I never lived up to him either. I have never not been lonely. I have never not been dead inside. I have been a fraud my entire life, and today, you exposed me for who I am. I don't know whether to hate you or thank you."

Ben looked at Marston with pity. "Marston, it's been a long couple of months. We are both exhausted. What we do is almost inhuman. We all struggle with our own demons. You are going to be fine. Go home and get some sleep.

CHAPTER 38

Monday morning, Ben and Stephanie appeared in Judge Jones' courtroom at the appointed time. Instead of Marston and his team, only Steve and Jack Martin, Marston's partner, appeared. Jack walked over to Ben and Stephanie.

"Good morning."

Ben asked, "Jack, what's up? Where is Marston?"

"Something terrible happened Saturday night. Rebecca called. Apparently, Marston had some sort of cardiac event last night and died."

"What?" Ben and Stephanie said in unison.

"Yes, she woke up to find him dead in his chair in his study Sunday morning."

"Oh, my gosh," Ben said. "I just saw him—we were just—"

"How terrible," Stephanie said, laying her hand on Jack's arm. He smiled wanly.

Ben blurted, "What happened? How? Is she going to have an autopsy done?"

"I certainly doubt it," Jack said. "There is really nothing to gain from it. He has passed, and we intend to give him the honor his career deserves."

"Yes," Ben said. "Absolutely. Of course. He should be given the funeral his life and career deserve. Are you taking over the case?"

"Ben, I have been on the phone with Dr. Kirkwood, the group, and the various insurance companies for the past day, and they want to try and resolve the case. I am just going to lay our cards on the table. We have a total of ten million dollars in total coverage. Will you be willing to recommend that to Ms. Landers?"

Ben considered for a moment. "Let Stephanie and me talk. We are going to step out in the hall. Please ask Judge Jones' clerk to tell him we need a few minutes."

Stephanie and Ben walked into the hall. "What do you think, Stephanie?"

"Are you freaking kidding me? When can they have the check?"

Ben sighed. "I know, I know, but I would really like to mess with them a little bit. Maybe we can get eleven."

"Ben Jennings, if you do not walk in there and take that money, I will stick this high heel I'm wearing so far up your ass, you will be singing soprano!"

Ben turned his back, bent over, put his hand over his mouth to prevent laughing out loud. "Come on, Steph. Just a little bit?"

"No!"

"You used to be fun."

"And you used to be poor, and now, you ain't." Stephanie shook her head and mumbled under her breath. "Crazy-ass White boy."

They entered the court room. Ben gave a nod and the thumbs-up to Jack, signaling an agreement. Stephanie let the bailiff know they were ready for Judge Jones.

"Jack, how soon can we get the check?"

"Ben, they are ready to close this one down. I am guessing within seven days."

"That's fine. We need to put the documents together so Judge Jones can approve the minor settlement." Ben looked earnestly. "And listen, Jack. I'm sorry about Marston. I know relationships with him are complicated. Mine certainly was. A lot of mixed emotions, a lot of memories. I know this will be hell on your firm."

"Thanks, Ben. I know that. He just lost his way. Who knows what goes on in someone's head? You have to be crazy to do what we do. Marston just got a much bigger dose of crazy than the rest of us."

The door to Judge Jones' chambers opened and he entered, stepped up to his chair, and sat. "Mr. Martin," he said, "I am sorry to hear about Mr. Owens. He was a powerful presence and a fine lawyer. He will be missed in this courthouse and city."

Jack Martin inclined his head. "Thank you, Your Honor. It is a dark day in our firm."

Judge Jones looked over to Ben. "Gentlemen, I guess we need to postpone this another week and reconvene."

Ben stood. "Judge Jones, if I may."

Judge Jones nodded. Ben gestured toward Jack. "I have spoken to Mr. Martin before court and believe we have come to an agreement to resolve the case."

Judge Jones looked surprised. "Really? That is excellent. So glad to hear it. If it works out, please let my clerk know as soon as you are able."

"We shall," Ben said. "May we be excused?"

"Yes, of course."

Ben and Stephanie shook hands with Jack and walked out together. When they turned the hallway and were out of sight, Stephanie looked at him with a gleam in her eye and said, "Hey, Ben, now you can get a new Escalade with even more bells and whistles. I see how hard you have been working for that honorary brother card."

Ben laughed. "Oh, yeah, maybe I can get some curb feelers and spinners on the next one."

Stephanie laughed, "You are so late. Those are passé. You will probably try to get some Jheri curls too. Now, you got to get the lift package and some cool lights." She turned serious. "Ten million will let Sydney get all the help she needs."

"Truly. I cannot tell you how happy I am for them. Their lives will always be a challenge, but now they both have hope. Maybe Alicia can go to law school. I bet she would be fantastic. She is so smart."

"And good looking?" Stephanie nudged him. "That's what you wanted to say."

"How dare you, Stephanie," Ben said in mock outrage. "I never—I only care about her brain and character."

"Hah! That's right. Ben Jennings, modern, evolved man."

Ben pounded his chest with his fist. "Down with the people, baby."

***

Ben walked out of the courthouse and crossed the street to Freddie's bail bond office. Freddie looked surprised to see his guest so early in the day.

"Hey, Freddie, what's shakin', big man?"

Freddie turned, "What were you doing in court?"

"Just settled the Landers case," Ben said plainly.

Freddie eyes got big. "What the fuck? Marston freaking Owens agreed to pay you?"

Ben tilted his head. "Well, not exactly."

"What do you mean, not exactly?"

"Marston died last night."

"What? Brother, what are you talking about?"

"When I got home Friday night, Marston was waiting on my porch with a gun."

"You shot Marston?"

Ben enjoyed toying with Freddie. "Not exactly. We had a discussion, and he went home. Got to court this morning, and Jack was there and said Marston died in his sleep and yada, yada, yada, they agreed to settle for a big chunk of change."

Freddie slapped the side of his head like he had water in his ear. "Look, Elaine, I am going to need some more than this yada-yada shit."

"I'll tell you tomorrow. Let's go play eighteen at Galloway."

"Galloway?" Freddie moaned. "Son, my game is far too sophisticated for a muni course like that. Those shitty greens are so slow. But I think I can get us a good money game out at Spring Creek tomorrow afternoon. We can stop by the Merc dealer and pick you up a new sled on the way."

Ben waved his palms down at him. "Easy, big fella. I don't have the money yet."

"Shit, boy. I know you like nobody else," Freddie teased. "Money will be burning a hole in your pocket. Can take the boy out of the hood but can't take the hood out of the boy, Benji Bear. Yes, indeed. I love watching you spend money. And if you putt worth a shit tomorrow, we may put a pretty good down payment on that thing."

Ben laughed. "Just set up the game for tomorrow afternoon."

"My man. I am going to need you to do a little better than last time," Freddie winked.

"Tomorrow. Pick you up at noon. We can grab some lunch and head out to Spring Creek. I will tell you the whole story then."

Ben got in the Escalade and called his sister, Kimberly. "Hey, big sis, how is it going?"

"Hey, Benji, I thought you were in court. Annie and I are working on some history. What's up?"

"My day just cleared up. I want spend the day with her." Ben pulled the Escalade out of the lot and headed for I-40.

"She would love that. Annie's been doing really well. She's all scrubbed and clean, and her hands are empty. We were about to grill some burgers. Come on over now, and I will have one ready for you. Cheddar or Swiss?"

"Cheddar. I will be there in thirty."

***

When Ben got to Kimberly's house, Annie looked shocked to see him. "Dad, what are you doing here? Don't you have to work?"

"Baby. Today is your day. Work can wait. After lunch, we can go by the house, and I can change, and we can take a walk. What do you say?"

Annie's face lit up and she smiled from ear to ear. "Oh, Dad. Sounds great."

They ate cheeseburgers, laughed, and talked. Ben told them about the settlement but not the amount. After lunch, they drove in the Escalade back to Midtown so Ben could change clothes. It was 80 degrees; the sun shone bright, and the hazy sky of summer had turned crystal blue. They walked the old trails of Overton Park. When they reached the beautiful modern building, Rust Hall, home of The Memphis College of Art, they took a break and sat on the steps. Ben opened his steel water bottle and handed it to Annie for the first drink. The cold water was refreshing. After enjoying a few minutes, Ben broke the silence. "Sweetie, how is it going?"

Annie turned to her dad and smiled broadly. "Dad, I'm great!"

"Really?"

"Yes, really." She handed him the water bottle. "I know I always say it, but this time, I really mean it. I finally get what you're saying about the medication. It's just like Mimi's high blood pressure or Kimberly's thyroid. I really thought about it, and you are right. It just comes down to chemistry. And the medicine really helps my chemistry."

Ben took a long drink of water. "I am glad you feel that way. You know I would never ask you to do anything that would harm you?"

She nodded. "Yes, Dad, I do know that. I promise I will do better."

"Honey, it isn't about doing better. You are great how you are. We just all want you to feel well. And if you're good, I'm good."

They sat a little while longer. Ben looked at her. "Do you know who Miles Davis is?"

Annie turned her head down and looked upward. "Of course, I do. You have made Max and me listen to him. You once said if you could only take one album to a deserted island, it would be *Kind of Blue*."

Ben laughed. "I had no idea you were paying attention. But my point is, Miles once said, 'Sometimes, it takes a while to sound like yourself.' I think it won't be very long until you start sounding like yourself."

Annie put her head on Ben's shoulder and smiled. "Thanks, Pops. We are going to get there. Thanks for sticking with me."

"You can't get rid of me that easy." Ben elbowed her in her arm. "Come on, punkin, let's go get some ice cream."

"Deal."

***

That night, Ben and Alexis made shrimp and grits with voodoo sauce. They drank Abita Amber beer, and Ben made his famous white-chocolate bread pudding with whiskey sauce. They sat on the patio and talked for a long time. Then, they settled into an easy silence, watching the river flow.

He finally broke the quiet. "I just don't know what this is all about."

"What, sugar?" Alexis asked. "Life?"

Ben nodded. "Yes, actually. I have run on this hamster wheel for all these years and for what?" He pulled a long swig of the Abita. "Is being a lawyer worth the emotional toll?

Alexis looked at him intently. After a pause, she asked, "Do you know who Jim Valvano is?"

"What? Jim Valvano?" he asked quizzically. "Of course, I know Jim Valvano, but how do *you* know Jim Valvano?"

"I do charity work for the V Foundation he started years ago."

"Really?" he asked. "I had no idea."

"What do you think I am, some vapid and shallow Instagram model?" Ben cocked his head, raised his eyebrows and index finger, and opened his mouth to begin to speak, and she put her finger over his lips. "Don't even think about it!" She turned serious. "The amazing speech he gave at the ESPYs when he was facing imminent death. Do you remember it?"

"Never give up."

"That was good, but the part that stuck with me was when he said every day, we should laugh, cry, and take time to reflect. And if you do that, it's a great day. From what I can see, cowboy, you get a lot of full days doing this work."

Ben stared into Alexis's eyes with a sense of wonder and affection and nodded his head thinking about what she had just said. It made sense to him. "And I have my own three things to suggest," she continued. "Seems to me, in the end, only three things matter: how much you loved, how gently you lived, and how gracefully you let go of things not meant for you." They sat in silence looking at each other. Ben realized he had vastly underestimated her. He gave her a tender smile. He was so content to be in her presence and unable to match her profundity. He thought of the Albert Camus line, "If those whom we begin to love could know us as we were before meeting them . . . they could perceive what they have made of us."

Alexis turned to him. "Benji, you make me not want to go back on the road without you."

He stared out at the river, not returning her glance, then finished the beer and smiled gently. "Who says you have to?"

He reached into the cooler beside him and pulled out two more cold ones, popped the tops, and handed one to Alexis. She took the beer in one hand and slipped her other hand into his. The two reclaimed their silence and watched the sun go down over the river on another day.

About the Author

Bill Walk is a Memphis trial lawyer and has enjoyed a varied practice over the past 31 years. He worked as a criminal defense attorney, defended doctors and hospitals, represented insurance companies, and, for the last 15 years, specialized in advocacy for persons who have suffered serious, sometimes catastrophic, personal injuries due to the negligence of doctors, hospitals, or other persons. Mr. Walk received both his undergraduate degree in Engineering Technology (Architecture) and Juris Doctor from the University of Memphis. He is married to Margaret Walk and has four children.

Mr. Walk successfully litigated and settled millions of dollars in claims on behalf of injured victims and their families, most notably obtaining a 12-million-dollar jury verdict on behalf of his client in 2011. In 2013, Mr. Walk obtained a jury verdict for over 4 million dollars, this time against a trucking company on behalf an injured motorcyclist.

In 2016, he, along with his three partners formed Walk Cook Lakey, PLC, located at 431 South Main Street, directly across from the National Civil Rights Museum. From this location he has continued work on behalf of injured persons, focusing his efforts on nursing home negligence, medical malpractice, trucking cases and a variety of wrongful death causes of action.

About the Publisher

The Sager Group was founded in 1984 by the journalist and author Mike Sager. In 2012 it was chartered as a multi-media content brand, with the intention of empowering people who create—an umbrella beneath which makers can pursue, and profit from, their craft directly, without gatekeepers. TSG publishes books and eBooks; ministers to artists and provides modest grants; designs products; and produces and distributes documentary, narrative and commercial films and music videos. By harnessing the means of production, The Sager Group helps artists help themselves. For more information: TheSagerGroup.net.

More From The Sager Group

Chains of Nobility: Brotherhood of the Mamluks (Book 1)
by Brad Graft

A Lion's Share: Brotherhood of the Mamluks (Book 2)
by Brad Graft

The Swamp: Deceit and Corruption in the CIA
(An Elizabeth Petrov Thriller)
by Jeff Grant

Meeting Mozart: A Novel Drawn From the Secret Diaries of Lorenzo Da Ponte
by Howard Jay Smith

Labyrinth of the Wind: A Novel of Love and Nuclear Secrets in Tehran
by Madhav Misra

The Living and the Dead
by Brian Mockenhaupt

Three Days in Gettysburg
by Brian Mockenhaupt

Senlac: A Novel of the Norman Conquest of England (Books 1 & 2)
by Julian de la Motte

Vetville: True Stories of the U.S. Marines
by Mike Sager

The Devil and John Holmes, and Other True Stories of Drugs, Porn and Murder
by Mike Sager

#MeAsWell, A Novel
by Peter Mehlman

Artifex Te Adiuva

Made in the USA
Monee, IL
22 March 2021